To Patty
with them,
[signature]

HANNA'S
ASCENT

HANNA'S ASCENT

Jayna Sheats

Bink Books

Bedazzled Ink Publishing Company • Fairfield, California

978-1-960373-07-6 paperback

Cover Design
by

"The Great Divide," by Kate Wolf, © 1980 Another Sundown Publishing Company
"Close to You," by Kate Wolf, © 1980 Another Sundown Publishing Company
"Brother Warrior," by Kate Wolf, © 1984 Another Sundown Publishing Company
Als ich vom Himmel fiel, by Juliane Koepcke, © 2011 (Piper Verlag GmbH, Munich)

Bink Books
a division of
Bedazzled Ink Publishing, LLC
Fairfield, California
http://www.bedazzledink.com

*To Esther, Ilana and Aaron, with gratitude for all their love
—and patience*

PART I:
FLYING WITH BROKEN WINGS

The finest hour, that I have seen
Is the one that comes between
The edge of night and the break of day
When the darkness rolls away

Kate Wolf, "The Great Divide"

CHAPTER 1

August 1956, near Paonia, Colorado

LANGUID HEAT WAVES shimmered over the tin roof of the weather-beaten cabin high in the Rocky Mountain foothills. But seven-year-old Johnny Shelby was shivering in his long-sleeved denim shirt. He had only one wish: to forget what had just happened.

His mother always used her hand for spanking. But his father's belt had been a battering ram, wielded with a hard-faced menace he'd never seen, pitiless as the rod packing hay into the baler. It left him even more frightened than bruised.

The day had started so well. The morning before, he'd shown his new doll to his cousin Dottie, who was visiting for a week from the east. She'd simply said, "Do you have a dollhouse and crib for her?" So he dusted off the cluttered bench in the dilapidated shed behind the cabin, and glued some boards together. The raft of whittled sticks he propped inside wasn't much like a crib, but it seemed okay for make-believe.

He'd gotten excused early from lunch and met Dottie in the shed. She handed him the doll. "She's crying."

He cradled it in his arms. "It's all right, sweetie," he cooed. "Mommy will rock you to sleep." Then he rocked the doll and sang the nursery rhyme he'd just learned.

> *Sleep, baby, sleep*
> *the father guards the sheep*
> *the mother shakes a little tree*
> *and down falls a little dream.*

He pretended to shake a tree trunk, but stopped when a shadow darkened the doorway.

"Jonathan Raymond Shelby." His mother's way of telling him he was in trouble.

His father pushed past her. "Dottie, go back to your grandmother's house this instant. Go!" he bellowed, and slammed the shed door after her. And then the horror had begun.

Afterward he brusquely ordered his two sons into the pickup. Following a jouncing ride over jagged ruts to the edge of the hayfield, he parked near a broken-down post-hole digger. Ten-year-old Danny watched with rapt attention as he bent his sturdy six-foot frame over the rusty machine and began hammering on a pin. Johnny kept his eyes firmly on the ground.

The rolling sagebrush and scrub-oak pastures next to the field were littered with pillow-sized hills of twigs and dried stems, crawling with thick tangles of savage-looking red ants. They gave him nightmares. Danny called him a coward, jumping heedlessly on the hills with his heavy boots and stamping away, laughing.

A sharp voice cut through his brooding. "Johnny, get me a quarter-twenty SAE two-inch bolt."

Several boxes of nuts and bolts, all jumbled together, were scattered around the pickup bed. He could never remember the names of the machines, cold and indifferent inside their rigid armor. But he was already in the doghouse. He had to try.

He found a bolt that looked about two inches long and summoned all his courage, holding it out at arm's reach. His father glanced briefly at it and grimaced. "Judas Priest, you'll never learn, will you? Danny, show him what I want."

"It's this one, stupid." Danny plunged his hand into one of the boxes, scarcely looking. On the way back, he dropped it onto one of the ant hills.

"Oops." He smirked. "Well, now whatcha gonna do?"

Johnny imagined the bolt disappearing deep into the hill. Fearing his father's anger more than he hated his brother's provocation, he grabbed it and threw it in the dirt several feet away, frantically brushing biting insects from his fingers.

He carried it like a prize to his father, who took it and turned back to his work without saying a word. Johnny returned to the pickup and sucked on his swelling fingers, imagining kneading soft, fragrant bread dough with his mother.

Twenty minutes later his father glanced up. "Go on back to the house and weed the garden. You won't be no use here today."

As he shambled down the dusty half-mile track through alfalfa stubble he was torn between shame and relief. His mother was standing on the stone porch— she'd probably seen him coming. Hands on her hips over her blue gingham dress, the thick black curls resting on her shoulders unruffled by the faint breeze, her expression was severe.

"Johnny, I'm very disappointed in you. You know boys don't play with dollhouses, and they *certainly* don't call themselves 'Mommy.'"

He looked down, dreading what was coming.

"After this you'll stay with your father in the shop and fields."

The pain of exile was almost worse than the thrashing. She was firm and demanding, but she was also tender, a patient and caring teacher. He wanted to be with her—and to be like her.

"But—can't I ever be with you again and help with bread and pies? And sewing?"

"Honey, you know that's girl's work. I shouldn't have let you do it in the first place."

"Doesn't it help? Especially the sewing? You say we can't afford new clothes."

"No. It's high time for you to start being a little man, like your brother."

He shuffled to the garden, his thin shoulders slumped. As he opened the gate, he saw a snail clinging to the post, probably trying to escape the hot soil. He stooped to pet the two kittens at his heels.

Before dinner, he did his usual chores: haul in firewood for the kitchen range and water from the well. Then he quickly put on clean jeans and shirt, pretending they were a skirt and blouse. No one could see those fantasies. He imagined his brown hair in pigtails tied with pink ribbons, bouncing in front of a pastel-flowered apron as he set the table.

Near bedtime, he snuck out to the shed. The eight-inch plastic doll lay in half a dozen pieces under the scattered boards. His treasure had been turned to trash.

Of course he shouldn't have brought her out here. His mother had given in to his begging under the condition that the doll stay in his bed, alongside his teddy bear. He knew that grown-ups didn't approve of boys playing with dolls, like the girls in his first readers did. And the boys in town would've given him a lot worse than the still-angry rash from his father's belt.

He'd named her Hanna, the girl's version of Johnny according to the encyclopedia. He liked calling himself Hanna. It came with a sweet lilac scent, as if a girl had hugged him as they laughed and played, or a grown-up had called him sweet. Despite the shame, the doll and his fantasies were like a warm fire on a cold winter day.

Hidden under the bedcovers, he glued the broken pieces together. But he couldn't make her smooth and pretty again. So he held her tightly in his hand under the pillow, hoping to ease her pain as she fell asleep for one last time. He was going to miss her.

Before anyone else was up in the morning, he combed her hair till it looked perfect, and wrapped her in a scrap of velour from his mother's sewing basket. He tried to think of a special gift he could give her, one that a girl would like.

In the little cigar box that held his only valuables, he found the tiny nugget of purple amethyst and placed it on her neck.

"It's from that rock shop in Rocky Mountain National Park," he told her. "You'll need a necklace in heaven."

He tiptoed through the house, trying to remember every creaky floorboard, not daring to imagine the consequences if his parents heard him. The dawn was deathly quiet—not even a bird singing.

He laid the doll in a small grave at the base of the lilac bush next to the shed, and sang the same lullaby as the day before. This time he remembered to use the German version that his mother had taught him. Then he placed a rock over the freshly turned dirt and scratched on it:

Hanna, August 1956

He wondered if grown-up mommies hurt the same way when their babies died.

A GRAY AUGUST drizzle set in soon after breakfast, melancholy as his mood. But it gave him a reprieve from yesterday's ultimatum. While his mother sterilized jars, he began peeling a bushel of peaches for canning, Maybe she'd even let him make a peach pie afterward. Then his father, welding a broken crankshaft in the shop, called him to operate the forge bellows.

Standing to his father's left, he thought the fire needed more air from the right. Quickly he moved to the other side and poked the snout of the bellows toward the coals, just as his father swung the glowing iron tongs toward the anvil. Johnny's bare arm was directly in line.

He screamed and dropped the bellows. His father examined the long, whitish blister, seeming more annoyed than concerned.

"Ah, it's not that bad. Have your mom put some Vaseline on it and come on back."

Danny, sharpening a chisel, grinned as he passed. "Shoulda named you Clumsy."

It wasn't, in fact, a very bad burn. But to Johnny, it was one more sign that he didn't belong there. A sign that no one else seemed able to read.

The sky cleared during the afternoon, and the weathered fenceposts were casting long shadows across the damp-dusty path to the corrals as he finished milking. If he hurried, he might still have one bright spot in the day. He wanted to use his ham radio that evening.

After he turned the milk cows out, the motherless calf he'd been feeding from a bucket until she was weaned less than a month earlier bounded up to him. She eagerly pushed her wet nose against the inside of his thigh. He let her suck on a finger before he hand-fed her some oats.

It was another way to play mommy. Luckily, he'd never let anyone see it. It could easily have been just as bad as with the doll.

Across the valley, the snow-clad summit of Ragged Peak didn't seem much different from its neighbors. But he knew the magic words that would open those cliffs, revealing the glittering palaces inside. There, Princess Hanna presided over elegant banquets with a lace dress, dainty shoes, and hair styled like the models in *The Ladies' Home Journal*. Visitors complimented her on her delicious pies and told her how pretty she was.

On his way to the house he passed through the shop. One wall was lined with the boxes of unsorted nuts and bolts. Above them was a hand-lettered sign:

The impossible we do immediately. Miracles take a little longer.

The owner of the hardware store in town had given it to him earlier that spring, along with a pat on the head. "You'll soon be old enough to be a real help to yer dad, son. This here's a good motto to remember."

He shuddered. The very thought squeezed his insides. He could almost imagine them in the vise on the bench. Helping his mother was hard, but it felt good. Sometimes she took him with her on errands in town. After she had coffee with a friend he would clear the cups from the table without being asked, and smile shyly at the woman's praise.

Tonight a family friend had stopped by and stayed for dinner. Afterward Johnny washed dishes as his mother put away leftovers. Danny eagerly listened while the men talked cows and machines, and the visitor offered to return the next day to help with the post-hole digger.

Danny finally asked a question of "Mr. Williams."

"Jis' call me Earl, Danny. Yer gittin' to be quite a man, ain'tcha?"

Johnny, wishing he were on the radio, mumbled, "Yeah, sure," under his breath. When his mother touched his hair he jumped, afraid he'd been heard.

"I think it's time for a haircut."

As badly as he wanted longer hair, it was still well above his ears, as usual. "Do I have to already? Couldn't it be just a tiny bit longer? It's not like Elvis Presley or anything."

"Hey, Johnny, c'mere." Earl's square chin jutted forward as he barked the command, glowering from under bushy eyebrows. Johnny felt his neck getting hotter. He approached gingerly.

"A guy lookin' like Elvis around here'd get his head shaved an' his butt kicked into the next county. You go down that trail an' you'll wish you hadn't."

Johnny stared at the floor. "I'm sorry."

"You know we don't cotton to sissies here. "

Johnny returned to the dishpan, glad that his fantasies couldn't be seen by anyone else.

His mother put her arms on his shoulders. "It's okay, honey. A little trim tomorrow will do it."

Her gentle gesture suggested an opening. "Could I still use the radio tonight, Mommy?"

"If you can start by nine-thirty. You need to finish the dishes, and empty the slop bucket and bring in wood. I'll turn the generator on in a few minutes."

He wished they had enough money to run the generator every night. But he was glad to have whatever time he could get. The radio wasn't like the farm machines. Its delicate coiled wires, glowing orange inside the tubes, were warm and friendly. And the rhythmic beeps of Morse code were a mysterious language, spoken in some enchanted world beyond the pastures.

Earl and his father were still in the dining room when he sat down in the little den. He knew the function of each of the gray-painted metal boxes with big black knobs and white dials with red needles: power supply, transmitter, antenna tuner, and receiver. After turning them on in sequence and adjusting each knob with confidence, he put the earphones on.

For a little while he would be in a world where he belonged. Code was his specialty. A high school teacher in town had given him a semiautomatic "bug," which used a side-to-side hand motion instead of the up and down of a key, and made the dots automatically. Despite his youth he'd placed in the top ten in the country at fifty words per minute.

He signed onto the traffic net and relayed some messages. Afterward he replied to a German call sign. Like Johnny, the other ham's speed was so great that he rarely used abbreviations. It was just like talking.

"Good evening, my name is Günther, location Hamburg."

"Good morning, I am in Colorado, my name is Hanna."

Johnny felt a pang of guilt for lying, even though his parents couldn't hear the code. But after yesterday's debacle it was a way to keep Hanna alive.

"Wow, you're the first female ham I've worked in the U.S. And we must be doing over 40 wpm."

A little girl glowed inside her shell, bright as the wires inside their glass envelopes. The ham in Germany had complimented *her*. She squirmed with pent-up excitement, basking in the recognition. "And you're my first contact in Germany. I'm 7 years old. I got my license in May."

"You're one smart girl, then. Good luck."

On her way to bed she got a drink of water from the kitchen. Earl turned toward her. He said nothing, but his face was hard as flint, like the rooster that used to torment her when she was younger, its head cocked from side to side as it sought the best time to strike.

During the night, Hanna dreamed she was in a classroom with other children instead of her isolated home school, wearing a pleated white skirt. A boy tried to pull her braids, but she squealed and ran away. After recess came geography, and she was the only pupil who could find Germany on a world map.

When Earl arrived in the morning, he got into the back of the truck. Johnny's father told him to ride there also. "Earl's got somethin' he wants to tell you."

His stomach tightened. "Does—does it have to do with . . . ?"

"We talked about it last night. He'll tell you." The door to the cab slammed shut, with Danny in front.

Johnny scrunched into the corner, expecting more berating about his hair. It hadn't occurred to him that his hidden dreams could be dangerous. But by the time the pickup stopped he knew they had to die, if he was to live. The seed of hope from the ham in Germany was a mistake. He had to replace it with another hope: that no one could ever breach the wall he would build around his forbidden longings—not even himself.

And he would bury that lecture with the dreams.

Bonn, Germany, 10 May 1970

JOHN'S CO-WORKERS FROM the embassy had gathered at the Restaurant Maternus, a favorite staff destination. This Sunday evening dinner was his farewell. After a reorganization he'd decided to go back to college rather than take a new job in a different department.

When the plates were clean, one of the men removed a chocolate cake from a box and inserted a blue candle in the center. He placed the cake on the table. "I know we're two days early. Don't worry, we won't embarrass you by singing here in the restaurant."

John looked more closely. Around the perimeter in blue icing was written: "Happy 21st Birthday, John, Our Man of the Year." In the middle was the outline of a quarterback with his arm back, ready to pass the ball.

The memory from high school struck his chest like a boulder falling from a cliff.

"I'm smelling a hell of a stench. John, did you shit in your pants out there?" The quarterback kept his face straight for only a few seconds before breaking into peals of laughter. Everyone else in the locker room joined in.

John continued removing his cleats.

After suffering their ridicule for three years, he'd been allowed to play for the final minute of the final game, with the Paonia team ahead by sixty points. Why had he even tried?

Because being a jock was the only way a guy got respect in high school.

He hated being a guy. But he would just as soon jump off a bridge as tell anyone that. The consequences might not be much different.

Though sometimes he thought of jumping off a bridge anyway.

John rose and grabbed his jacket. "I'm sorry, guys. I really don't feel well. Can you just enjoy the cake without me tonight?"

"Hey, John, what's wrong?"

"I'm fine, really. I must've had too much beer. Don't worry about me." He hurried out, nearly knocking his chair over.

Not until he heard the gentle gurgling of water nearby did he realize he was on the Kennedy Bridge, with no memory of how he'd gotten there. He peered over the railing into the depths of the Rhine, dimly illuminated by a slim crescent moon whose reflection wobbled erratically on the water. He'd read that after the frantic demand of the lungs for air overcame the instinct to survive, drowning was easy. He would pass calmly into unconsciousness and freedom.

Only that moon, its edges scalloped like a mountain range by the rippling current, stood between him and blissful relief. It seemed as if the life he longed for was always just beyond a mountain. Inside the one to the east of his childhood home, those elegant castles had offered his feminine self freedom from her shackles. Then he'd crossed the Continental Divide for college in Boulder, hoping the big city social life would solve his problems.

On his first Christmas Eve there, he'd emerged after a solitary meal into a few inches of fresh snow on the nearly deserted campus. Flakes fluttered like frost-covered fireflies into the scattered circles of illumination cast by the streetlights. He'd walked westward, toward the hills.

In the four months of fall semester he'd really not made a single friend. His midterm grades were dismal; he'd probably soon lose his prestigious scholarship. He was even getting a C in calculus. The only A he could hope for was in German, which was a snap. But he didn't know why he was taking it. Or why he was there at all, for that matter.

In high school he'd managed to get straight A's, even as he doggedly spent each afternoon at football practice. And then spent part of each evening reading copies of *Hairdo* and *Seventeen* that he slipped in with groceries for his mother to make the purchase seem innocuous. Afterward he'd feel guilty and dirty, ashamed of his very existence.

Boulder had brought no relief. He couldn't stomach going home for the holidays even though he had nothing to stay at school for. In fact, he had nothing to stay anywhere for.

He hadn't dressed for the temperature, and both fingers and feet were growing numb. He was near the edge of Chautauqua Park. The trails up Flagstaff Mountain and the Flatirons were just ahead. The thought suddenly seemed attractive. According to Jack London, freezing to death really wasn't so unpleasant.

A small Christmas tree with only white lights in the two-story house on the hillside above caught his eye. He wondered if they were Germans—he'd read that this was the custom there. The soft orange glow behind the curtain looked so friendly and warm. A faint resonance stirred, misty and aching, echoing a faded dream, hinting of a reason to return.

But that presented a dilemma. Staying in school was no longer an option.

It wasn't the first time he'd thought of leaving. He'd already gone to the library several times, groping for ways to avoid the draft and Vietnam. Certain "essential defense-related jobs" offered a deferment. But how to get one wasn't clear.

One government publication had mentioned communications intelligence, which he understood to mean electronic eavesdropping. The name of a CIA department spokesman was given. That night he decided to write a letter. It was an absurdly long shot, but maybe they'd like his combination of skills in radio, typing, and German.

Four months later he was at the embassy in Bonn, ready to spend the next two years analyzing East German communications. And trying to analyze himself, hoping to understand and vanquish his demons.

After many hours in the libraries he learned that such a thing as transsexuality was known to psychiatrists. Someone named George Jorgensen had become Christine Jorgensen in Denmark in 1952. She'd written an autobiography, which he ordered. For the first time in his life John knew he wasn't alone, and he wasn't a horrible pervert. And change was possible.

Bonn had no mountains, and at Christmas he'd felt irresistibly drawn to the Alps. And so it was that exactly one year after his nighttime excursion in Boulder, he'd left his pension in Garmisch-Partenkirchen, alone as before. The air was crisp and calm, forming a fog of breath while snow crunched underfoot. The ordinary tourist wares—coffee cups, tiny alpine houses, candles—in the dimly lit storefronts seemed charming, even elegant.

A murmur grew steadily from around a corner. People in a procession carrying candles were singing solemnly in a cadence that seemed familiar despite the foreign language. Its meaning was a mystery, but this call from a different culture was magical. It made him feel at home, as though he belonged somewhere for the first time in his life.

But when the midnight procession faded away, the empty silence drowned his moment of elation, and the sharp alpine skyline seemed no different from the one in Colorado. Whether in Boulder or Bonn, change wasn't possible. It would violate rules as rigid as the laws of physics in the eyes of everyone he knew. Those people would consider him a horrible pervert, Jorgensen's doctors notwithstanding. He'd become an untouchable exile.

He'd shuffled slowly back to his room, grimly stuffing his feelings back in the closet. Where they'd stayed, grumbling occasionally, until tonight.

The ink-black Rhine beckoned under the bridge. The devil and the deep blue sea—never had a timeworn expression been so timely. He thought briefly of praying. *To your parents' God? Are you out of your mind?* He put one leg of his rangy six-foot-two-inch frame over the railing, instinct fighting every inch, despair pushing relentlessly forward. *Just do it. Nothing's worked. You're out of options. You won't regret it.*

But he stopped and turned back. Somewhere in his miserable childhood, there must have been a moment of hope. Hanna had never quite given up. And now she insisted loudly on her right to come out. This was *her* body. She wouldn't let John destroy it.

Back in her studio apartment, Hanna found the little girl's diary deep in the bottom dresser drawer. She slid the catch back on the tiny lock. Inside its pink cover, decorated with sparkly butterflies, sprays of purple lilacs in the margins framed a pale pink background. She turned to the first blank page and wrote slowly.

11 May 1970

How many times have I wondered if life was worth it? But I'd always swallow hard and plow back into the grind. Tonight seemed different.

Why shouldn't the guys have brought that cake? Of course they couldn't have known that being the man of anything was my ongoing worst nightmare. And no one will ever give me the cake of my dreams, with a pink-ribboned Barbie in a flowing white dress on top and pink candles around the base.

Not unless I tell them the truth.

I've done all the library research I can. I know what I am. I'm a girl, and I always have been. And my name is Hanna, not John. I know there are others like me. But I'm afraid to do what they've done. I'm afraid of being an outcast. Or even dying. What would I tell my parents? How would I even start? I've denied it so long, just to live.

But I can't live with that denial anymore either.

She closed the diary and put it in the bottom of her suitcase. Those white Christmas lights had saved her life the first time. Another formless memory had done it tonight. Would she be so lucky the next time?

She didn't know the answers to any of the questions she'd just asked. But she hadn't yet written the most important one of all.

Her father's cousin had dropped out of high school to enlist in the Navy, and spent most of World War II in a Japanese prisoner of war camp. Afterward he rose to the rank of master diver, and became a leader in experimental undersea operations. Some had included NATO and the German navy.

After the untimely death of his mother he'd lived with his aunt and uncle and was treated like a sibling to Hanna's father. Later he'd taken an extra special interest in her. After visiting her in Germany he began to correspond frequently. His descriptions of how he'd survived the horrific challenges of the war without bitterness toward his captors had deeply impressed her, and he'd become a very special friend and mentor. What would he say?

She wrote a note on a page torn from the end of the diary, which she would airmail on arrival at the Frankfurt airport.

Dear Richard,

This will be unlike any of my previous letters. There's no suitable introduction, so I'll come straight to the point.

For as long as I can remember, I've felt like I was really a girl, and I simply can't live the way I am any more. I've come close to killing myself twice.

Psychiatrists call this transsexuality, and it's possible to take female hormones and have a sex-change operation. There's a book about it by Dr. Harry Benjamin. I'm considering doing this when I get home. If you're not too angry with me, maybe you'll only give me a stern lecture about how despicable it is. You're the only person I've told so far; it could just stay that way.

I'll be at the Lazy J Motel in Boulder till I find a place to live.

Sincerely,

Hanna Shelby

A few hours later she rose, groggy and bleary-eyed, and donned a sports coat for the trip home. Standing at a table in the train station with coffee to counter the morning chill, listening to the familiar screeching wheels and muddled echoing voices, she tried to quell her qualms about the future. She started when her boss tapped her on the shoulder.

"John, thanks for a great job. Here's a recommendation letter." He cracked a wry smile. "You're leaving just in time—I think you couldn't have put off that haircut much longer."

Her nervous laugh sounded a lot like a giggle, and she wondered once again if he had any inkling of her struggle. She'd been keenly aware of the critical stares as her hair crept down her earlobes and over her shirt collar.

As the train that would take her to the Frankfurt airport pulled away, Hanna closed her eyes. The rhythmic clacking under the carriage calmed her churning thoughts a little.

Christine Jorgensen's autobiography had offered a tantalizing glimmer of hope. She'd gained respect, even admiration, finding fulfillment in a rewarding career. Yet it still seemed impossible. Demons from a fear-laced childhood screamed at her like jackals. And the closer she got to Colorado the louder those voices were sure to become.

CHAPTER 2

GISELA HOFFMANN WATCHED her husband unfold the Sunday *Denver Post* and fish out one section: an in-depth report on the near-disastrous Apollo 13 moon mission one month ago. Breakfast conversation was over for a while. With a faint sigh, she downed the last of her coffee and went upstairs.

She rarely opened the door of the first room at the top. Nothing could compensate for the absence of the precious spirit who had given it life before. Not the east-facing picture window with its expansive view toward the University of Colorado, nor the pink and white flowers painted on the pastel blue wall, nor the quixotic bedspread with its mixture of kittens and puppies frolicking in a cloud of butterflies.

This morning was different. Elisabeth had been looking forward to seeing the first human on the moon. She'd missed it by two days.

But her presence lingered. A glint from the glitter-and-sticker encrusted diary on the top nightstand shelf caught Gisela's eye.

Ich heisse Elisabeth Hoffmann, it began in precise block letters. *If I haven't given you permission to read this, please put it down now!!!*

She didn't obey. A few tears trickled down her cheeks as she leafed through the pages, observing the third-grade German turn into fluent English. She couldn't remember a time when she hadn't been in awe of those writing skills.

She set the diary down and went to her own bedroom. The collection of mementos on her dresser was like a shrine, where she could commune with her daughter's spirit. Of course she didn't take such mysticism seriously. Yet those things made the world feel softer and more nurturing, the way the sharp contrasts in the foothills behind the house blended harmoniously in the light of a full moon, reflecting the sun that had gone down.

The center was occupied by a portrait-size photograph in the typical pose that high-school yearbook photographers coax from their clients. Short, winsome brown curls framed her brown eyes and heart-shaped face, but her demeanor was serious, like a professor.

On either side were smaller photos. A little dancer on stage, in a tutu. A young skier, triumphantly holding a medal aloft. A preteen in her nightgown, hair in curlers, petting the kitten purring in her lap. One more like the portrait, behind a microphone on a podium. Accompanying the photos lay a throng of stuffed animals and a polished cedar jewelry box with a pearl-inlaid hairbrush resting on top.

She'd struggled with her feelings for ten months. But resolution hadn't come. The past wasn't coming back. Many times she'd thought that a new occupant for the room could help her move on. But she could never bring herself to do it.

She carefully placed the diary in the drawer of the nightstand and went back downstairs.

HANNA RETRIEVED HER Fiat sport coupe at the New Jersey port the day after landing. For two days she meandered through upstate New York and past the Great Lakes, sleeping in hostels and eating carrots and potato chips, trying hard not to think about what awaited her in Boulder. Finally she crossed the plains nonstop, pulled into the Lazy J parking lot late Friday night, and fell exhausted into bed.

She spent the weekend wandering the streets, seeking insight from familiar scenes that were now incomprehensibly foreign. At ten Monday morning she was still in her room when the phone rang. "Airmail letter here for you, Miss Shelby."

The sleepy woman on night shift hadn't shown any reaction when Hanna signed in. But as she introduced herself to the receptionist now, his surprised expression quickly twisted into a sneer. "You—Hanna? Like 'A Boy Named Sue'?"

She snatched the envelope and nearly ran out the door to escape his guffaw. In her room she opened it with shaking fingers. So much depended on it. She could still change her mind.

> *Dear Hanna,*
>
> *Your news came as a surprise, but your openness embodies the integrity that I've come to expect from you.*
>
> *As I've stated in our previous conversations, men and women everywhere act from the same basic motivations driven by our glandular impulses and fundamental instincts for family, personal fulfillment and peer-group recognition.*

Hanna couldn't resist a smile. Despite his lack of formal education, Richard was more of an intellectual than many Ivy League graduates.

> *Every person is responsible for his own personal search for truth. I know nothing about the details of your situation, but it appears that you have looked deeply and seriously for that truth.*
>
> *That is what is also best for those around you, but many, if not most, will not see that. You will have to decide which path to take: the one that is right for you, or the one that others say is right for you. If you decide on the former, you may have to face unpalatable consequences. In times of uncertainty, a leader cannot look back.*

When you confront this choice, remember that in the end, it is your decision alone. You will never regret making the right one.
      I'll write more when I have learned more. In the meantime, I wish you good luck.
      Very sincerely,
      Richard Shelby, TMCM, USN (ret.)

She held the letter briefly to her bosom, wanting to pull it inside her, to meld with it. This man, with an exterior of quintessential macho toughness, had given her his blessing. What was inside wasn't always what was outside.

Just like her.

With her mind cleared like the air after a mountain thunderstorm, she walked the half-mile to the university admissions office and started perusing psychology course catalogs. The name Carl Rogers caught her attention. His concept of "unconditional positive regard" had been a prominent discovery in her research. To Rogers, the authentically expressed self was the key to health.

She was reading the synopsis of a course taught by a former student of his, Dr. Pamela Preston. Hanna located her office—and kept going, as the imperious guard still lodged inside her silently screamed: *if someone knows, it will destroy your future.*

Then she thought of the bridge. She'd made a decision. And the one person she'd confided in had said: don't look back.

She returned to Preston's door. The cheerful voice that answered her hesitant knock belonged to a woman with an Afro and an open smile, half hidden behind scattered stacks of papers and books and a small nameplate.

"What can I do for you?"

"Uh, umm, uh . . ."

"Relax. Something about finals?"

"I'm sorry, I'm being silly, I know. It's hard to talk about. I came to ask you for some advice."

"Please, sit down." Preston's smile morphed into a more serious though still friendly mien. "University professors love to give advice. Now what's the question?"

Hanna was seized with panic. What made her think this unknown professor could be trusted with a secret she barely trusted herself with? And what if she did? There couldn't possibly be any future for her. Christine Jorgensen became a nightclub entertainer. That wasn't her.

"Well, um, do you know anything about transsexuality?" There. She'd said it. She braced herself for a laugh, a frown, a sneer, anything but acceptance.

"A little, though I'm far from an expert. Tell me more about your interest."

"I—I think I am one. I've read as much as I could, and I've spent a lot of time thinking about it. But I've never told anyone." She gripped the arms of the chair till her knuckles were white. She was breaching protective mental habits built with daily reinforcement for years. "It seems like most people find it shameful or perverted or sinful. I don't know what to do. And I don't know how to do it. Or what's even possible."

"I can't tell you what to do. You have to decide that for yourself. But I can listen, and I can help you realize your thoughts are valid. You have to accept yourself if you want to be a full and healthy person. You are who you are, and you're okay. That's the starting point."

Preston reached across her desk and placed her hand on Hanna's. "How about if we walk over to the Student Union and get a cup of coffee, and you can tell me more?" She stood up and pulled a packet of Kleenex from her desk drawer.

Hanna held back until they were seated at a table in a corner, with no one close by. Then the dam broke. She cried more than she spoke. She spoke of her childhood yearnings, her doll, her high school torment, her malaise in college. And about nearly jumping from a bridge in Bonn.

She didn't talk about the thrashing from her father, the very thought of which left her frozen with foreboding. Nor about the ride in the pickup truck and the lecture that had been so terrifying that she'd stolidly resolved not to remember it.

Preston listened patiently. "Hanna, you're speaking from your heart, that's clear. Your attitude is awesome. You already know the path will be hard. You have to be determined."

"I am—I think." She smiled weakly. "I'm so afraid. I mean, I don't know the first thing. Like, just for clothing—how would I know what to buy, or what sizes, or anything? And I'd be laughed out of the store."

"That, Miss Shelby, is the easy part. We can go shopping this afternoon, and I'll make an appointment for you with my hair stylist. It's the therapist part we need to worry about. You'll need hormones, and that takes an MD."

"Won't that cost a fortune?"

"Not necessarily. I'm thinking of one who's a good prospect. I've talked to him a few times at local conferences. He's different—came here from San Francisco instead of a prestigious big city because he loves fly fishing." She flashed her compassionate smile. "Sometimes even before work. I think he may understand you. He has empathy."

Hanna tried to process her feelings as they returned to Preston's office. From abject despondency to emerging hope—the world looked so different from a mere hour ago.

"Dr. Preston, if you don't mind, can I ask you why you're doing this? I mean, I guess I was wishing the name of Carl Rogers could mean something good. But I didn't expect . . ."

"Your expectation wasn't wrong. A few years ago a paper reported a survey of MDs. Over eighty percent of psychiatrists thought someone like you was severely neurotic, and only ten percent would approve the surgery you want. For surgeons in general it's three percent. Many of these learned doctors consider you 'morally depraved' and a 'threat to society.' But enough depressing statistics. Hopefully Doctor Feinstein will be among the ten percent. I need to make two phone calls, and then we'll do that shopping."

She asked her secretary to arrange a call with Feinstein, and told Hanna to wait there. She disappeared into her own office and emerged barely a minute later. "Your hair appointment is at four thirty. Now let's get you some nice clothes."

During her first year of college Hanna had sometimes walked hastily through the women's sections of department stores, imagining buying something. She'd always left quickly, ashamed and guilty. She still felt like she was trespassing in a forbidden space. But behind her benefactor's protecting shield she tasted a hint of belonging. Could she really come here on her own, breezily chattering with the salesgirls about styles and fabrics?

After Preston dropped her off at her motel with a promise to call with any word from Feinstein, Hanna impatiently pulled the packages out of the shopping bags. She was glad she'd been carefully saving her money in Germany. She tore the wrappings off the half dozen skirts and blouses, three pairs of shoes, bra, purse, and basic makeup bag and arranged them in neat rows on the bed. And then she danced around the room with childlike abandon, a colt discovering the freedom of a field for the first time.

She finally chose a purple A-line skirt with a ruffled hem and a matching ruffled blouse, with black T-strap wedge sandals. As she looked in the mirror she was both euphoric and dejected. The image she'd dreamed of so often was almost there, and yet so far away.

Underneath, her body was the same angular abomination—nearly a perfect rectangle. And her boyish hair didn't even cover her ears.

Still, as she walked to her car and felt the gentle swish of the skirt on her bare legs, sat down and swung them into the car in one smooth motion, and placed a sandaled foot on the clutch pedal, the euphoria started to get the upper hand.

Until she got to the salon. It was the ultimate insanity to think she could come in here. She braced herself for a chorus of laughter. But one of the women immediately approached her with a smile. "Hi, my name's Trisha. Pam told me you haven't had a perm before. Would you like to choose a style from our book?"

Of course—Dr. Preston had told Trisha about her. But still—all those hours with the magazines in high school, imagining—it couldn't possibly be for real. Dreams didn't actually come true.

"I'm sorry—I'm not sure . . . do—do you think this would be okay with my hair?" Hanna kept her eyes down as she pointed to a photo with soft, intricate curls and feathery bangs. She had to be glowing crimson.

"Oh, that's a super selection, Hanna—it matches your heart-shaped face really well. You'll look like Petula Clark with tighter curls. Ready to go downtown tonight for sure."

Trisha soon put her at ease, assured her that the noxious smell from the perm would dissipate after a day, and sketched a setting pattern which Hanna reverently tucked into her purse.

She finished with a makeup tutorial. "No charge for the makeup. That's my gift to Pam. And to you—hoping you come back."

After Trisha brushed the last curl into place, she held up a mirror. "How do you like it?"

But Hanna didn't see a twenty-one-year-old woman. She saw a seven-year-old girl, shyly offering a freshly baked pie to waiting guests in her make-believe palace.

This was who she was. Who she'd always been. The girl who longed to come out of her hiding place, holding her head high, and laugh and play and cry with the others. To simply be with the others. And to be herself.

And now she could do it. Apparently dreams *did* come true.

"It's perfect."

Now she just had to learn to actually be the girl she saw.

AT EIGHT O'CLOCK in the morning two days later, Hanna entered the wood-paneled office of Dr. Morris Feinstein, M.D. His lanky frame, wavy black hair and open-collar blue shirt completely confounded her expectations for the appearance of a psychiatrist. He listened with unwavering focus.

"You're not alone, Hanna, and I'll do my best to support you. I haven't actually had a transsexual client before, but in my residency I became acquainted with Harry Benjamin. The *Benjamin Standards of Care* define the field. I copied these excerpts for you."

He fished a small sheaf of papers from a drawer and placed them on the desk. "You need to spend a year, preferably two, living as a woman before the operation. That's to make sure you aren't making a mistake that you'll regret. The effects of the testosterone blockers and the estrogen are reversible, especially in the early stages, but surgery is not. So I need you to think very carefully about your answer to this question. Do you have any doubt about what you're doing?"

She shook her head. Her makeover had opened a door from hell to paradise: veiled, full of daunting challenges—but the promise of life.

Dr. Feinstein smiled. "I didn't think so. What you've told me was remarkably well thought through. I'll give you the hormone prescriptions today."

Hanna had difficulty concentrating as he talked about breast growth, hormone side effects, and blood tests. Visions of her feminine future floated through her mind like movie scenes, with her the star.

"Fortunately, one of the few clinics where these operations are done is right here in Colorado next to New Mexico, in Trinidad."

She snapped back to attention. "How much does it cost?"

"More than I do." He smiled. "You'll have to save some money. But with planning you can do it. Even as a student." He handed her more papers. "In the meantime, you're dressing superbly. I really like your hair—very elegant."

Hanna flushed as she touched her hair. "I know this is out of date. But I've spent my life envying girls and their neat hairstyles. I'm probably obsessed, but I wanted the curls so badly."

"You're how tall?"

"Six-two."

"So when heads turn at the sight of this really tall woman, they'll see a hairdo that's unambiguously feminine—no chance of confusion with hippies there. I'd say it's a definite plus for passing. Do you have an electrologist?"

She'd never heard the word. "I beg your pardon?"

"For your beard. Once you've gone through puberty you're stuck with it. The procedure isn't complicated. The electrologist sticks a tiny needle in your skin next to the hair and gives it a short electrical stimulus. It can feel like anything from a little pinprick to a nasty sting. Unfortunately, it has to be done for each hair, and there can be a few hundred thousand."

Hanna gulped and tried to hide her shock. Feinstein smiled. "A good electrologist can move quickly. Usually a few hundred hours is enough. My secretary can give you a recommendation."

He leaned forward intently. "Now, Hanna, you've lived twenty-one years with constant reinforcement of masculine attitudes, masculine language, masculine culture. But now you're entering a new culture. You'll be the same person, and yet everything is affected—it isn't only clothing and makeup. A culture is made by a society. To become a part of that society you have to learn its language. Do you have woman friends ready to help you?"

Hanna shook her head again. How could she make those friendships unless the women knew her as a woman? And she couldn't pass as a woman without knowing their language. She'd hardly begun her journey, and already she was stuck.

She looked down at her lap. "That's what I'm most afraid of. Changing how I look—I was worried, because I didn't know how, but it seems maybe that's not so hard. But knowing how to act . . . I mean, I *don't* know, and it's scary." For a moment the fear welled up and she wanted to go back to a safe space.

But there was no safe space.

"Dr. Feinstein, there are people who would kill me. That's why I thought for so long that I couldn't do this. Maybe I can't."

"Hanna, I know the hate is real. And the ignorance is pervasive. But that ignorance can also help you. Most people have never even heard of a transsexual, let alone known one. As long as you present a reasonably feminine image, that's how you'll be seen. I think you'll pass well, your height notwithstanding. And I'm here to help."

This was so complicated. But she was feeling better. It seemed like it was all possible. There was only one hurdle left. "I have one question. Registration is in, umm, about two weeks. How can I be Hanna—and female—on my student ID?"

"Changing your name is a simple court procedure, though it takes a few months to finalize. But being legally identified as a female requires a change on your birth certificate, which requires the surgery. It's just like Catch-22."

He pushed the papers toward her. "Dr. Benjamin's clients, as far as I knew, either had fake IDs or jobs where they didn't need one. I'm afraid working the streets isn't an uncommon situation for transsexuals."

The time was up and he was walking toward the door. "I wish I had a solution. I'm sorry. I'll be happy to talk to the university administrators if it'll help. That's as much as I can do."

Hanna drove back to the motel feeling like she'd grasped a tiny ledge and was now dangling from it.

This couldn't work. A professor would call her "John," and students would see her hairdo and clothes and double over in laughter—if she was lucky. She pictured Earl Williams riding up to the house and dismounting, spurs jangling, grabbing her hat and examining her hair. "Thought I tole you yesterday to get a haircut. Don't lemme see this again or you'll be eatin' Rocky Mountain Oysters fer dinner."

Dr. Preston had made it seem so simple. But the exit from hell opened onto an abyss that she couldn't jump, and its depths were still more fearsome. A long-haired guy might get harassed, even in the era of hippies and rock stars. But actually looking like a girl was a path to merciless contempt and ostracism.

Besides the psychologists she'd only told Richard. She could still go back.

To what?

She locked her room and began to walk. She had no destination but away. Away from her past, away from the future. Away from any thoughts at all. Let the universe decide her fate.

She followed Colorado Avenue onto the campus. She was hungry—since arriving in Boulder she'd subsisted mainly on vending machine snacks. She found a café on The Hill and ordered eggs and coffee. As she stared idly at the *Daily Camera* that someone had left on the table, the waitress delivered her order and asked if she wanted anything more.

"Thanks, that's all. But can you tell me where the restroom is?"

"At the end of that hall, past the men's room, and downstairs. I don't know why they make *us* go so far—but that's men for you. They design the buildings."

Us.

Two days after emerging from her crusty cocoon and gently flexing her rainbow wings, she'd passed! Yes, it was only a casual encounter, a few words. But she'd done it. Roller coaster, whiplash, yo-yo, see-saw—from guarded anticipation through excited optimism, dashed hopes and hopeless misery, to success in this ultimate challenge, all in one day, no metaphor could even come close.

She fairly gobbled the eggs. She would not disappoint her cousin—or herself. With a slurp of coffee she slapped two dollars onto the table, grabbed the newspaper, and half-ran back to her room. At the very bottom of her suitcase was her diary. She read the last words.

But I can't live with that denial anymore either.

Underneath she wrote:

Nor will I.

Then she locked the diary. It was time to say good-bye to those days. She drove to Chautauqua Park, where she knew she would find a lilac bush, and buried the book as she'd once buried her broken doll.

She'd thought then that her dream was over. But it hadn't been. Maybe dreams were immortal, growing back from the graves of their fractured fragments.

Her new life would be nurtured by the tears from all those years of grief.

In her room she found another letter from her cousin. So soon—for a moment she was paralyzed by fear. Maybe after he'd learned more, as he'd promised, would come disapproval.

> *Dear Hanna,*
>
> *Another team leader in one of my NATO exercises was a German diver named Werner Jendrossek. More than once he spoke of a high school classmate who had moved to Colorado several years ago. After I received your letter, I called Werner. He offered to connect you with his friend: Hermann Hoffmann, HIllcrest 2-7240. They live close to the university.*
>
> *Werner was sure that Hermann and his wife would be pleased to meet you. In your current circumstances, you will probably need to make new friends, and this couple may even introduce you to others.*
>
> *With best wishes,*
> *Richard*

She felt much more than mere relief. Richard was showing her that intense trials were likely to lead to greater understanding. Obvious in hindsight, perhaps, but *she* hadn't thought of it. Probably a lot of others didn't, either.

She sat down at the little motel room desk and removed a sheet of paper from the drawer. Two years ago a couple had said a stilted goodbye to their son, not understanding why he was leaving. And she hadn't been able to explain how he'd never been there.

The wastebasket contained four crumpled wads before she finished the letter.

Dear Mom and Dad,

    I hope you're well. I'm safely back in Boulder.

    This letter will come as a shock, but I don't know how to cushion it. I know you're going to be upset and angry.

    For as long as I can remember, I've felt like I was really a girl.

    I've felt so much shame, and tried every possible way to make it go away, but nothing changes it. I just can't live the way I am any more. I've thought—often—of killing myself.

    While I was in Germany I learned about transsexuality in the libraries, and I've seen a psychiatrist here. The only resolution is to take female hormones and have an operation that produces female anatomy. A new first name goes with the new identity. Before the operation you live as a woman for a year, which I've started doing.

    I'm sorry. I love you very much. I'll come visit next Monday, but I needed to tell you this way first.

    Love, Hanna

She slumped in her chair, drained by the emotional marathon she'd just run. She had to get out of this motel. She gloomily scanned the newspaper classifieds. Even with a private room—which she probably couldn't afford—passing still seemed unfathomable. But wait: there was the number Richard had given her. Maybe they could suggest some options.

Nostalgia flooded in as she heard Gisela Hoffmann's accent. Had she really left Germany only nine days ago? It seemed like another lifetime. Nervously, she gave only a brief introduction, mentioning that her cousin knew Werner Jendrossek. Gisela sounded astonished, and extended an invitation for coffee the next day at noon.

Hanna bought a stamp at the front desk and left the envelope to be mailed. The news would spread quickly. Her aunts and uncles would say she was selfish and irresponsible, a dishonor to her family. Cousins would ridicule her. Family friends in Paonia would shake their heads. None of them would ever talk to her again except with scorn. Certainly she could never expect help from any of them.

Back in her room, she took off all her clothes and hung them carefully in the closet. She looked at herself in the mirror for a long time, crawled into bed, and sobbed.

CHAPTER 3

GISELA WAS SURPRISED when the doorbell rang precisely at noon—Americans were rarely so punctual.

"Hello," the visitor said, with apparent nervousness. "I'm Hanna Shelby—the girl who called yesterday."

"Please come in." Gisela averted her gaze to hide her astonishment. The visitor was a little taller than Elisabeth had been. But the face and hair were eerily similar.

Hanna stepped hesitantly inside. *"Danke schön. Ich hoffe, ich komme nicht ungelegen."*

Gisela looked back up sharply, now thoroughly unsettled.

"Sie sprechen also Deutsch? Wo haben Sie das gelernt?"

"I lived in Germany for two years," Hanna continued in English. "I'm still a beginner."

"You speak quite well, really. And no, this isn't at all inconvenient. Please come this way." In the dim interior light, the likeness to Elisabeth was even more compelling. That it was impossible didn't lessen her disorientation.

Then the radiance of sunlight from the east-facing living room window fell on her visitor's blue eyes, and the spell was broken. But as her heart slowed, Gisela realized how fast it had been beating. Her reaction had surely been noticed and ought to be explained.

She gestured toward the senior yearbook portrait on the wall as they sat down to the coffee. "My daughter, Elisabeth. The resemblance is striking, no? And then to hear you speak German—it was so unexpected."

Hanna's gaze lingered on the photo. "Yes, it's amazing. Is she in college also?"

"She died last year."

"Oh, I'm so sorry. I can't even imagine how difficult that must be. Maybe—should I leave? I certainly don't want to be the cause of painful memories for you."

"No, no, it's all right. So many connections to someone I didn't know existed only a day ago. How did your cousin meet Werner?"

Hanna began matter-of-factly, but there was something deeper than nostalgia in her recollections and resonance with the German culture. This wasn't quite the casual meeting that Gisela had expected. Under the salon-perfect hair and salmon cowl-neck top with coordinated skirt, so unlike the prevailing student fashions, she sensed a vulnerable girl, hiding some unhealed hurt.

And it was bringing up her most motherly feelings.

When Hanna mentioned that she'd started looking for a room, Gisela abruptly stood up. "I'm very sorry. Will you excuse me for a moment? I'll be right back."

She called her husband on the phone in their bedroom. "Hermann, the girl I told you about is looking for a room to rent. I'd like to offer her Elisabeth's room."

"That's rather sudden, isn't it? You've agonized over this for so long."

"I know. I just have a feeling about her. You'll understand when you meet her."

Back in the living room, she apologized for the interruption. "Hanna, would you like to see Elisabeth's room? It might be suitable for you."

"Really? Are you sure? I mean—wouldn't that be too painful?"

"Thank you for being so sensitive. First let's see if you like it."

Hanna entered the room in slow, delicate steps, as if afraid of something. "It's spectacular."

Gisela strove to act professionally. "The bathroom is private. There's a door to the other bedroom, but that's only a hobby room."

Hanna sat on the edge of the bed and briefly placed her head in her hands. "There must be so much of her here. For you to share it with a stranger—I'm humbled beyond words. But I feel like I'd be an intrusion."

When Hanna looked up again, Gisela saw the expression of a child fearing a reprimand, but not understanding why. Or an orphan, lost and confused. She moved a little closer. "My daughter had planned a life of learning. She would want that to continue. The way I think of it is that the living can continue the life of those who've passed away."

"That's so beautiful. But I can't imagine being capable of it."

"The renter doesn't have to do anything other than use the room. If I left it untouched for the rest of my life, it wouldn't get any easier. Just doing something is important."

"You're sure?"

"I'm very sure. Is thirty-five dollars a month okay? You can use the kitchen also."

"That would be awesome."

As they returned to the living room, the air was charged with thunderstorm intensity. Hanna twisted her fingers and smoothed her skirt repeatedly as she sat down. "Frau Hoffmann, there's something very important I have to tell you. It might change your mind."

Gisela waited.

"I-I was so nervous . . . obviously I'm still nervous—have you ever heard the word 'transsexual'?"

"No, I don't think so."

Gisela didn't think she'd ever seen someone look so mortified as Hanna stammered out her secret, perspiring and looking mostly at her lap.

Was this a red flag? Gisela hadn't planned on becoming a therapist. She was in no place to assuage someone else's pain. She had enough of her own. Yet her desire to reach out to this girl with her conflicted spirit had only grown.

Gisela was a reasonable woman, and reason said Hanna should go. But emotion said stay. And emotion seemed to be winning.

"Well, that explains your height and voice. I wondered about that, but I've seen women as tall as you. Elisabeth was actually close to your height. You seem naturally feminine, though, and I took that at face value. But you tell me, Hanna. Why should it matter?"

"I—I, well, I mean . . . it shouldn't. One is the same person, really, before and after. It doesn't change one's basic character. For other people, it's just the, you know, traditional femininity and masculinity things."

"Exactly. What stood out to me is how you spoke of my daughter and respected my feelings. I can't say I understand your experience, but it's none of my business, really."

Hanna seemed on the verge of tears. "Thank you. I—I'm sort of overwhelmed. This is all happening so fast."

"What does your family think?"

"I haven't seen them yet, I just wrote to them. I don't expect—they're very religious and politically conservative. But maybe I'm wrong about them too."

After an awkward silence Gisela stood up. "I wish you luck. We'll have occasions to talk more. You may move in whenever you're ready."

Near the door she paused. "A month after Elisabeth died, I cleaned out the room. I've been thinking of renting it for ages, but it was always too hard. Now I don't even know you yet, and you seem like more than a renter. It feels somehow— what's the English word?—auspicious. Anyway, I'm happy you came."

Alone again, Gisela sat quietly on the sofa for a few minutes, remembering a conversation over coffee ten years ago, shortly before they left Germany.

Soon after a friend's son graduated from college, his parents discovered he was gay. A huge row followed, with his father threatening to forbid him to visit. His mother was caught between the two. "What did I do wrong?" she wailed. "And what should I do now?"

Gisela thought for a few moments. She didn't know anyone who was a homosexual, and she didn't understand it. It seemed illogical, to love someone of the same sex romantically.

But what if her daughter turned out to be one? Would it change her love as a mother? That certainly wasn't logical either. She would always love her child.

"Bettina, he's your son. He graduated, he's got a job offer, he's doing what he wants to do. And he loves you. What more can we hope for from our children?"

Bettina sighed. "Tell that to my husband."

Of course Gisela had not inserted herself into this quarrel. But she hadn't forgotten it. Throughout the sixties she watched in amazement as parents and principals turned into tyrants when boys' hair began to touch ears and collars. Neither hair length nor sexual orientation was anyone else's business but the owner.

She didn't know how her new renter felt. She couldn't even imagine it. But she understood something about the hurt done by prejudice. Elisabeth's childhood stuttering had seen to that. It hadn't lasted long, but it was enough.

Prejudice could not survive the light of knowledge. She had the rest of the day off. She might as well go to the library and start learning.

After a few trips between the card catalog and stacks, she had what she thought she wanted: *Christine Jorgensen: A Personal Autobiography.*

As the desk clerk filled in the book card and due date slip, the librarian passed by. "That was such a weird book. I don't know why we got it. Well, this *is* Boulder."

Gisela looked up. "Yes. A good place to live."

The woman made an indistinct noise. Gisela watched her disappear behind a partition. Boulder was indeed a diverse community, not all of which was open-minded and welcoming.

She'd barely finished the book when her husband arrived home. "*Hallo, mein Schatz.*" She gave him a quick kiss. "*Das Zimmer ist vermietet.*"

"That was quick."

"But I think you should read this book."

Hermann raised his eyebrows when he read the jacket blurb. "I assume this is relevant to her?"

"Yes, she's a transsexual. She's also polite, quiet, and caring. And she speaks some German. I think I'm going to like her."

"You've always talked about renting the room, not looking for a friend."

"I know."

He was right, of course. She hadn't planned on this. But Hanna needed someone to look out for her. And Gisela knew how to do it.

AFTER MOVING IN the next day, Hanna got her first experience of electrolysis, and scheduled another session for Saturday. The electrologist advised against using makeup for at least a day, but she couldn't wait. She needed practice before visiting her parents.

About seven-thirty a.m. Monday she pulled into the Mobil station near the southern edge of town. A young crew-cut attendant, mechanically chewing gum, rested one hand casually on his hip while the other dangled at his side.

Confronting the world again was almost scarier than before she'd found the Hoffmanns. This man stirred her worst fears.

She rolled her window down, stomach churning, and he moved closer. "Fill 'er up?"

Little more than a whisper emerged. "Yes, with premium, please."

After inserting the nozzle and locking the catch on the lever, he circled the car and washed the windows with practiced strokes. "Check the oil, miss?"

"Yes, please. I came across the country a few days ago and haven't had it checked yet." Her voice was suddenly clear, her tone fluent. All from the power of one word.

He fumbled for a moment before finding the hood release catch. "Hmm, I haven't seen one of these before."

"It's a Fiat. I bought it in Germany. I guess they aren't so popular here in Boulder."

"Ah." He peered at the dipstick after cleaning and reinserting it. "Well, your oil's fine. It's barely half a quart down. Myself, I've never heard of a Fiat. But you won't catch me insultin' a customer, especially if she's pretty." He pulled out the gas nozzle. "Just over twelve gallons; that'll be four sixty-two."

Pretty.

Finally her fumbling fingers found her purse and a five-dollar bill.

"You have a real nice day now and thanks for stoppin' by," the attendant said as he returned her change.

With that she might indeed have a real nice day. She remained in this bubble of euphoria all the way through the pine-forested foothills of the Front Range to Monarch Pass. The Fiat's murmuring drone added base to Joni Mitchell's "Both Sides Now" on the stereo. Twice she stopped to listen to the newly sprouted quaking aspen leaves whispering a gentle spring greeting.

But the all-too-familiar farmland on the west slope was like a dreary autumn drizzle on her fragile hopes. And after downtown Paonia came a descent through a chasm of menacing memories on the rutted dirt road that ascended a thousand feet to her childhood home in the picture-postcard mountains.

Above the sagebrush flats, cottonwoods in front of a low sandstone cliff marked the small creek where she'd played among the dandelions and irises. When she thought no adults were looking, she made flower chains that she put in her hair and around her neck.

Then a sharp bend brought into view the pinyons that had been knocked down by a monstrous chain towed between two caterpillar tractors. It was meant to allow more grass to grow. But it looked to her like a sea of scars, ridges of dead trees between twisted trenches.

Finally, she passed through the barbed wire gate onto the gravel parking apron. Before approaching the house, she glanced into the dilapidated machine shop.

The nuts and bolts, the ancient forge, the rusty machines—everything she'd tried to forget was there. Trembling, she focused her thoughts on her new hairdo and smart black pencil skirt with white blouse and white T-strap sandals.

With unsteady legs she walked quickly around to the side of the little shed and parted the branches of the lilac. A few purple irises sprouted next to the rock. Gently she touched the epitaph—*Hanna, August 1956.* Silly superstition, but maybe it might bring her luck in the coming meeting.

At the front door her mother's fleeting display of shock was quickly followed by something more like dismay and disappointment. But she said nothing.

Hanna was totally unprepared for this. She'd expected some sort of stern admonishment. Finally she smiled awkwardly. "Hi, Mom."

Her mother turned away to the kitchen. "Would you like some coffee? We just finished lunch and it's still hot. Dad should be back any minute. He's checking the water for the horses."

Hanna nodded, glad to put off the inevitable unpleasant exchange, and sought the relative safety of her old bedroom. Next to the tiny desk the old manual sewing machine, with its treadle that she'd struggled to reach, threatened to disappear under layers of dust.

Above it, similarly dusty, was her crystal collection. The colors were mainly food coloring, since they'd been too poor to afford anything else. But the fake amethyst actually had real chromium in it. In high school she'd taken chemistry, eager to learn how the element that looked shiny on car bumpers could also look purple. The teacher didn't know.

Over the bed hung the photo of her two cats curled up together on the stone porch, and she almost reached out to pet them. Prince, black except for a white spot on his neck, and his sister Princess in perfect tone reversal, had stayed with her like escorts as she strolled for miles through the pine forests, daydreaming of lush flowering gardens. A year old when her doll was smashed, they'd both died within a few months of her departure for college.

In the living room an east-facing picture window had been added in a remodel ten years ago. Ragged Peak with its fantastic castles occupied its center. Beyond the fields to the north were the pastures—and the ants.

Those ants. Now she understood her nightmares a little better. Menacing creatures had always been ready to swarm over her in a careless moment, a veiled danger embedded in every nook of every pastoral place she looked to for refuge. Far more serious than mere mindless insects, they couldn't be stomped on or crushed by brushing them off. That's what they did to their victims—people like her who somehow threatened their world order.

The sound of the front door opening called Hanna back to the dining room. Her father avoided looking directly at her as they all awkwardly sat down at the table. But she could see the tightness in his face. The anger that had been the bane of her childhood had mellowed over the years, but traces still remained.

She took a deep breath and tried to sound calm. "I know this is probably a shock." Then she had to pause for a long time. "It isn't something recent. I've known it since I was a young child. I fantasized about it from the moment I knew what a girl was, in fact. I'm sure you remember that time with the doll. And how I'd wear my belt so tight." That had gotten her several spankings.

She hadn't expected her mother to shout, but the complete lack of response was unnerving. She dried her sweating palms on a napkin before continuing.

"I tried my best to be the boy that you and everyone else expected, but the girl never went away. I was this male facade over a female self. I don't blame you or anyone for this. It's just a biological fact. People say it's probably caused by hormones in the womb. I guess I'm hoping you can accept that without judgment."

She paused and looked at each of them, willing them to come around, wanting the silence to be a good omen. Her father shifted in his chair and said nothing. But the pain in his eyes was like a hundred barbed hooks in her heart.

Her mother finally spoke, in her familiar parental-lecture mode. "John—I know you want the name Hanna, but I can't imagine using it—we've tried to understand what you wrote. Yes, it *is* a shock. It just doesn't make sense to us. We've always loved you and always will. But this is so far outside our comprehension."

Hanna felt encouraged. This calm, measured response could be an opening to appreciation, maybe even accommodation. She waited quietly.

"The Bible tells us God created men and women separately, and He doesn't make mistakes. We can't see how to reconcile that with what you're doing. On the other hand, the Bible also teaches love and compassion. We still don't know what to think. We prayed a lot after getting your letter and have asked God for guidance, but He hasn't revealed it to us yet."

The moment of hope faded. Hanna knew only too well how strongly those beliefs bound them. The dogma always prevailed over the love.

"Until we know more from Him, I can only say what I think, and Dad agrees with me. You're throwing your life away, for something that's probably a passing phase—a misunderstanding. I cannot for the life of me see how any good could come from it. What if people find out, in spite of how you look? You'd become an outcast. This *can't* be the right way."

Her mother had a point. She needed to pass successfully, for which she needed the ID that she couldn't get for years. The obstacles were like those ant hills. There was no way past them without being eaten alive.

But she'd be eaten alive if she stayed where she was.

"Mom, do you still have my pie pans?"

Her mother sighed deeply. "As well as the stool you used to stand on. John, I know how much you wanted to stay in the house with me. And you were a good helper—you kneaded a lot of bread dough standing on that stool. But you were a boy, and your place was in the fields."

She looked at her husband as if for support. Hanna watched closely, fearing an explosion. But his only reaction was a tightening of the lines that radiated away from his eyes.

"I know we can't wish this away, but I hope you'll consider praying about it—even though I know you don't believe in that now—and maybe something will change. There *has* to be some way to deal with these feelings that isn't so destructive."

"Thank you for not saying anything more negative. I really appreciate it. As to praying—well, what you said is correct. But maybe we can leave it at that and we'll find a way to come together in time."

No one said any more. Eventually Hanna stood up. "I'm sorry," she said. "I do love you. But I have to do this."

"We're sorry too," her mother said. "And we do love you, too."

They hugged briefly, tensely. Hanna walked slowly to her car. As she opened the door, her eyes wandered from the mountain peaks to the lilac. She saw a little girl with pigtails huddled under it, a broken doll cradled in her arms, her princess dress torn and greasy. She looked up, frightened eyes begging for rescue.

With tears trickling down her cheeks, Hanna realized she could never return.

CHAPTER 4

BACK AT THE Hoffmanns, Hanna found a message from Joanna Nyland, Department of Motor Vehicles branch manager in the little town of Granby, southwest of Rocky Mountain National Park.

When she called in the morning, the secretary said Ms. Nyland wished to see her regarding her Colorado driver's license. Her name change application would be needed. A flash of excitement faded into a pounding headache—how did the DMV even know about that? She made an appointment for the next day.

Beyond the Winter Park ski area, the road straightened into the hay fields and grasslands around Fraser, often the coldest weather station in the country during the winter. The little Fiat picked up speed as if it were on a German *Autobahn*, and Hanna's anticipation sped up with it. But the flashing red and blue lights in her rearview mirror brought her back to the present.

The officer grinned. "Late for a party, miss? This won't take long. I'll just need your driver's license and registration."

The friendly grin disappeared abruptly a moment later. "Mr. Shelby, step out of the car."

He held up her license as she obeyed, defenseless as a field mouse under the talons of a hawk. Time came to a halt before he spoke again. "You do know that female impersonation in public is illegal, don't you?"

"I—I don't . . ."

"Wait in your car."

He strode back to his patrol car. Hanna sat motionless, her throat desiccated. She knew stories of redneck policemen beating up homosexuals and hippies. An eternity of ten minutes passed. Plenty of time to imagine the swing of a nightstick against her head.

Finally a sheriff's car pulled in ahead of her. The officer came back, leering.

"Follow that car. If you even think of driving off—well, I recommend against it."

The distant mountain horizon closed in like the walls in a horror movie. She was about to be one of those stories, and no one would even know what had happened to her. Her mind went numb.

Her legs were as leaden as the lump in her stomach, and simply steering in a straight line was a struggle. At the first traffic light she forgot to shift into neutral, killing the engine in a lurching stop.

Inside the Granby courthouse she was ushered into a spartan room with olive-drab walls and dull green window trim, furnished with a few utilitarian desks. A woman in uniform behind one of them gestured toward an ink pad.

"Left thumb first."

"Um, may I—may I just ask . . ."

"Cross-dressing is a crime. A crackdown on perverts like you started in Denver about a year ago, but it's being enforced statewide now."

Her frozen thoughts finally thawed enough to think of an action. "May I make one phone call first?

"Wanna call your lawyer, huh? Yeah, Miranda and all. There's the phone." She pointed to the wall.

Hanna wasn't thinking of a lawyer. If she ever got out of there, she wanted Joanna Nyland to know she'd tried to come. She explained to the secretary in a stammer that she was at the sheriff's office and might miss the appointment.

The woman's voice was crisp and professional. "Thank you for calling us. I'll let Ms. Nyland know."

Her heart went into free fall. When she might be able to speak with another friendly person she had no idea. Moments later a beer-bellied, balding man with a large ring of keys ushered her through a heavy door with a tiny window into a small concrete-lined hall. He patted her down roughly, digging his fingers hard into her crotch with a repulsive grin, before pushing her inside one of two cells whose barred doors were visible.

The guard's voice seemed almost gleeful. "We'll find out later today if you can get out on bail or not. It usually gets crowded here on Wednesday night—midweek bar specials. Some o' them guys might have a good time with you."

And then she was alone. Just on the other side of that wall were people, and a world of light and freedom one door beyond. But she might as well have been in Siberia. She searched for any idea to cling to, anything she could do. But she couldn't even call the guard. The cell had nothing in it but a wood bench and an open toilet bowl below a metal sink at one end. There was no way to tell time.

She wanted to think positively, to keep her mind away from the terror that kept poking in. But there was no way out of this that preserved even a shred of her previous prospects. The guard's implicit threat grew into a certainty. Her life was effectively over.

As she stared vacantly at the floor, head throbbing till she could no longer see clearly, the outer door abruptly opened. The guard shoved an even bigger man through it, and moments later into her cell. He landed on one end of the bench with a thud.

Hanna jumped up, fright quenching the headache for at least a moment. "Wait—it's not night yet. Don't you have another cell?"

The guard's leer made her skin crawl. "Sorry, babe, the other one's out of service. But don't worry—Doug's a choice hunk. You'll have a ball." He bent over in a guffaw.

Her new cellmate looked as though he'd just noticed her. "Why, honey, how nice of you to visit me." His slurred speech matched the stench of alcoholic breath. But his eyes began to clear noticeably as they focused on her. Eons passed before he stood and grabbed her shoulders.

Hanna tried to wrench herself away, but his bearpaw hands wouldn't budge. A little drool dripped from his twisted mouth. "I dunno why they put me in here with you, honeypot, but I'm sure's hell happy 'bout it. You might as well lay back an' like it." He unzipped his fly and let the bulge burst free before he pushed her roughly onto the bench.

She was paralyzed. If she resisted he could easily beat her to a pulp. If she didn't resist he would find out and beat her anyway. For both options the end would be the same.

The clang of the cell door drew his attention, and she jumped up. The guard's dour face was darker than the sky before a thunderstorm. "Well, smartass bastard. Seems someone just *has* to talk to you right this instant." He yanked her out and shoved her into the front office.

The intake clerk held her purse as though it were soaked in sewage. "Who'd've pegged *you* to have friends in high places? But if I were you I'd get the hell out of here pretty fast anyway."

She burst outside and descended the steps with legs so weak she was sure they would collapse like twigs under a falling log. Once in her car she sat for a long time, crying spasmodically.

Eventually she reached the DMV. The secretary greeted her pleasantly. "I'm sorry that took so long. Ms. Nyland will explain." But Nyland acted as if nothing had happened. "Hello, Hanna. You have your name change application and a photo ID?"

Hanna fumbled in her purse with fear-frozen hands. Finally, she extracted the court papers and her old driver's license and passport. Nyland scanned them and passed them to an assistant. She motioned Hanna to a chair.

"Let me explain. Your psychiatrist Morris Feinstein helped me immeasurably with my son a few years ago, when we lived near Denver. So, when he called me last week I said I'd certainly do what I could. Then when I looked up your records, I remembered something. You used to live in Paonia, correct?"

Hanna nodded.

"About five years ago, one of my son's high school classmates was visiting Paonia with his family. He was attacked and seriously hurt, apparently because he had a Beatle haircut. Did you know about that?"

She nodded. She'd last thought of it as she stared into the Rhine River a little over two weeks ago. She'd overheard the quarterback of the football team chortling quietly to the halfback during practice.

Who knew a Coke bottle could go so far in there?

"It made me think extra hard about your case." Nyland shook her head slowly. "What just happened to you is unfortunately not surprising. There *is* such an ordinance in Denver, by the way, but not here. I'm sorry it took so long—I had to get hold of a lawyer. The threat of having him show up with a TV reporter in tow was enough to call their bluff. Otherwise they might have gotten away with it. Who's going to check up on them?"

The assistant came back with a packet of papers which Nyland handed to Hanna.

"Anyway, the sex on your driver's license is normally the one on your birth certificate. But a few people, even today, don't have birth certificates or can't locate them—remnants of the frontier era—and we do have other options. My boss said if your treatment were reversible, I couldn't use them. So, I pointed out that if you stopped taking hormones, whatever breasts you'd grown wouldn't go away. And electrolysis is permanent also."

Hanna held her breath. For the entire last week she'd tried to pretend this dilemma didn't exist. But the morning had made it clear that wasn't an option.

"I'm giving you a temporary license, good for ninety days. You'll get the card with your photo in about two weeks. I'll renew it—ninety days again—as long as Dr. Feinstein certifies and documents your steady progress toward surgery within two years. I'll need to see you here myself each time."

Such a simple thing: the tiny letter "F" on a card. But it had the power to change her life. College seemed possible again. And the hell she'd just gone through wouldn't be repeated. Her spirits were soaring now, on the wings of an official's simple signature. But she dared not show it. That could jinx everything. "Ms. Nyland, I—well, thank you."

"Good luck, Hanna. They'll take your photo right over there. And feel free to use the restroom first if you wish. You probably want your makeup to look its very best."

As she stepped back onto the street, the control disappeared. She skipped down the steps onto the sidewalk, threw her arms in the air like a cheerleader, and hummed a couple of bars of "Climb Every Mountain." She looked furtively around, expecting people to be staring at her. No one was.

She bought a bag of potato chips in a nearby store. The clerk gave her change and smiled. "Have a nice day, hon."

Her car was fifty feet away. She could reach it in a single leap and not dent her energy. Passing was so much more than clothes and hair, just as Dr. Feinstein had said. How she behaved changed how people saw her. And how she felt changed how she behaved.

She'd jumped over the edge of destruction to reclaim her future. But on this roller-coaster another plunge should be imminent.

THE NEXT MORNING began a series of daily electrolysis sessions. She'd already learned that an hour was a very long time to endure electric shocks every few seconds, even if they were tiny ones. Afterward the reddened skin had to be calmed with gobs of aloe vera. But she was determined to make as much progress as possible before classes began. So, against the advice of her electrologist she actually doubled the sessions, rationalizing that she didn't have to show her face to anyone except the Hoffmans. The week seemed like one long operation without anesthetic, but several square inches of her cheeks were free of five o'clock shadow. She was exultant.

Finally, registration day arrived. She handed her temporary driver's license to the clerk, who riffled quickly through the pre-registration forms and pulled one out.

"Umm, I see a 'John Shelby' here, but no 'Hanna Shelby.' Were you pre-registered?"

"Yes, the other name was—umm, a mistake. I've just changed it."

The clerk looked at her intently, and back down at the form. "It seems like more than your name has changed."

Hanna was sure her face was the color of a beet. "Yes," she said finally.

"Wait a moment. I need to talk with my supervisor."

He disappeared behind a partition, and Hanna glanced nervously over her shoulder at the queue snaking out the door and down the sidewalk. Suddenly every student seemed like a leering cowboy eager to pounce on her. The humiliation in Granby was far from healed.

The clerk returned with another man, who studied the papers briefly. "I don't understand what's going on. Your license says you're Hanna Shelby but you claim to also be John Shelby? Which is it?"

His voice was loud enough for a classroom. Snickers punctuated the murmuring behind her. What if one of them came from a future classmate? The roller coaster was dipping toward the depths.

"I'm sorry." Her voice was barely a croak. "Here are the papers I've submitted to the court for changing my name. It takes a few weeks. But they show both names."

The supervisor examined them for a long time while the voices swelled steadily, threatening to rip her fragile self-confidence asunder in a torrent of taunts. She clenched her fists. *Pretend you don't hear them. It'll soon be over.*

"So, are you actually a guy or a girl then? Or something in between? This is very confusing."

Open laughter rippled down the line. The supervisor shook his head. "You need to come with me."

In his office, he sat down behind the unoccupied half of an L-shaped desk, made a brief phone call, and smirked at Hanna, who tried to melt into the wall. "So what kind of queen don't you want to see at your wedding? A *drag queen*, of course."

His colleague snickered. "Yeah, that would be a *drag*, wouldn't it?"

A third man entered and scrutinized the papers. Time stood still. She felt drenched in a downpour of sweat. But eventually he looked up. "The seal on this driver's license appears genuine. You can accept it."

After a few more snide comments she emerged with the registration form bearing her new name and correct sex, which would be her ticket to a student ID with photo. She went home and collapsed on her bed, bedraggled and beaten, wondering how many students in that line might remember her.

And what was she even doing? Where was she going? Was there a solid shore in this new life? Two weeks after moving in, her room was still nearly bare. A few clothes in the closet, university brochures and class schedules, the latest *Time* magazine and *Der Spiegel* next to the Hans Hellmut Kirst novel she'd started in Germany. It was so much like a hotel room that she actually opened the bedside drawer to check for the Gideon Bible.

There was indeed a book there, but not a Bible.

She washed her tear-stained face, refreshed her makeup, and went downstairs, where Gisela had just returned from work.

"Gisela, this book was in the drawer of the nightstand. I think . . ."

Gisela took it tenderly. "Yes, that's her diary. *Was* her diary. But you may read it if you like."

Hanna felt like she was holding a sacred object. On the way to her room she pondered why a near-stranger would be entrusted with something so personal. Gisela had talked about continuing Elisabeth's life. Maybe this was part of what she'd meant.

If so, she'd been entrusted with an assignment, not a privilege.

Elisabeth had been a keen observer and a good reporter. Near the beginning she'd written, still in German: *Papa is a big boss for a company from Germany that makes hi-fi stuff, and Mama works in an office. She takes care of everyone and keeps them in line. He's very tall and she's very short. They have brown hair. Mama's is longer than mine now because I got a pixie bob just before we came. But I still curl it.*

Hanna smiled. From the perspective of a nine-year-old, the six-inch difference between Hermann's six-foot frame and Gisela's was undoubtedly dramatic.

The neat cursive writing was adorned by little sketches in the margins. Some showed the calico kitten her parents had given her soon after they arrived. *Mama says the Americans don't let their children wander like Germans do,* read one entry. *But I can go on the trails wherever I want. Of course I'm careful. And Minka goes with me. Right in the pocket of my backpack.* Hanna's eyes misted. Apparently Minka didn't go out anymore. A quite sedentary calico cat could usually be found lying in the sun near the living room window.

Other pages spoke of skiing, and some races she'd won. But it wasn't long before the main topic, now in English, had become school and books. She unleashed an acerbic wit on writing that she judged to be awful, punctuating her critiques with large exclamation marks. By her sophomore year in high school, Elisabeth had been sure that literature and language teaching would be her professional future. But then the diary went silent.

Hanna was aching to know more. "Gisela, thank you so much for allowing me to read Elisabeth's diary," she said that evening as they sat in the living room. "She was a precious soul. She had so much ahead of her."

Gisela's stony visage made it clear that Hanna was intruding on sensitive territory. Clearly a lighter tack was called for.

"You know, most of those hairstyles she made sketches of were ones I fantasized having, at about the same time, probably. I used to buy the little booklets and magazines at the grocery store, and pretend they were for my mom."

Gisela laughed then. "If I'd spent that much time on my hair, I would've for sure never gotten her grades. Not that I did. What about you? Have you decided on a major?"

"I haven't. I'm a little frustrated. Elisabeth was so clear about her plans."

"You're having a hard time with your parents, aren't you?"

"Yes." Hanna sighed. She was clearly getting nowhere regarding Elisabeth. "I got a letter yesterday from them."

"Tell me about it."

"They're still torn between love and prejudice. Their world just isn't friendly to me."

"You're a brave young woman, Hanna. This must be incredibly hard for you."

If only she could tell Gisela every detail of the hopes and fears clamoring in her chaotic mind. The hopes for happiness of her still-fragile feminine spirit; fears of humiliation if her old form was recognized. Hopes for a normal, uncomplicated life like everyone else seemed to have; fear of its impossibility. Longing for her family to accept her, and near certainty that they never would.

But that would all be far too personal. Gisela wasn't her confidant. She swallowed hard. "It's nothing compared to losing a daughter."

"You didn't answer my question. Will you follow the engineering major again?"

Hanna shook her head vigorously. "The only thing I'm really excited about right now is language and culture. I've been interested in Germany for a long time. My mom—she'd been a first-grade teacher before she got married— taught me some children's songs in German. I learned a few other phrases then, too."

"Wait." Gisela left the room. A few minutes later she returned and handed Hanna a stapled paper. "Elisabeth wrote this essay as part of the Stanford admission process—for her language major."

When Hanna looked up, she found herself alone again. Gisela's behavior seemed doubly perplexing—sharing Elisabeth's private things, yet apparently unwilling to talk about them. But there was no misunderstanding the relevance to their conversation. The essay's theme was Elisabeth's experience learning a new language and culture, and her delight in novel American practices. She saw this as the foundation for a career that would foster bicultural appreciation.

Hanna recalled her first impressions of Bonn: cobblestoned streets, compact cars with a "D" in a white oval on the bumper, traffic circles with arrows pointing in so many directions, signals with a little person in red or green. Tasteful, understated window displays. Her first *Weihnachtsmarkt*: strains of music echoing her mother's piano, crowded tables of crafts and kitsch under strings of lights, *Glühwein* with *Bratwurst* and mustard fresh from the grill, seasoned with magic.

The message was clear: Her major should be foreign languages with a specialization in German. Next year she could attend a foreign studies program at the University of Stuttgart, near where Gisela's sister lived. Perhaps she could even go to Stanford for her PhD.

The next day she told Gisela and Hermann. Hermann nodded. "We could speak only in German with you if you'd like—as close to immersion learning as you can get without being there. And you could share meals with us." He glanced at his wife. "That would be okay, wouldn't it, dear?"

"Thanks for checking with me." Gisela's wry smile spoke of tenacity leavened by resilience and love. "Yes, your help in the kitchen would be most welcome."

Hanna was grateful—and nervous. That night she wrote to Richard about her conflicted feelings. She felt like she was deserting her parents. But the path that was right for her had led to the house of this couple who accepted her for who she was.

Where it might lead after that she told herself to not even think about.

CHAPTER 5

THE LAST LITTLE witches and ghosts had sung "trick-or-treat" fifteen minutes ago. Hanna, who'd interrupted her non-stop studying to help with the boisterous visitors, settled on the sofa alongside the Hoffmanns in front of a crackling fire and some leftover candy. The evening news led off with the last battle near the Vietnamese Demilitarized Zone, which had been briefly quieted by Tropical Storm Louise.

The cozy conviviality was everything she'd hoped for—almost. Five and half months of dinners and dishwashing had made her feel at home. But the butterfly bedspread reminded her every night of how much she didn't know about its original owner.

The local news was up next. "An accident caused by ice on Highway 40 claimed the lives of two drivers in a head-on collision this afternoon."

Hermann immediately switched the TV off. "Excuse me, I'll be back in a minute." He left the room.

Hanna glanced at Gisela, whose face was immobile. "Gisela, was Elisabeth in a car accident? Isn't there a way—couldn't you tell me even a little . . . You know I care about you so much." She held her breath through an oppressive silence.

Finally Gisela's expression softened ever so slightly. "It was the summer after she graduated. She'd gone to a seminar in Denver in the morning, and was on her way to another in Ft. Collins. A heavy thunderstorm opened up about halfway, and a tractor-trailer going the other way jackknifed and skidded. It killed her instantly."

Hanna slid across the space left by Hermann, and Gisela leaned on her shoulder as tears flowed freely.

Anything she said would probably be intrusive. Yet she ought to do something. As she fretted and reproached herself, Gisela straightened and looked her directly in the eye. Hanna waited for the words she thought were coming, but instead Gisela stood up and left the room. Now Hanna was furious with herself. She shouldn't have pushed. Why couldn't she have been more patient?

Three nerve-wracking minutes later Gisela returned and placed a shoebox on the dining room table. She sat down and motioned to the chair next to her. She took the photos out one by one and laid them on the table like playing cards. A little girl on skis barely three feet long, doing the snowplow. Birthday parties, sleepovers, laughing faces in snowsuits, serious faces in classrooms.

And still not one word. Hanna was afraid to move, afraid of whatever explosive emotions might be behind this astonishing self-control.

There were photos of Nutcracker scenes. One showed Elisabeth, probably about eleven, posing by herself, so serious and earnest and proud. Hanna ached with envy.

"Hanna, you should take dance lessons. It's something you have to know. And it will help your feminine presentation. When shall we schedule them?"

When, not if?

Gisela seemed completely serious, authoritative. Almost like a parent. "We need to get you some dresses. Let's go shopping tomorrow afternoon."

Hanna tried to imagine what it would've been like. To have bounced and twirled down the aisles looking for a flouncy dress for a special birthday party, maybe at the start of first grade. A little more serious search before a music recital. Later, her first prom dress.

Neither anger nor tears could bring back that lost childhood. No matter what her parents finally decided, her mother would never go shopping for dresses with her. And here was a woman who would.

The thought of shopping with Gisela was daunting. The language of fabrics and styles was still foreign to her. She didn't even know what the skirt she was wearing was made of. But she remembered the tiny patch of fabric she'd wrapped her doll in before burying her. It was soft, the way she'd felt, the way she'd wanted to treat her baby. The way she wanted her mother to treat her.

DURING THE PROMISED shopping trip, Hanna had chosen a cotton surplice dress whose patterns evoked a sense of seamlessly melding with the fall foliage. With a new red bead necklace, it would be perfect for her first speech in Public Speaking 101, about *The Feminine Mystique* and the importance of the feminist movement.

Admiring herself in the mirror before leaving the house, the folly of her choice hit her with full force. Even her blouses and skirts contrasted starkly with the faded blue jeans and tie-dyed T-shirts favored by most students. But there was no time to change now.

After a stilted introduction she forgot her self-consciousness. Looking up from her notecards as the teacher had emphasized, she saw faces ranging from politely interested with a few nods of approval, to glazed-over bored. She hurried back to her desk, glad it was over.

In the hallway, she found herself behind two men.

"Do you think she's really a girl? I mean, she looks like one, but with that deep a voice? And Jesus, she's tall."

Ears nearly aflame, Hanna dropped back a little. She didn't want them to see her, but she couldn't stop herself from listening, her confidence shaken to the core. This hadn't happened before.

"I was thinkin' the same thing. But that *couldn't* be a guy, could it? I guess he could be wearin' a wig. Pretty convincing if so. Why would anyone do that, fer chrissakes?"

"Weird, isn't it? You ever hear of drag queens? I saw a show in San Francisco once. But they were obviously an act. She—he's really good if that's what he is. I can't tell."

She ducked into the restroom. She didn't need to go, but she needed to get away.

She always feared that people were thinking these very thoughts about her privately. A brief look of confusion when she first spoke was an all-too-familiar routine. She'd learned that coaching could increase her basic pitch by up to an octave, and give it a more feminine timbre. But despite her diligence, the lessons were slow going.

After washing her hands, she took her makeup kit from her purse and fiddled with her already perfect eyeliner. Any distraction from that turmoil.

"Hanna, that was a great presentation." With a start she noticed that one of her classmates was brushing her hair a few feet away. "Male chauvinism is *so* insidious, isn't it? They act like it's for our own good."

"Oh, thank you so much, Beth. I really appreciate that. I was so nervous."

"It didn't show. It was totally rad. And by the way, I love your dress. It looks super nice on you."

Hanna started to touch up her lipstick, flustered. "You're too kind." She took a deep breath, feeling as clumsy as she must have sounded. "I'm *really* looking forward to hearing you. Aren't you on soon?"

"Next week. First speech after break." She tossed her hair back. "Have a nice Thanksgiving."

Hanna exhaled deeply and spent another minute in front of the mirror. It hadn't really dawned on her till then how few people she could count as friends. Beth might never know what a lifesaver she'd been.

She rushed home. Gisela, who did Thanksgiving dinners like an American, would be in the kitchen immersed in day-before preparations. She was making bread, which she would parbake. "We have another guest to cook for. Hermann invited a colleague from Germany who's here for a few months of training."

Hanna took the dough and started kneading. She'd blocked a lot of painful childhood memories, but she remembered the bread. How happy she'd been alongside her mother, eagerly learning every measure, every secret to a perfect loaf. Hoping it would please her father.

She would never have that bond. She had to stop thinking about it. Then she became aware of Gisela's intense look. "Elisabeth used to stand in exactly that spot."

Hanna turned back to her work and punched the dough with extra vigor. She thought she saw something wistful in Gisela's face. Or did she just imagine it because she wanted it? Gisela continued chopping vegetables.

At dinner, Hermann stood and walked around the table to pour wine for Gisela and Hanna, who didn't remember him ever doing that before. "Last Thanksgiving there were only two of us. We have much to be thankful for." He raised his glass. "*Prost.*"

Gisela kept her gaze on her husband. "*Wo Schatten ist, ist auch Licht.* Or as the Americans say, 'Every cloud has a silver lining.' I'm grateful that Hanna is sharing our home."

Hanna's throat was so dry she could barely swallow the sip of wine. "I don't think there's ever been a time in my life when I've had more to be thankful for than today."

Despite these welcoming vibes, it was pure fantasy to imagine herself being part of this family. And yet—she'd seen the photo of her in her new dress on Gisela's bureau a few days previously. It was propped against the framed photo of Elisabeth.

TWO DAYS BEFORE Christmas, Hanna received an envelope with her brother's return address in Ft. Lauderdale, Florida. It was written in his wife's handwriting and included an evangelical proselytizing tract.

> *Dear John,*
>
> *Your behavior is so far from the Way that we think it may be a sign of demonic possession. We are both praying that this demon will be cast out, though this would require a strong Christian warrior with the strength that comes from a personal relationship with Jesus, and it appears that you have banished all such people from your life.*
>
> *Nevertheless, we're writing to make a last attempt to get you to understand that you are now on a one-way path to hell to join Satan. There is no place in the Kingdom of God for such perversion as you have described, and if you are not for Him you are against Him. We will not communicate again with you unless you demonstrate that you have repented and turned back to God.*
>
> *Phyllis and Daniel*

Hanna thought of all the times she'd yearned for a brother or sister she could confide in, who would comfort her, offer a shoulder to cry on. But when she'd merely hinted at her discontent he thundered like a revivalist preacher. "Get that thought out of your head right now. God made men and women totally different. Confusing them is a serious sin."

With trembling fingers she slowly tore the letter into tinier and tinier shreds, until she could not find one with a complete word on it and carried the pieces to the fireplace.

She put on her coat and the boots with kitten heels. The stars brought the foot of Flagstaff Mountain behind the house into stark relief as she carefully descended the steep driveway. The December air was like crystals in her lungs. The crunching snow made her think of running on a sub-zero night to the outhouse on the ranch. She ran for a few wobbly steps and laughed.

She'd left that ranch behind. And there was nothing she could do about the hate.

She wondered how she would react if her parents' decision were the same as her brother's. It didn't matter. She was doing what was right for her.

Above her, behind the curtains in the living room window, the white lights glowed softly on the tree. The shiver in her spine felt like a convulsion. That scene had saved her life three years ago, like a lighthouse leading her back to land. She'd been so despondent then that she hadn't even known where she was, nor had she cared. Now she was living in that very house, with the life she'd only imagined in hidden fantasies. In a few moments she'd be in the kitchen, helping Gisela bake a *Stollen*. The next day they'd roast a goose. She was a part of their lives, giving and receiving—belonging and valued for who she was.

She tried not to think about the years that were lost. If she died tomorrow, these moments would be enough. She had only one more wish.

A mother who loved her as a daughter.

THE LETTER CAME in the middle of February.

Dear John,

It is with heavy hearts that we convey this news to you.

We love you, but we cannot approve of a path that is not only destructive to you, but hurtful to all those who have loved and nurtured you.

God loves you dearly, but He is just and demands allegiance to His laws. What you're doing is contrary to them. It is painful for us to say it, but it's become clear that you cannot continue as you're doing and remain in either His good graces or ours.

You are our son, and we pray that, like the prodigal son of the Bible, you will repent and return to us.

Sincerely,

Mom and Dad

She'd expected it, but it still hurt. She felt like a powerless spacecraft, drifting beyond the last planet, cut off from all family connections—except the thin lifeline to her cousin.

She described the letter during dinner, staying stoic. She'd done her crying and cursing. That part of her life was past.

"I'm sorry, Hanna." Hermann sighed. "To base such an uncharitable attitude on religion is incomprehensible to us."

Gisela nodded. "Friedrich Schiller said it: *Mit der Dummheit kämpfen Götter selbst vergebens.*"

Hanna smiled wanly. "What irony. Schiller says the gods can't beat stupidity, and my parents attribute something stupid to God."

They continued to eat in silence. Afterward Hanna began clearing the table. When she came back from the kitchen the dining room was deserted. Anxiety welled up. They'd been very nice to her, but this was so personal. It was selfish of her to have introduced it at dinner.

She was finishing the dishes when Gisela returned. "Hanna, can you come to the living room for a moment?"

Hermann was already sitting on the sofa at one end. When Gisela sat down she left a space between them. She took Hanna's hand and turned toward her. "You've lost your family. Would you like to join ours?"

Touching a live electrical wire would've had a milder effect. "Do you mean . . . Gisela, are you—I mean, am I—I've probably misunderstood, I don't . . ."

Gisela smiled. "Yes, Hermann and I would like you to be our daughter, if you'd consent."

"Really? I mean . . ." She started to cry. "Gisela, I'd be in heaven. Oh, that would be so awesome. You know, I've fantasized about being part of your family. But—isn't adoption just for babies and children?"

"No, a person who is legally of age can give consent to be adopted, and anyone can adopt them. It's very straightforward. Hermann and I have been talking about it for a few months. Ever since that night when you let me cry on your shoulder—that's when I realized that I was thinking of you as a daughter."

She lifted Hanna's hand and put it under hers on her lap. "No amount of crying or denial will bring Elisabeth back. And no one can replace her. But together we can honor her."

Hanna scrunched down until she could put her head against Gisela's shoulder. "Is this really forever? No going back?"

"Adoption is forever, Hanna. But there's one thing I must be clear about. We're German citizens. You're becoming part of a German family, not an American one. Is that okay?"

Hanna didn't hesitate. "Mama, whatever it takes to be your daughter."

Her mind was like a crowded dance floor, myriad thoughts jostling each other wildly. A calm space was needed to digest them. But at that moment, all that mattered was the blissful sense of belonging. She had a home.

THE NEXT DAY the threesome went to the consulate in Denver to start the paperwork for adoption. Hanna broke into sobs as they left. Having a family who accepted all of her had been only a dream for so long.

A firm yet soft hand squeezed hers. "Hanna, we should celebrate. Do you ski?"

"Sort of. I started in Germany—in Garmisch-Partenkirchen. I'm just a middling weekend skier, but I do love it."

"Okay, at spring break we're going to Steamboat Springs. Last week of March, right?"

Back at home, Hanna went to her room and started writing a letter to her other parents—they weren't her parents any more, but it was hard to think of them that way. She wrote a dozen drafts, and crumpled each one into a wad.

Days turned into weeks. Spring break arrived and she'd gotten no further. The hurt of their rejection didn't make her feel any better about rejecting them. Stern religious language notwithstanding, they'd done a lot for her. She owed them something.

But not her life.

The ski resort's spruce-green islands in a sun-sparkled sea of snow distracted her from this dilemma. But Gisela and Hermann were both expert skiers, and Hanna struggled to keep up. Gisela waited impatiently at the bottom. "You're taking private lessons this week. No backtalk. It's decided."

"Yes, Mama," Hanna replied with mock meekness. Inside, she was euphoric.

With team sports came hated memories of high school. But in skiing it was just her, the snow and gravity. As she learned to move in harmony with the hill, she realized how much she'd changed.

In her male mode her body had been a tool, to be used to achieve certain objectives. As a woman, its form was a thing of beauty—not for others, just for herself. Underneath the stretch pants, she felt sensuous. Alive. Energetic. Comfortable with how she moved. And *very* feminine. She really could be who she was. Without fear. She didn't have to hide it from anyone.

Her skis were less cooperative. She couldn't count the number of falls in the first day. But her instructor was patient and encouraging. On Friday afternoon she entered a local competition and placed third in the giant slalom. The instructor seemed more excited than she was, giving her an ecstatic high five and a bear hug.

Back home, they'd barely unpacked when Gisela took Hanna's hand. "Come, there's something I want to show you. And something I want to give you."

In their master bedroom, Gisela pointed to a plaque on her dresser. "This is from the Steamboat Springs Winter Sports Club—the sponsor of your race. The cup is from Elisabeth's last regional division race. It qualified her to compete for the national team."

Hanna felt a warm pulse of fusion. She would never match her sister's skiing, but this was one more way to continue her life.

"But *this* is what I want you to have." Gisela handed her the carved wooden jewelry box, the hairbrush, and a teddy bear.

Tears flowed once again as Hanna sat on the bed and clasped the bear. "After my doll was smashed, my parents took my teddy bear away, too. I was supposed to get it back after a year if I behaved like they wanted. But they never found it."

No seal from the German government could ever match that. After a lingering hug she returned to her room and wrote the letter without changing a word.

> *Dear Mom and Dad,*
>
> *This is the hardest letter to write that I have ever even imagined. I still love you, and nothing you've said to me makes me want to change that. But the dogma of religion has come between us and opened a gulf that apparently cannot be bridged. It's true that I don't believe in God in the way you do. But if I did (and I don't rule out the existence of some kind of divine presence), that God would not reject people with the characteristics He gave them.*
>
> *Phyllis wrote to me several weeks ago. You probably know what she said. They don't want anything to do with me, and quite frankly, the feeling is mutual. What you wrote is quite different, and I appreciate the distinction. But I can't meet the requirements you put in your letter.*
>
> *Gisela and Hermann Hoffmann, the couple I've been living with, offered to adopt me. And I accepted their offer.*
>
> *Sincerely,*
> *Hanna*

Then she took another sheet of lilac-bordered stationary and wrote to her cousin. Besides unlocking the decision that had saved her life, he'd connected her to this couple who'd taken her in. His words now seemed prescient, as if he'd known all about the bitterness and beauty that were to come.

She wondered what other wisdom might be in those words. They had emerged from so much suffering.

CHAPTER 6

AS THE WEATHER warmed with the arrival of spring, the new family often hiked the Flatiron mountain trails behind their house, the steeply tilted slabs of reddish sandstone watching over them. As a child Hanna had eagerly looked for the first snowflowers, buttercups, and spring beauties. Now, the blossoms on the crusty bare ground glistened with the promise of her new life. Later, their moonlight-conjured images blended in harmony with the rocky hillside behind her balcony.

In early May, a few weeks after her adoption was legally complete, the Hoffmanns headed for a weekend in Estes Park. After dinner, they strolled through the town in the early twilight. Hanna dawdled in front of the clothing stores, reveling in her new parents' fond expressions.

On Saturday morning, after visiting the MacGregor Ranch Museum, they came across a pair of rock climbers. As she watched, spellbound, the one on the ground glanced at her from time to time. Finally, he grinned and motioned for her to come closer. "You wanna try it?"

She shook her head. Climbers were death-defying daredevils. "Are you serious? I don't know anything about that stuff."

"It's not hard. We can show you how. You don't have to know how to tie knots or nothin'. You just put your hands and feet on the rock and up you go."

The two steep faces, joined at a crack and angled like a partially open book, had no apparent holds or ledges. What the guy said was clearly absurd. "No way. I wouldn't be strong enough."

"Honey, you don't need strength. Did you see how my friend did it? You put all your weight on your feet. Your hands are only for balance." He chuckled as he looked at her hands. "Hell, you won't even scratch your nail polish on this climb. If you can hike up here, you can do it."

She examined him more closely. He was lean and muscular, but not brawny. A few locks of curly black hair hung casually over his forehead. Apart from the skinniness of her jeans and the scoop neck on her long-sleeved tee, they were dressed quite similarly. And he seemed nice.

Hanna turned toward her parents. "Go ahead, dear," Gisela said. "We'll wait for you."

She swiveled back to the climber. "Okay, I want to. What do I do?"

"Let me clean the pitch so you don't have to worry about the pro—that's what we call the gear we put in—getting' in the way. I'll just be a minute. My name's Daryl, by the way. My buddy's Joe."

"Hi, I'm Hanna."

Joe pulled in the gold-colored rope from the top as Daryl swarmed up the cliff, deftly removing metal wedges and oval rings with spring-loaded gates. They reminded Hanna of giant safety pins—she had some earrings with similarly shaped clips. Joe then lowered him to the ground.

"Now, come over here and I'll tie the rope around your waist. Joe'll belay you from the top. If you fall, you won't go nowhere. The rope'll hold you."

Daryl pointed to tiny flakes on the rock. "See these? They may not look like much, but even with your tennis shoes you can step on 'em. Then you just put your hands into the crack like this and twist, lightly. No need to hurt that delicate skin. You only want enough force to give you balance."

Hanna slipped several times as she attempted to take the first step, and she wondered if this had been a mistake.

"You're huggin' the rock, Hanna," Daryl said. "Close your eyes for a moment. Feel where your body is. Then concentrate on standin' up straight."

To her astonishment, a moment later she was several feet off the ground, her feet apparently planted securely on nearly vertical rock. Soon she was twenty feet up, and the crack widened, making the jamming technique impossible.

"Now you're at the hardest part. Just remember your balance. That's what rock climbin's all about."

Hanna became increasingly frantic before resting on the rope, stymied. "I can't do it."

"All right, Hanna, trust me on this. Put both hands in that crack there and pull to the left, keepin' your feet on the right-hand wall. The pullin' puts pressure on your feet against the wall, and they'll stay. Give it a try."

"Oh my god, that really works!" Seemingly only moments later she was untying the rope and handing it to Joe, then skipping down the faint dirt path behind the outcrop, feeling like she'd just done something impossible.

As she approached Daryl, a solitary lupine caught her eye. She didn't want to disturb it, so instead picked a daisy and put it in her hair.

Daryl grinned. "Shall we call you Daisy instead of Hanna?"

Three preteen boys were hiking down a trail toward a creek where they intended to fish. One of them picked a lupine and put it in his hair, which had grown longer than usual during the summer.

"Well, if it isn't John the flower girl," one of the others said before breaking into peals of laughter. The third boy joined in, then stopped. "You can go back now. I always thought you were a sissy anyway. Bye-bye, sweetie pie." The two went on, cackling.

John only felt relief as he walked slowly back home. He'd been afraid they would beat him up after his reckless impulse.

Hanna blinked and hoped her momentary reverie hadn't been noticed. "Hanna the flower girl," she said, trying to be nonchalant.

Joe came up behind her. "You are definitely the tallest chick I've ever seen."

"But cute." Daryl picked up the sling. "You wanna do some more? We're not in any big hurry. This is only the start of the season, of course, and we're just gettin' in shape a little. It's not hard to belay you."

The flower blossoming inside her was much more than a daisy. Up to now she had little experience with sexual desire. Attractive girls had stirred envy, not passion. And society branded romantic thoughts about boys a quintessential evil in her previous guise. But that guise wasn't hers anymore, was it? And she definitely had a feeling about this guy. A mysterious aching energy, a yearning to go somewhere she'd never been.

She faced her parents, eyes imploring as she pressed her hands together. "I know we're supposed to be hiking together. But this is so awesome. Is it okay?"

"Don't you want lunch?" Gisela's frown seemed like a cloud in an otherwise clear sky.

"Not now." She was too keyed up to even think about eating.

"All right, how about a couple of hours? That still leaves most of the afternoon."

She turned back to Daryl. "If you'll have me, I'm ready to try. I can't believe I'm doing this."

"Hey, maybe we'll make a climber of you." He winked mischievously. "That voice—kinda like Lauren Bacall's."

If he knew Bacall's movies, he might know one of her most famous lines, that packed essence of implied sexual tension. "You *do* know how to whistle, don't you, Steve?"

Daryl puckered his lips for a moment. "How little we all know."

That, Hanna realized, was just what she was thinking. The electricity between Bogart and Bacall as she sang that song had never really stirred her emotions—until now.

Joe grinned. "I don't see many chicks out here, but the ones I know are damn good. Diana Bowman puts me to shame any day." He led off toward another part of the crag.

The afternoon's climbs were sometimes frustrating. But after saying goodbye and leaving her phone number with Daryl, she was hooked. Instead of a world of macho musclemen she'd found a delicate, very feminine dance of mind, body, and rock.

And a boy who thought she was cute.

The sun was already well below the peaks when she met her parents sitting on a bench near the parking lot. Gisela looked somber. "You were so punctual when you first came to our house. What happened to you?"

This was awful. She'd never actually upset them before. "I'm sorry, Mama. I was having so much fun and lost track of the time."

"Never mind, we've got all day tomorrow. I'm glad you enjoyed it."

Sitting in the back seat, Hanna tried without success to quell the fierce argument raging in her head. One side was full of remorse. The other side said, *But look what you found out.* The second side won decisively as they passed a Virginia Slims advertisement and she recalled those two guys in her Public Speaking 101 class.

Yes, she'd come a long way, baby.

TEN DAYS LATER, Hanna spread out some notes in the Student Union coffeeshop, hoping the hubbub would help her focus on the final exam starting in an hour. At home, all she could think of was rock climbing—and Daryl.

As she sipped her coffee, she sensed someone standing close by. She looked up and nearly dropped the cup. She hadn't realized the cousin she'd known as Dottie so long ago was at the university.

Dorothy looked both embarrassed and perplexed. "Excuse me, I didn't mean to be rude. You look really similar to someone I know."

Hanna shuddered inwardly. Dorothy's family was among the worst—especially her grandmother. She thought of feigning ignorance. But that would make *her* rude, and she felt strangely impelled to keep the connection if she could.

"My name is Hanna Hoffmann. I doubt you've heard of me. But you knew Johnny Shelby."

"That's who I was thinking of. This is crazy—I know he didn't have a twin sister."

"I used to be Johnny."

Hanna thought she'd never seen such astonishment. Her chest tightened—it would probably get worse. But she could only keep going now. She pointed to an empty chair. "Here, if you have time we can talk."

As Hanna spoke, Dorothy's shock transitioned to puzzlement punctuated by a few frowns. "Sorry, Johnny—I mean Hanna, this is a lot to take in. Wait—when we were playing with your doll, in that shed, and your dad got so angry—was that part of it?"

Your dad got so angry . . . Hanna's nervousness went up another octave. More than anger—and more than she dared think about. "I've tried to block that out. But I'll never forget the doll."

"Now I remember something else. You know how Rhonda and I used to set our hair each night? We would've never let a boy see us like that back in New Jersey. But we'd sit in that little den and talk to you, just like a girlfriend. I thought then you were different from other boys—maybe, you know, queer, but I never imagined anything like this."

"And you never knew how much I envied you."

She laughed. "Well, I'm glad you're happy, even if it still seems a little strange."

Hanna's tension dropped back a few notches. This mild reaction was so far from what she'd feared. "Thanks. But what's happening with you?"

"I'm getting married."

"Oh, that's wonderful—congratulations. When? Who's the lucky guy?"

"Thank you, May 26, Gary. It'll be in Pueblo." She reached into her purse. "Sorry, it's only a sample invitation. I know a week's pretty short notice, but I'd love it if you came."

As Hanna walked to her class, unsettled thoughts swirled around like a spring snow flurry, dotting the flowers with reminders of the winter just past. The thought of the other relatives who would be there filled her with dread.

But all the way back to that childhood, Dorothy had been the image of what Hanna longed for. Maybe she didn't have to worry. She'd come so far in her new life. Those relatives really didn't matter to her anymore—she had new relatives. And it would be a fancy event, where she could wear something fancy. Almost like a red carpet. She had to go.

She rushed straight from her exam to the first store. At the third she found the perfect dress—expensive, but it would be worth it. Its palatinate purple chiffon with ruched waist and flutter sleeves was exquisitely elegant and feminine. The boat neck helped conceal how little cleavage she had. She could pair it with her light silvery strap sandals with low block heels, and Elisabeth's amethyst earrings and necklace.

And feel like the princess of her dreams.

She burst into the house, effusing over it before she even saw her mother. But Gisela frowned when she heard what it was for. "Hanna, it really wasn't so long ago that you spoke of your relatives as though they were dangerous. This isn't wise."

An unaccustomed irritation welled up. What made her mother suddenly such an expert on her relatives? She didn't need anyone spoiling her vision. "Why? It's a wedding in a church. How am I going to get hurt?"

"You're a woman, with no self-defense training, and alone. You won't always be in the church. And you said your car needed service."

"I'll take the bus, if it makes you feel better."

"I'd feel best if you didn't go at all."

If Daryl asked her out, she wouldn't accept parental interference in that—how was this different? In the dressing room she'd glimpsed a bit of the life she might have had. She couldn't pass it up. "Mama, this is important to me."

Gisela's fixed stare was like a weight. "I can see that, Hanna. It's also important to both of us that you come back safely."

Hanna threw the package on the sofa and drove downtown in a huff, furious at this absurd overreaction. She found the office of a travel agent, where she purchased bus tickets and reserved a hotel close to the Greyhound station in

Pueblo. The church was across the street from a bus stop. The hotel included breakfast, and the reception would be dinner. She'd only need enough cash for the room and lunch before the two o'clock wedding.

By the time she returned home, her pique had transmuted into anxiety. She'd be devastated if she couldn't go, but the reservation could be cancelled and the tickets refunded—she'd made sure of that.

As Hanna entered the house, Gisela descended the stairs slowly. Her stern countenance gave no hint of any change of attitude. But then she spoke quietly. "At least don't travel at night. And call me if there's *any* problem at all."

"I promise."

She breathed a sigh of relief. She was baffled by this quarrel, but at least she was going.

HANNA FOUND THE entrance to the church with only seconds to spare and tiptoed toward a seat in the very back. It had taken her much longer than expected to change from the black skirt and lace-trimmed white blouse that she'd worn on the bus. She'd had no time for lunch.

Otherwise the morning had gone exactly as planned. She'd set her hair the night before, knowing she'd be searching in vain for a comfortable position on her pillow, but she wanted it to look perfect. Rising before dawn, she brushed and teased each curl with equal care. After the last puff of hairspray, she lingered in front of the mirror. Mary Tyler Moore would surely approve, even though the style was long out of date. The little country girl hadn't quite grown up yet.

After the ceremony, guests were asked to leave the chapel in order from front to rear. The couple would greet everyone at the reception entrance. Dorothy seemed genuinely pleased to see Hanna and returned her wishes for happiness with a bright smile. "Thanks so much, Hanna. I'm so glad you could come."

But when Hanna saw her relatives standing in a group barely twenty feet away, her stomach tightened. This wasn't a friendly place for her. And Dorothy would be busy and unlikely to notice her absence. The sooner she left the better.

She moved slowly toward the exit, pretending to mingle with the guests. Then Dorothy's grandmother, standing next to Hanna's estranged parents, gestured toward her. "Norma, is that your son—the one who now thinks he's a woman? How perverted can someone get, anyway?"

The woman's husband snickered and turned to the man next to him. "Yeah, Chris, what happened, anyway?"

Chris glowered back. "My son screwed that up first rate. He shoulda whipped the kid to hell and back. But lemme be clear. He ain't no grandson o' mine now."

That day when I was playing with my doll, that wasn't whipping enough? And the other thing, that she'd put out of her mind so firmly. She didn't know how, but she was sure her life had been threatened. It might be threatened again now.

In panic she ran outside, and seeing a taxi nearby, jumped in and asked to go to the bus station. She had only one thought: to be back with her beloved parents, sleeping safely with Elisabeth's comforting spirit.

As the taxi pulled away, she thought of her belongings in the hotel. It didn't matter; she'd get them somehow. Once on the bus, she closed her eyes and sunk into a bath of relief.

In Denver she found the connection to Boulder cancelled due to equipment failure; she had a three-hour layover. After an hour she gave up trying to ignore her hunger and asked the ticket agent if there was a cheap place to eat nearby.

He gave her three options: *The Alpine Inn, Pizzeria Romano,* and *Norm's Diner.* She chose the first, hoping it might at least have German beer. That would be all she could afford, as the taxi had taken almost all of her money. Maybe they'd offer free pretzels.

The only seats open were at the counter. She waited till she had her beer to ask about the pretzels. The proprietor smiled faintly and handed her a menu. "No one is allowed to leave Otto Wolf's café hungry. Especially not a German. Order what you like—on the house."

Her spirits leapt at the thought of a real meal. But whatever had made him say that? "Thank you, but I'm not a German. Is it still okay?"

"Your accent is weak, but not gone."

She replied in German. "Wow, I had no idea. English is actually my native language. But I've been speaking only German with my family for almost a year now, so I guess the accent has rubbed off on me."

Toying with her clutch, she told him she was waiting for the bus to Boulder and was anxious to be back home. She said nothing about the reason for her trip. They talked about the weather and accents.

As she ate her *Bratwurst* and fried potatoes, she became vaguely aware of someone staring at her. She looked over to see a tall, burly man with thinning gray hair across the café, playing cards with three other men. He seemed creepy, but she didn't know why. She decided to ignore him.

A few minutes later he passed her on the way to the bathroom and pinched her on the butt. Apart from a reflexive jerk she didn't respond. On his return, he paused and slipped his hand to the inside of her thigh as he whispered in her ear. "Come join us. Free beer and a guaranteed good time."

Hanna stared straight ahead, feeling ashamed, wishing he'd go away. She just wanted to get home.

She watched him return to his table. He didn't appear to be drunk. Wearing a gray tweed jacket and khaki pants, his self-assured bearing gave the impression of social class.

A while later he passed her again, and stopped to put his arm around her, resting his hand briefly on her breast. This time she jerked away and said emphatically: "Get away from me!" He snickered. As he walked casually away, his right hand nearly struck the top of her beer glass.

Otto looked up sharply from pouring a beer at the other end of the bar. "What did he do?" he asked quietly, as soon as he was able to come back to Hanna.

"He actually put his hand on my breast." She shook her head. "I was so surprised, even after he touched me the first time, too. That's never happened to me before."

"Listen, if this guy is a pervert, I'll have him thrown out. I'm sorry about this."

"Thank you, I really appreciate that. The first time I didn't say anything, and I felt bad about that. This time I said something. I don't think he'll come back." She finished her beer.

Not long after that, she began to feel sleepy. Otto was saying something, but she couldn't understand it. She had to get fresh air. "Thanks ever so much for dinner—you're an angel in disguise. But I really ought to get to the station now. I don't want to miss the bus." She jumped to her feet and headed unsteadily for the door.

Outside, she stumbled. An arm encircled her waist. One wrist was jerked up and around something—a neck? Then darkness descended as her muscles stopped responding.

CHAPTER 7

GISELA WATCHED THE last passenger disembark from the third bus of the afternoon. Annoyance had given way to gnawing worry. She called the hotel in Pueblo.

Then she immediately called the police. "My daughter Hanna was expected on the 12:50 bus from Denver. She was staying at the De Remer Hotel in Pueblo, but she didn't check out and they haven't seen her since yesterday. I'm very worried."

"Yes, ma'am. Her description?"

"She's twenty-two, six feet two inches, slim, with shoulder-length brown hair and blue eyes. She was probably wearing a white U-neck blouse with shoulder ruffles, and a black skirt."

Half an hour later the call was returned at her home. "Ms. Hoffmann, the person you reported missing is your daughter, correct?"

"Yes." Her pulse quickened.

"I thought so. Never mind."

One second of silence was enough to imagine a profusion of possibilities, though she knew exactly what was coming. "Wait. What do you mean?"

"A man otherwise matching the description you gave was brought to the Denver General Hospital early this morning."

"Without identification?"

"Neither personal effects nor clothing."

"This patient can't talk?"

"Not so far."

Gisela swallowed hard, resolutely ignoring the bile. "Please, just one more question. What size breasts does this 'man' have?"

There was a pause. "He does have breasts like a woman. But definitely male genitals, there's no doubt that he's a man."

"With a teased bouffant hairstyle?"

"Yes, but . . ."

Her worst nightmare. Hanna had been far too naïve about the dangers a woman faced. "This is *very* likely my daughter. She is a transsexual, and her genital surgery was scheduled for this summer. I have pictures that will identify her."

Another silence.

"Ms. Hoffmann, I don't know what you mean by 'transsexual.'"

Gisela tried to keep her explanation succinct and simple. She doubted she was getting through anyway. And fear made her trip over anything but the simplest words.

"I see. Well, I think you should speak with the homicide detective in Denver."

Gisela's heart stopped for at least two beats. *"Homicide?* You didn't say she was dead."

"Yes, ma'am. That's all I know. I'll ask Captain Alda to call you right away."

She put the handset on the cradle with infinite care, half-consciously hoping that would heal this fathomless rift in the universe. The red brick university buildings, normally so reassuringly solid, were swaying as if there'd been an earthquake. Her home of so many years might collapse at any moment. *Take it one second at a time.*

But time had ceased to be a line. A second or a year might have passed before the phone rang again.

"Ms. Hoffmann? This is Captain John Alda, Denver police. I'm in contact with the Boulder department. My young intern gave me a primer on transsexuality, so I think I understand the situation with your daughter. Can you tell me why she—you said Hanna, correct?"

"That's right."

"Why she was in Denver?"

She told him about the wedding and Hanna's expected itinerary.

"And you're from where?"

"Germany. She's American, but we adopted her this spring."

"Can you describe her dress?"

Dress, not skirt. So Hanna hadn't even changed after the wedding. "A purple evening gown, with a boat neck and flutter sleeves?"

"You pass. Can you come to the hospital to identify her? Right now she's a nameless body."

"Do you mean she's . . . dead?"

"Last report she was in the ICU in a coma."

Gisela caught her breath involuntarily. Perhaps not the best news, but it was a narrow bridge across the rift. "Can I come right this instant?"

"I'll be at the main intake desk at five-thirty."

She grabbed Hanna's passport and a couple of photographs, and drove the thirty miles to Denver at *Autobahn* speed, still refusing to think about what she'd heard. Luck was with her, and she wasn't stopped. She arrived at the entrance exactly on time.

The policeman, though in plain clothes, was easily identified. Six feet tall and trim, with close-cropped black hair, his demeanor and bearing were what she expected. With him was a skinny girl with a shoulder-length bob who looked barely over five feet.

"Ms. Hoffmann? This is the assistant I mentioned: Kirstie Wolf. She just graduated from high school, but she's sharp."

He led the way to the elevator and up three floors, relaying along the way what Otto Wolf had told them. A hawk-faced man whose desk would nearly fill Gisela's office introduced himself as Ronald Ridgeway, assistant director for emergency services.

"I guess I'm still not understanding this," he said after looking at the documents Gisela had brought. "We're discussing a patient who is unambiguously a male, apparently a transvestite—besides the effeminate hair, he had nail polish on both fingers and toes, and earrings and a necklace—and yet you're calling him your 'daughter.' And how exactly are this passport photo of a man and some snapshots of a woman supposed to be relevant?"

He looked at Alda. "I presume the police have taken note of this kinky sex stuff, since there *has* been a crime. Perhaps the 'victim' isn't so innocent."

At that moment Gisela wanted to commit a crime herself. Instead she took several long, deep breaths before speaking. "Mr. Ridgeway, perhaps the photos would seem more relevant if you looked at them. The face is clearly the same. I don't have other photo IDs because she was carrying her driver's license and student ID. I've told Captain Alda facts which he said his detective had learned independently."

"I'm sorry, but we require actual evidence for identification. You can come back and talk to the director tomorrow if you wish." He stood up. "I have to leave now. Good evening."

Gisela put her hand on the hallway wall, seeking to avoid falling into the infinite void that again yawned underneath the tiny pedestals she stood on. Images of Elisabeth's mangled body floated in front of her.

And then she felt a small, feminine hand in her own.

"Ms. Hoffmann, I'm so sorry. I can see the resemblance in the photos. And of course the victim is your daughter. This must be just horrible for you. We're here to help."

The calm resolution in the young woman's intense, unwavering brown eyes was as unexpected as it was comforting. She clung to it as a stout tree in a storm.

"Kirstie, thank you. Could we go somewhere and talk for a few minutes? I gather you know something about what happened. I'm—it's important for me to know everything I can."

"My father's café would be just the place."

THEY SETTLED AT a window table after Gisela was introduced to Kirstie's father. "Now that I know you as someone other than Captain Alda's assistant, I have so many questions. How did you start working with a detective? And how did Captain Alda know what Hanna's dress looked like? The dispatcher said she came to the hospital naked."

Kirstie smiled. "I've been interested in detective stuff for as long as I can remember. My father got me my first Nancy Drew book when I was in second grade, and I finished all of them that year. Sherlock Holmes, Agatha Christie— while my friends were reading fairy tales or books about horses or something, that's what I read."

Otto set two cups of tea on their table. "She did occasionally look up from her books. She may have even taken time to eat now and then."

Kirstie's indulgent demeanor told Gisela a lot. "His brother's a lawyer, and knew people in the department. He got me my first internship two years ago. For me it was a dream come true. So when I found Hanna in the morning, I called Captain Alda, and he hired me again for the summer."

"*You found her?* Where? How?"

Kirstie paused. "She was wrapped in bedsheets, lying on top of the trash in the dumpster behind this café."

Gisela gripped the arms of her chair for a moment. *She's alive. And she's going to stay that way. That's all that counts.* "How . . . ?"

"I have this Siamese cat who's very independent and curious, and there's a cat door, so he can come and go as he pleases. He woke me up and led me to the dumpster. I felt her pulse—there almost wasn't one." She set her teacup down and reached across the table. "If it weren't for him, Gisela, your daughter would not be alive."

Gisela tried in vain to imagine Elisabeth, who'd been the same age as Kirstie only a year ago, talking about finding what probably looked like a bloody corpse as though it had been just another school assignment. This slight girl was stronger than any giant.

"Kirstie, your captain said you educated him about transsexuals, which is a topic most people know little about. How did you learn this?"

"My school had a lot of political activism and social awareness stuff going on, especially about race and women's lib. I worked on the newspaper and yearbook, and learned a lot of little tidbits. Homosexuals and transsexuals have been the object of such terrible discrimination."

"You're amazing. And the dress?"

"My dad's usually here, just like now. He remembered her well—she didn't have enough money to buy food. He said she was very attractive—and he doesn't usually say things like that. He really admired her dress, but he thought it seemed out of place for a bus trip. I found it in a nearby trashcan."

Gisela was still struggling to comprehend the tempered steel behind Kirstie's peaceful poise. "You know, you haven't said anything about your mother. Doesn't she worry about you?"

Another pause. "My mother passed away when I was three. From cancer."

"Oh, I'm so sorry."

"It's all right. I really don't remember her. Dad didn't talk about her much. He wouldn't remarry. No one else could be good enough for him. When he was putting me to sleep, he'd sing the songs that she used to sing, and tell me how brave and noble she was, and how I should be the same. I think that for him, I'm what's left of her."

Gisela felt that tightness in her head again. "That's probably not the healthiest attitude for you to have to live with, but I understand it. My first daughter Elisabeth was killed in a car accident. I've often felt as if she sent Hanna to be her substitute. Crazy, I know. But Hanna felt—feels—that way too."

She only realized after she felt the girl's hands in hers that she'd finally responded to Kirstie's gesture. "She's not going to die, Kirstie. She can't. Not without me."

She firmly believed this. But her rational mind had never been so frightened in her life.

EARLY THE NEXT morning Gisela called Dr. Feinstein's office, only to get his call service, which connected her to Dr. Samuel Harris.

"He's gone fishing," Harris sounded nonchalant. "Sounds like a comic strip, I know. But with Memorial Day on Monday, he took an extra day. I'm covering for emergencies."

After Gisela's briefing he agreed to accompany her to the hospital, armed with Hanna's file. Their visit was clearly not a bright spot in Ridgeway's morning. "Dr. Harris, the injured party found near the Alpine Inn is a man. This is clear. What isn't clear is the source of your confusion."

"Mr. Ridgeway, my colleague Dr. Feinstein has been treating Hanna Hoffmann for several months." Harris's voice was a model of patience. "She's what is called a 'transsexual,' a relatively rare but certainly not unknown condition. She was living as a woman, and was scheduled to undergo genital surgery this summer. These records of her hormone treatments since June may be helpful."

Ridgeway glanced at the papers. "I've no idea why a physician would prescribe estradiol to a man, but it doesn't make him a woman. But I won't report you to the medical board, since he's under our care now. Good day."

"What are we going to do?" Gisela paced in circles in the hallway. She wasn't one to cry easily, but she was close at that moment. "He can't keep me away from my daughter."

Harris walked alongside her, staring at the floor. Finally he stopped. "Gisela, you need a lawyer. And I think I know who can help. It's a slim chance that we get him on short notice, but let's try." He led the way to a public phone in the lobby.

Gisela tried to let some of Harris's professional calm seep into her anguished nerves while she stood by. She should've asked Hermann to come with her. She hadn't imagined it would be so difficult. How could such an idiot become an assistant director?

Harris looked satisfied as he hung up. "He's going to call the hospital director right now. I'm to call him again in thirty minutes. I see a cafeteria here—we can have coffee while we wait."

She barely touched her coffee while Harris told her about the lawyer, grateful for distraction. Anything to avoid thinking about her daughter lying alone and deserted in a sterile ICU room, clinging to life.

"I worked with Connelly on a couple of cases involving mental health and malpractice. Kind of like a wolf. Not a big man, just understated toughness that comes out when it's needed. You'll be glad he's on our side."

Harris was positively jaunty after the next call. "He's still got the touch. He'll join us in the director's office at noon."

James Connelly reminded Gisela of Perry Mason, only smaller. Without fanfare he led the party to the director's office. The tone of Don Orliss's disdainful greeting was one he might have used with janitors requesting overtime pay for working at night. But Connelly's thin smile didn't flicker as he offered his business card, which said simply: "Partner, Connelly and Pritiker."

"Mr. Orliss, I really appreciate your taking time from lunch for us. I understand you have some questions about the identification of my client Gisela Hoffmann's daughter."

"We have an unidentified male patient whom Ms. Hoffmann says is her daughter. Mr. Ridgeway tried to educate her and her so-called psychiatrist about elementary biology, but didn't get anywhere. Are we talking about the same case?"

"Mr. Orliss, I believe I understand your point of view. The patient hasn't yet had sex reassignment surgery. She's still marked 'male' on her passport. However, her driver's license and university records identify her as female. The surgery is scheduled for August."

Gisela's knuckles were white in her lap as she listened. She wanted to be tough herself. But this was Connelly's play. "Wolf" was an apt characterization.

"This young woman's mental health is affected by how she's known to the public, and by whether she has family members present in the hospital. I've no desire for a legal battle. I think we both want what's best for the patient. Wouldn't you agree?"

Orliss snorted. "Are you telling me you'll try to compel me to classify this man as a female for his mental health?"

"Please believe me—I don't want to compel you to do anything. You have a difficult job, and the responsibility for a severely injured patient. Let's do what we can to help her recover from this trauma."

"I'd say I was doing my part. What is the lawyer doing?"

Connelly's sigh was barely audible. "Remember Helen Hotchkiss?"

"The 7-11 clerk, assaulted late at night?"

"Resulting in severe mental trauma."

"Why are you bringing this up?"

"Do you remember how the hospital treated her?"

"Connelly, I'm not in your courtroom. Do you have a point?"

"I do. One of your doctors misdiagnosed her, and it was proved to be because of her race. It made her treatment much harder. The hospital never admitted guilt. But there was a confidential settlement. I wrote the terms."

The only sound Gisela heard for a long time was her heart. Fortunately it was a strong heart. She put her will behind the lawyer's, even if it was superfluous.

Orliss grunted. "All right. Give me a letter with all Hoffmann's medical records and the other information."

"You'll have them in three hours."

By six-thirty Gisela was in the office of Dr. Alan Hempstead, chief of trauma surgery.

"Ms. Hoffmann, it won't help if I sugar-coat your daughter's prognosis. She lost two liters of blood, which should have killed her. It quite possibly caused brain damage. She's been in a coma since her arrival, and may never wake up. But if she does, it will help if you're here. It's up to you, but we can give you special hours and try to make you comfortable."

"My comfort is the least of my concerns, Doctor Hempstead. Being with her is all I care about. I lost one daughter already. I don't intend to lose another."

GISELA SETTLED IN beside Hanna's bed with a copy of *War and Peace*, judging its contents a suitable distraction from her emotions. Hermann brought her dinners of cold cuts and black bread with pickles. Otherwise she ate hospital meals and napped in empty examination rooms. The racks of monitors humming and blinking throughout the night offered equivocal comfort. She had her own connection to her daughter's vital signs. Occasionally she sang, stretching her spirit toward the life that might be struggling to reach the light.

Late in the morning on the fifth day, Gisela saw Hanna's eyes open briefly. She continued singing, her gaze fixed as if frozen. Four hours later it happened again—along with a word, "Mama." With racing heart, she called the nurse. But despite a flurry of attention, Hanna didn't respond further until after dinner.

"Mama, wo bin ich? Wer sind all die Leute? Und warum tut mir alles Weh?"

"You're in a hospital, with special doctors and nurses," Gisela said softly, also in German. "The pain will get better. Just rest."

"But why were the other people talking so strangely?" Hanna closed her eyes again.

Gisela's felt a small chill. What was strange? And why was her daughter's tone so childish?

"Let's leave her alone tonight," the resident who came around said. "That she's speaking in whole sentences right after such a long coma is incredible. We'll do an exam as soon as the surgeon comes in the morning."

The next time Gisela sang "Der Mond ist aufgegangen," Hanna joined in. She knew the words perfectly. But at the line "Der Wald steht schwarz und schweiget" she interjected in German, "Mama, it makes no sense. Forests are green. Why does the song say they're black? And they don't stand up or sit down, only people do that."

"Hanna, how do you know forests are green?"

"I don't know, you told me, right? Or from school?"

"What school, darling?"

She looked exasperated. "Kindergarten, of course. Where else?"

"Sweetheart," Gisela responded in English, "what are they teaching you there?"

Hanna looked at her blankly. "*Was? Mama, was ist los mit dir?*"

"Hanna, what did you do before Kindergarten?" Gisela asked in German.

Hanna furrowed her brow. "I—I don't know what you mean. Isn't that just what I do?" Concentration turned to a pout. "Can I have my pacifier now?"

Gisela dwelt for only a moment on the implications. Then she forced her forebodings into mental crevices from which she fervently hoped they could not return. Of course this was a major trauma. She couldn't waver now.

Frantically fighting sleep, she vowed to remain vigilant. Her presence might be critical when Hanna awakened. But she herself awakened to a pair of orderlies wheeling a gurney into the room.

"The surgeon's ready to see her now," one of the men said cheerfully as he slid his hands under the patient, while the other started to move her IV drip chamber. Hanna jerked away with a panicked expression and tried to curl into a fetal position, grimacing in obvious pain.

"What's wrong, dear?" Gisela spoke softly. Getting no answer, she tried the same motion as the orderly had used, and the nurse quickly assisted. Hanna did not object.

It soon became evident that she would not tolerate male attendants. The resident who'd seen her the day before shrugged. "Yeah, the police report says she was probably assaulted. I guess woman doctors are good for something after all."

Twenty minutes later a dark-haired woman with a stethoscope showed up. "I'm Doctor Anna Lamola. I'm finishing my residency in trauma surgery this month. It seems I'm needed here."

Dr. Hempstead appeared in the doorway, said, "You're in good hands," then moved on.

Dr. Lamola returned later with some Polaroid photos. "Your daughter was sexually assaulted, and there's necrotic tissue on her perineum. I think that will heal. There are also other wounds. But the most urgent issue is this abrasion burn over her entire back. Treatment is the same as for a thermal burn: tissue excision and skin grafts. The sooner we start, the less severe the scarring will be."

"I appreciate your explaining." Gisela had a host of questions, but now didn't seem the time to raise them.

"We'll do the first one tomorrow. Can you be my translator?"

"One more part of my job as mother. I'll do it for the nurses, too."

She called Dr. Feinstein after Hanna returned to the room. "What are we going to do? Besides the amnesia, and the childlike behavior—now this fear of men. We need you, but she's not going to let you near her."

Feinstein was silent for a moment. "Let me call Ellen Beattie. She's on the faculty at the university med school. Specializes in child development and trauma, and she did her internship in Germany. If she can take this on, she'd be a really good fit. Hanna won't care since she can't even remember me."

Dr. Beattie came the next day. A stocky woman with long blonde hair and a distinct Scottish accent, she was intrigued but cautious. "Try to ignore me. I'll need to observe her for a few days to get an idea of what's going on."

Dr. Lamola found a room for Gisela at the university, a three-mile bus ride away, affording her the first real night's sleep she'd had in a week. She brought in a cassette player and recorded herself reading books from Elisabeth's childhood: *Die kleine Hexe*, *Pünktchen und Anton*, and several from Astrid Lindgren.

Hanna was heavily sedated most of the time, but she wanted the tapes every waking second. After one, she looked especially animated. "Mama, can you tell me some stories about yourself when you were a child?"

"I'm afraid they won't be very exciting, sweetie. I didn't have a talking raven, and I certainly couldn't lift a horse."

"Well, then, you can just make something up. That's what they did. I mean, a girl can't *really* lift a horse—can she?"

From the questioning uptick and uncertain manner, Gisela realized she really didn't know.

When she called Hermann that night, she described the event with adamant detachment. Dr. Beattie and the hospital staff seemed very competent, but this was trackless terrain, where emotions might trip her up so easily. Her mind had to stay absolutely clear.

A WEEK LATER, a memo was given to all the hospital staff with any role in Hanna's care. Dr. Beattie was ready to present her current conclusions. Gisela was moved by the number of attendees.

After thanking Dr. Lamola for the introduction Beattie began slowly, as if searching for words. "I have to state clearly at the beginning that I've only been observing Hanna for seven days. And hers is a *very* unusual case. I know of no other like it.

"Many of her symptoms are typical of severe trauma: anxiety, distrust, and fearfulness, a tendency to be easily frustrated, moodiness, and nightmares. She also has severe amnesia, with almost no memory of anything before her injury.

"She recognized her mother, and interacts with her normally. She was guarded but also accepting on seeing her father. But she's fearful of all other men. Fortunately, Denver General has an excellent female trauma surgeon." She nodded toward Dr. Lamola, eliciting a smattering of applause from the nurses.

"There are two other critical symptoms. First, she not only cannot remember any English, she almost immediately forgets whatever we try to teach her. Yet she remembers German—at about a six-year-old level."

A Latina nurse raised her hand. "Doctor Beattie, a couple of days ago I greeted her in Spanish—just for fun, you know—and she repeated it back to me. We started a game, and she can now say several phrases in Spanish."

"Thanks for mentioning this, Luz. Yes, the disability is restricted to English. My working hypothesis is that it's part of her subconscious protection strategy. Language is at the heart of culture, and therefore our entire perspective on life. English was the language she probably last heard when she thought she was being murdered—that's what the police think happened. German is the language of her loving family.

"That explanation connects with her regressive behavior. Episodes of childish behavior by an adult are actually well known, especially in the case of sexual abuse trauma. The brain tries to return to a time before the trauma in order to escape it."

"Like an attempt at time travel." Gisela wanted to simplify the complex jargon.

"That's one way to put it, yes. But why the childhood age? Also permanent regression is less common. Episodes may occur frequently, but typically last less than a day.

"Hanna, as a transsexual, has experienced other threats that at least to her may have seemed life-threatening. Dr. Morris Feinstein—sitting over there—gave me a crash course in this remarkable phenomenon during the week. Hanna was previously his client. She told him some things about her childhood, though she seemed to either not remember or hold back a lot.

"From that, we believe she had a very traumatic experience much earlier in her life—perhaps around the age of seven. Combined with this recent assault, the effects may now be embedded in her neurochemistry. There is some evidence of such changes associated with severe war injuries and torture.

"That's as much as I can say. Be gentle and patient with her, and let's hope we can bring her back. To some extent she has to grow up all over again."

Gisela told herself not to be discouraged. Pessimism was forbidden. Whatever the obstacles, she would be there, and her daughter would be all right.

CHAPTER 8

THREE DAYS LATER Dr. Lamola strode briskly up to Hanna's bed. *"Hanna, wie geht es dir heute?"*

"Besser, danke," Hanna smiled weakly at the greeting, turning her head from the bookstand beside her bed.

Dr. Lamola nodded to Gisela. "I got Ellen to teach me that. Maybe it'll make me seem a little more human to her. Now it's back to you translating." She turned to Hanna again. "I thought maybe you'd like to try sitting up in bed for a while."

"Can I?" The weak smile broadened. Except when she was being bathed, the injuries on her back kept her mostly on her stomach.

"I think so. You've been here two weeks now. The last time the nurses changed your bandages they thought you'd healed enough to handle it for at least a couple of hours. It'll be a welcome break from staring at the floor, don't you think?"

Hanna nodded vigorously.

They got her positioned, and she wiggled her toes and kicked her feet with a little giggle. She smoothed the sheets and pulled them aside. "This is nice—I have a body I hardly even knew about."

Then she frowned. "Doctor Lamola, those are boy things down there, aren't they? I'm a girl. What's wrong with me?"

Dr. Lamola sighed. "Hanna, dear, Doctor Beattie will have to talk to you about that." She turned to Gisela. "I'll call her."

Hanna scowled as she grabbed her pacifier and sucked on it furiously.

When Beattie arrived she took Hanna's hand. "Hanna, don't worry. Sometimes nature makes mistakes, and people are born with the wrong parts. It's possible to have an operation to fix this problem. It takes some preparation first, though."

She pouted and whined. "Why me? Why am *I* a mistake? And why do I have to wait? I want it now." She rolled over and burrowed into her pillow.

Beattie walked around the bed closer to Gisela, though there was no sign that Hanna was listening. "I wish I'd had a chance to prepare her. I'm sure she thinks of herself as a girl and never even questioned it. Her penis inside the catheter would be just another noxious part of her injury. But seeing it is a different experience."

The next day Hanna remained withdrawn and silent, scarcely acknowledging her surroundings. Gisela pushed her qualms away. This would pass. In the meantime, there were things she could do.

Dr. Feinstein had been so impressed with Hanna's progress that he'd approved her genital surgery for the summer. The date had been set for August 17 with Dr. Stanley Biber. But her competence to make this decision was no longer clear. Beattie called Feinstein from a conference room speakerphone, as Gisela listened.

Feinstein was hesitant. "This is obviously a very unusual case. Ellen, what's your current prognosis?"

"It's very hard to say. Hanna's acting a lot like some traumatized children I've known who took literally years to progress. On the other hand, she has the mental resources to recover quickly—*if* she can access them."

"Then it's up to me to get her back," Gisela declared with a conviction that masked her uneasiness. The psychologist's pessimism irritated her. This had to be a minor setback.

And she didn't want another ignorant administrator interfering with its cure.

As a foreign-born adult, Hanna's adoption had not made her a German citizen. The law provided that status only for minors, or adults for whom there was a demonstrated parent-child relationship in practice. There wasn't much doubt about that relationship now.

Gisela went to the consulate and applied for conversion of the adoption to the strong form. She left exhausted by the bureaucracy and more anxious than ever about the future. The decision was now in the hands of a judge, five thousand miles away.

FOUR DAYS AFTER noticing her penis, Hanna still hadn't spoken a word. Dr. Lamola came in to see Gisela.

"Dr. Feinstein and Dr. Biber have agreed that Hanna should proceed with the vaginoplasty once she can tell us she's ready. It's a long operation—about six hours. She has to understand what's coming."

"It's hard to know how much she's hearing, but I think it's something. I'll do my best."

She tried the story that Hanna had described as one of her favorite childhood fantasies. A boy was lost, and walked miles through a forbidding forest to the base of a steep peak. When he said, "My name is Hanna," the rock briefly opened and let her inside. Now a girl with long, flowing hair and sparkling armor, she made her way through fierce battles and narrow escapes to a glittering palace covered in gems. After passing tests of beauty and wits, the girl found her mother, who introduced her to a prince who asked her to marry him.

Hanna slept fitfully that night. In the morning she demanded to sit in her mother's lap. The nurses could barely suppress their mirth. Gisela groaned and rolled her eyes, flooded with optimism. The story had unlocked something.

Hanna rubbed her face. "Could the operation be scheduled now?" she asked, as if the last five days had never happened.

Told that Dr. Biber was awaiting her request, she responded with the biggest smile of her entire post-trauma life. For the rest of the day, she sat up and hugged every woman she saw.

Gisela hadn't ever seen Beattie looking so pleased.

Hanna was moved out of the ICU the next week, after a stay of thirty-three days. Her daily walking exercises lengthened and physical therapy on her skin intensified. Dr. Biber drove up from Trinidad to do the vaginoplasty. He insisted on a pre-op consultation, even though he'd discussed it with both Gisela and Hanna months ago.

"Hanna, do you understand what the operation will do?"

"Sure, it'll make my body right." She acted as if the question was stupid.

Biber gave Gisela a knowing look. "Okay, that's true, but let's go into a tiny bit more detail. We'll take the penis away, but we keep a piece of its skin and put it where a girl's skin has a special nice feeling. Your mom can explain all that to you. Then we make a little space inside your body, right where a girl's private parts are, with more skin grafts, and some outside too. You'll look and feel just the way you think you should."

Hanna appeared unperturbed. "If Mama trusts you, then I do."

Afterward, confined once again to bed and a soup-and-juice diet for the next three days, she complained volubly. "I want to see it. Why do I have to wait for two weeks? I can't stand it!"

Gisela was amused, but also proud. Patience had paid off. Hanna's childish behavior was disconcerting, but it showed progress. And it was telling that she hadn't objected to having a male surgeon for her operation.

When the packing finally came off, and a nurse taught her how to do the vaginal dilation exercises, her face glowed. "I have to do it for forty minutes, three times a day," she told her mother with a broad grin, as if it were a special privilege.

Gisela squeezed back a lump in her throat. What a privilege, to witness this lustrous moment in a life otherwise perfused by pain, with no end in sight that Hanna would be able to see. This small reconciliation of her body with its image in her mind would be a lifeline.

Hermann's evening visits were Hanna's only connection to the rest of the world. Toward the end of July Gisela asked Kirstie Wolf if she'd be willing to come. "I'd just introduce you as a friend. Nothing about the assault."

"That would be awesome. You know I barely saw her before. The EMT people only took the sheets off after she was in the truck."

Hanna beamed at her unexpected guest. "Oh, how exciting—you speak German. You know, you're the only girl I've ever spoken to. Except for my friend Elke. But that was in kindergarten."

In the hallway afterward, Kirstie gave Gisela a quick hug. "What a delight she is. But I can see the challenges. Getting her back into the world won't be easy."

That's the understatement of the year. "Please keep in touch—and thanks."

Beattie suggested a journal. Gisela brought in a girl's diary and a lap desk. Hanna spent an hour on it, carefully printing neat letters in the hand of an eight-year-old.

> *I'm in a hospital with lots of doctors and nurses. My body hurts a lot. I'm glad my mother is here most of the time. I get anxious when she isn't. She tells me I'm getting better. I hope so. I hate lying in bed all the time, and all the pain.*
>
> *My father comes sometimes. He's very busy. I love him too. I wish I saw him more.*
>
> *My therapist comes every other day. She's the only other person who speaks my language. She wants me to tell her about my feelings. But that makes me afraid. There's something really bad there. She says I'll understand it and make it go away someday. I hope so.*
>
> *At night sometimes I have horrible dreams, with monsters trying to kill me. I wake up crying. It helps when Mama holds me, but if I'm alone it's really scary.*
>
> *For a while I was in a sort of dream even in the daytime. I couldn't say anything because I was afraid the monster would hear me. I stayed hidden for a long time, but finally I had to risk getting chased because I had to come back to Mama.*
>
> *Here's a picture of myself when I was younger. I used to really like my special friend Elke. I wish she were here now. We could talk about so many things. Here's another picture of me now.*

Her first sketch showed a young girl with long bangs and pigtails, running and playing with another girl under a sunny sky. The second showed a sad girl with short hair, alone under heavy clouds. Alongside was a third, looking confused.

Beattie appeared pleased. "This is just what I'd hoped for. Maybe more will come out that she won't tell us. Also, we should encourage her to talk more to that nurse in Spanish."

Gisela nodded. "English notwithstanding, language seems to be alive and well for her."

"Her mental age has jumped by a few years in the month since her setback. She really needs to make more emotional progress. I want to try some playacting with dolls."

"Are you sure it's not too soon? She still seems so frail. The diary really underscores that."

"We'll give her another week. But I think she's ready."

HANNA THOUGHT HER therapy sessions were boring. Mostly they talked about what she was learning. So she was excited when Dr. Beattie showed her a doll house and furniture. It seemed a little like the outside world that she'd never seen. (Well, she *had*, but no one believed her.)

"I'd like us to create a play together. I'm hoping you'll have some ideas about what the actors should say and do."

Hanna nodded. It sounded like fun.

"This is a restaurant, where a man cooks some food—here's the kitchen—and serves it to these customers. The restaurant is part of a hotel, where people can spend the night in these rooms. What do you think the people at the tables are talking about?"

"Hmm. I think this couple is worried about their baby at home, and those men probably want to be at a football game."

The half hour went quickly. This was definitely the highlight of her week.

The next week, the couple went to one of the hotel rooms. She puzzled over that for a while. "I guess maybe they have a babysitter, and they're going to spend the night away from home."

In the third session, a different couple left the restaurant and went to a bedroom. The man pushed the woman and started to take her clothes off.

Hanna suddenly hurt all over. She grabbed the dolls and threw them into a corner of the room. "No, no, no!" The game had turned into a nightmare.

"I'm sorry, Doctor Beattie," she said through intermittent sobs. "Please don't do that again. I—that was too scary. Something felt—like someone was about to come out and kill me."

"Hanna, try to tell me a little more. What did you think was happening with the dolls?"

"I'm not sure. For sure the man was going to do something bad to the girl. He was angry, and she was afraid and weaker. I think he was going to hit her."

"You've read fairy tales where someone, even a child, was hit by an evil person, and you didn't react that way. Why is this different?"

"I—I don't know. Those are stories. This seemed—I sort of felt like the doll could turn into a man and hurt me. I know that's silly—it's impossible, right?"

"Do you think something like that happened to you in the past?"

"It seems like—oh, I don't know." She buried her face in her hands and began to cry in earnest again. There was danger in that room, and it wasn't like a story at all.

"Okay, Hanna. We won't do that again soon. One step at a time."

Dr. Beattie walked her back to her room. She was barely past the door when she broke into a run, dodged around the bed, and threw herself into Gisela's lap, heart pounding. She wanted to tell her mother about what she'd seen during the session. She'd been afraid to tell her therapist that a fiendish giant had appeared behind the doll house—it was way too crazy.

But now she couldn't tell her mother either. Anything she said might make it reappear. Then it would be real, and it was far too powerful for anyone to stop. She clung to her mother all evening until it was time to turn the lights out.

A little girl was in a large room with chandeliers and a marble floor where people were dancing after a wedding. Then her pretty lace dress turned into greasy baggy overalls, and the people all merged into a giant human-like monster waving a belt, snarling at her.

She awakened and screamed. The wall clock read 1:10. She didn't go back to sleep.

After a breakfast that she ate little of, she stalked down the hall toward physical therapy. Every door seemed to be hiding some danger. She shivered despite the summer warmth.

A new therapist was waiting for her. "Your usual therapist is out today, Hanna. Before we start, I'd like to take a quick peek at your bare back—just to see the progress. So I'll have to take the pressure garments off."

She brushed the skin with a feather-light touch. "Ah, this is good, healing nicely."

A nurse handed her a note. "Please excuse me for a moment—I'll be right back." She followed the nurse out of the room.

Hanna saw a mirror in one corner. She went up to it and looked over her shoulder. Her entire back was a twisted landscape of trenches between ridges and knots of scar tissue. The skin was a sea of choppy waves, mottled and distorted. Nothing smooth remained.

Heedless of wearing nothing but the skimpy hospital gown, she screamed and ran out. After turning down a few corridors she crumpled onto the floor in exhaustion. White-coated orderlies gathered around and lifted her onto a gurney.

Her mother was beside her. "Honey, it's all right. You're completely normal."

That didn't make sense. She wasn't normal.

The world wasn't normal, and nothing made sense.

CHAPTER 9

IT WAS ONLY plain white paper, five by seven inches, but Dr. Beattie's note seemed like a flashing beacon of hope, and Gisela certainly needed one. After three weeks of vain attempts to coax some response from her emotionally disconnected daughter she'd exhausted all her fuel and was beginning to burn furniture. The psychologist hadn't actually said much—"I have an important proposal to discuss with you"—but it was enough to fan her faltering hopes.

Those hopes dimmed the moment she opened the office door to find both Beattie and Lamola, looking certifiably funereal. She sat on the edge of her chair, as if being able to make a quick exit would improve the prospects.

"Gisela, this hasn't been a pleasant ride, I know." Beattie neatened a stack of papers on her desk. "This is very hard for me to say. In my profession, pessimism tends to be self-fulfilling—not a good strategy."

"I've never been partial to pessimism."

"But we have to face the facts. Hanna is exhibiting classic symptoms of trauma-induced dissociation and acute psychosis. There's simply no way to predict how long it may continue."

She'd never liked Beattie's tentativeness. "A mother doesn't give up, Ellen."

"We're not giving up, but we may need a new approach—in a different environment."

Gisela raised her eyebrows and folded her arms. Something new was what she was expecting. But what? Medication? A different therapy regimen?

The surgeon leaned forward. "What Ellen is trying to say is that it may be better if Hanna were in an institution that can serve her current needs better."

Gisela jerked to attention as if she'd been jabbed. *An institution?* That would swallow her daughter and never give her back? The burst of rage was uncontainable despite her best attempts. "So now the body mechanic is done with her job and doesn't give a damn what's inside the sack of skin she's patched up?"

"Gisela, I didn't say that. But patching the body is indeed what we're set up to do here. We're not experts in psychological illness. Up to now it's seemed that Hanna was making good progress. But this is different. We're thinking of what's best for the patient."

"Your patch job isn't done yet."

"No, it isn't. But we could bring Hanna back to the hospital for operations. It's a trade-off either way, to be sure."

"And my daughter's life is what's being traded."

Beattie sighed as she turned toward her colleague and back. "This isn't an easy situation for any of us. Maybe we should take a break."

Gisela stood. There was a rushing sound in her ears, as if the unleashed emotions were actually thundering out from a broken dam. "I'll be here when you're done." Her tone was clipped. "If you think you're going to separate me from Hanna—maybe I should find someone else. Are you the only German-speaking child therapist in the world?"

"Gisela—please. You're not helping."

"Maybe not. But neither are you."

"Look, I'm sorry. There wasn't really a way to broach it less harshly. I understand your anger. But it's not a situation with any simple answer."

"That may be. But the answer has to include my staying with my daughter. And not in some faceless institution. I still can't believe you suggested it. And after you caused the setback—how can you live with yourself?"

She was surprised at her outburst. It was rude, and it wasn't her way. But she'd reached her limit with patience. She'd done her part; the experts needed to do theirs.

"As a professional, I do my best. It doesn't always work," Beattie said after a long silence. "It isn't clear to me whether the doll scene or the effect of seeing her scars was more important in triggering this setback. I suspect both. But here we are now. We can't change the past."

"Yes but we can change the future, dammit."

"Your patience brought her back before. Maybe it will again. But if she doesn't respond within a week, I think we have no choice but to move on."

"She's going to make it, Ellen. That's my mother's diagnosis."

Gisela closed the door very softly behind her. She felt like she was on a battlefield: tense and focused, but unsure where the greatest danger lay. Only one thing was clear: she wasn't moving anywhere without her daughter.

IN THE LAST hundred days Gisela had been home twice, both in the first week after Hanna's injury. The thought of seeing her room without her in it was unbearable. Once down that path was more than enough.

She gave no hint of what had transpired when she phoned Hermann that afternoon. This could only be shared in person. She told him she was coming home for dinner. His tone betrayed his surprise, but he didn't express it.

"To what do I owe this honor?" he asked with a grin as she opened the front door. "I almost feel like we're dating again."

He talked mostly about their neighbors' remodeling project as he drove to an upscale restaurant that they enjoyed. Gisela said little.

She was still studying her menu when he put his down. "I've gotten a new customer in San Diego. It's potentially a really big contract. So I'll have to spend several days out there, starting Monday."

She looked up. "Good. You can take up surfing while you're there. Don't get eaten by a shark, though. We still need your health insurance."

"What . . . ?" He reached across the table. "Gisela, I know this has been a huge strain for you. It has for me too."

"Of course it has. You have to make your own breakfast, schedule the housekeeper's visits, watch TV alone. A huge strain." She got up, bumping the table. "Excuse me. I have to go to the bathroom."

Hermann half rose from his seat and put his hand on her arm. "Please—stop. Tell me what's wrong."

She brushed his hand off, but didn't continue walking. After a long pause she sat back down. "When I told you about Hanna's detachment I didn't think it was a big worry. But Doctor Beattie says she's psychotic and doesn't know if she will ever come out of it. And wants her to go to an institution."

Then, after pushing her salad plate aside and spilling the water glass, she put her head on her arms, crying softly.

Hermann leaned across the table. "Honey, let's go home. I'll get something for us later."

She lifted her head slightly and nodded. She was ashamed of making such a scene in public, but she'd been powerless to stop. She'd spent her anger on the doctors. Now she was exhausted—and not a little bitter.

They returned home in silence. Hermann ordered a pizza. Then he opened a bottle of wine and brought two glasses to the living room. "Will you give me a chance to show that I'm not a completely insensitive oaf?"

Slouched against a sofa cushion, she raised her glass in the gesture of a toast. "To our daughter's health."

Then she told him all she could remember about the meeting. "I was so angry I didn't even think about asking any questions. Hermann, I am not going to let them put Hanna in some mental institution. What sort of mother do they think I am?"

She downed a large gulp. "I saw what happened in the PT room. She's frightened. I can understand that. Those scars are not pretty. But she needs love, not some strange cold place that only makes it worse."

The bottle of wine disappeared quickly. She saw Hermann's look when she went to the cupboard. But she knew he wouldn't say anything now.

Gisela couldn't remember the last time she'd been drunk. That was immature and self-indulgent. She was a sensible woman, a wife and mother with responsibilities. But her discipline was crumbling under this onslaught. What if Beattie was right? What if her purpose in living disappeared a second time?

And not even with finality. Hanna could linger in this dissociated state indefinitely, leaving her with dwindling hope but without closure. Always on the other side of a window, beyond her touch.

Why had she ever allowed Hanna to go to that wretched wedding? She was a mother, dammit. She should've been firm.

The TV was no help. Everything pointed back to her daughter in some way. Her husband was trying to be solicitous, but her body was stiff and closed. She couldn't share her grief.

The second bottle was empty, and she'd had the lion's share of it. Without saying goodnight she stumbled up the stairs and into the bedroom she hadn't seen for three months.

But sleep was far away. Guilt, frustration, rage, emptiness—a maelstrom of emotions she rarely felt were now all she felt. She paced around the entire upstairs, seeking solace that she didn't expect to find. Certainly not in Hanna's room, where Elisabeth's teddy bear was propped against one pillow.

Then Gisela remembered Hanna's joyful tears at the gift, and snapped back to sobriety as if she'd been slapped.

It was ten-thirty, but she called Beattie at her home number. "I've never discussed my other daughter with you, have I? She is—was—three years younger than Hanna. She was killed in a traffic accident the year before I met Hanna."

"I assume Hanna knew about her." Beattie sounded tired.

"She felt extremely close. As if she was in some way continuing her sister's life. I gave her some belongings that she treasured. Mightn't they be a way to get through to her now?"

"It's definitely worth a try," Beattie replied after a pause. "Let's do it."

"And I want to be there in the room with you. Maybe that will give her some sense of safety." *And give me some sense of control.* After her last meeting with the psychologist, that was a requirement.

She gathered all the things she'd given Hanna: stuffed animals, jewelry box, and hairbrush. Fortunately Hanna hadn't taken that with her. She added Elisabeth's diary and the photos from her own dresser.

She opened the jewelry box to add the purple amethyst earrings that Hanna still had on when she was found. In a pocket in the lid was a photo of Elisabeth in a Nutcracker dance costume.

She held it for a long time. It was one of the photos they'd been looking at just after she told Hanna how Elisabeth had died. Obviously it had meant something extraordinary, for Hanna to take it without permission. Why hadn't she asked? Gisela would happily have given it to her.

Of course they hadn't been a family then. Yet it was that very evening that Gisela had first thought of Hanna as part of her family.

Maybe it would now help make that family whole again.

GISELA CAME TO Beattie's office ten minutes early the next morning and helped set up. They put Elisabeth's senior class photo on one side of the desk and the teddy bear on the other, the hairbrush tucked into its waistband. The other animals clustered around the jewelry box and diary, with the little dancer photo in front. Gisela then sat in a chair in a corner and waited.

Hanna approached the desk, her focus moving from one object to another. "Where . . . where did these come from? Why—what are they?"

"Do you remember your sister?" Beattie asked.

"I . . . I have a sister? Where is she? Why hasn't she come?"

"She was killed in a car accident, Hanna. She died without ever meeting you. But she is a part of your family. And before your injury, you knew about her and loved her."

Hanna looked totally bewildered. "That's . . . that's her?" she asked, pointing to Elisabeth's photo.

"Yes."

"She looks so much—so much like me. I didn't know . . . I know these things somehow, the animals, the box. I don't know. Were they hers?"

"Yes, Hanna, they were. And your mother gave them to you."

Hanna walked around, touching not only Elisabeth's things but Beattie's pens and notebooks. "But these are not . . . are they? I've seen these. Haven't I? They're—they're not hers. Are they mine? No. I don't recognize . . ."

A trickle of tears turned into a stream. "I'm crying. Why? I cry so much. Why cry? Why am I afraid of these things? They can't hurt me. Can they?"

"These things are not harmful. In fact, they belonged to someone you loved. You are afraid of memories of something that hurt you and took you away from these things. Your tears are for your loss. They make perfect sense."

Hanna wiped her face but started crying again. "I . . . don't remember. How could I have a sister and not even remember her name?"

"Hanna, your memory was badly damaged by what happened to you. Now some of those memories are coming back, but they're coming back as a sort of patchwork. That makes it confusing for you."

She picked up the dancer photo and looked directly at her mother. "This must be her when she was little, right?"

"Yes, sweetie." Gisela's heart leapt even as it was torn. She'd rebelled against thinking of Hanna as a little girl from the moment she'd awakened from the coma. But just then it seemed as if the girl in the photo was the one holding it. Or the other way around.

Hanna studied it carefully. "But in the other picture she's a grown-up. How was she so much older than I am?"

The drum that had been beating steadily in Gisela's chest was now pounding wildly. The sun had shattered its shroud, at least for a moment. She willed this rational speech to continue. "You are actually a little older than Elisabeth."

Hanna furrowed her brow and stared at the photo as if it held the secret to her life. "So—that's why I'm your size and not child size?"

"That's right." Gisela gripped her chair. They were so close to breaking through.

"This . . . it's so confusing. My childhood, Elke, that's imaginary?" Her attention went back to Beattie.

"Right again, Hanna. Your real childhood, from before you were hurt, is blocked from your consciousness along with so much else. But sometimes, something like the memory of your sister's things comes through a little."

Hanna picked up the big teddy bear, cradled it in her arms, and held it to her face. She pulled the hairbrush gently through her hair. Finally she opened the jewelry box and fingered the earrings.

"I don't know these things, but . . . but I do, in a way. Now I really don't know what is real and what isn't. I'm so confused. But there's something here. I want to understand it. I *have* to understand it."

"Hanna, I know it's confusing—and painful. The pain of your recent injury is mixed with that from your childhood. Just remember your life is important. To others as well as to yourself."

Hanna's eyes remained wet, but the flood had abated. Beattie stood up and laid her hand on her shoulder. "This is a lot to take in at once. Let's talk again tomorrow, okay?"

"Thanks, Doctor Beattie. Yes, I need time to think. Maybe Mama can help me." She turned to the desk. "May I take the bear?"

"Of course."

As they left the room, Gisela couldn't resist a quiet aside.

"Mother's instinct wins again."

CHAPTER 10

GISELA HAD JUST gotten a cup of coffee the next morning when Hanna sat up and hugged the teddy bear.

"Mama, tell me about Elisabeth."

"Elisabeth was my only child for eighteen years. Then she was killed in an accident. I was terribly sad, as you can imagine. But ten months later, you walked into my life and stayed there, never to leave. Hermann and I adopted you as our daughter."

Hanna knit her brows again. "This is so weird. So, I first met you when I was big? I wasn't born from you? But somehow, I came right after her? Is there some connection between us? How come I don't know any of this? But of course, I know why. Doctor Beattie said the injury did it. There is so much I don't know now, life is suddenly so complicated."

She got out of bed and paced around. "So, what is adoption about? Where did I come from? What happened to my parents who gave birth to me? Didn't they want me?"

Gisela didn't want to speak ill of people whom neither she nor Hanna were likely to meet again. But in the more than three months that Hanna had been in the hospital they hadn't reached out once. The publicity had been voluminous and mostly virulent. Wouldn't a caring parent have at least tried?

It was such a contrast with Hanna's cousin Richard, whose last letter to her had arrived mid-summer. Along with his gracious reply to Gisela's explanation he enclosed a short note, to be translated and given to Hanna when appropriate. He'd also asked permission to tell their mutual friend Werner Jendrossek, in case he might somehow help.

Hanna should be told that she had a cousin who cared deeply about her. But nothing about her parents. Gisela chose her words carefully. "They weren't able to take care of you the way you needed, even as a college student, and so you came to us."

"It sounds like they didn't want me. There must've been something wrong with me."

The memory was etched in her mind like acid on copper: the young woman tiptoeing around the bare bedroom in Boulder, her emotional wounds displayed as though on a billboard. "No, Hanna, there was something wrong with them."

"Was it because of my genitals?" Her eyes flashed with anger. "That I had the operation for?"

"Hanna," Gisela said softly as she held her daughter's hands, "parts of your life before your trauma are still hard to explain to you, and you will have to trust us that we loved you before, we love you now, and we will always love you. And there is nothing wrong with you."

Hanna appeared to relax. "All right. It makes me sad to think about a mama and papa not wanting me, but I'm glad my real Mama and Papa love me. And my sister—she must've been so nice, to have these stuffed animals—so cute and cuddly. Do you think she would've liked me?"

"I do, Hanna. We can never know what didn't happen. But as the mother of both of you, I think you would've been beautiful sisters. You probably would've even fought like sisters do."

The sweet music of her daughter's laugh was both exhilarating and a little nerve-wracking. Twice things had gone terribly wrong just when she seemed to be doing well.

Hanna took the picture of the little dancer from its place in her jewelry box and held it tenderly, her look distant and dreamy. She carried it to her physical therapy session, where she struck sassy poses in front of the mirror. "I'm still as beautiful as ever, and nothing can take that away," she told the girl who returned her solemn stare.

Gisela saw something different: Hanna picking her way gingerly across an avalanche-swept slope near Trail Ridge Road strewn with broken boulders and twisted, stunted trees that were the only survivors at timberline, passing brilliant blue and white columbines half-concealed behind the rocks.

When she returned, Hanna wrote in her diary again.

I've seen myself now, all of me. I can't cover it up with fantasies any more. I have a hideous-looking back, and this is the way it is going to look forever.

I'm very sad, but I'm also feeling grateful because of what so many people have done for me. I know that the girl who speaks German and visited me has a cat who found me, and she's a detective who spent her whole summer looking for the man who hurt me. They haven't found him, but she's still trying.

I have a sister. She was a lot like me. She died so I'll never meet her, but I still love her. Mama tells me she liked a movie called "The Sound of Music." I love those songs. I memorized some of the words even though I don't understand them.

Dr. Beattie told me that some bad person caused my injuries, but I don't remember it. It's too scary to think about. She says I have to get stronger first.

In last night's nightmare, I was in a dark, dirty room with a rough wood floor. There were metal scraps and nuts and bolts all over, and I was wearing

horrid-looking greasy clothing. A monster was snarling at me, horribly ugly,
with strands of gray wire on its head. I thought that if I could sort out all of
the nuts and bolts, then I'd be safe, but I couldn't do it.

My scars are just skin. They aren't the real me. I'm like a wounded bird.
My wings were broken, but I can still fly on them.

Gisela gave the diary to Beattie, who returned it with her final report one
week later, the day before Hanna's scheduled discharge. "I want to read you one
section for emphasis."

Since the end of her last and most severe setback, she is behaving more
or less like a typical pre-adolescent. If this pattern continues, her mental age
may jump forward again once she experiences more emotional progress. But
the setbacks are worrying, especially the second with its dissociation and
acute psychosis. Her trauma is very deep, and some symptoms may never be
eliminated.

Hanna's case, despite its unique features, resembles some combination
of head trauma and severe emotional abuse. In those patients, intellectual
development is almost invariably stunted. I recommend that college not be
considered; even high school will be a serious challenge. Her future prospects
should be considered in this light.

She handed the stapled papers to Gisela.

"Gisela, the mismatch of mental age and body will be a huge problem for her,
even in a special needs school. Children can be cruel, and this is one of the worst
ages for bullying. On the other hand, home-schooling would be terrible for her
social development."

"I've already been thinking about it. There's a type of school in Germany
that'll be right for her. The only problem is that we'll have to be separated for a
few weeks. I don't relish that, but I see no other way."

The bureaucratic preparations had been comparatively easy. Her daughter
was a full German citizen, with a birth certificate showing her proper name and
gender. And a passport. Her old country was no more accepting than her old
family. She should be where that history wasn't known.

Sixteen months ago, Hanna had come to her door as if sent by the gods. From
the ashes of grief new life had sprouted. Then evil had almost effaced it for a
second time. Almost. But not quite. It would continue in a different way.

The psychological preparation for this transition would be anything but easy.

"Honey, there's something very important we have to talk about now." She
placed Hanna's hand between hers. "It appears that your inability to speak
English may be permanent. And there's no school here that can teach you in
German. So Papa and I have decided to move back to Germany."

Hanna looked surprised but excited. "So I get to finally see the place I still think I was born in?"

"That's right. Not only see it—it will be your home. There's just one small problem. Papa can't leave his job right away, and I have to pack everything that we want to ship. It should only take a few weeks."

She paused, wanting to cushion what was coming, wanting it not to come at all. "In the meantime school starts September twentieth, already only four days from now. It's important for you to miss as little as possible. Until I get there, we want you to stay with your aunt—my sister Heidi—and uncle Georg."

The sunshine on Hanna's face disappeared. She turned and said woodenly to the wall, "Don't worry about me, Mama. I'll be fine."

Then she shook with wrenching sobs, violently pushing her mother's embrace aside.

The emotional adjustment ahead was clearly a very long and twisted road.

HANNA BLINKED REPEATEDLY as she stepped hesitantly outside the hospital.

"Wow—this is so cool." She looked up and down the street. "But I never imagined all this noise."

Her mother laughed. "It'll take some getting used to. There's a café two blocks away. We'll have breakfast and then drop Papa off at his work before driving through the foothills. You used to love Estes Park."

Soon the car was rounding curves no longer familiar to her. It made her feel nervous. "Mama, is there really a school in Germany where I'll be accepted, in spite of how big I am? It's all so hard to picture, and I don't even know what a school is like."

"It's called a *Volkshochschule*." Gisela's voice was even and soothing. "It's for adults, including pupils who failed their exams before. So you'll get the same certificate as regular graduates of the *Hauptschule*."

"That's the easiest secondary school, right? And then I can get a job?"

"Yes, honey. For that you'll attend a *Berufsschule*."

"Good." If she understood it all correctly, the others wouldn't know a lot more than she did. "So I won't be too far behind?"

"Your classmates will be reviewing the last three grades, the same material you need to learn. Also we can hire a private tutor to help you."

Hanna relaxed, then sat up with a new thought. "What about friends my own age?"

"Heidi and Georg have lived in Waldenheim all their lives, and they know just about everyone, including families with children in the seventh grade. They'll take care of you, Hanna. Try not to worry."

She pressed her nose against the window. Jagged ravines plunged into mysterious unseen depths beneath broken cliffs. Scattered trees clung precariously to the tiny sandy ledges. But the tires hummed smoothly on the road as her mother's strong hands turned the steering wheel.

"I guess it'll be fine. It has to be. Thank you, Mama."

An hour later her spirits took a wild leap as she opened the door of her room. "Oh my—a real bed, with no IV stand!"

Her mother, standing in the harsh light from the picture window, looked tired, even frowzy. "Mama, you haven't taken care of your hair."

Immediately she felt horrible. After all that selfless woman had done for her—how could she have even thought such a thing? She only looked decent because one of the nurses had given her a blow dryer that morning. She'd better make amends, quickly. "Could I do it for you now?"

"That would be lovely."

Her guilt ebbed a little after her mother showered and was comfortably seated. "You know, I could learn how to cut hair, too, I'm sure. Wouldn't I be good at it?"

"I believe you would."

"What else would I do, anyway? I guess I could do secretarial stuff, but they might want me to speak English. This way I'd only need German."

She stopped with a curler in one hand and a lock of hair in the other. "Wait, how do I know anything about this? This is so weird. It just popped into my head. So what's with me and hairstyling?" Planting her feet apart and hands on her hips, she glared at her mother.

Gisela smiled. "You used to love it, and you liked helping me. You made me feel like my daughter was really coming back to life. It was a precious moment, Hanna."

"So, things *will* come back—more than recognizing a picture." Now she felt embarrassed. What did her mother remember? There was a person she would never know, who was her and yet not her. Someone Mama had loved as much as her.

"We really don't know what will happen to your memory, dear. We have to be patient."

Hanna started back to work. "Well, anyway, I can be friendly and helpful. That's good. I can be useful. I think I'd listen to people, too. I should be able to make people feel better about themselves."

"That's the young woman I was proud of before, and I'm proud of you now. I know you'll do well."

She was glad for her mother's words. She knew so little about the world outside the hospital, and the specters of her nightmares were never far in the background.

THE NEXT FEW days were a scramble of preparation. Hanna's old books and notes meant nothing to her now. But she wanted all of the mementos from Elisabeth. Another print was made of the portrait.

On the evening of September 21, Hermann lit a small fire in the fireplace even though the weather had yet to turn cold. Hanna nestled next to Gisela on the sofa.

Hermann sat down in his leather-covered armchair. "Hanna, I wish we were just enjoying the evening with each other, happy with your homecoming. But you're not leaving us for long. Now, for a few weeks you have to be more brave and grown up than you should at this age."

Gisela smiled wanly. "As you can see, both of us have gotten used to thinking of you as a child, and not how you were before your injury."

"Oh, shut up."

They were right, and she hated it. She didn't want to be grown up. She wanted to be cuddled and protected, here in this house that was her home. And she wanted this unknown person who was her before the assault to go away. She was confusing and dangerous. Anything from before the assault might be part of it. Just like with the dolls.

She hated her anger. She loved her parents, and knew what sacrifices they'd made. She clenched her fists and tried to send her fury somewhere else.

But she was the one being sent somewhere else.

"Hanna, dear . . . I know it's hard. Believe me, if there were any other way, we'd do it."

She clutched her knees, trying to quench the rebellion in her heart. "I know, of course." Her voice was dull, but the fire was still there.

Then those strong, sensitive fingers gently touched her shoulders. Not firm, not pulling or pushing. Just a touch, but the tension drained away as if a valve had been opened. She put her head on her mother's lap and cried in silent, heaving sobs.

Finally she straightened up. "I'm sorry. I won't let you down. Excuse me." She went to the bathroom to dry her eyes and blow her nose. The question she had to ask wasn't an easy one.

She sat next to her mother again. "On the day before I left the hospital, Doctor Beattie told me about rape—that a few bad men sometimes hurt women in their private parts. Now I understand why it was so upsetting to see the male doll attacking the girl doll. That's what happened to me, wasn't it?"

"Yes, sweetie, it was. Part of it."

"Why would a man do that, Mama? In the stories, when a boy meets a girl and they fall in love, it's a beautiful thing and everyone is happy. Why would a man want to hurt me?"

"We wish we had an answer for that," Hermann said softly. "I don't think anyone knows. There are a few men who just seem to be defective."

"But *I* was defective." Hanna turned toward him. "My genitals were wrong. That didn't make me want to hurt anyone. It doesn't make sense."

"No, it doesn't. Just remember that most men are not like that at all." Hermann crossed over to the sofa and put his arm gently around her.

Hanna gave him a peck on the cheek before standing up. "Come, I want to hug you both. I'm going to make you proud of me. You'll see. I just wish . . ."

Her throat tightened and she couldn't say any more. She wanted to be brave and grown up. But in fact she was neither.

PART 2:
AN IMMIGRANT IN THE MOTHERLAND

But I'm a child of the wind
I've been blown away
but I'm back again.
I just don't know
if you really understand

Kate Wolf, "Close to You"

CHAPTER 11

THE NEXT MORNING, Hanna followed her mother with furtive sideways glances through the chaos of Stapleton Field. At the United Airlines gate she was introduced to the flight attendant who would look out for her on the plane and take her to the Lufthansa desk in New York.

Hanna stolidly denied any nervousness, though her stomach felt like a miniature of the bat cave in New Mexico she'd just read about. She checked the contents of her bag over and over, and made a dozen drawings of the doll she wanted.

But as she hugged her mother for the last time, she lost it. After spending an hour on makeup that morning, now she could only hide her tear-stained face behind her stuffed leopard as she followed the solicitous woman who settled her in her seat with words she didn't understand, but whose tone she did.

As her mother had promised, she was treated as a special guest in New York. "We've been expecting you," the clerk said. "As we understand it, you're traveling to Germany to live with your aunt and uncle, and you don't speak English, is that right?"

"Yes, that's right. I hope I'm not being too much trouble." It was immensely reassuring to hear a complete stranger talking in her own language.

"It's no trouble. We're happy to be of service to you."

She pressed her face to the window next to her spacious seat until the light gave out, transfixed by the shoreless waves that were now her whole universe. After what seemed like a sumptuous dinner she dozed briefly. But her rambling thoughts wouldn't rest. From a home she barely knew she was traveling alone with a small suitcase of hope to an unknown land that she felt was hers. So much promise, so much to go wrong. She put on the headphones and kept a tight grip on her leopard.

Eight hours after boarding, a customs agent at Frankfurt International Airport examined her passport. "Ah, you're the girl who grew up in the United States but only speaks German?"

Hanna opened her mouth and closed it again. How could this man, who was like a policeman, know this? Finally she responded as she thought one should to authorities. "Yes, sir."

"Wait a moment." He gestured to another agent a few stations away, who finished with the person he was talking to and then brought a small plaque over. It was engraved with an ornate inscription:

The undersigned greeted Fräulein Hoffmann upon her arrival in Germany and wish her the best of luck for the future.

"How did you know? Does everyone—no, surely, how can that . . ."

The man grinned. "The embassy told us a little about you. The agents all thought it would be a pleasant touch to welcome you with this little memento. We know it won't be easy to adjust to a new country with no friends, and not even your parents close by."

Her face still felt flushed. "I don't know what to say. Thank you so much."

"It's our pleasure," he said. "I'll help you through customs."

Finally she reached the exit, where she was greeted with a fierce hug. Heidi's face was rounder than her sister's, and her hair was shorter, but she was the same height. Unlike Hermann, however, Georg wasn't much taller. But he was sturdy and self-assured. He took her suitcase and extended his hand. "You must be exhausted, Hanna. But your room and bed are all ready."

"Oh, Uncle Georg, don't worry about me—I'm too excited to sleep. I can't wait to see your house. I wonder if it will look the way I imagine it."

A taxi took them to the *Hauptbahnhof.* The huge glass ceiling was like a castle entrance, big enough for magical mythical creatures. A giant river of iron rails, wide as the pictures she'd seen of the Rhine, rippled out into the city. In the distance, tall buildings were topped with massive signs solemnly announcing lofty company names. She was enchanted.

After two and a half hours they arrived in Böblingen, where the Baumanns' car was parked. Finally, a short drive through dense forests led to Waldenheim. Hanna found the tall, narrow white houses with their flat red rooftiles strangely comforting. Her books were coming to life.

But reading had not prepared her for the feeling of the narrow, winding cobblestone streets. A single building seemed to line each side, all light-colored stone and plaster, with direct, understated advertising and tasteful window displays. Intersections were festooned with signs like bushes, with branches pointing to streets and nearby towns. A picture of a person turned green or red in the traffic lights.

She felt ready to burst. This was home, even though her parents weren't there. Her mother was coming soon. It was all going to be a dream come true—a good dream finally.

The Baumanns' house, like its neighbors, had three stories under a steeply sloping roof. Hanna barely glimpsed the kitchen and dining area on her way up the stairs. After dropping her suitcase, she scampered further upward to find a study, sewing room, and small sitting room with a dormer and skylight.

She returned more slowly to her room where she pushed back the curtains on a small window. The view wasn't expansive, like Boulder, but cozy, like her bedroom. It made her feel safe. Back downstairs, the kitchen gleamed in white with shiny black backsplash and chrome trim on the appliances. Compared to the pastel colors and flower patterns she'd known in Boulder, it evoked a space-age boldness.

Georg smiled and set a cup of hot chocolate on the table. "Enjoy this now, because you'll probably crash well before dinner. You'll have the weekend to relax and get to know your new home, and then start school Monday."

Excitement mixed with anxiety as she drank the rich liquid. Her background was so different from anyone else. They would know so much that she didn't.

ON MONDAY, HANNA arose early after a nearly sleepless night and agonized over what to wear. She was too nervous for breakfast. Heidi had explained the commuting process the evening before. "I'll drive you this week. After that I'll take you to the Echterdingen station, where you can catch the *S-Bahn* to downtown Stuttgart. Once you're comfortable with making connections, there's a bus between Waldenheim and Echterdingen. The whole trip is just under an hour."

Thoughts jostled each other impatiently as they approached the school. Would she be able to follow the lessons? What would the other pupils be like? What could she talk about?

A labyrinth of dim, unadorned hallways led to the director's office. One of the three women in the crowded, windowless outer section ushered them to Lothar Braunschweig's private room. A tall man in a gray tweed jacket greeted her professionally.

"Fräulein Hoffmann, welcome. I wish we could give you more individual attention. The most I can do is to take you to your first class. When you're finished, you may come back here and someone will show you to the entrance, where you'll find Frau Baumann."

Hanna fought back tears as Heidi said goodbye. The enchanted new land suddenly seemed forbidding and frightening. She couldn't imagine introducing herself and her singular story to strangers without adult help.

Four hours later, she fell into her aunt's arms. Then she straightened quickly. "Aunt Heidi, it was *so* fascinating. And the other pupils were really nice."

The first statement was true. The sense of childlike delight that she'd felt on her arrival in her new homeland had only increased. Despite having arrived a week into the school year, she'd been able to keep up with geography, and German was a breeze.

The second statement was an outright lie.

Besides the director and his assistant, and the teachers calling roll, no one had spoken a word to her all day. She'd expected her size to attract attention, but instead she seemed invisible. Perhaps she was so strange that no one wanted anything to do with her. But she couldn't give even a hint of this to her aunt. So many people had worked so hard to get her there.

"I'm glad, Hanna. I'm sure there'll be hard moments at first until you get used to it. Rest a little before the coffee and cake I told you about yesterday. Two girls your age are coming with their mothers at four."

She tried to focus on her new books, far too keyed up to rest. These girls would be the age that she felt herself to be, but they wouldn't see her that way.

Voices announced the arrival of guests. She came hesitantly down the stairs.

"Hanna, I'd like you to meet Sabine and her mother Frau Brinkhaus." Heidi turned immediately to the door as the other pair arrived. Sabine kept her eyes on her gold ballet flats with a chain across the dainty pointed toes, her face half hidden by gentle waves of long blond hair.

Heidi served the cake and drinks, and asked the other girls to introduce themselves. Then she turned to Hanna. "Now, I know you've just arrived. But what do you think of our little town?"

She couldn't express her apprehensions to these strangers. She wanted them to like her. "I—I, um, think it's lovely. Everyone is very nice."

"Why don't you show the girls your room?"

"Well, I—okay. Can I show them the study up above?" There was nothing in her room but the precious things from Elisabeth, carefully arrayed on her dresser. Probably boring—and also private. As she climbed the stairs she talked about what she'd found so exciting in Germany. But they lagged behind, chattering to each other.

"Sabine, how's your puppy? Is he cute?"

"Oh, he's adorable. But housetraining him is *so* much work. You have to come over and help me walk him."

"The moment we get out of this place."

Sabine replied quietly, but Hanna still heard her. "Soon. She's so weird. There's something not right."

Soon after they returned to the living room, Frau Brinkhaus apologized for leaving suddenly because her daughter had developed a splitting headache.

Hanna trudged back upstairs. Instead of her fabled promised land she was wandering in a barren wilderness. Maybe no place would be friendly to her. Maybe some curse from her past had caused her to be assaulted and had now followed her here. She clung to a slender hope that she'd meet some nice friends. But she dreaded the next day.

Deep in one of her dresser drawers, she found the bag with her pacifier. She ignored the knock on the door and sat on her bed, trying to picture her room in Boulder.

HEIDI INVITED ANOTHER family with a seventh-grade girl to dinner on Wednesday, but she was as uninterested as the others. Again Hanna went to her room and put herself to sleep with her pacifier. The next morning she carefully colored in another red heart on her calendar, and wrote the number of days until her mother would arrive on 7 November.

Frequent episodes of regression followed. Her childish voice was met with stares at first, and then snickers. She buried herself in her books. If she could memorize every word, perhaps she would get a chance to show her classmates that she wasn't stupid. Math offered a chance: after two weeks of lectures the pupils would start doing problems at the blackboard.

Monday was surprisingly sunny, and it was her first day to take the bus from Waldenheim. Buoyed by pride in this responsibility, she approached hopefully. But she blanked at the equation—why was "x" there with the numbers? The class erupted in raucous laughter.

She hurried out after class as fast as she could, her cheeks still burning, trying to ignore the two men laughing about "that feeble-minded girl from America." She scrunched down in her seat on the train and hoped she was invisible. At least she would please her aunt and uncle by taking the bus.

A short distance from the bus stop she encountered a small cluster of school-age children. She recognized Sabine.

"Why, if it isn't the American rocket scientist—who I hear is going to graduate from kindergarten soon."

"I don't think so, Sabine, she doesn't know how to walk yet." Hanna heard these words just before she tripped over a stick that a boy suddenly thrust in front of her ankles.

She picked herself up, carefully smoothed her torn skirt, and continued walking, stonily ignoring their laughter. Only when she got home and closed the door to her room did she break down, sobbing in wrenching heaves that left her stomach in pain.

For the rest of the week Heidi drove her to and from the bus stop. But today she was nowhere in sight. Hanna pulled her scarf a little more tightly around her neck and sighed with resignation. After half an hour the family's VW pulled up with Georg behind the wheel.

He seemed unhurried. "My entire department is starting the weekend early today. We finally finished a big project after lots of overtime. Do you mind if we stop by the house of one of my coworkers?"

Of course I mind. It was another moment in a life that no one understood. "What if I do? I'm sure it doesn't matter."

If he was annoyed, he didn't show it. A few minutes later he introduced her to Emma and Paul Giesselmann.

"Paul and I have worked together for many years. Their daughter is about your age. Emma, is she here now?"

"Upstairs with her usual clan. I'll get her." Frau Giesselmann returned with a sturdily built girl of above-average height with long brown hair swept across her forehead and tucked behind her left ear.

Georg nodded to her. "Hi, Doris. This is my niece from America. I'll let her tell you her story herself. Paul and I want to have a beer, so you'll have time."

Hanna caught Doris's quizzical look. At least she wasn't being ignored. She followed as Doris silently motioned her toward the stairs. A much shorter girl with thick wavy black hair met them on the landing. "This is Clara."

"You have a lovely necklace." Hanna hoped a compliment might help her connect. The pendant was a delicately wrought gold-colored ring of tiny birds with a six-pointed star in the center.

"Thank you, I'm so glad you like it."

"And this is Annika." Doris clearly wasn't one for long-winded introductions.

Annika was as tall and thin under her tousled blond curls as Clara was short and stocky. *She must be a nordic princess.*

As they continued down the hall, an open door revealed three more girls standing around a long table. Dowels and string were scattered amongst tubes of glue, files, clamps, and other woodworking tools.

But it was the sewing machine in the corner that caught Hanna's attention. She went over to it and put her fingers on the presser foot. Something felt familiar. "It's electric, right? Could you turn it on?"

She had no idea why she'd asked. But a moment later she'd sewn two scraps of fabric together. She got up and returned to the door, her face warm. "Sorry, that was weird, I know. Just ignore me."

Doris and Annika exchanged glances, but continued down the hall. Doris sat down last in the study. "So, what's this story of yours? How can you be from America and speak perfect German?"

"I was hurt and lost all memory of my past, including English. And every time I try to learn it again I forget it immediately. The Hoffmanns adopted me."

"Wait a minute." She disappeared down the hall, reappearing a moment later with the three girls who had been in the workshop. "This is Lena, Frieda, and Amelie. Now, tell us about it."

There was nothing subtle about Doris Giesselmann.

Hanna was afraid to talk about the most personal parts of her life to six girls whom she'd never met. But she longed for companionship. For three weeks her only friendly contacts had been her aunt and uncle. So she told them about her countless skin graft operations, how she'd had to learn everything again starting with kindergarten, and that a cat had found her.

She didn't tell them that she'd had an operation on her genitals. The books she'd read never talked about anything like it. She didn't understand it, but there was clearly a sense of shame around it.

Doris's large brown eyes remained fixed steadily on her the whole time. "You don't need to worry about your scars around us. There's something odd about each of us. But we don't let anyone mess with us. Now, about those nails."

She took Hanna's carefully manicured hands in her own. "Can you help us do this? We've just been allowed to use nail polish this year."

"Sure. I learned in the hospital from a Mexican nurse. She was so awesome."

"You speak Spanish?"

"Some. It was easy to learn. I'm even studying French now. It's only English I can't do."

"Do you know any swear words?"

"A few." Hanna felt herself blush. "The worst one she taught me is for a really nasty person."

"Tell us, come on."

"*Gilipollas*—it means asshole."

They all giggled as Hanna's cheeks burned.

After the polish was dry, Doris suggested they all go to Café Schilling for pastries and chocolate. There was no discussion—the others all just got up and looked for their coats.

They passed several other children of similar age as they neared the small downtown area. Then Hanna froze as she saw Sabine.

"Nice afternoon for a walk, isn't it, retard?" Hanna recognized the voice of the boy who'd tripped her. She saw now that he was both taller and heavier than the other boys in the group. Though none of them were anywhere close to her height, she started to duck into a store.

Doris grabbed her arm. "Hey, come back here—you can't run from these clowns."

"Be careful, Franz. Doris is with her. Why, is beyond me."

"A lot of things are beyond you and Franz, Sabine." She whispered to Hanna, "Tell him the Spanish you just taught us—and do it loudly."

Hanna responded without hesitation. She regretted it instantly. But Doris's tone commanded obedience.

Franz looked perplexed. Doris laughed. "A little too much, huh? You should try learning a foreign language, like the girl you called a 'retard.' Hanna, tell him what it means."

Again she worried, but obeyed.

He raised his arm as if to shove her. "Watch it, stupid cow—nobody talks that way to me. *Ouch!*" The arm dropped to his thigh and he bent over, dancing about on one foot.

"Why Franz, you can't get stung by a bee in October." Doris casually picked up a six-inch-long wooden rod with a rubber tip from where he'd been standing. "Such an imagination." Watching Franz hobble down the sidewalk with his friends,' she slipped it into the pocket of her jacket. Then Annika emerged from behind a parked car.

Hanna was bewildered. "What on earth is going on?"

But Doris offered no explanation. "Nothing at all. Let's go. I'm hungry, aren't you?"

HER NEW FRIENDSHIPS transformed Hanna's social life. Now she went directly from the bus stop to Doris's house, no longer afraid to walk. She still sat to one side of the others as she studied her own lessons, worried she'd annoy them or be ridiculed for saying something foolish.

Gradually she realized they weren't going to laugh at her. Doris insisted she teach them what she knew about sewing. Though it made her nervous, it also made her talk, and she savored the thought that she actually knew more about something than they did. She began to join in their idle banter.

A week before she thought her mother was coming, a letter was waiting when she got home. Excitedly she tore it open. *There've been complications getting the house ready for sale. I won't be able to come until December.*

To Hanna that might as well have been forever. She ran into her room and slammed the door, screaming at Heidi to go away. But her aunt refused to leave her alone. Grumbling, she agreed to go to Doris's house, where she walked wordlessly past Annika and sat in a corner of the den, arms folded, staring fixedly at the wall.

Doris pulled her onto the sofa. "If you're going to be here you have to talk. What's wrong?"

"Doris, whatever made you want to be friends with me? Didn't I seem way too strange?"

"Of course you seemed strange—you *are* strange." Doris raised her eyebrows slightly. "I knew you'd fit in. It was obvious."

"I haven't driven you crazy, being such a wimp?"

"Well, there are times." Hanna's scowl softened, and after a moment they giggled.

Doris tossed her hair back. "It's gotta be hard. Probably no one wants to talk to you at the school you're going to, 'cause they think you're childish. They think you're an overgrown retarded seventh-grader, but seventh-graders think you're a retarded grown-up. Right?"

Hanna nodded, more than a little amazed. These girls really understood her. And they were being sympathetic and understanding. Probably a lot more than she was. She felt ashamed of her churlishness.

"My advice: Ignore them. You're way better. Look at what you've been through. And you study more than anyone. You show *us* up sometimes. You know, there've been strong women who changed the world in spite of all the bad things that men did to them. You're going to be one of them."

Hanna shook her head. "Why would you ever say that? I'm a moody wreck. I don't know how to just be happy like you. I'm anxious and afraid all the time. Then I get angry. I try to not show it, but I must be beastly."

"Silly goose, most of the time you're way too nice."

"I'm always afraid of what people will think about me."

"You shouldn't give a hoot what other people think. Stand up for yourself and don't apologize. That's what we do." She pointed at Annika. "Her grandfather was an SS officer, in charge of Norway. He was tried and executed there after the war. That didn't stop Clara from being her best friend."

Hanna looked up sharply. "Really?"

"We're unusual, it's true." Clara's tone was matter-of-fact. "Our parents got us together when we were toddlers. Then when we learned this—we were seven—I just thought, 'Well, so? It wasn't *you*.' It didn't change her."

Annika put her arm around her friend. "And Doris said 'That's what I expected.' But I think that was our first lesson about what prejudice—and empathy—is really about."

Hanna hesitated. Dare she tell them? A loud voice inside said no. But sitting in a classroom every day with strangers who ignored her when they weren't making fun of her, she longed to be accepted as she was. Whatever she was.

She didn't want to be an outsider. She wanted to belong. Without secrets.

She looked at her lap, still uncertain. "There's something else. I've been told some people think it's awful, though I don't know why."

"All right, out with it."

"Have you heard of transsexuals?"

"I've heard of transvestites. Guys who like to dress up as girls. Which clearly isn't you."

When Hanna finished, Doris looked at the others for what seemed like forever. No one showed a reaction. Hanna felt sick. She should've listened to that cautious voice.

Finally Doris swiveled back. "Hanna, that you're on the odd side isn't in question. But this is how I described you to another friend: absurdly tall with a voice like Marlene Dietrich, speaks way more French and Spanish than anyone else we know, and never goes anywhere with a hair out of place. Oh, and would kill for *Currywurst*."

Her gaze was like a musician: intense, calm, and inwardly focused. She seemed to be having several conversations at once, only one of which was out loud.

"As for this other thing: well, so what? Like I said before, there's something about each of us that's like a scar. You're sincere— no pretense. That's what's important to me."

The others nodded. Hanna swallowed hard, relief flooding in, calming her churning stomach. "I hope you'll all be my friends forever. How can I thank you?"

"I don't care about thanks. Only strong friends."

For the first time in her life, she had a friend. Strength—that she wasn't so sure of.

IN DECEMBER THE famous Stuttgart *Weihnachtsmarkt* became a regular weekend destination. Hanna was enthralled. Ambling past brightly lit tables under wooden awnings, admiring the carved figurines and candles, trying to avoid spilling her *Kinderpunsch* as she ate *Bratwurst* with mustard hot off the grill—all stirred something deep inside. She was where she belonged.

This was what she'd dreamed of in the hospital. She crunched through the snow and hummed songs that she knew well, even though she'd never heard them. Soon her parents would come and the picture would be complete.

Gisela and Hermann arrived at the Böblingen train station two weeks before Christmas. Hanna wanted to be there an hour ahead of schedule. Eventually she compromised on half an hour and paced up and down the platform.

"How can you not know what car they'll be in? Where am I supposed to wait, then?" She vented her irritation at Heidi and Georg as they calmly sipped coffee near the station entrance.

When the train came to a halt and they stepped out, Hanna was at the far end. She broke into a run, stumbled, and fell. By the time she'd picked herself up, they'd made their way to her.

"Hanna, I hope you're taking better care of yourself than this," Hermann said dryly. Then they both laughed as she put her arms around them and squeezed with all her strength.

"Oh, Mama, Papa—oh god, I'm so glad . . ." She thought of how to stop the tears that would certainly smudge her mascara. She couldn't do it. But she still smiled so widely her face hurt.

They started toward the exit. "Mama, Papa, I have to tell you about the *Weihnachtsmarkt*. I know you know all about it, but I didn't. I got you something, but I don't have it with me, and I couldn't tell you what it was anyway, of course. And did you know that moss is super-important for water storage? And there are Roman ruins just outside of our town? And I've been sewing—I give my friends lessons. They're so awesome . . ."

She didn't stop while Georg fetched the car and she sat in between her parents. Only when they passed through the center of town and she saw Doris coming out of a government building did she suddenly fall silent.

She hadn't written anything about the bullying to her parents because she didn't want to worry them. Should she talk about it now?

She decided not to. She was afraid of reopening the wounds.

CHAPTER 12

DORIS STOOD NEARLY at attention in front of the desk of Uwe Kellermann, member of the *Bundestag* for her district. He pushed a large envelope toward her.

"Here's the report, Fräulein Giesselmann. The very brief summary is that, as you suspected, your grandfather was not a robber as the newspaper clipping claimed. The so-called police, who were indeed SS troops, executed him after finding him in a gay bar."

Doris flinched. She'd been expecting something shocking, but not that.

Kellermann must have noticed. "I'm sorry. This is a bit much to drop on a twelve-year-old girl, isn't it?"

"It's all right, Herr Kellermann. The clipping has been driving me crazy ever since I saw it. Of course I was never meant to—my mother had it in a locked file cabinet."

"And you found the key. Snooping, hmm?"

Doris hesitated. But he'd been so helpful. Impulsively she decided to be open. "Actually, I picked the lock."

"Now that's interesting. What led you to do that?"

"My mother seemed so defensive, I thought she must be hiding something. She got really mad after I pestered her about him. So I decided I had to find out what she knew."

"Well, then, you could be a budding detective. Or thief."

She grinned. "A friend of my father's showed me how. I think he expects me to be the first female auto mechanic in town. I *am* handy with stuff. Anyway, thanks. Now I have to figure out what all this means."

"I'm glad I could be of service. Don't forget the SPD was the party that helped you." His eyes twinkled as he shook her hand.

Doris shuffled down the hall with uncharacteristic gloom as she scanned the report's summary.

Her mother had told a different lie: She'd said her father was a soldier, killed early in the war. She was obviously ashamed of him. Because he'd been a homosexual? Doris was pretty sure that would pose a problem for her.

She was indeed handy with mechanical stuff. She also knew by now that she was a natural leader. After all, who else formed a band of mavericks in the second grade, modeled after mythical female nordic warriors, and took on the world?

She was proud of her *Schildmaiden*. With her leadership, Lena, Frieda, and Amelie had become playful and confident, and no bully dared touch them. She and Annika were a fierce duo, and Clara had learned quickly.

What was the deal with the Nazis about "different" people, anyway? She knew a lot of people who thought Jews were "different." If she hadn't known Clara, maybe she would've thought that too.

Grown-ups often didn't tell the truth. She could handle that. But this report left her feeling adrift. Its other revelation, about Annika's grandfather, was a little unsettling. Added to what she was just learning about herself and daren't tell even her friends, it was indeed a bit much.

As she left the building, she saw the Baumanns' car pass. She knew Hanna was expecting her parents to come from America. Hanna—that strange girl in a strange body with the condition that nobody had even heard of: maybe she would understand.

IT WAS THE second day of the new year. Hanna was relaxing in the living room with her parents, trying not to think about their impending departure. Gisela would come back in three weeks, with the house sold and everything shipped. But her father's employment contract required him to stay until April.

Gisela finished a piece of *Stollen* that Hanna had baked a week earlier. "You helped me make one of these during your first year with us."

"I hope it was better than this one. I think I didn't knead the dough enough. Whatever it was, I messed up."

"Hanna, don't do that to yourself." Gisela shook her finger. "Nothing is perfect the first time. Be proud of what you've done."

"I'm sorry, Mama. I know my self-confidence is awful. I'm doing better, though. And my friends help me a lot."

In the morning Hanna said goodbye and plodded down the sidewalk to the bus stop, eyes on her feet, using all her resolve to resist running back.

Doris called her in the afternoon. "Come to my house and we'll play Monopoly, or *Mensch ärgere dich nicht* if you prefer."

Anger and resentment surged. Her friends obviously didn't understand her after all. "That's stupid. Don't you realize how much homework I have?"

But she didn't do homework. Instead she stared out the window of her bedroom, wishing that the woman downstairs was the one who had read and sung to her through all the dark times of her short childhood.

She just wanted a regular home. Like what other children had.

The next day she came to Doris's house, but sat alone and refused to talk. Finally Doris handed her a note.

If you don't start talking to us, we're going to use only English around you.

Hanna looked at Doris as if the note were a string of curses. "You *what . . .* ? And you're supposed to be my friends?"

But then she realized how selfish she was being. They'd done so much for her. And her father was probably sacrificing his career for her, and both parents were working overtime to make this change. It wasn't so easy for them, either, was it? Now she felt even worse.

"I'm being an absolute shrew, aren't I?" The tears that always seemed so close came yet again. "It—it's so hard without them. It made me feel almost like everything was normal again. And then I snapped at you, after all you've done. You should just give up on me."

"Silly goose, we're not letting you off that easy. Suppose you give us a quiz on the Roman Empire stuff that we were studying before Christmas. And make sure you have the weekend after next open. We're going skiing in Oberstdorf. Chaperoned trip—no parents."

Hanna was tired by bedtime, but sleep still came slowly.

> *A girl had been ordered to organize some jumbled nuts and bolts in a shop. It seemed impossible. She felt that on the other side of one wall someone knew how to do it. There was a crack in the wall—but it was too small to get through.*
>
> *But then she heard a monster snort, and the shop became a cave. Seeing a wide crack in one side of the cave, she ran desperately. There was barely enough room for her to squeeze in as the beast bore down on her, snarling and cursing. She huddled there petrified, just out of reach of its vicious claws.*

She flung the duvet aside, looking for her enemy, unsure at first if she was dreaming or awake. In the corner of her bedroom demons were cackling in obvious glee over their plans for her when she fell back to sleep.

Yet hadn't she done something to escape the monster? Which meant, if one took lessons from dreams, that fighting back against her fears wouldn't kill her.

The very thought was frightening.

OBERSTDORF WAS ONLY 160 kilometers southeast of Waldenheim but over four hours on the train. Shop windows lighted the way as several gaggles of schoolchildren found their hotel. The chaperones sternly quelled the chaotic hubbub in the lobby and shepherded everyone to their rooms, where tonight's dinner would be what they'd brought from home.

In the morning, the forbidding flanks of the Nebelhorn glistened under a picture-perfect Alpine sun. The girls signed up for a beginner's lesson. The instructor, who introduced himself as Ulrich, looked quizzically at Hanna. "Are you sure you're in the right place?"

"Yes, she's one of us," Doris answered before Hanna could even speak.

He gave them a brief lecture about technique and a demonstration of the snowplow turn over a short section of hill, and then directed them to try.

The nebulous anxiety that was always in the background intensified. She'd never done anything like this. Skiing was bound to painfully stretch her scars. She would never keep up with her friends. She was about to make a fool of herself.

Yet the skis felt comfortable, even vaguely familiar. With barely a passing thought for the instructions she'd just heard, she bent her knees deeply, moved into the snowplow position, and executed a flawless turn with her weight on the downhill ski and upper shoulder forward. Ulrich didn't hide his shock.

"Fräulein," he said, "this is a beginner's class. You should be in at least a beginning advanced class. If you go back to the place where we met, someone will direct you to the right place."

"But I've never had a pair of skis on my feet in my life," Hanna protested, embarrassed.

"Really, it's not a joke for the others who need this instruction." His voice was sharp and dismissive. "You can't stay here; it will disrupt the class."

Hanna felt tears coming. She couldn't stand the thought of leaving her friends.

"Please, I can explain." Doris stepped awkwardly forward, sliding backward half a step for every one she took toward the still-annoyed instructor. "It's true that Hanna isn't in our school. But she's really a seventh-grader—she's doing *Hauptschulabschluss* preparation in a *Volkshochschule,* and we study together. She was hurt and lost her memory. Now she's learning everything all over again. I think something she knew before came back to her."

Hanna tried to reach over and hug Doris, in the process falling against her. Together they tumbled to the ground. The other girls cheered as they struggled to their feet.

Ulrich was silent for several seconds, his face impassive. "You *really* don't remember skiing?"

"No. Mostly I just did what my legs wanted to do. Honestly, no one could have been more surprised than I."

"Well, let's see how much those legs know. Do the turn again and tell us what you think your body is doing."

In a short time he had her critiquing her friends. The group split into two and traded "instructors" after an hour. By noon the six true novices were sailing through stem turns on intermediate slopes. Hanna forgot her embarrassment. All she had to do was concentrate on what her body could do, and forget about what people thought of it.

Ulrich left them for one lift cycle, and when they returned to the base, with Hanna in the lead, they found him watching with three of his peers.

"You see," he said solemnly to his companions. "If you know the right technique, you can bring beginners to this level in a two-hour lesson. Why can't you klutzes do this?"

One of them snickered. "Ulrich, this is worrying. You need good eyesight to be a ski instructor. At least good enough to see the difference between a young girl and an adult."

"This is a class of seventh graders. They had a chaperone with them when I met them."

"If she's a twelve-year-old, then I'm Jean-Claude Killy."

Ulrich turned toward Doris, who nodded. "Hanna is one of us."

The other man turned toward his ski tips.

Ulrich smiled a little. "She's a genuine beginner all right—at first, she couldn't tell me a thing about how to ski. And yet somehow she does know."

He put his hand on her shoulder. "I'll make two bets. Take her up a black diamond slope right now. First bet: she'll tell you she's never done it before and is petrified. Second bet: she'll be able to ski it right behind you."

Hanna didn't need to be staring down a vertical cliff to be petrified. But they started for the lift and obviously expected her to follow.

"Don't worry about it, Hanna." Ulrich's voice was soft and sincere. "Let your body do its magic. You'll be fine."

As the lift rose higher and higher, Hanna closed her eyes and tried to concentrate on her body, imagining each muscle in action. The silence of the snow-covered mountain calmed her nerves.

At the top of the lift she followed the others in a U-turn to face a forty-degree mogul-covered slope that eased off fifty meters below. As the instructors took off, executing a flawless series of rapid sharp turns, panic gripped her.

Then she closed her eyes again, positioned herself as she knew was right, opened her eyes, and pushed off. Her body *did* do the rest—just as Ulrich had predicted. When she skied up to the waiting men, they looked at each other and back at her. "Nice," the one who'd doubted Ulrich said. "Let's go, then."

For the rest of the day Hanna taught the other girls, enjoying the friendly, easy laughter of the group, her scars forgotten. Skiing ahead of her friends, she felt graceful and feminine.

It was nearly eleven before the girls stumbled exhausted to bed that night. But Hanna's mind was still buzzing.

What had made Ulrich believe in her? Hadn't he taken a huge chance? She wondered where her ability came from—and whether she would ever know. What else didn't she know about herself? And would she ever be able to anticipate when these mysterious reverberations from the past would arise?

Whatever the answer, she needed to be strong for her parents. She had to snap out of her funk.

For more than an hour, these thoughts danced chaotically in her mind. But when she finally drifted into dreamland, this time there was no monster. Instead she flew through the air on her skis, lithe and graceful, passing the gates of a giant slalom as a crowd cheered.

WHEN SHE GOT home, Hanna was greeted at the door by Gisela, who had arrived earlier than expected. She tried not to show her surprise. She wanted to spring her own.

"Mama, I can ski!"

"Of course you can."

But as Hanna's mouth opened, her mother's amused look turned somber. "I'm sorry, Hanna. Doctor Beattie told us not to talk about your past till you were stronger. After those setbacks, I think she was afraid that almost anything from before the assault could trigger another one."

"It's okay, Mama. I've been thinking about myself. Doctor Beattie's right. I'm afraid of memories. But the sewing and skiing were good. Let me tell you what happened."

Her mother's demeanor grew ever more somber till it was unsettling. "You're discovering more than skills, sweetie. Now I understand your reaction to Doris's sewing machine. You told us a little about what sewing meant to you as a child. Speaking of which, look at this article."

She handed Hanna a newspaper. "Papa's new job is in Frankfurt. Don't worry—we'll stay here together till the end of this school term at least. But while I was apartment-hunting, I met the founder of this new children's theater. She's so creative and energetic, but short on cash. She's doing most of the work herself. Volunteers would help her a lot. So of course I thought of you."

"Me? For what?"

"Sewing costumes. And Doris and her friends could help make props."

"That's crazy—I'm only an amateur. And Frankfurt's so far from home. Anyway, what will they think of me?"

"You can stay with Papa on weekends. Let's go up and meet her. I'll simply tell Frau Bachmann you're studying for your *Hauptschulabschluss*, planning to be a hairstylist, and Doris is a close friend at our local *Hauptschule*. She doesn't need any more details."

The theater was in northwest Frankfurt, half an hour by *U-Bahn* from the train station. Margarete Bachmann's office was piled with costumes, wigs, puppets, and bits of furniture around a baby grand piano. Wearing a red dress with rose-like ruffles around the neck and matching shoes, she projected the enthusiasm of an entrepreneur filled with love for her art. She immediately plunged into a description of her next project.

"So far I've done old standbys—folk stories and fairy tales. This one's new: about a girl who overcomes prejudice to become a star football player. The script comes from Frauke Zwiebel—have you heard of her?"

Hanna nodded vigorously. "A friend of mine gave me one of her plays for grown-ups. It was awesome. Really inspiring to me as a girl." She paused. "Would it be possible—I mean, would she ever come to see us?"

"Definitely. She's married to my principal financial backer. They're strong art patrons—they very much want to see this theater succeed."

Frauke Zwiebel's visit came about halfway through the rehearsals. Speaking to the entire cast and crew, she praised their work and extolled its value for combating negative stereotypes about women and girls.

Hanna was star-struck. The playwright signed autographs for both Doris and her, and smiled indulgently at her schoolgirlish infatuation. Afterward, Hanna was so excited that she used white thread for the seams of an entire armful of dark-colored pants, and had to rip them all out and start over. As soon as she was home, she put the autographed book on her dresser, right next to Elisabeth's portrait.

AT THE OPENING Sunday matinee performance on May seventh, Margarete Bachmann brought the crew onstage after the performers for a curtain call in front of a standing-room-only crowd, with Hanna introduced first. On their way out Hanna noticed Frauke Zwiebel. She toyed briefly with the thought of waving hello, but quickly dismissed it. The playwright's attention was completely engaged by a man walking alongside her.

Friday was Hanna's birthday. As her friends looked on, Gisela brought out a *Schwarzwälder Kirschtorte* topped with thirteen pink candles and an eight-inch-tall doll with a dress made of pink and white icing. Hanna burst into tears.

"What's wrong?" Gisela looked perplexed.

Hanna quickly hugged her mother, shielding her face. "I don't know what made me cry," she whispered. "It just made me feel so good. Like something happened that I'd dreamed of. I'm so silly. I'm sorry, Mama."

"Life would be so boring without you. Now get back to your party."

After a hike and picnic the next day, the two couples and Hanna stopped in town for afternoon coffee and cake. Georg idly leafed through the *Anzeigenblatt*. Hanna saw his expression suddenly darken, but she didn't want to spoil the idyllic mood with a question.

When they got home, he came to her room. "Hanna, a Stuttgart real estate developer named Volker Zwiebel was also at the play. He's easily recognized—short, portly, curly black hair. Just before you joined us on the way out he said rather loudly to his wife: 'You're right: there's no way in hell that could be a girl.'"

"Wait a second." The implication was too bizarre to digest quickly. "Is his wife Frauke Zwiebel?"

"Yes, the playwright. The local paper has a letter from him questioning your sex, and demanding that the authorities either produce physiological proof or change your identification. Lothar Braunschweig received the same letter. He just telephoned me."

Her head responded with a reverberating throb that frightened her almost as much as the news. "Why—why would they do this? I don't understand . . ."

"Neither do I. Hold tight and be patient. You'll be safe."

Be safe?

The woman she idolized, as much for her advocacy for women and stance against prejudice as for her art, was attacking her for reasons that sounded a lot like raw prejudice.

She forced herself to eat a little despite the pit in her stomach. Afterward, they watched the news on TV. Frauke Zwiebel was frequently interviewed as a commentator on the arts. Tonight she talked about the political consequences of the recent showing on TV of a film with men kissing. Her finishing broadside left Hanna numb.

"Removing sanctions against gay men by the repeal of Paragraph 175 three years ago was a welcome development. The fear of older homosexuals harming younger men with unwanted advances was unfounded. But equal rights for transsexuals is a very different matter, some liberal politicians notwithstanding. Let them dress however they want, but sex is real. Men in dresses invading women's spaces would profoundly endanger real women."

In the morning Hanna found a poster on a kiosk near her bus stop captioned in large handwritten print: "Danger—suspected man masquerading as a girl in Waldenheim." Underneath was a photo of her, along with a list of statistics regarding male and female bodies.

Why was this happening?

She wasn't happy with her body. It wasn't only height: she still wore an A cup bra, and hips broader than her shoulders were a fond hope. But all the girls complained about their bodies. Hers was just a little worse. She hated it, but she didn't think of it as hateful.

She hoped her friends hadn't seen the poster. Though she was only vaguely recognizable in the low-resolution black-and-white photocopy, it was still a personal attack. One that came from someone who presented herself as an advocate of girls' and women's rights. A humanist.

Clara had heard about an American rock band that would give only one show in Stuttgart mid-week. Her older sister volunteered to accompany the seventh-graders. Its name seemed almost sinister—The Grateful Dead—and they had a reputation for drug use. But maybe it would take her mind off the menace in her real world.

Hanna had no idea what to expect—she'd never been to a concert. The Stuttgart Liederhalle seemed like a very fancy place for rock and roll. They found their seats, and the eight-o'clock starting time came and went. Finally, at the appearance of a few men who didn't seem to her any different from the technicians who'd wandered on and off stage for more than half an hour, a raucous cheer erupted and the music began.

She'd never imagined such music. Rhythms flowed like a river from crashing rapids to placid streams, guitar notes soared like flocks of starlings, and voices of haunting emotion left her in tears of joy. She left with the feeling that a window onto a new life had been opened.

But the next morning, the accusing poster drowned her rekindled spirits like a deluge on a campfire. It was right—she could never be normal. She looked at other girls with their cute little shoes and slender fingers, and looked away. She didn't want to even think about her own.

She *was* a misfit. Perhaps her body was hateful after all.

Her concentration in class vanished. She came home and slammed the door. "I can't do it. Why do I have to solve equations to be a hairstylist? I can use numbers but the x and y stuff makes no sense. I'm never going to graduate."

"Dear, you've been doing that all year," Gisela asked gently. "Why is it different now?"

Hanna didn't want to talk about her turmoil to the grown-ups who'd done so much for her. Maybe this was all her fault. But where had she gone wrong? This was who she was. She couldn't change that.

She flung herself onto the sofa and pummeled the cushions. "I don't know. It just is."

"I know it's hard to ignore them, but it's best to. The Zwiebels' bigotry is their problem, not yours."

Hanna wasn't about to be comforted. They couldn't possibly understand. It wasn't only insults: Frauke Zwiebel had assailed her basic rights as a human. Someone could take that as justification for a violent attack.

A WEEK LATER, as she passed a small park on her way home from the bus, five men were loitering on the grass.

"Have you heard about the guy who's pretending to be a girl here?"

Hanna looked straight ahead and pretended to ignore them.

"*It* is not a guy. It's a sick animal."

"A creepy pervert—straight from the devil. Should be a crime."

Hanna quickened her pace.

"Yet our commie government and university psychologists make this crap legal and protect him."

"I say it's the fault of the stinkin' parents who want to be homo friendly. Put 'em in jail."

"Yeah, and put the kid in an asylum, so he can't do damage to real girls. That's what the woman on TV was talking about."

One of the men pulled a wide black belt from his pants. "Nah, just give the sissy a good whippin'. He'll get straightened out."

At the sight of the belt, Hanna felt her head tighten as if in a vise, and her vision blurred. She spurted forward in blind panic. The uproarious laughter licked at her heels like flames.

She burst through the door of her home, sobbing, and vaulted up the stairs to her room. She grabbed her pacifier from the back of a dresser drawer. And when she told her mother what the men in the park had said, it was in the voice of her five-year-old self after the coma.

She clamped her eyes shut and tried to nestle in her mother's lap as she'd done in the hospital. She hated herself for being this way. She was supposed to be strong and grown-up.

But at that moment, she was a frightened child again.

She curled up on her bed, ignoring her mother's struggle to pull the duvet out and cover her. "I'm sorry I'm being such a baby."

A girl was walking through a forest toward a mountain that she'd been told contained a palace inside. She knew there was a vicious monster nearby, but if she was really quiet she could avoid it. But she was still a long ways from the cliff when the monster jumped out from behind a tree and grabbed her.

It pulled her into a dark cave with jagged ceiling formations festooned by old rusty chains. A sawhorse stood next to a forge, draped with several belts.

Hanna awoke in the darkness with a scream, her back throbbing. She remained awake, shivering, until morning.

CHAPTER 13

HANNA DIDN'T LEAVE her house the next day. Jumping into a den of jackals would've been preferable to confronting those men. She wouldn't even let her mother drive her. After school was out she called Doris, who seemed unruffled. "We were taken in badly by that scumbag woman, weren't we? But just ignore those lowlifes in the park."

"*What?* You can't be serious. Don't you understand?"

"I do—completely. They're nothing but witless lackeys who worship the Zwiebels and think they're doing what their idols want. Not much going on upstairs. Trust us, Hanna. We'll have you covered. I'm calling it 'Operation Porgeror.'"

She *did* trust her friends. But she couldn't relax. The menacing insults had rekindled more pain in her back than she'd felt in months. Nevertheless she approached the park again the next day, though it was like walking toward a ticking bomb. The men were there, snickering as before. "Ah, Herr Pussywillow found us. Heinrich, don't you think his hair's rather long for a guy?"

"Definitely. I can take care of that. But maybe he should get a trim in other places as well. Since he doesn't seem to value them very much."

Heinrich was the one who'd threatened her with a belt before. Now he was brandishing a pair of scissors.

There'd been something more ominous about that belt than his promise to "give her a good whippin." She knew that on this day one year ago, a man had beaten and nearly killed her. That was still all she knew. Doctor Beattie had said to wait until she was stronger. How strong did she have to be to face down the terror these men aroused in her?

The man who spoke first was leering at her. "Good idea. And you can give it a nice tattoo at the same time. Carve 'IT' on its forehead."

She answered her question by breaking into a run. A second later she heard a loud yell and looked over her shoulder. Then she stopped.

Heinrich was holding his thigh and groaning. A rubber-tipped dart like the one she'd seen next to Franz last fall was lying on the sidewalk. A moment later all of the men were yelling and jumping spasmodically. They scattered frantically, but darts homed in on them like angry hornets. Heinrich slipped and fell on the grass where he was peppered by an extra fusillade.

An eerie silence descended over the park. The contrast conjured a vision of a horde of dinosaurs thundering out of nowhere and then fleeing, frightened by an unseen enemy. Hanna's heartrate slowed. Eventually, it seemed there was nothing to do but go.

Near the end of the block, she caught a fleeting motion in her peripheral vision. She turned to see a rotund man holding a tire iron like a baton, less than two meters away. Then he dropped it with a yell, grasped his thigh with both hands, and hobbled to a Mercedes double-parked across the street. The rear window shattered as the car screeched away, laying thick rubber tracks.

From an alley mid-block, Doris peered around the corner, waved, and disappeared.

Once again the world was calm and peaceful. Hanna picked up the tire iron and looked at it for some time before placing it carefully on the grass next to the sidewalk. Then she continued on at a slow pace, fiercely telling herself she wasn't afraid.

All six girls cheered as she approached her doorstep. Doris was grinning broadly. "You're such a slowpoke. No matter—we wanted to get here ahead of you. Now invite us in so I can tell you the whole story."

They gathered in the upstairs study. "Thanks to Annika and her Swedish mom, I've been obsessed by myths and legends about female Nordic warriors for ages. One involved two goddesses named Porgeror and Irpa who shot arrows from the tips of their fingers. Crossbows were our best substitute."

"Where on earth did you learn to make crossbows?"

"They're well-known in European military history. We had to tinker a lot to control the force. We can go from a little ping to a nasty wound, with a twenty meter range."

"That's what Annika used on Franz?"

"Yes, but that was nothing compared to this time. And of course we used a metal tip for the car."

"Won't the police investigate?"

"There's nothing that can give us away. I'm certain no one saw us. Amelie and Frieda scooped up all the darts right behind you. And Zwiebel's prints are on that tire iron." Doris shook her head. "I only realized he'd been watching when he drove up from down the street. I guess he just had to enjoy the show."

Hanna looked from one to the other. "I don't know why you did this for me. But I love you."

They looked at each other and giggled. "It was actually a lot of fun," Annika said finally.

"Almost as much fun as we'll have this next week," Doris said. "Hanna, you know Corpus Christi holiday is coming up. We're all going to Oberstdorf with my parents, leaving Wednesday after school. You're coming, naturally."

"Let me check with my mom."

"Tell her I said you *have* to come. But come directly to the train station in Tübingen, not to my house. Departure is 2:42." Doris's tone was more imperious than usual.

Hanna found Gisela in the kitchen and returned with the desired permission along with an invitation to a dinner of *Käsebrot* and ham. She finally tumbled into bed long after dark.

A girl with two cats, one black and one white, came to a steep, monolithic granite face. Her fingers briefly brushed the rock as she whispered, "My name is Hanna Hoffmann."

A crack formed just long enough to allow them into a vast, dimly lit cavern. A monster standing next to a glowing tunnel ran toward them, waving a massive evil-looking belt. The girl leapt and squeezed into an alcove. At that moment the cats jumped onto a ledge, yowling fiercely, and dislodged some rocks onto the monster's head. It ran cursing into the dim depths of the cave.

The dream faded away, and she slept peacefully the rest of the night.

AS HANNA ENTERED the station, she saw Doris and her mother standing at a table behind a small kiosk, glaring at each other. Feeling a little alarmed, she hesitated about twenty feet away, shielded by the kiosk. Their voices weren't hard to hear.

"Mama, could you please just stop this nonsense? That poster was a pack of libels and you know it."

"I don't know. I know sex is not a choice. That transsexual thing is even worse than homosexuals."

Hanna backed up carefully, half afraid her heart's pounding would betray her, and approached again facing Doris, who nearly shouted her greeting.

The anger and anguish in that face were enough to finally convince Hanna of what she'd gradually come to suspect: Like her, Doris lived with something that society condemned. Now she knew that her friend's mother, like her previous parents, was a part of the problem. She could only imagine the difficulty. She didn't know what to say—if anything. Maybe Annika could help.

Emma Giesselmann turned and smiled sweetly. Hanna waved weakly. Her relationship with this family had just become a lot more complicated.

Doris's father arrived, and they were soon on the train. Doris squeezed the girls into an unreserved compartment. "The police chief came to my house Saturday. I expected that—our group's retribution to bullies is well known. I said I didn't know what he was talking about. He didn't give anything away, but he really didn't seem to care much."

Her nonchalance seemed a little restrained at first. But she soon regained her aplomb and the girls passed the time in relaxed adolescent babble. Four and a half hours later, they stepped out to see the last waning sparkles on the Nebelhorn. Above the shadowed town, the foothills and flanks of the scalloped peaks glowed with the verdant green that came with sunset. The valley had emerged from its winter hibernation, reborn into a new cycle of life.

They savored an outdoor dinner of *Käsespätzle* followed by a leisurely stroll around town. If Frau Giesselmann's attitude toward Hanna had changed, she kept it well hidden.

For the next two days they would use one of the cable cars to reach some high-elevation hikes. On Saturday, if the weather forecast held, the girls wanted to take a *via ferrata*. Doris explained it to Hanna.

"It's a way to climb steep places without being a technical climber. You clip a safety sling around fixed cables with carabiners. When you get to an anchor point, you clip a second carabiner onto the leading side, and then take the first one off. In a few *really* steep places there'll be a metal ladder. Don't worry, we've done this before. My parents trust me."

The day dawned bright as predicted. The trail was dry; only the highest points had a little snow. Lingering over the panoramic view till after noon, they were the last to descend. A few clouds hinted at rain later in the afternoon. They had plenty of time to get back safe and dry.

Under those conditions, a loud thunder-like rumbling sound was startling. Moments later, a cloud of dust settled a few hundred meters in front of them. Above and to the right was a prominent new scar.

It was apparent that the rockslide was very close to their route. Their chatter about the awe-inspiring power and indifference of nature stopped abruptly after they topped a small ridge.

One of the ladders had been dislodged from a nearly vertical section about thirty feet high. They were trapped.

The girls looked at each other and the path silently. Climbing down the cliff was out of the question. They could only wait until they were missed. But their light raincoats weren't meant for spending the night on an alpine peak. The statuesque pinnacles they'd been admiring moments ago looked cold and unforgiving under the rapidly gathering clouds. At best they would be miserable. At worst, if the storm were serious . . . it wasn't a pleasant thought.

Lena's wide eyes exuded rising panic. Amelie got completely stuck on her second word. That was especially alarming—stutterers were always able to continue eventually. Not this time.

Frieda held them both. "Don't worry, we'll keep each other warm," she said with a slight quiver. But tears slowly ran down one cheek. Doris put her arm around Frieda, but she was uncharacteristically silent.

Hanna shuddered as she peered over the edge of the cliff. Something nagged at the edge of her mind. There *was* a way down. Their slings could be connected together like rungs of a ladder. If this ladder could be anchored at the top, they could climb down it.

There were no rocks in the right place for an anchor, and the bolts that had held the metal ladder to the rock had been hopelessly bent. However, if someone stayed at the top of the cliff and braced her feet against one side of a crack in the flat rock at the top, she could be the anchor while the others descended.

But then how would *she* get down?

"Doris," she said with a firmness that surprised herself, "we have to go. The weather looks too dangerous."

"It's bad, but we have no choice. The cliff is clearly impossible. Frieda was right—we'll just have to stay really close together."

"I thought of a way to do it. You'll have to trust me. I'll hold the slings for the rest of you, and then I'll drop them and come down."

"That's a perfectly blank wall. What's come over you?"

Indeed, what had? What made her think she could climb vertical rock with no ledges? Her mind said she'd lost all sense. Her stomach was glad she hadn't eaten any lunch. But her fingers could already feel the tiny flakes, and the pain as she dug in and balanced delicately on them.

"I really don't know, but I'm sure I can do it. I don't know why, I just feel it."

Doris regarded her for a long time.

"Hanna, you're nuts. But since you trusted us, I guess we have to trust you. I only hope I don't have to go back and explain to my parents why you're not with us."

"So do I." Hanna grinned. "But at least *I* won't have to explain it."

"You're doubly nuts. Make that triply. Okay, let's get going."

Hanna quickly attached the slings to each other with the carabiners. Then she braced her feet against one edge of the crack she'd seen and looped the end sling around her waist while each of her friends climbed down.

Finally, she closed her eyes and gritted her teeth as she dropped the slings. Now it was just her and the rock. And Doris was right, of course. She had no idea what she was doing. Yet her body felt like a taut string, already creeping toward the face.

Ignoring the pit of ice in her stomach, she lay face down and gingerly dangled her legs over the edge, holding onto the crack where her feet had been only moments before. Her feet found a tiny ledge about three inches wide, sloping slightly downward. She put her weight carefully on it and looked down. A horizontal crack, big enough to fit her toes into, was another three feet lower.

Without thinking, she placed her left hand around a half-inch thick knob of rock. There was nothing comparable for her right hand. But eventually her fingers found a tiny but firm flake she could pull on to balance her weight as she moved first her right foot down, and then her left. Though the foothold was miniscule, she was standing comfortably again. In front of her was a vertical crack in the rock into which she could put her fingers for balance.

The vertical crack became wider below that, and she examined it for a long time. If she put her hand into it and spread it, would it hold her?

She looked down and saw her six friends, watching in stunned and frightened silence.

Wincing slightly as she pushed her knuckles against the rough surface of the rock, Hanna put some of her weight onto the wedge she'd created from her own flesh and lowered her feet to the next small ledge. She put her hands on the sloping ledge above her head for balance. Breathing deeply, she looked around. Ten feet down, twenty more to go.

Her classmates stared back up, faces frozen. Could they catch her? She pushed the thought away.

The rock below her was impossibly blank. To the right was a corner, like a half open book, with a crack where the two faces joined. Most of it was wider than her hands. But at its top, level with where she stood, it was still hand-sized. The crack attracted her attention like a magnet. She imagined her feet pushing on one side and her hands pulling on the other. It was a crazy vision.

She looked back up. There was no going back.

Pulling on the vertical crack with her left hand as she'd done at the top, she inched her feet to the right until there was no more ledge. Then she stretched her right leg toward the corner, ignoring the stabs of pain in her back. As tall as she was, she still could not quite reach the corner.

Her legs were quivering. She couldn't stay where she was.

Without thinking she pushed off with her left foot and lunged, thrusting her hand toward the crack and jamming it in as tightly as she could. It hurt, but it would not come out until she was ready.

The rest of the climb took only seconds. The motions seemed eerily familiar. It felt like her body had a mind of its own. On touching the flat ledge, she looked around in a daze, and then collapsed. The girls pulled her back onto her feet and cheered wildly as they clustered into a giant hug.

"You realize you've done this before." Doris's manner contained equal parts of annoyance and admiration.

"Of course I haven't, why do you say that?"

"Like your sewing and skiing, silly goose. Anyone could see it. Well, anyone except you."

Hanna saw it quite well. She simply didn't want to admit it. These memories brought her closer to something both fearsome and fascinating. Even more than the others, the climb evoked an aching, painful yearning. Almost seductive.

And scary. "Let's go. I'm ready to get back on level ground."

Doris's parents were so relieved that they didn't get angry at first. But during a late dinner, listening to heavy rain and watching lightning strike the peaks, they swore they would never allow such an unchaperoned expedition again.

"Mama, stop it, enough already. We were fine, okay?" Doris scowled at her mother and turned to Hanna. "And you're one of my *Schildmaiden*, just as if you'd been there at the beginning, Seven girls—seven years old. What a coincidence."

Hanna's vision blurred. When it refocused, she saw a seven-year-old girl, with bangs and long pigtails tied with pink ribbons, looking shyly up at Doris, who said, "Of course you're a girl, Hanna. And now you're safe with us."

"Hanna, are you all right?" Doris looked worried.

Hanna blinked. "I'm fine. Absolutely fine."

WHEN HANNA ARRIVED home on Sunday evening, her mother listened quietly and without interruption.

"You did one day of rock climbing before the assault. But no lessons, like with skiing. You may be a natural climber, Hanna."

The poster was gone. Her friends had saved her from serious harm, and she'd paid them back. She'd been accepted into Doris's exclusive group of warrior girls. Yet she was frightened. Her life was like a haunted maze, where unseen hideous creatures threatened her without warning.

The bullying had made her angry, but she understood it. Kids with differences got picked on. It happened to others also. But Zwiebel's attack must have had a cause. Just like the one that had hurt her so much. Maybe there really *was* something bad about being a transsexual. Maybe Frauke Zwiebel was right, and she was an imposter.

And didn't the fact that her most devoted defender was a lesbian leave her even more exposed?

Sleep finally quieted this cacophony of conflicting thoughts. But her scars were aching when she woke up. Especially those two thin lines around her wrists. The doctor had said they looked as if they'd been made by ropes, but no one really knew. For a long time they'd been numb, but recently some feeling had returned.

She wanted to make them numb again. She *had* to make them numb. Then maybe her other pains would be numb, too.

That night she found the rope that Heidi and her mother sometimes used to hang clothing in their laundry room. She tied nooses in the ends of a piece about four feet long, and pulled them tight against her wrists. She put her foot against the rope and pushed until she winced with the pain. And then she pushed more.

When the sensation in her fingers was gone she tried to loosen the knots, but she couldn't.

She stifled a scream. A huge weight seemed to be pulling on her arms, forcing the rope deep into the flesh. She heard the voice of the man in the park, pulling out his belt. "Just give the sissy a good whippin'."

She lay on her bed immersed in pain, feeling utterly helpless. Why had she done this? The last thing she wanted in her life was more pain. Yet she'd attacked herself, as if there was something inside that she needed to destroy—or release.

Her shoulders ached. She stretched her toes toward a floor that wasn't there, finally realizing she was lying flat on her back. But when she stood up the pain was the same.

She was going to die. The monster would win after all.

She crawled into bed. She should at least be covered when she died.

But under the sheets, in the darkness, she felt a presence that was not the monster. It was gentle, feminine, touching her wrists. She thought she heard singing.

She jerked upright, suddenly remembering there were scissors in the medicine cabinet. But her wooden fingers fumbled and dropped them repeatedly. It took forever to cut the ropes.

She sat on the floor for a few minutes before throwing up. The nausea was from shame: shame for what she'd just done, for what she didn't know if she'd done, for what she was, for what she wasn't.

Back in bed, but free of her bonds, she breathed slowly and deeply for a long time. Clara had talked about people meditating this way to find inner peace. She really didn't know what peace would feel like. But she definitely knew its opposite.

CHAPTER 14

THE NEXT MORNING Hanna quickly dismissed the thought of wearing long sleeves to hide the angry red rings—the weather was far too warm. She smeared on some concealer. But her mother's face told her the attempt was as pathetic as she thought. She covered one with a cloth bracelet and the other with a wide ribbon. After school her mother told her to get in the car. Hermann would meet them at the office of a Stuttgart psychologist to whom Dr. Beattie had introduced them.

Hanna approached Dr. Angela Meissner's office with what felt like a vise in her gut. But the psychologist said nothing about the self-harm episode. After a respectful greeting and casual questions about schoolwork, she rested her arms on her desk and leaned forward. "Building self-esteem after what you've been through is a long path. In everything you've done already, what do you regard as your most important achievement?"

Hanna looked at her lap, taken aback by this unexpected twist. "Umm, maybe getting through school this year?"

"Think harder, Hanna."

"Well, the work that I did for Frau Bachmann on the play was sort of nice."

"Indeed it was, and more than 'sort of.' You earned your applause—and *you* were the leader for that project, not your friend Doris."

"That's silly—all I did for the others was encourage them."

"The beginning of true leadership. And your rock climbing?"

The thought redoubled her doubts. What was that supposed to mean? She'd only done what came to her naturally. "But it was Doris and her friends who saved me from those men. I felt helpless."

"And yet you faced them, with no one else around."

She thought of their taunts, and then of picking up the tire iron. Dr. Meissner was right. She still couldn't believe in herself. That's why she'd attacked herself, wasn't it—she was her own worst critic. Because she wasn't everything she wanted to be, she hadn't accepted who she was.

The emotional shield from her unknown past was a straitjacket, keeping her from finding the fearless freedom she'd glimpsed in those moments of self-confidence. It still held her in its tenacious grip.

She turned away, not wanting her therapist to see her tears—or her turmoil. Finally she turned back. "But do other people really think about me like those horrible men? And Frau Zwiebel—why is *she* on their side? That I don't get."

"People with deep insecurities often show the greatest intolerance. Frauke Zwiebel may be projecting her own self-loathing because she's threatened by a woman who feels empowered to fully accept and express herself. The Zwiebels took a very reckless gamble. Strangers don't normally think anything but 'Wow, she's tall' when they look at you."

Hanna sighed. "I'm just a girl trying to do my lessons and have fun with my friends. I don't threaten anyone."

"Hanna, those people are the ones with a problem, not you. They were cowards. You're a courageous young woman, and you should be proud of yourself."

Hanna blushed. Was she really a woman now? The day she'd left the hospital, her mother had said "the young woman I knew." But *she* didn't know that woman. Nor did she feel courageous. She was trying to make sense of a world that made no sense.

Meissner handed her a folder. "Here are some practical exercises to help you deal with negative feelings like the ones you had yesterday. And don't hesitate to call me anytime you feel the need."

On the way back to Waldenheim, she leafed through the handouts. They included a history of Germany's leading role prior to the Nazi era in allowing transsexuals to embrace their identity, and some recent progress. Behind that was a clipping from *Stern* in January, entitled, "*So habe ich überlebt.*"

Juliane Koepcke, a seventeen-year-old girl on her way with her mother to her parents' biological research station in eastern Peru on Christmas Eve, had awakened on the jungle floor, still strapped to the seat of the airplane in which she'd been flying next to her mother. She found no wreckage around her, no people, either alive or dead, nothing but her seat and a small bag of candy. Her glasses were gone.

With a broken collarbone and some deep cuts, wearing a minidress and one sandal, the candy her only food, she followed streams downhill, swimming past caimans and piranhas, stepping carefully around stingrays in the shallows. After ten days she came across a boat and used some of its gasoline to extract thirty maggots from one of her wounds. The next day the owners of the boat found her and took her to safety.

She described her feelings near the end. "*Hat es einen Sinn, weiterzumachen? Ja, sage ich mir unter Aufbietung aller Kräfte, du musst weiter. Weiter. Hier gehst du zugrunde.*"

Hanna put the clipping down and stared again at the trees. So many times she, too, had wondered if there was any point in going on. Would she ever find a safe place? Would the world ever let her be? But Juliane had confronted the hardships and pushed onward—*weiter*—because that was the way to life.

That is what she had to do also. Her family loved her. She had to finish school and become a certified hairdresser. With that job she would make her parents proud of her. And maybe she could even be proud of herself.

She wrote her own version of Koepcke's resolution and taped the paper over her desk. "Summoning all my strength, I'll keep going. I refuse to die." For the next six weeks she dove into studying and scarcely saw anyone.

At the end of the term Lothar Braunschweig called her into his office. "Fräulein Hoffmann, your therapist Dr. Meissner has provided me with some records which your mother felt could be helpful for me to know about. Please don't worry: I maintain the strictest confidentiality."

Her annoyance at her mother for not asking her permission was allayed somewhat by Braunschweig's gentle tone. She waited silently.

"During the last two months your work has been, in a word, outstanding. You should be preparing for the *Realschulabschluss* next year."

She was surprised at how quickly her shock turned to curiosity. Why did he think she could handle the higher level? Why didn't *she* think she could?

He seemed to read her mind. "You underestimate your abilities. That incident with Volker Zwiebel strengthened you. You're ready to begin your career."

My career. It always seemed so distant and unattainable, like a rainbow. Yet that's where she'd promised herself she was going, wasn't it? And the idea of more learning stirred an inchoate longing, though it, too, remained out of reach.

"But the *Realschule*—that's heavy academic work. I'm nowhere near smart enough."

"It's more a matter of whether you want it enough."

A YEAR AND a month later, that career was no longer at the end of a rainbow. Her workplace would be the upscale *Friseursalon Petra* on the Marienplatz. Petra Klinger had called her for an interview the week before the *Berufsschule* classes began, casually mentioning a phone call from Lothar Braunschweig, who'd recommended "a very promising student." Half an hour later she had the offer.

Choosing a seat near the back of the classroom, her hopeful anticipation mingled with the frolicsome energy of a gaggle of new students. This was her first experience of school with only other girls around her.

The instructor reviewed the syllabus and basic expectations for the term. Then she paused and let her gaze roam over the class. "As hairstylists, you want to help your customers look their best. Have you considered that you can also help them look and feel worse?"

Her somber tone sounded even more ominous in the dead silence that followed. "Your work will bring you into frequent and close contact with a plethora of pathogenic bacteria inhabiting human skin, which can cause disfiguring illness in your customers. State inspectors may close the salon for minor infractions. So mastery of the rules of hygiene will be our first requirement."

Hanna left the class feeling as dismal as the scenarios that were presented. This was nothing like the level of science she'd learned before. She was glad she'd be in the salon tomorrow.

But her ostensible boss was nowhere to be seen. Instead one of the stylists curtly instructed her to sweep the floor and disinfect all the used tools. Around noon she was handed a receipt and told to fetch some laundry for a customer. Petra Klinger came by midafternoon, said "Welcome to the salon," and continued to her office without another word.

Hanna went home wondering if she'd made a serious mistake. For eight hours she'd felt as if she were walking on eggshells, afraid of angering a stylist—or worse, a customer. Her appetite for dinner had vanished.

The students had been told to expect verbal questioning after a week of hygiene lectures. All Hanna could think of was the moment of ridicule three years ago when she couldn't do the elementary math problem at the blackboard. This was sure to be a repeat.

"What is Methicillin-resistant Staphylococcus aureus?"

She stood up in a rush of adrenaline. "A bacterial strain that cannot be killed by beta-lactam antibiotics, which are the most useful ones available. The first outbreak, in the United States, was six years ago. It isn't common, but the resistance is worrisome and reminds us to be even more vigilant about hygiene."

The instructor pursed her lips briefly. "Very good, Fräulein Hoffmann. You may sit down." She paused. "Did anyone else study the optional reading material?"

Getting no response, she looked directly at Hanna. "When we do the first exercises with mannequins, I want you to be prepared to demonstrate washing technique for the class."

Anxiety notwithstanding, she received a nod of approval afterward. A week later she was ordered to a washing station in the salon. "Here, come do the drying. Pay attention, now—this isn't a mannequin, you know."

She did what she'd done in class, and observed with a careful sidelong glance that the stylist looked slightly shocked. Soon she was called on regularly for washing and drying. The change in tone was dramatic. She'd been accepted into their circle.

Frau Klinger rarely spoke to her other than to give curt directives. So she was both surprised and terrified on being told near the start of the second term that she'd be the first in her class to cut a real customer's hair.

The girl wanted to change her chin-length bob to an A-line cut. Simple enough, but precision was essential. As she began, Hanna's only uncertainty was about how disaster would unfold. But when she finished, the smile on the girl's face told a different story.

She belonged here.

She was also ready to live on her own. Being together with her parents again in Frankfurt was lovely, but they were even further away than Waldenheim. With their offer of financial help, she searched for an apartment in Stuttgart. Near the end of April she found it: a third-floor flat close to the Leipziger Platz, ten minutes by bus from work. On days off she could easily enjoy the view from the Karlshöhe, or simply watch children in the Elisabethen Anlage playground.

And fantasize what it might be like to have children of her own.

She moved in twelve days before her birthday. Which one she wasn't sure. To belong with her classmates like a normal student she should be seventeen. But she also still felt closely connected to her ninth-grade friends from Waldenheim. She dismissed the date listed on her birth certificate: she certainly wasn't twenty-five. Dr. Meissner, who still had official responsibility for her mental health, suggested compromising on sixteen.

Two more weeks passed before her friends, still in Waldenheim, could all come for dinner. She fixed *Schwäbische Maultaschen*, following appetizers of cheese with freshly baked *Brötchen*. She borrowed extra dishes and a set of beer glasses from a neighbor. The tasteful table arrangement embodied thoughtfulness and delicacy. Like the feelings she longed to share—about children, about love, about who she really was.

Clara hugged the giant teddy bear that lolled on one end of the sofa. "Hanna, you know your place is even cuter than a button. But it's just what I expected of you. I'll bet that's the Nutcracker you got on your first trip to the *Weihnachtsmarkt* here."

Hanna tried not to show her emotions. Someday, she would be stronger. But for now they had to remain silent, like the snowflakes that swirled and drifted down on the little skier inside her glass globe, or the stunted, twisted-wire trees hanging tenaciously onto jagged cliffs in her miniature bonsai sculpture.

The three girls she'd invited to this special party had been her first friends in Germany. Two and a half years later, she still didn't trust anyone else to touch those feelings.

"You all knew my goal was to have a stuffed animal nearby no matter where I was in the apartment. Whenever I had a dream without monsters, there was usually one in it."

Doris fingered the tiny people in Hanna's dollhouse. "You sewed these doll clothes, didn't you?"

"I know, some of the seams are crooked."

"Hanna, you can be so annoying." Doris scowled at her. "I remember you telling us about your therapist's dolls, and how much they frightened you."

"There's something about dolls that I don't understand. That was awful. But I still love them. The one my parents gave me—remember the birthday cake?—I feel like a little girl when I hold her. So silly, I know."

Annika's grin showed only in her eyes. "We won't tell anyone."

There was much to catch up on. Hanna wasn't the only one no longer in the same class: Clara had been promoted to Gymnasium. The plates emptied quickly as they chattered. Back on the sofa, Clara poured more coffee. "Annika, I see you with your new boyfriend pretty often."

"He's a maybe. He's hot, but . . ." As if on cue, Doris's posture had closed in like a flower folding up for the night.

Hanna had been nominated by the others to speak up when the time came. "Doris, please don't worry. When you're ready to introduce a girlfriend to us, we're all anxious to meet her."

Annika's poker face didn't change. "It's okay if you curse at us. You can even do it in Swedish."

"So you know," Doris said finally. "I mean, is it really so obvious?"

"It's obvious that you're not giving us credit for being your friends." Hanna felt like she was walking on paper-thin ice. Whatever she said would probably be irritating. She ached for her friend.

Doris seemed not to have heard. "Do you know how my mom is driving me absolutely insane?"

"We don't actually have a spy bug in your room."

Annika matched her tone. "Only the insanity part we knew."

Doris sighed and looked at Hanna. "Did I ever tell you how the *Schildmaiden* started? We were in second grade—we'd just heard about the Holocaust."

Annika and Clara looked wistful as Doris continued. "I thought about some other friends who were vulnerable in some way. Amelie and her stuttering. Lena's non-family—her mother claims not to even know who her father is. And Frieda has an uncle who molested her. I knew she needed a friend, and finally she told us."

"All of which is precisely why *you* should confide in *us* now."

"Yeah, I know. It's hard, Hanna. It's scary."

"I happen to know a bit about that."

Doris smiled sourly. "I guess I've been bested." Then her smile faded. "It's hell. There isn't a peaceful moment with her. She bugs me all the time, and there's no way I can tell her anything."

"I can introduce you to a great therapist. I'm sure she could help somehow. I also think you should get the *Jugendamt* involved. Maybe they can calm your mother down. And if you need to force the issue with her, you could just move in with me for a few days."

"You're serious? You'd do that?"

Hanna had never seen Doris show any mood but unflappable self-control. She felt humbled. That she could really help was so unexpected. "You're my friend. Why wouldn't I?"

A few tears rolled down Doris's cheeks—another first. "Thanks. Hanna, you've grown up. Look at you. Turning the tables like this."

"We get by with a little help from our friends."

Doris reached for a deck of cards on the small shelf mantel. "All right, who wants to play *Böse Dame?*"

Hanna was relieved that the conversation about romance had been cut short. Sex was for normal girls. Doctor Biber had assured her that no one would know the difference between her vagina and any other. But there were so many worrisome unknowns. Whether being that close to a man was safe was just one of them.

Sleep drifted in quickly, mingled with the sensuous aroma of Annika's Eternity Peach perfume. So lovely—she'd have to get some right away. *After a long hike the girl's path was blocked by a steep cliff. Undaunted, she began to climb, trusting her weight to flakes she could barely see. A wiry man with curly black hair and a kind grin murmured encouragement as she inched her way up toward his outstretched arms.*

The telephone intruded just as her hands touched the rim, and for a few more sleepy moments she tried to hold onto her triumph. Her mother greeted her. "Hanna, your attacker in America has been arrested. The trial is scheduled for the fifth of August. You have to testify."

She put the receiver back slowly, silently. Three years of steady struggle had brought her serenity. Confrontation with the assault could destroy it all—what if it sparked an episode like the one in the hospital? On the other hand, if it brought her English back, maybe she wouldn't feel so much like an oddball.

Both prospects were unsettling.

CHAPTER 15

Thursday, 1 August 1974

Hanna arrived in Boulder with her mother four days before the trial. Hermann would come when he got vacation ten days later.

Despite the distance to the Denver courthouse, Gisela had insisted they stay in Boulder, not far from their old house. While Hanna went shopping and hiking with Kirstie, she checked in with Chief Deputy District Attorney Karen Dickenson. Afterward they sipped ice tea in the dry Colorado heat under a patio umbrella.

Gisela seemed satisfied. "The DA's going to prosecute the case herself. She expects the defense attorney to exploit anti-transsexual prejudice to the hilt, and she wants the jury to see you as a real human being. We talked to Doctor Beattie—she feels it'll be safe."

To Hanna that didn't sound very encouraging, and two and a half days of pointless-sounding questions during jury selection was no help. The glass shield that kept her translator's voice from disturbing the court distorted the incomprehensible babble even further. Her mother, sitting next to her at the table in a rear corner of the main hearing room, held her hand as she fidgeted. Dickenson looked cool and confident with her trim padded shoulder jacket and pixie bob. But the defense attorney towered over her.

Finally the jury was seated, and after lunch Dickenson gave her opening statement. "May it please the court, counsel, ladies and gentlemen of the jury: We are here for a very simple reason. The defendant—the man sitting over there—felt that satisfying his sexual appetite and preserving his ego unbruised took precedence over the life of a woman, and her right to live without pain.

"A little more than three years ago, on May twenty-sixth of 1971, the defendant, William Staunton, put a sedating drug into Hanna Hoffmann's beer as she sat at the bar of the Alpine Inn. He then grabbed her as she stumbled into the street, carried her to the Paradise Hotel next door, and asked the owner, Victor Vronsky, to leave her in room 18. Then when he discovered that her anatomy was not what he expected, he decided to kill her, as brutally and painfully as he could. He took her to the empty storage room next to the kitchen on the ground floor of the hotel, raped her, and beat her on the back until there was no skin left. Then he wrapped her in the sheets from the hotel bed and dumped her in the trash behind the Alpine Inn, leaving her for dead.

"But though she lost two liters of blood, she did not die. She did lose all memory of her past life, and is not able to identify him. No eyewitnesses have been found. Nevertheless, after we present the evidence, we are confident that you will find it unimpeachable."

Twenty minutes later Fred Miller rose from his seat next to the defendant. His alternating cadence contrasted dramatically to Dickenson's crisp delivery. Hanna cringed as he slouched his large frame over the defense's desk. The physical challenge to the prosecutor was unmistakable.

"Ladies and gentlemen, you will hear many claims from the counsel for the state in this trial. I urge you to listen to them carefully. If you do, you will find that there is not a single shred of direct evidence for the guilt of my client.

"You will hear about fingerprints on a dress, on bedsheets, on a doorknob. You won't hear anything about when those fingerprints were put there, or under what circumstances. You'll hear about blood spots in the hotel. But nothing about how they connect my client to the injury that was done to the victim. That is because he did not do it.

"You will hear about a sedating drug. You will hear no evidence that my client possessed this drug, or gave it to the victim. There will be no weapons or instruments identified. And no motive—only imaginary prejudice.

"The prosecution will tell you how circumstantial evidence fits together to form an uncontestable whole, like the pieces of a puzzle. Ladies and gentlemen, this puzzle has more holes than actual pieces."

And with that he sat down.

THE STATE'S CASE was complete by Thursday noon except for Hanna's testimony. Miller asked few questions. He zeroed in on the identification of chloral hydrate metabolites in Hanna's blood, and forced the analyst to admit that the values were only marginally significant. He also highlighted the absence of direct evidence that either Staunton or Hanna had been in the storage room—not a single blood spot or fingerprint had been found.

Hanna stared straight ahead as she passed Staunton on her way to the witness stand. Once seated, she dared look. His face showed all the emotion of a stone.

The prosecutor began in a compassionate tone, which the translator did her best to reproduce in German. "Hanna, we appreciate your courage in taking the stand. Let me first ask: Do you remember being attacked and beaten by anyone?"

"No."

"What is the earliest memory of life that you have?"

"I was in a hospital with my mother. I was about five or six."

"You don't remember ever being a teenager or adult?"

"No. I just remembered being in kindergarten. That wasn't real, but I didn't know it then. I only understood later that my body was older. I felt like I was the same age as the girls in the children's books my mother gave me."

Dickenson continued through a series of questions about Hanna's perceived age, the operations she'd endured, and the pain that she still felt nearly every day. She answered earnestly, in her most grown-up voice. Her mother looked pleased.

"Just one more question, Hanna. Even though you don't have memories of the event that hurt you, do you have dreams about it, or nightmares?"

"I definitely have nightmares. Often. Lots of times it's really scary and I wake up, and have a hard time going back to sleep. Sometimes there are scenes that I remember. Like with monsters and things. When I've had a good day at work, or had a lot of fun with my friends, then I may not have a nightmare. But if the day's been hard, then I'm likely to."

"Thank you again, Hanna, for answering these questions. I know these are not pleasant memories for you. I have no more questions. The lawyer for the defendant may wish to question you now."

Miller began his cross-examination in a quiet, even gentle, voice. "Miss Hoffmann, when you were a man—"

"Objection, Your Honor. The witness has already stated that her earliest memories are of being a girl."

"Sustained. Counsel, you must restrict your questions to those which have not been asked and answered."

"Miss Hoffmann, you did testify earlier that you had an operation to, and I quote: 'fix the defect in my genitals.' What was that defect?"

"I had a penis."

"And why do you say that you were a girl, if you had a penis?"

The judge's gavel came down vigorously as titters rippled through the audience. A flash of anger burned Hanna's cheeks, but she tried to stay calm. "Because I *was* a girl."

"Do you know what a girl is, Miss Hoffmann?"

"Objection—the defense counsel is badgering the witness."

"Sustained."

Hanna felt beads of sweat on her face. She felt like prey to a heartless hunter.

"Your surgeon, Doctor Lamola, testified that you had marks on your wrists which were suggestive of ropes cutting into the flesh." Miller paused for several seconds. "Now, whatever it is that a transsexual does for fun, does it involve having someone tie them up?"

Hanna couldn't decide afterward if it was the implicit insult or the unwitting evocation of her self-injury attempt. But the scene erupted in her mind before Dickenson could open her mouth, and she couldn't stay silent. If she did, wouldn't that be letting Miller smear her character, just what she was there to prevent?

"It wasn't for fun. He was angry. He tore my dress before he took my nylons off and tied me up while I was lying on the bed."

A collective gasp arose in the courtroom. Miller snapped to attention. "Who is 'he'?"

"The man over there." She pointed to Staunton.

Dickenson moved quickly to the bench. "Your Honor, may we have a short break?"

Several minutes later the attorneys and judge returned. Dickenson said something to Gisela about a gay panic defense. When Hanna looked puzzled, her mother just squeezed her hand. "Don't worry, honey, you'll be all right."

She didn't feel all right, as Miller loomed over her again. "Miss Hoffmann, how sure are you that Mr. Staunton is the man who tied you up?"

"He was right on top of me, before he turned me over."

"Did he say anything?"

Did he say anything? The vision was as pitilessly vivid as the lawyer himself. Though the English that came with it was garbled gibberish, she somehow knew exactly what he'd said, and repeated it in German. "That I was a perverted fucking bastard who'd tricked him, and he was going to teach me a lesson."

"I have no further questions."

Hanna felt alone and afraid. She wished she hadn't said anything. She wished she weren't there at all.

No one was stirring when Dickenson approached her. "Miss Hoffmann, normally a witness is questioned only once by each lawyer. But today, we will have something called 'redirect.' The defense attorney wishes the jury to believe your attacker's crime was justified. So I will now continue my questions. I want you to tell the court everything you can remember about your experience."

Hanna fidgeted and looked down.

"That man"—she looked up and pointed at Staunton again—"reached up my dress and touched my genitals. Then he tore the dress and tied me up, like I said. I couldn't move—I was too scared.

"He used the phone and said he was in room 18 and needed help. A few minutes later someone came in. I was on my stomach then. Also my hair was messed up and in my eyes. But he sounded just like the man who testified earlier."

Dickenson interrupted. "Let the record show that Miss Hoffman is pointing to Mr. Vronsky, the owner of the Paradise Hotel. Please continue, Hanna."

"They put a pole under the knot where they'd tied my hands and feet together, and lifted me up and started walking. All I could see was the floor and a bit of the walls near the floor. I was afraid to scream—I didn't know what they might do.

"Finally they got to some stairs. I could see metal steps with open spaces in them. It was a long way. I tried to count the steps, but I lost track. I was so scared and hurting. I felt like my arms might come out of my shoulders.

"At the bottom they put something under my hands and feet that felt like a chain, and left me hanging from it instead of the pole. It hurt even more. The second man said, 'Have fun,' and left."

Hanna locked eyes with her mother. "For awhile it was quiet except for the sound of heavy breathing. Then he grabbed me and I felt a horrible pain in my anus. I screamed at the top of my lungs. He laughed."

The courtroom floor was undulating slightly—*it has to be just a mirage*—and filmy spectral fragments bubbled up and swirled over the murky water-like surface as they turned into remembered scenes. But there were more that lurked underneath, stretching away from the basement into a past where vaguely familiar people threatened violence worse than what she'd just recalled. She clenched her chair and tried to focus.

"I felt like I'd been torn apart. It went on for a long time. Finally he stopped. I was sobbing. My skin felt wet where it hurt. Then it happened again."

Glancing at Staunton, she shivered.

"He said, 'Now there's a taste of your own medicine.' I said I didn't understand what he meant. He laughed and said, 'Of course you do, scumbag. That was as natural as you are.'"

She stopped. Finally Dickenson approached the stand. "Hanna, I know this must be unspeakably painful for you. But I must ask you to continue. Take your time, take deep breaths, pause when you need to. I can get you a glass of water if you wish. But your testimony is vital."

Hanna took several swallows of water. "He put a sawhorse underneath me, and cut part of the pantyhose so my legs were free. Then he let me down so I was sitting with my crotch on the rail. He pulled the laces from his shoes and tied my ankles to the legs of the sawhorse near the floor."

Her voice broke. The heaving of the courtroom had worsened, and she felt nauseous. Staunton resembled a grotesque gargoyle. Could he hurt her even now? *No, the lawyer will protect me.* Her vision cleared, and she looked up at the judge.

"I'm sorry, I really don't know how to describe it very well. All of my weight was pressing on the flesh in between my . . . umm, groin I think it's called, and this little rail. And it pressed and pressed, there's not an instant of relief. There was nothing I could do—it just got worse and worse. It was—it was . . ."

She turned back toward Dickenson. "He asked me how it felt. I begged him to let me go. But he said, 'I want you to feel it right there. That'll teach you not to trick men.' Then he went up the stairs and I heard the door close."

The courtroom was pin-drop still.

Where was she? She was alone and helpless. She didn't want to remember any more. She wanted to pull up the covers and cuddle with her teddy bear. She wanted to burrow into her mother's lap and find safety.

Or just die.

Then she heard the prosecutor's voice, soft and reassuring. The translator matched both the tone and volume. "Hanna, you've come this far. You survived all of it; you're alive today, and you're telling your story so it doesn't get lost. You have a few more steps to go. Only a few more to the end. Don't give up now."

Hanna twisted her fingers around each other as if trying to tie them in knots, and smoothed her skirt several times. She felt a hand on her shoulder. A soft, feminine voice was whispering something.

"Weiter, weiter."

She turned, but no one was there.

The sense returned that she was fighting more than one man's sadistic fit, that others had come before him, and she'd never be whole if she didn't stay with it. She straightened her back and imagined shooting Doris's darts at the shell hiding Staunton's face.

"I just wanted to die. Anything to end the pain. I felt like I would really go insane. Maybe I already had. Finally, he was there again, and I asked if he could just kill me, quickly. But he didn't say anything. He cut the pantyhose. Then he untied my legs and tied the laces around my wrists and pulled my arms toward the ceiling, in a sort of V, and took away the sawhorse.

"My chest and arms seemed like they would break, but my wrists were the worst. He stood right in front of me—I can still remember how he sounded— *Now this is where you get what you really deserve*, and took his belt off and started hitting me on the back."

Only then did she tremble all over and stammered out, "I don't know how many times he hit me before the pain just went beyond what I could stand, and I thought that I was dying and would be at peace and . . ." She barely heard the judge's voice interrupting the translator before everything went black.

HANNA AWAKENED SURROUNDED by paramedics, who helped her to Gisela's car where she curled up in the rear seat. The next thing she knew there was sunlight outside her room. Dr. Beattie asked a lot of questions, and then told her she'd been very brave and ought to spend the day relaxing—she didn't need to hear the defense testimony. Her father arrived the next morning, tired and anxious to see her. After extensive reassurances regarding Hanna's health, he led his family on a hike in the familiar hills, holding her hand tightly the whole way.

On Monday morning Hermann squeezed into the little booth next to Gisela, ready for Dickenson's closing statement.

"Ladies and gentlemen, this trial has been a difficult experience for all of us, and especially, I am sure, for you. What you heard Miss Hoffmann describe seems straight out of the Spanish Inquisition, or perhaps a Gestapo interrogation.

"At the opening I said this case is very simply about a man who felt that satisfying his sexual appetite and preserving his ego unbruised took precedence over the life of a woman, and her right to live without pain. Now let's review the facts that we have established in the last two days.

"We heard the testimony of Mr. Otto Wolf, proprietor of the Alpine Inn, that the defendant harassed the victim with unwanted sexual advances while she attempted to eat dinner at his bar, and followed her when she left. Shortly afterward Mr. Vronsky brought her to the registration desk of the Paradise Hotel, mumbling that she was drunk and needed a room to sleep it off. He signed in as a guest in room 18, using an assumed name."

Dickenson set up an easel with a layout drawing, and pointed out the locations of rooms in the hotel as she traced the route from entrance to room 18 to the empty storage room. She went over the details of the lab analysis of Hanna's blood, the origin of the sheets, and Staunton's fingerprints on the dress, sheets, and doorknob of the bedroom. She dwelt for some time on the potential of the kitchen to enable cleanup of the blood so that no trace was left at the alleged site of the crime. Hanna felt profusely grateful to this self-assured, imperturbable defender of her honor. After all the horror, justice was coming.

"Miss Hoffmann testified, after unexpectedly regaining some memory, that she was carried down metal stairs to the location of her torture. There are no stairs between room 18 and the storage room, and indeed no such stairs anywhere in the hotel. But imagine for yourself, ladies and gentlemen, how you might feel if you were being carried, naked, suspended by your hands and feet bound behind your back, by a man who has threatened to kill you. Would you remember every detail precisely?"

Hanna gasped slightly. Under so much stress, she hadn't appreciated the dilemma she'd introduced. Now who would the jury believe? Was she even right? The whole experience on the witness stand had been so surreal.

Dickenson finished five minutes later. "Facing likely death, it is understandable that Miss Hoffmann should have a confused recollection of the building. But her description of her injuries is exactly what the surgeon reported.

"The defendant's desire for sex with an attractive woman was thwarted and he was angry, like a spoiled child who finds that the candy inside the wrapper isn't what he expected. Except this was a human life. One that will always live with disfigurement and pain, because of the actions of the defendant—who didn't regard her as human.

"While a guilty verdict cannot restore her body, it is what you can give her. And it is what justice requires."

After a break Miller began. His voice was soft, his cadence measured. "Ladies and gentlemen of the jury, you have an awe-inspiring responsibility. If you return a guilty verdict, Mr. Staunton will likely go to prison for the rest of his life. If he were not guilty of these accusations, an innocent life would be ruined. What you determine is what will happen. That is the power of the jury, and its role in our great system of justice.

"My job, at this point, is not to argue the case, but simply to review and try to remember what we have learned during this trial. We have learned that fingerprints were left in certain places, blood spots in others. There were signatures and sedatives.

"What we have *not* learned is how these observations are connected to the crime. Counsel for the state has assured you that circumstantial evidence is solid because it doesn't change; it cannot be influenced by changeable opinions. But its interpretation is subjective. And there are many interpretations to these observations."

He led the jury through each key point of the state's case before coming back to the beginning, in the café.

"Mr. Wolf says the victim reported being harassed. But the victim can't remember it. And Mr. Roy Moore, who had a clear view from Mr. Staunton's table in the café, testified that there was no harassment. So we don't know."

Miller's voice began to rise and fall in wide swings. "Perhaps Mr. Staunton, seeing someone he thought was a woman leave the café in distress, went to help. Perhaps the person fainted then. Perhaps Staunton arranged for this person to have a hotel room, and then went to check up on her. Of course, if he had, he would not have found a woman."

Dickenson rose quickly. "Objection, Your Honor. Miss Hoffmann's name and female sex were on her driver's license."

"Your Honor, his birth certificate identified him as 'male' at that time."

"Sustained. The defendant had no access to either document—only to the victim's appearance. Mr. Miller, you must stick with the testimony given."

Miller turned to the jury. "Yet another way for Mr. Staunton's prints to be on the sheets would be if he had turned the bedcovers down for this person he thought was a woman, trying to be helpful. The victim testified to being threatened in the hotel room. But that same testimony speaks of stairs that don't exist—and a sawhorse that mysteriously evaporated. You will have to decide if you believe anything whatever of that story."

He pushed the easel roughly to the side of the courtroom, nearly knocking it over. Even sitting behind her plexiglas shield, Hanna felt like he'd punched her and cast her aside.

"We have heard direct testimony from Mr. Moore that Mr. Staunton was kind and generous to the transvestites who hung around the club he runs. Men masquerading as women, just like the victim—"

"Objection, Your Honor."

"Sustained."

"I want to read a short excerpt of the transcript from Mr. Moore's testimony. 'As an investor in Staunton's Mile-High Swingers Club, I visited from time to time. It was a very high-class place, with well-dressed men meeting well-dressed women for drinks and dancing. But there were a couple of trannies who hung around, working the streets—that's about all those people ever did, since no one else wanted them. Staunton often let them use the club restrooms, and even stay in the lobby when it was cold outside.'"

Miller looked directly at the jury foreman. "This does not sound to me like the behavior of a man who is prejudiced against transsexuals, let alone hates them."

He put the transcript back on his desk. "Ladies and gentlemen, the trial record is consistent with the complete innocence of Mr. Staunton. However, I remind you that proof of innocence is not required by the law. Proof of the defendant's *guilt* is required beyond a reasonable doubt. Absent such proof, you must return a verdict of not guilty."

Jury deliberations continued through the rest of the week, and notes asking for instructions came out twice.

At ten a.m. on Friday Judge Gilford gaveled the court into session. The jury was ready to give its conclusion.

CHAPTER 16

JUDGE GILFORD ASKED the jury foreman to stand. "Has the jury reached a unanimous verdict?"

"No, Your honor. And the votes have been unchanged for two days. We don't see any possibility of coming to a unanimous agreement."

"Thank you all for your service. You may go home now. Ms. Dickenson, under these circumstances I have no option but to declare a mistrial." He turned to Staunton. "You will be remanded to the county jail to finish your current sentence for distribution of pornography. You will be eligible for parole in six months. Court is adjourned."

Hanna stood up unsteadily, so lightheaded she was afraid of collapsing. Cuddling with her parents on the sofa of their rented apartment, walking the trails where the spirit of her sister spoke to her, listening to the sibilant patter of the English-speakers, her hopes for the trial had grown into a crescendo. She would regain the language that had been taken from her, her lost memories, her peace of mind. Maybe they would even move back here.

She'd revisited hell to tell the jury her story. How could they not hear her?

But in fact none of it would ever come back. Nor would she ever be free of her nightmares and nebulous fears. Like the scars on her back, they would be there forever. She pictured the familiar streets and shops in Germany, where her friends were stronger than her foes. Colorado was an evil wasteland.

She didn't scream or cry. Her mind was numb. She turned to her mother and spoke in a voice that seemed distant, muffled. She wondered if it was even hers. "Can we go back home now? Is there a flight still today?"

And then the tears came.

Her mother held her as she always had. "Hanna, dear, let's go to Estes Park for the afternoon. It will help."

Hanna wiped her face. "All right."

But she wasn't looking forward to it. Mountains couldn't heal her hurt. She stolidly ignored the scenery as they drove.

Dickenson had decided to take the afternoon off and join them. Kirstie and Beattie came with her, and they all gathered in a café just off the main highway. Hanna's gloom had lifted a little, matching the light filtered by the clearing thunderclouds. "I wonder why I love these mountains so much. After all, I've only barely seen them once."

Gisela and Hermann smiled.

As they placed their orders, a small herd of elk wandered down the street directly in front of the café.

The waiter chuckled. "This has been happening every day since last week, when some guy who didn't know the area very well left a pickup load of apples open in front of the grocery store at the end of this street. The elk sniffed out the apples, found their way from their usual crossing down the street to the pickup, and did some serious damage."

He waved toward the street. "It's odd, though. They always follow exactly the same route now instead of just cutting directly across from the forest. I guess there are cues that remind them how they got to those apples."

Hanna grinned as Kirstie translated, but her friend and advocate looked deadly serious, eyes locked on the last few elk, as if trying to spear one with her gaze.

"Hanna, I don't doubt you—there has to be a basement. But after your testimony Captain Alda had the hotel closed and searched for a whole day, and he's out of ideas. So here's mine. The elk remember how to find the apples by following subtle sensory cues in exactly the same sequence. So if you were in exactly the same position as that night, maybe memories would come back to tell you exactly where the turns on your route were."

Hanna winced. She was trying to leave that house of horrors behind. How could Kirstie do this to her? "You can't be serious. I'd be tied up and naked like I was before?"

"Yes, but only with your friends—the hotel's still closed. The four women right here could do it. And of course we'd have a stretcher, so you wouldn't feel any pain."

She stared across the street, her body rigid. She didn't want to. But Kirstie had already turned to Beattie. "Is this out of line, Dr. Beattie? I know it's a long shot, but—we can't just let this guy get away with it. I believe Hanna."

Beattie turned away from the disappearing elk. "I think it has to be up to Hanna and her mother. We know how easily symbols can trigger devastating memories. None of us predicted what happened at the trial. On the other hand, she survived that in excellent condition as far as I can tell. She's a very different girl from the one who had such difficulties in the hospital."

Gisela turned to Hanna. "Yes, after every battle you get a little stronger." She placed her hand on Hanna's shoulder. "But it's your decision. And we'll support and love you whatever you decide."

Hanna shook her head slowly, eyes averted. But she'd seen the love in her mother's face, and the pride in the psychologist's. Juliane would've done it. Surely Elisabeth would've done it.

Seized with enthusiasm, she leapt up. "Okay, I'll do it—let's go." Then she sat back down, cheeks burning with embarrassment. "Well—I guess we should eat first, shouldn't we?"

Dickenson had observed this untranslated exchange in German with bemused detachment. But when Kirstie gave her a summary, she immediately left the table and headed for the pay phone. She returned visibly energized. "Captain Alda will be there at four o'clock with a stretcher and pole. It's a completely crazy idea. But we're ready to try it."

APPREHENSION BUILT INTO sweaty agitation as Hanna was tied up with nylons that Gisela had brought—they might even be hers. As the pole touched her hands and feet, a wave of nausea engulfed her. She took that as a good omen.

Alda had cut holes in the fabric so she would see the floor in the same way as before. Dickenson and Kirstie carried the stretcher slowly along the corridor while Gisela and Beattie held the pole.

The gray-brown mottled carpet, bordered with tan cable molding at the periphery of her vision, was familiar and undistinguished. A gap in the molding, presumably a hallway, didn't change her feeling. But the next one was subtly disturbing. "Turn left here."

She felt nothing unusual as they passed two doors. Then something changed. As if an invisible toxic fog was oozing down the hall—she was astonished as well as frightened. "Turn right."

"Are you sure?" Dickenson asked. "To the right is the door to a service closet."

She was sure. But why? She didn't believe in psychics. Yet the menace was palpable. The carpet was somehow different. Every thread stood out like a living, writhing worm, threatening to swarm over her.

"As sure as before. I know I must sound crazy, but it feels evil."

Dickenson opened the door with the master key Alda had provided. Inside was a spacious closet with largely bare shelves on one wall and tools on the other, leaving four feet of clear aisle way.

"The stairs are here," Hanna said matter-of-factly as they brought her in. "Can you take me away now?" She started to struggle. "I can't stand this anymore."

In an adjacent room Kirstie quickly freed her while Gisela retrieved her clothes. She rubbed her wrists and stretched, slowly and deliberately, breathing deeply. Her voluntary bondage had felt all too real. The women returned to the closet where Alda and Sgt. Manuel Barrios were doing their detective duties. Hanna watched from the entrance.

Alda was staring at the back wall. "Nothing odd here. Of course we searched this room before. Hanna, you're sure you were carried through a door."

"Whatever it was, the pole was horizontal and then they tilted it down for the stairs. But I really couldn't see anything around me." She shivered a little.

Barrios stood up. "I can't see a thing that's different from the other service closet. Maybe we need a magnifying glass, like Sherlock Holmes." He ran his finger slowly over the wood-paneled walls, frustration evident in his face.

His companion stepped into the hallway. "Let's check the adjacent rooms again. Maybe she's off by one door." While the two men spent the next ten minutes inspecting both rooms, Hanna's anxiety mixed with growing embarrassment.

Alda shook his head as the pair returned. "Looks like it was a dead end. Happens often enough, unfortunately." He turned to pick up the stretcher.

Hanna felt a wave of panic. This hadn't been her idea, but now she couldn't give up. She looked beseechingly at Barrios. "Isn't there *anything* you can do?"

"I wish." He returned to the rear of the closet and idly put his finger on one of the shallow rabbets. Then he jerked it away as if it had been burned. "Boss— look, this is tongue and groove paneling, but there's a joint there."

Alda used his pocketknife to enlarge the hairline crack. "Could've used that magnifying glass for real." Soon a shiny metal sheet emerged, revealing a barely visible gap perfectly aligned with the crack in the paneling. Then he put the knife blade into the rabbet about three feet to the right. "Over here, too. So, a door that opens by sliding perpendicularly to the wall? Looks like it's time for some demolition work."

He called the dispatcher with a message for his assistant. Five minutes later the radio crackled back to life and informed him that All-American Rentals would deliver an acetylene cutting torch in twenty minutes, along with a prybar and tape measure.

"Good work. And thank Nancy for me also, will you?"

Gisela went to get some soda and chips from the café. Occasionally someone sat down, but mostly they paced around the lobby impatiently.

As soon as the truck arrived they used the prybar to rip away the paneling, which was glued to the metal. After ten minutes Barrios had cut a slot about twelve inches long. "This'll be slow going. It appears to be hardened steel, a quarter of an inch thick."

Hanna felt a chill. "Mama, I'm sorry, I really am . . . can I go to the café? This is just too creepy."

Gisela took her hand and left, followed by Beattie.

In the café, Hanna still felt cold. "I know it's so important. But I'm afraid of having to feel all that again, like I did in the trial."

Gisela shifted in her chair. "You can sit on my lap if that will make you feel safer."

"*Mama!* Just because I'm afraid doesn't mean I'm a baby."

"You don't remember doing that in the hospital?"

She made a face that she hoped conveyed her annoyance. But then she scrunched her frame down enough to put her head on her mother's breast.

She wasn't only afraid. She was ashamed of being afraid. She ought to be stronger than this specter.

Then she stood up, as if at attention. "Okay, I'm ready to act grown-up. Let's go back."

The slits were two feet long vertically and three horizontally, and coming close to meeting. Alda looked up. "I stuck the tape measure through the slot—nothing stopped it on the other side. There's definitely a room there. One hell of a lot of work went into hiding it."

Finally the two cuts met. They pried the loose plate toward them, where it landed with a dull thud.

Barrios shone his flashlight downward. "Oh my God." His voice seemed truly reverent. "Perforated metal steps. Looks like knotted nylons at the bottom. And the blood—Jesus, I guess I never saw two liters of it before." He quickly descended, followed closely by Alda, and flicked the light switch.

Hanna put her shoulders through the hole. "I'm not coming down. I only want to see a little bit."

What she wanted was to run away as fast as she possibly could. But she was powerless to stop. Stepping on the tread as though it were an eggshell, she looked over her shoulder. "That's it. No more."

Yet she continued her descent, moving with the same infinite caution. Once on the floor, she stretched a hand toward the shoelaces, as if saluting them. She rubbed her wrists, crouching to get closer to the congealed dark splatter, undisturbed since it had trickled to the floor three years ago.

Nearly taking her life with it.

Shaking, she started toward the sawhorse that was off to one side, the metal-studded belt underneath. Barrios gently blocked her motion.

She saw alarm in his face. He moved closer and she put an arm around his shoulder.

"*Gracias, Senõr.*"

And then panic seized her entire being. "*Ayúdame a salir de aqui. Rápido, por favor. Lo siento.*"

With neither surprise nor apparent exertion, he slung her over his shoulder, carried her up the steps, and passed her through the hole. As she curled into a fetal ball on the floor she heard herself, as if she were outside her body, wailing like a baby. Then all went dark once again.

GROGGILY SHE PULLED herself upright. "Where . . . where am I?" But even as she said this, she realized she was in a car. Her parents' car. Kirstie was next to her.

Through the window she saw the jagged ravines and twisted trees of the foothills. "Are we going to Estes Park? What happened? The last I remember I was in that building, that . . . hellhole. How did I get in the car?"

Kirstie laughed. "We carried you. It was like you were in a coma again. But the medics said your vital signs were fine, and Doctor Beattie said you'd probably wake up today. Which is just what you've done."

"My god, you always seem to be there when I need rescuing. It's so embarrassing. Whatever will I do when you're not there?"

"I hardly did anything. But I do have a little surprise for you." Her mischievous smile communicated no more.

"We're going to camp for three days," her mother said.

They devoted one day to a hike near Longs Peak with a picnic in the grass beside the Wind River. A light breeze gently rustled the cottonwood leaves as the waves rippled relentlessly past. Water striders scampered across the stranded pools of placid backwater on the shore while Hanna scampered over the rocks alongside Kirstie with childlike abandon, bathed in her parents' radiant bliss.

After Hermann had delighted Hanna with Currywurst for dinner, the four settled in a line on a log and savored the aroma of coffee and hot chocolate mingled with campfire smoke. Hanna sat between her parents with an arm around each of them.

"Mama, I wish . . . I'm so happy Kirstie is here with us. We had so much fun today."

She caught herself just in time before saying Elisabeth's name. Her sister's spirit hovered over them, protecting like a guardian angel. Through her untimely death, she'd given birth to this extended family.

Gisela put an arm around her. "Hanna, we're all glad that Kirstie is with us."

Kirstie said nothing. But the flickering firelight illuminated a tear trickling down her cheek. "You're both the most wonderful friends," she finally managed to say. "I'm very lucky to know you."

"But how can it be," Hanna continued, "that of all the places where that vile man might've attacked me, it was right next to your house? And that you and my mother would get to know each other so well?"

Kirstie stood and walked slowly into the darkness behind the log, returning after what seemed forever.

Gisela broke the awkward silence. "Hanna, I think these are things we have to accept."

Kirstie fairly glowed. "And about that surprise I mentioned. Your mom told me about your rock climbing escapade in the Alps. I guess you're serious about the sport."

"Are you kidding? I was so scared . . ."

"You know, when you were climbing here before the assault, you were actually flirting with one of the guys." Hanna felt her face flush as red as the coals. "They told you about a woman named Diana Bowman, who they said was one of the best climbers in the country. And she's going to be here tomorrow just for you."

"Oh—my—god."

THE FIRST RAYS of sun were peeking through the trees the next morning when Hanna crawled out of the tent she shared with Kirstie and paced around the forest. She'd been awake since before dawn. The thought of climbing with such a legendary woman was both terrifying and enchanting. She wondered if any more memories would return.

And what she might learn about herself.

An ancient Volkswagen Beetle braked abruptly behind the Hoffmanns' car, and its driver seemed to materialize by the picnic table even before the motor had quieted.

"Is there a Hanna Hoffmann here?" The woman's voice echoed through the still-sleeping campground.

Hanna scrambled over from behind a tree. "*Ich bin hier!*"

"I guess that must mean 'Okay, let's go then.'" Bowman grinned. "I've got climbing shoes and a harness for you. We've got a lot to do today."

Kirstie joined them and translated Diana's rapid-fire chatter about her plans for their day. A short walk from the Lumpy Ridge parking area, Diana handed Hanna a pair of shoes with smooth rubber soles.

"Climbing shoes need to fit close so you can really be in touch with the rock." She buckled the straps for Hanna and then turned away to put her own shoes on.

"Now for a lesson in belaying. The leader depends on her partner. The rope runs around your waist and up to me, through the carabiners that I clip to the pro. That's these metal things—they're called 'chocks'—that go into cracks in the rock. If I fall, you just cinch the rope tight against your waist."

Diana virtually danced up the cliff. Hanna didn't believe she would get more than a foot off the ground. Yet in a short time, they were shaking hands at the top as Kirstie joined them.

"You're a natural climber, Hanna. You use your body gracefully—balance instead of brawn. That's how women succeed in this sport."

Bowman's tone was matter-of-fact. But what Hanna heard was the same message she'd heard from Doris after her impromptu climb in the Alps. You belong. As a woman.

After the previous week that reassurance meant a lot.

After a few more short climbs Diana gestured toward a sheer eight-hundred-foot buttress under a looming peak. "Hanna, that was first done by one of the best climbers in the world. It's six pitches, and steep—it probably looks intimidating, but I'm sure you can do it. Shall we?"

Intimidating? The buttress looked completely impossible. But she was ready to follow.

She had little in common with this woman's indefatigable energy and self-confidence. Yet she felt a kinship. Maybe Diana had also been a frightened, shy little girl at one point. Maybe she too could become a climber.

Three hours later she was standing at the top of what Diana called Kor's Flake, but to her was the top of the world. Her hands were scratched, her muscles ached, and her back throbbed with pain. But she felt like a mountain goddess.

The feeling was still there as she went to sleep that night.

A girl was hiding in a narrow crack in the wall of a rock cavern, where she'd been chased by a monster. Her two cats sat on their haunches at her feet. The cats started walking toward a glowing tunnel, hugging the wall. Seeing and hearing no other creature, the girl followed them.

Soon she saw another giant cavern beyond the opening. The cats arched their backs and hissed as they looked back into the gloom, but nothing blocked their progress into the new cavern, whose many-hued stalactites and amethyst geode-studded walls were dimly illuminated by light from a distant castle.

BACK IN STUTTGART, she wrote a letter of appreciation to Barrios. In that moment of need, he'd been there. His sympathetic reply included a brief update on their investigation.

"We knew that Staunton's club had a pornographic side that the public didn't see, but we missed his affection for bondage. Besides watching it, he'd planned to make money from photography, and was smart enough to find a different location so as not to jeopardize the club. I apologize for failing to find the clues. They were as well hidden as the door itself."

Images from that basement would lie in wait, ready to pounce on her peace of mind with little provocation. Nylons, metal stairs, shoelaces, studded belts, and most of all sawhorses—she'd have to avoid them all. But she hadn't run away. As a result, Staunton would be brought to justice after all. Maybe it wasn't all in vain.

In the meantime, despite her disappointment, the trial had made her stronger, just as her mother had said. She had a lot to be pleased about—a career she loved, cherished friends, and her own apartment. And her precious mementos.

On top of the dollhouse the leopard that had watched over her on her first flight to Germany stood guard, and her growing collection of other stuffed animals had found snug shelters in every nook. The bonsai and globe occupied the windowsill.

Elisabeth's animals would stay on her bed, assuaging her fears as she fought the fiends in her nightmares. On top of her dresser, the little doll that had been in her birthday cake had her own bed.

And soon the doll would have a necklace, made from amethyst nuggets that Hanna had bought in Estes Park. They'd sent shivers through her whole body when she saw them in the rock shop—it was very strange, but she'd known instantly what she would do with them.

Her mother had arranged an appointment with Dr. Meissner. Remembering her dream with the castle, she shuffled through her closet searching for a defiant statement of femininity. There it was—the pink sheath dress with asymmetrical neck that she'd bought before the trial but never worn.

It didn't escape the psychologist's notice. "Very nice, Hanna. Sophisticated yet tasteful. A new dress for a new phase of life, perhaps?"

"Thanks. I guess you have a report from Doctor Beattie about the trial."

"I do. And I'm very, very impressed with your courage. I know you don't feel like you got what you wanted. But this is a huge step. You know already that mental healing doesn't come quickly."

"I thought I might get my English back. Maybe after he's sentenced."

"Does it affect your life?"

"It bothers me because it's a sign of being an outsider. So many other Germans seem to know it."

The hour passed quickly. Then it came. "Now, Hanna, how is your love life?"

Dr. Meissner had surely meant well. But the question clenched gnarled claws around her gut.

Only two months ago that climber in her dream had radiated real warmth, the first man besides her father and uncle who hadn't seemed suspicious. She'd awakened with a tiny bud of hope for romance. But the trial hadn't merely smashed that hope, it had vaporized, atomized, and stripped it to the naked nucleus, ready to devour any feeling that came close.

She struggled to compose tactful words that wouldn't convey her seething froth of fear and anger to the therapist. This wasn't Dr. Meissner's fault. "I'm not sure a lover is possible for me. I don't think anyone will want me, the way I am."

"Hanna, you have to change that attitude. Don't doubt your ability to love or be loved. You faced the monster. Now it's time to reclaim what you lost."

She fervently wished she could. But the emotional wall she'd put up against the threat of men was an equally effective barrier to keep love securely inside.

CHAPTER 17

Five months later: 4 February 1975

HANNA HAD SCARCELY hung up her coat at the *Friseursalon Petra* when her boss poked her head in. "Good morning, Hanna. Can you come by my office for a moment? Coffee is waiting."

The offer of coffee—it would be espresso—signified a session involving praise for a job well done. It was one of Petra Klinger's trademarks.

She waited till Hanna had taken a sip before speaking. "Have you ever heard of Annemarie Renger?"

"She's the parliamentary leader for the Social Democrats, right?" Hanna remembered the name from school.

"Who needs an encyclopedia with you around? Yes, she's been a force for democracy—and feminism—since before the war. She's also famous for her style. Dagmar Schoenberg is one of her protégés—and has very similar expectations for her appearance. I'm sending her to you."

A brief flash of pride quickly gave way to alarm. She certainly wasn't ready for such a client. This was a prescription for a debacle. "Frau Klinger, I'm flattered, but . . . surely she's expecting one of the experienced stylists."

"Naturally she's coming here because of my reputation. But you know the quality of your technique. And personal rapport is critical in this business. You're the right choice."

Hanna left sweating. She was about to enter a trial more stressful than last summer's. If she passed this test, the state exam would feel like an insignificant afterthought.

Her concentration evaporated. She vacillated endlessly about the color mix for her first customer, and the woman left without her usual compliment. Whatever had possessed Petra Klinger to make this rash decision, the truth would soon come out, in disastrous fashion. Her gut churned till she wondered if she'd have to go home.

Dagmar Schoenberg came at eleven. And Hanna's day was transformed in an instant.

Her new client's hairstyle was very similar to her own when she first came to Germany. Her friends had poked fun at what they called her old ladies' hairdo: medium length with precise waves that curled under just below her ears. As her hair grew longer she'd grown out of the style. But she hadn't forgotten what to do.

She greeted her client with solemn formality and went through an intake consultation as she'd been taught. But she was already sure of the answers. The butterflies in her stomach gradually settled back to sleep.

There was little conversation for a long time. Hanna didn't mind. It gave her space to convince that unrelenting critic in the back of her head that she really did have a worthy talent. It was a difficult debate, but she was beginning to believe her side had a chance to win.

"Hanna, do you pay attention to politics?" Frau Schoenberg asked as Hanna brushed the curls into place using small spritzes of hairspray.

"Not as much as I should, I'm afraid. I did well in my lessons on government and current events only because I've a good memory. I know I could learn a lot from you."

"I wouldn't want to bore you. What do you like to do in your spare time?"

"Talk about boring—that's me. Let's see. I read mysteries and romances. I like cooking when I can have friends over. And sewing. I make clothing for little dolls, that go in dollhouses. But I've also given some clothing to the *Arbeiter-Samariter-Bund*."

"What a coincidence—as the chairwoman for the Baden-Württemberg section, I want to thank you for that donation."

After she left, Petra Klinger came to Hanna's station again. "Her next appointment is in five weeks—with you, of course."

The butterflies stirred in their cage as ecstasy vied with fear. So often something good in her life presaged something bad.

SHE WAS EAGER to talk about that appointment during her next meeting with Angela Meissner. Dagmar Schoenberg had related some political stories after all, leaving Hanna thoroughly starstruck.

But the psychologist had something else in mind. "The personality inventory I gave you last month says you're a shockingly normal eighteen-year-old. It's April fifteenth—just in time for your birthday next month. Four years after your injury, you can begin to think of your body and mind as being in step again. And I don't need to see you anymore."

She handed Hanna a letter, stamped with an official seal. "You're on your own."

Though the letter listed her age as twenty-five, she really felt like she'd just triumphed over adolescence. How keenly she'd looked forward to this—and how apprehensive it left her. "I don't know, I'm not sure I can handle being 'normal.' Well, I guess my panic attacks aren't going away, are they? If I could only have a magic pill for those."

"I wish. Don't expect your anxiety and nightmares to go away soon either. But you've got the resources to handle them."

She handed Hanna a gift-wrapped package tied with a ribbon. "Good luck. You can still call, anytime you need me. And be proud of yourself. Remember pride isn't the same as arrogance."

Hanna left feeling light-headed and lead-footed. To be truly on her own was both exhilarating and frightening. Each step forward risked a fall.

Her first customer that morning was Dagmar Schoenberg, who seemed more animated than before. "My son Erik just started his new job at the university. He moved into his apartment last week, and now he has to get used to the area again."

"He is on the faculty of the university here in Stuttgart?"

"Yes, in physics. He defended his doctoral thesis in Munich last fall, but didn't do a *Habilitation*. To become a professor without that is extremely unusual. He got the offer just before Christmas. He's very excited."

Hanna's curiosity was piqued. She didn't know what a *Habilitation* was, but the way this woman was speaking of her son seemed unusually personal.

"But after being away for so long—he did his *Diplom* there also—he's out of touch. All those important little things like where to get your coffee and cheese. And where to get a haircut. Of course I gave him my advice."

"Ah, does that mean I have a prospective client?"

"Don't be silly. Who else would I send him to? He's rather hard to please. I think you'll like him."

"And did you tell him that also?"

"Of course. You *can* be dense at times, Hanna." The look of exasperation came with an unmistakable twinkle in her eyes, a welcome distraction from the feeling that she'd just encountered a disquieting crack in this world where she thought she was safe.

"Seriously, my son is not typical of his peers. You're younger, so you don't remember those days after the war when the past was a nightmare, the present rubble, and the future a thin sliver of hope. That's what he grew up in. And we did well. My husband is now a vice president at Bosch, and you know what I do. But there were days then when we were grateful to have an hour of heat in the evening during the winter."

The crack was growing. From its depths a huge cage of emotions growled "Danger—disturb at your own risk."

"I can't remember a time when Erik didn't look out for others. When we got the first bar of chocolate we'd seen for years, I gave him a small piece. He broke it into four quarters and gave three to his friends."

Hanna was concentrating on her work, but couldn't avoid occasional glances at the mirror. She'd never seen such seriousness in a client's expression. "As he grew up, he demanded more of himself than anyone else did. And he had a hard time accepting other people, because he didn't see them as having the same integrity. So now do you see why I think you might like each other?"

"Actually, I'm totally mystified. I'd be the last person on earth to satisfy someone so amazing."

"Hanna, this is our third meeting, and I already know some things about you that you don't know about yourself."

That was easy to believe. What she knew about herself was far outweighed by what she didn't know. But of one thing she was certain: she wasn't the slightest bit ready for the relationship she was being led toward.

WHEN ERIK CAME later that week, they were both very professional and courteous. Hanna couldn't help but admire his high cheekbones, gently curved jaw, and soft blond hair. He was also taller than she—enough to put her head on his shoulder? She put that thought out quickly.

He asked about her doll clothes (*Wow—Dagmar told him that*), and seemed genuinely interested. Finally she got up the nerve to ask about his job at the university.

"It's like moving into a new house. You're all excited, but first you have to find the broom closet. And there's no broom in it."

After he left Petra gave her that now-familiar exasperated look. "He's not a full two meters tall. Two centimeters short of it."

Hanna felt her face flush. "How do you know?"

"I asked him."

Three weeks later he clearly was not in serious need of a haircut. Within a few minutes he asked her if she liked music.

"Yes, very much. Do you have a favorite?"

"Just now I was thinking about classical. Munich has a superb orchestra, which I enjoyed immensely. But Stuttgart is also very nice. Only a highly trained ear will notice the difference. Would you be interested in going sometime?"

That the question was obviously coming didn't make it easier to respond to. Dagmar Schoenberg had described a man who ought to be any girl's dream come true. She should feel like a princess, after being plucked from a crowd of peasants. Why couldn't she just accept it?

"I—I'm sorry, I've never been to the symphony before. My aunt and uncle had some records that I've listened to. I know so little. Some Beethoven and Mozart. Oh—and the Trout Quintet. That feels so moving."

Erik's face became distinctly dreamy under a faint smile. "Seems to me you know quite a lot—it's a masterpiece of lyrical emotion. Mendelssohn's Third Symphony is the main feature this Saturday night. It's also called the 'Scottish symphony.' Very romantic, evocative of nature, and easy to listen to. I think you might like it."

"It sounds wonderful. May I . . . call you tomorrow?" The words came out in little more than a croak. Erik's graceful "Of course" made her feel even more horrible.

After barely making it through the rest of the day, she rushed through a perfunctory cleanup and dashed out the door with no destination in mind, except that it wouldn't be home. She needed solitude and distraction. Maybe the hiking area near Echterdingen where her parents had taken her on her thirteenth birthday, suffused with the comfort of the doll whose magical radiance she still pondered. She wasn't dressed for hiking, but the forest would exude its balm even from a distance.

But as the train approached Möhringen, she remembered the botanical garden in Hohenheim, where cherries, hibiscus, rhododendrons and magnolias would be blooming lavishly. Flowers were what her spirit needed. Twenty minutes later she was ambling down the manicured paths, nearly forgetting for a few moments the intractable dilemma that had brought her there.

Nearly, but not quite. What was she going to do? During the last three weeks, every time she tried to banish Erik from her mind, she found herself looking up at the smooth sweep of hair across his forehead and the twinkle at the corners of his eyes. Those eyes that seemed as large as her dreams. If only she could get even a little closer to them—exactly the chance she'd been offered.

Nonsense. No man could be serious about her. A peasant, indeed. A tall, leggy one with a waist more like a dent than an hourglass. Whatever she said to this man of the world would be clumsy and uncultured. Not to mention the panic attack she'd probably have if he actually embraced her. At best the evening would be unbearably awkward; more likely he'd be offended and never come back to the salon. If she politely said no, she might at least keep her job.

I can't remember a time when Erik didn't look out for others. Couldn't she just accept what his mother had said? Why did she let her paranoia control her?

On one side of the path was a lilac, thick lavender sprays luxuriant in the sun. Still obsessing over her dilemma, she idly observed the irises near its base. *Wow, such an exquisite purple—someone must have put something magical in that dirt underneath them.*

Her heart nearly stopped, her feet rooted to the sidewalk.

She closed her eyes and felt the profusion of blossoming plants around her as a living force, the spirit that winter could not extinguish, determined to find its place in the light.

Wasn't that who she was?

Of course I should go. The fearful phantasms hadn't vanished, but they weren't as strong as the promise of love. She ran as fast as she could to the entrance to find a telephone.

She spent the next week in frantic dress-search mode. Finally she settled on a black chiffon with a waistband and ruched hip embellishment. She added silver and onyx earrings and necklace and put her hair in a French twist.

Erik came to her apartment precisely at six with a bouquet of three pink roses, which she put into a vase after profusely thanking him. He was dressed in a smartly tailored suit with a white shirt and a black bow tie. With the lightest touch he guided her to his Audi, where he opened the door and delicately held her hand to help her in.

Not only didn't she panic, she began to relax. All she had to do tonight was follow his lead. He was almost a stereotype of old-fashioned chivalry. But he was also very direct and genuine.

A few stones crumbled almost imperceptibly from that wall.

Her heart did a little flip as she recognized the hall where she'd seen the Grateful Dead. Could this startling contrast really be an auspicious portent? She was a child exploring the castle of her dreams as she followed Erik to their seats. He nodded casually to other couples several times, once stopping to exchange greetings and introduce Hanna as his "special friend."

"And lovely she is," the man said. "Fräulein Hoffmann, Erik is very lucky to have you with him tonight." Hanna felt sure her legs would crumple directly under her.

The symphony began with a pair of overtures. Beethoven's Egmont preceded one composed by Mendelssohn's sister Fanny. The sense of auspiciousness grew. She'd never heard of a woman composer.

During the intermission Erik took her backstage without explaining, and she followed without questioning. His effortless confidence made any possibility seem plausible. But when he introduced her to the conductor, she suppressed a gasp. He bowed slightly. "Welcome, Fräulein Hoffmann. I'm so glad you've come." He turned to Erik. "Erik, what a superb performance you gave us last week."

Hanna looked at him with wide-eyed astonishment.

"I'm not in the symphony, but I play regularly in chamber music recitals," he said matter-of-factly.

"He's fantastic," the conductor assured her. "If he weren't a scientist, he'd surely be performing here with us. Have you not heard him play?"

Hanna shook her head.

The conductor turned to the first violinist, standing just behind him, and raised his eyebrows. "Perhaps Günther would allow you to give the young lady a sample." The other man nodded and handed Erik his violin and bow.

Hanna thought that Erik blushed slightly as he took the violin and played the beginning of the fourth movement of the Trout Quintet. She was transfixed. The peasant turned princess-for-a-day had been given a private audience with a musical genius.

Finally she recovered her wits. "Erik, that is amazingly beautiful. And you remembered that it's my favorite piece."

Erik smiled slightly and handed the violin back to its owner.

Mendelssohn was nothing like the delicate dance of Mozart or the strength and passion of Beethoven. Here was something soft and haunting, then bursting with energy that seemed to come directly from the wind and waves. On the way home, she wanted to know more about both of the Mendelssohns. Erik's account of how the brother had supported his sister's career privately but held back publicly was sympathetic and respectful.

He is so caring and gentle. Whatever he does, I think he will never hurt me.

He helped her out of the car and walked her to the door of her building. After she'd unlocked it, she turned and looked up at him. He took her hand and kissed it gently. "Thank you for such a wonderful evening."

"I should be thanking you. It was delightful."

"Perhaps you might like to do it again?"

"I would. Good night, Erik."

She sat on the balcony and watched the waning gibbous moon sink toward the horizon, carrying the magic of the evening into a new cycle. During the last few hours there hadn't been even the faintest rustle of a monster in her life.

The thought of love was so tantalizing, and yet still so terrifying.

WARMER DAYS AND spring flowers heralded a new season. When Erik phoned on Monday, he suggested she wear comfortable shoes suitable for a stroll along the Neckar on Saturday, and afterward they would enjoy a late lunch sitting outside overlooking the river. She should bring a sweater for the evening.

She told him it sounded beautiful, but she felt near panic as she hung up. What if 'comfortable shoes' were running shoes with laces? That image was one of her demons.

There was nothing she could do. To avoid obsessing over it she went shopping. She met him wearing a black A-line cotton dress with a bright blue and red floral hem, and more flowers scattered around the top. Her hair was in a high ponytail held by a yellow band.

"If you stray into a meadow along the way I might lose you." Erik seemed serious, but for the twinkle in his eyes.

Hanna tossed her head and gave him her brightest smile, now breathing normally after noting his dark gray canvas slip-on shoes.

"There's a trail that starts in Esslingen along the river and then climbs above it, with spectacular views. It goes all the way to Bad Cannstatt, but we can go only part way—enough for the view—and come back in time to eat."

"You lead and I'll follow, Herr Schoenberg."

"You probably won't even have to swim. The river looks pretty calm today."

She'd already realized that the slightest hint of a smile, seen mostly around his eyes, likely presaged a silly joke, often followed by something more serious. A few minutes later, walking hand in hand along the path close to the river, she got both at once as she pointed out the daisies, thale cress, and buttercups.

"You'll have to be the botanist, Hanna. I only know where to buy roses."

She laughed. "Okay, I accept the assignment. I doubt that anyone would confuse me with a botanist, but I did pay attention during the lessons on German flora."

They made their way gradually upward, passing wild cherries bordering vineyards where buds were beginning to break. With the pretext of enjoying the increasingly wide vistas, Hanna stole surreptitious glances at her companion, taking in the curve of his chin, his long slender fingers, his graceful shoulders and lithe legs.

And her trust was growing along with the inkling that love might be possible after all.

"Did you notice that some of the flowers have fallen off your dress and are now growing alongside the path?" Erik sounded earnest.

"You said you didn't know anything about flowers." She tried to sound reproachful, but it came out more like shy adoration.

"But forget-me-nots one cannot forget."

Her heart was practicing flips and flops in earnest. "They are a sign of love, you know."

"And you have them on your dress, interspersed with wild red roses. Which must mean that you are either a lover of nature or a natural lover."

"Maybe just lovably natural."

"Naturally lovable." Erik stooped and selected a single forget-me-not. "I don't usually pick wildflowers. They should be left for everyone to enjoy. But this may be time for an exception."

Erik gently held her ponytail with one hand and inserted the stem under the band with the other, leaving the tiny blue flower peeking out from the top of her head. Hanna tried not to look directly at his eyes, but they drew her in irresistibly. Intense and deep, matching the flower, they hinted of a refuge whose serenity seemed fathomless.

Was it attainable? Would *she* be welcome there?

She pushed these frightening questions aside. *Stay in the moment.*

Bathed in the warmth of a windless sunny afternoon in the low seventies, they strolled upward until they found themselves a short distance from the *Grabkapelle Württemberg.* Erik stopped. "How do you feel? We needn't go any further. This wasn't supposed to be a forced march."

Tired or not, she would've continued till she collapsed to keep this moment alive. "It's lovely, Erik. Of course, we should go up there. It looks fascinating."

It was nearly six o'clock by the time they were finally seated on the terrace of a small café in Esslingen. The sun was already dipping into the low western hills. They'd put on their sweaters near the end of their walk, but the day's warmth still lingered.

"Well, so much for a late lunch. I promise my scheduling is usually better than this."

Hanna gazed across the valley and back at Erik. Her first date had been a moment of pure magic, unbidden and unexpected. She'd followed her leader with all analysis suspended, as if the whole evening had been a dance. Today she was the hostess for a jostling crowd of unsettling thoughts.

Barely a month ago she'd told her therapist that she was too ugly to have a lover. But even if she could hide her scars, what would come next? So far everything had been simple. But what would she do when he wanted to kiss her? Or more? Could a man really be trusted? What would happen if he found out? *When* he found out—he surely would.

She wanted so badly for this past not to exist, to be a normal girl like her friends, with normal problems and fears. For just a little while, for this man who had been sent by the gods, maybe she could deny it.

"Erik, this is perfect. I love the light at this time of day. We shouldn't have arrived a minute earlier."

"I agree, the light is perfect. Do you know your hair in the afternoon sun is showing all the colors in the spectrum?"

Hanna's cheeks warmed. "How can brown hair do that? Really, isn't that impossible? How does a physicist explain that?"

"What the physicist says is that your hair can act as a diffraction grating if the sun strikes it at exactly the right angle, and that separates the light into the different colors."

He said this in his professorial lecture tone. But what followed was as gentle and melodic to her ear as the violin he'd played on their first date. "And because yours is so soft and smooth, it really does exactly that."

"Erik . . ." Hanna didn't know how to talk romance. She might spoil everything by saying the wrong thing. All she could do was speak her heart. "You are so sensitive. I've never met a man who notices things the way you do."

"And I've never met a girl with more to notice. Every time we meet your hair is in a different style, each somehow more beautiful than the last. That's your profession, true. But you do it so artfully. And then you wear something like your tanzanite earrings, with a blue that perfectly matches the forget-me-nots on your dress."

"I can't believe it. How could you know they're tanzanite?"

He actually looked embarrassed. "I'm sorry. Minerals and gems are a sort of hobby."

"Oh, Erik, don't be sorry—I love that you know all these things. I was just surprised. You must know where it comes from, then."

The boyish grin that she loved reappeared. "I may not know everything."

"Of course, it's from Tanzania. The mines are right next to Mt. Kilimanjaro. So the gem is a gift of the mountain. Or so says Tiffany, anyway."

"I know the mineralogy. The message will have to come from you."

She didn't reply. Her heart was too full of too many emotions to speak, and she was terrified of marring the moment even slightly. So she simply reached across the table and squeezed his hand tightly.

When Erik next came to her apartment, the roses he brought were red. Impulsively she took one of them and put it in her hair as she walked toward his car. She held the other two with her clutch, treating them as tenderly as a kitten.

Of all the delicate strands in her heart, the possibility of love was the most fragile. Out of the fear of so many years, Erik had awakened a dream that was growing into a thread of hope. A mere whisper of wind from the past might break it.

CHAPTER 18

ERIK WASN'T ACCUSTOMED to receiving pale pink envelopes. When he saw one slide through the slot next to his apartment door late Saturday morning in the middle of July, he picked it up immediately. The return address gave him goosebumps.

Hanna hadn't written to him during the nearly two months they'd been dating. After all, they'd been seeing each other weekly and often spoke on the phone. The pretty pastel stationary with soft-hued alpine flowers in the background wasn't propitious.

> *Dear Erik,*
> *I cannot continue our relationship. I'm sorry. It is not your fault. It is entirely mine. I will love you forever.*
> *Hanna*

The enigmatic note struck him like a last cry for help from someone disappearing into the depths of a turbulent river. And he might be the only witness. He grabbed the phone and called her number. After a dozen rings with no answer, he hung up and called information in Frankfurt, where he knew her parents lived.

"Erik, I'm so glad you called." Gisela sounded both relieved and distraught. "Hanna is in a very bad way. This is like one of the crises she went through in her first year of recovery."

Recovery? "What is this about? I just received a letter mailed three days ago, saying she is breaking off our relationship. I was expecting to see her this evening."

"She received word that Staunton escaped. Wait, do you know about what happened to her in America?" Gisela's voice quavered.

"America? Apparently, there are things I don't know."

"Erik, I really need to see you in person. This can't be done over the phone. I hope you don't think I'm being melodramatic, but Hanna's life may depend on us."

He felt distinctly colder. "Would you like to come to my flat or shall I come to you?"

"Give me your address. I can be there in an hour."

He tried to keep his mind off of her cryptic comment by practicing his violin. No matter what he started playing, snatches of the 'Trout' would creep in.

Gisela was precisely on time. But she was silent for half a minute after sitting down. She clutched and smoothed her skirt repeatedly. "Erik, it should have been Hanna's decision how and when to tell you this. But I think now I have to. Hanna was originally an American. She was renting a room from us at college— we were living in Boulder, Colorado. She was at odds with her parents, and we adopted her after several months."

She brushed lightly at the corner of one eye. "Soon afterward, she was kidnapped, raped, and tortured almost to death by a man named William Staunton. It left her with complete amnesia, speaking only German."

There were indeed things he didn't know.

It was hard to imagine the insecurity that women lived with. Mostly he'd tried not to think about it. Physics and music were his world. But Hanna, whom he simply could not picture as an American, was now a part of it also.

The thought of this injury made him want to hold and comfort her like a fragile child. She really was rather childlike in some ways. Her lack of guile was part of the charm that had captivated him. She never seemed to be playing games with him. No hidden agenda.

Yet there was this secret history. Could he still trust her?

Gisela was quite still now, hands in her lap. He needed to match her calm. His first real love affair had become a mystery. But it couldn't be any easier for the mother of this enigma.

"I'm so sorry, please go on. That must have been unspeakably difficult for you, and I'm very grateful. You probably know how much I love her."

Gisela briefly described Hanna's hospitalization, the trial, and its outcome. "A second trial, with the new evidence, was scheduled for this summer. Then four days ago Staunton escaped from prison and got over the border into Mexico. The police say it's unlikely he'll ever be found there."

"How could he have escaped? Surely someone like that would've been held in a high security facility."

"One of the police officers was in league with Staunton. The chief detective was finally closing in on him. Apparently the rogue officer saw it coming, and they went to Mexico together."

"Where is she? Has she talked about it?"

Gisela's eyes seemed haunted. She looked away for a moment before replying. "She's back at my sister's house in Waldenheim, since that's closer than our home in Frankfurt. She threatened to kill herself, and wouldn't talk to me at all when I came. I'm at my wit's end."

Erik played idly with the letter with its flowered border, and thought about the forget-me-not. The way her ponytail swung as she laughed. The music of her touch.

"You lead and I'll follow, Herr Schoenberg." Though her cornflower blue eyes twinkled, her expression had been earnest.

He'd not yet said those magic words to her: "I love you." He'd carefully constructed a plan for how to get there, and beyond. But would he be able now?

"Is there anything you think I can do?"

"If you're still willing to talk to her, she may listen to you. Of course, this isn't rational. We know her trauma is still intense. The doctor in Colorado said she might not ever fully recover from it. But she's done so much. You know what she's like."

"I thought I knew."

"This was a shock to my husband and me also. Staunton's escape triggered something very deep in her that I can only guess at. The assault took away her new life in her new family, and her subconscious may still want to go back there. I think part of her believes she'll get all her memories back if he's punished."

"Frau Hoffmann, I can't even begin to imagine what all this must've been like for her. But to be perfectly honest with you, I don't know if I'm the right person to help. I need time to think about what all this means. I hope you understand."

"That goes without saying. May I leave my sister's address and phone number with you? Of course, what you do with it is entirely up to you."

He handed her his notebook. "Certainly."

Before she left she stood on the threshold for some time.

"Erik, since that day Hanna walked up to my house and entered my life, three times it seemed she might not survive a crisis. Each time I tried to be patient and show my love. Always I sang to her, and always she came back."

He extended his hand. "Perhaps this time she has to bring herself back."

ERIK CLOSED THE door very softly, and paced slowly around the room for three complete circuits. In the wake of the small cyclone that had just blown through, walking was the only way to restore order. For him it was part of being a physicist. Had he been born about fifty years earlier he would certainly have been right at Neils Bohr's side on those storied long walks around the Copenhagen Institute. In Munich he'd created his own version, leading other students on day hikes around the Starnberger See as he sought to perfect the clarity that he would demand as a professor.

He fetched his car and pointed it northeast, intending to make his way to the forest preserves near Korb. Driving reflexively, he replayed the conversation with Gisela like an endless tape loop. Obviously this was a painful subject for Hanna, but if she couldn't share it with him, what did that portend? He very much wanted to extend his sympathy and emotional support, but not if she wasn't trusting him.

The carefully cultivated fields and tidy houses brought some comfort. Growing up watching them sprout from the wasteland of the war, he'd built his own mental structures, imposing an order that rested on the immutable foundations of science, something safe from human folly. He didn't want to be reminded how fragile it really was.

The same discipline that governed his professional life had been extended to the personal. Ever since he'd become aware of such matters he'd imagined having a wife who looked up to him in his sphere, and he would do the same for her. He knew little of that sphere, and was anxious to learn, in exchanges of candid mutual openness. Instead he'd just experienced the very opposite.

A factory for building materials abruptly appeared on the right, and he realized with a shock that he was on Esslinger Strasse, far south of where he'd thought he was. His mood became even gloomier. The expanse of blighted earth was a dissonant tear in the elegant harmony of the forest, crushing any hope for a restorative walk.

The town of Esslingen was only a few miles ahead. The river might at least offer some solace. The reminder of his second date with Hanna could perhaps be suppressed.

He arrived less than a quarter of an hour later. It wasn't the forest he'd been thinking of, but his spirits brightened almost immediately as he strode along the path. A slight breeze rustled the leaves of the birch trees along the bank, filtering flecks of light through their bright green foliage. The smooth, steady flow of the water seemed gentle, even soothing, yet under the surface was a relentless power whose progress could not be altered by any storm.

Exactly how he had long aspired to be.

How could he allow himself to be deterred by this little tempest? What did he even know about it? Hadn't he just told Gisela that he couldn't imagine what Hanna's experience had been like?

He couldn't, and probably never would. But he could and would find out the facts. He headed for the train station to find a telephone.

HEIDI BAUMANN GREETED him warmly. "Thank you for coming, Herr Schoenberg. I apologize for the mess. But please make yourself comfortable, and I'll do my best to get Hanna to come out."

Erik could see no mess in the tidy living room. The mess was in his mind, where the uncertainty that had led him here still rumbled like the remnants of a storm.

Finally, Hanna slowly descended the stairs, and the uncertainty vanished as if by command. Her eyes were red and puffy, her face haggard. It was the first time he'd seen her with no makeup, and her always immaculately styled hair was wildly unkempt.

Whatever twists of the mind had led her to this state would not change his love. This raw, naked pain was not deception.

She crossed the living room tentatively, as if she didn't belong there, and sat as far from Erik as she could get. She was holding a small child's blanket, staring at her lap with her shoulders hunched together.

He wanted badly to reach out to her. Instead he leaned a little forward and placed his palms upward on his thighs. "'Hanna, please tell me what you're thinking. You know I won't criticize you."

When she finally spoke her voice was flat, emotionless, like a recording. "Erik, I've not been honest with you. I so much wanted it to work for us, and I was afraid to say anything that wasn't a part of my fairy-tale vision. But now it doesn't matter."

"Perhaps you can stop pre-judging me for a moment and tell me your story. I've been a pretty decent listener up to now, have I not?"

She twisted the blanket into a tighter knot. "You found me here, so that means you probably talked to my mother. What did she tell you?"

"That she isn't going to fail you now, any more than she did in the past. Hanna, are you going to let this man who hurt you so much hurt you yet again?"

"So you know that he escaped into Mexico where he can hide from the police and probably never be found."

"The first part of that sentence is fact. The second part is baseless speculation."

She shook her head. "Erik, everything is over. All my hopes for healing are gone. I can't go on. And I can't drag anyone else down with me. I'm sorry I hurt you. I've hurt everyone. I wanted so much and look what I've done to them. I'm sorry."

"Hanna, please listen to me. I can't imagine the hurt that's been done to you. But it doesn't makes me love you less."

She was silent again. "You won't love me when you find out about me."

"I love you, not your skin. Not your birthplace. Just you."

She hunched forward, eyes averted from him.

"No one can love me the way I am. Look at me. I can't wear a dress cut below the neck because my skin looks like tangled rope. I'm a bundle of nerves with panic attacks at random times. I wake up from a nightmare and can't sleep, and my skin hurts all the time. I can't wear pantyhose or even look at the laces of running shoes. I'm an outcast; I should have been left in the trash bin where he threw me. I want to be seen as an ordinary girl but I'm so much taller, I can never fit in, I'm ugly and I'll never have children, and . . ." Her wobbling voice broke and she sobbed uncontrollably.

Erik moved closer to her, and she didn't move away. He gently guided her head onto his shoulder and then onto his breast, where she lay weeping for uncounted minutes.

He was trained to give answers. But he realized that there might be no words to answer this cry from the heart. So, he stroked her hair and was silent.

Finally, he took a handkerchief from his pocket and dabbed gently around her eyes. "Hanna, I love you. That's it."

"Even with all of that?"

"With all of that and anything else."

Hanna sat up. He'd never seen such intensity in someone's eyes. They seemed to be imploring him to approve of her. Or maybe demanding.

"If you're not telling the truth, please just go away now."

"You and your aunt will have to carry me out of the house if you want me to leave you."

The tears came again. But the head nestled on his shoulder made no attempt to move.

He ran his fingers carefully through her hair, gently removing the tangles one by one, and smoothed it in a fan over her shoulders and down her back. Little by little, he felt her sinking into him.

"May I make a suggestion? Come to my chamber music recital tomorrow at seven. We can have dinner afterward. There's a place I've been thinking about that I haven't taken you. I think you'll like it. It has a nice view. It will be an even nicer view if you're part of it."

"You're crazy. How can you even think that?"

"Because I'm crazy, obviously."

She snorted, quietly but unmistakably. "You're insufferable, Herr Schoenberg."

"And persistent." For her to say that meant there was hope.

She straightened again and rubbed her eyes.

"Erik, what should I do? I can't trust my own feelings. Part of me never wants to let you out of my sight again. The other part of me is so afraid—afraid of hurting you, afraid of something that will hurt me, afraid of—of I don't know what."

He had no idea how to assuage those fears. Saying the wrong thing could send her backward again. And tied to that thought was another: If she did marry him, these emotions would be part of the package.

But maybe that was just what his orderly life needed.

Anyway, the only rational response was the honest one. That was his rule. "Hanna, I can't really know about the things you fear. What I can and do know about is how much I love you. It's up to you to decide between me or the demons."

"You're a clever one, Herr Schoenberg. Okay. I need some time to think. I'll call you in the morning."

CHAPTER 19

ERIK GLANCED AT his watch as he pressed the doorbell, but he knew it was precisely six-thirty, just as Hanna had requested. She met him at the entrance instead of buzzing him inside as usual. He handed her the white rose.

She looked questioningly at him. "Erik, is it . . . is it okay if I wear the rose? A white one? I mean . . . 'innocence and devotion'—I've got the second part, but I'm not sure about the first. But this *is* a new beginning."

He hadn't been certain till that moment that she understood his game with the roses. And it still wasn't clear if she thought the 'new beginning' might include marriage. He could only hope.

"Hanna," he said sternly, "you *must* wear it."

She threaded the stem through her bun, leaving the flower resting on the thin silver headband with purple beads. Around the base of the bun were two short braids, held in place on either side by tiny purple orchid barrettes.

As he stepped around behind her to bend the rose stem into a circle, he saw her back for the first time: the cruelly contorted scars bared above the bold palatinate purple tulle of her strapless column dress. He drew a sharp breath and averted his eyes. Then he forced himself to look closely and grapple with the grotesque spectacle. Behind it, he realized, was a feminine but very fierce warrior, challenging the monsters from her past to an uncompromising duel.

He nestled the stem under her braids so that it resembled a garland of victory. How long ago had she bought that dress? She must have planned to wear it for him as she was now doing. The way he'd made his own plans. The little package in his pocket had been wrapped weeks ago.

He lifted her bangs for a moment and kissed her lightly on the forehead. "You are as lovely as a lotus." His fingers brushed against her amethyst earrings. Then with the lightest touch he guided her to the curb. As always, he held her hand until she was seated.

The concert hall stood behind a fountain and formal garden. From her hair ornaments to the bows on her shoes, she was another flower in the sea of variegated purple bordering the walkways. He held her hand tightly as they followed the curving path. Occasionally their eyes met, launching little messages of adoration to flutter across the narrow gap.

He led her to a seat next to his parents. After introducing his father, he bowed slightly. "The three of you have the best seats in the house. I hope you enjoy the music."

Hanna's brief astonishment amused him. Apparently she'd forgotten he would be playing.

"Oh, Erik, good luck," she said. "I can't wait to hear you."

After opening with Mozart's Violin Sonata No. 18 in G major, he would be the soloist for the Violin Concerto in A major. Though his mind was on the music, he felt her eyes riveted on him with each stroke of his bow.

THOUGH THE APPLAUSE had faded, Hanna was still basking in the beauty of the music, savoring each radiant note, visualizing them dance past like sparks of light. She and Erik bid his parents goodnight and drove to a restaurant with a panoramic view of the city's hills.

The restaurant, with its ivy-robed stone walls and cobblestone drive flanked by statues of lions, reminded her of a castle. A fantasy of glittering chandeliers and ornate tables with elegantly dressed guests flashed through her mind. She shuddered, imagining what the people inside would think of her ugly back.

"Herr Schoenberg and Fräulein Hoffmann, welcome." The maître d' ushered them to a table near the window, lights in the hills twinkling like a stage set. Rather than a castle, perhaps she was in a theater. Did she then have a role in the play?

"Herr Schoenberg ordered the appetizers ahead of time." The man now had the faintest hint of a smile. "So now you must tell us if he chose well."

A waiter arrived bearing a bottle of wine and a broad platter. He poured a small amount of Mosel in Hanna's glass. She swirled the wine a little and tried to look serious. "This is perfect, thank you."

Erik raised his glass as their eyes met. "*Prost*," he said simply.

As they ate the gravlax with capers, pickle, and dark rye bread, Hanna became aware of a small ensemble playing "Something Good," from *The Sound of Music*.

Had she told Erik that was one of her favorite songs? Indeed, somewhere in her mysterious, bumbling past, she'd somehow done something right that brought her to him. She hoped they could continue dating, despite the wretched way she'd behaved.

As the song drew to a close, Erik pushed a small package with a bow across the table toward her. Hanna gasped.

What . . . is this—can it be? No, don't be silly. But what then? "Erik, what . . ."

He was smiling broadly, almost as if enjoying her confusion. "Why don't you just open it and find out?"

She was trembling so much that she dropped it twice as she got the paper off. *The white rose—could her dream . . . ?* She held her breath until she could actually see a jewelry box. Caressing the velvet cover, she turned it over—and then put it down. Yearning for the ring till it hurt, loath to learn she was wrong, certain only of pain, she couldn't move. But finally the box was open and the small tanzanite stone sparkled softly in between its two tiny sapphire companions.

"Oh my god, Erik, oh my god." And then she became aware that the music had stopped, and the other patrons had become a rapt audience. Flustered, she looked back up, her mouth still open.

"Well," Erik said in his calm, soft, matter-of-fact way. "Will you?"

"Erik, are you sure this isn't a dream? I mean, it's a dream anyway. No matter what it is."

"Put it on. See if it fits."

She slipped it onto her finger. The fit was perfect.

"You still haven't said yes—or no," Erik reminded her.

"Yes, yes, yes; a million times yes! Of course, I said yes, didn't you hear me? Can't you hear at all? What's wrong with you?" She heard applause and turned, embarrassed at her tears but smiling through them.

When the music started again, Erik stood up and led her to the small dance floor. She lay her head on his shoulder and felt his strength. When she looked up into his clear blue eyes, the radiance of his love cast the rest of the world in dim shadow. She didn't think about herself until he smiled and softly whispered to her.

"Hanna, you know you are always beautiful to me, but every memory is pale compared to the present."

It seemed like barely yesterday that she'd hesitated to picture herself touching him, fearing to so much as dream of this intimacy. Now she was dreaming of an intimacy that was far more fearsome still.

AS THE CAR came to a stop in front of her apartment, she said, "Would you like to come in? I mean, just to say goodnight. Or have a drink. I probably have some sherry or something."

"That would be lovely. Just for a moment."

It was too dark to see his face clearly, but she felt his closeness. She longed for what was coming as much as she was terrified of it. Annika had told her the first time might be painful, but it was nice the next time. Desire argued loudly with dread while her legs ignored the debate and steadily climbed the stairs. Once inside, they didn't pause on the way to her bedroom.

Hanna sat down on the edge of the bed, and Erik followed. She embraced him with a passion she didn't know she had. As his tongue felt each corner of her mouth, her hands pulled fiercely against his neck, as if she could pull him inside of her entirely. Without stopping he took the pins from her hair and unbraided it, all the while kissing her as tenderly as at the beginning. She began to unbutton his shirt.

She longed to unite her body with his, to melt into it, to fuse together. She stroked his hair and ran her fingers down his back, pulling on his waist with her other hand. She continued to hold his head, her fingers caressing his cheeks and neck, as he slipped her dress down.

Her entire body went rigid as the memory burst through the thin shell she'd put around it after the trial.

She knew he would be surprised and confused, but she was powerless to move. One part of her mind was begging the other to shut up and let her live this moment. But the basement pushed that thought brutally aside. She willed herself to get up and run.

But just as before, she couldn't even scream.

Erik had stopped instantly. Now she felt his fingers on her cheeks, tracing intricate love letters with a gossamer touch. No one had ever touched her like that. As strong as it was delicate and nurturing, it carried the promise of compassion.

Whatever he does, I think he will never hurt me.

He continued to hold her head as if it were a fragile globe, softly massaging her hair. Finally, she relaxed, ever so slowly. She wanted to apologize, but the words still didn't come.

Instead she pushed her dress down and then helped him remove his pants.

She lay down, legs open, hugging him. She was breathing faster than she'd thought possible. His fingertips lightly stroked her scars, and all the pain and fear that they carried surged back. But there was nothing but love and compassion in his eyes. She felt a solitary tear rolling slowly down her cheek, carrying the hurt away. *Not only won't he hurt me, he really and truly loves me. Even if I don't deserve it.*

No fantasy had prepared her for the waves of infinite warmth now spreading throughout her body. She thought of all the hours spent on dilation, twice daily for months after the surgery, now twice weekly forever. She'd often wondered if it wasn't a waste of time. *No, it wasn't.* He reached his climax slowly, as her taught muscles relaxed. Afterward she lay still, afraid of disturbing the soft, euphoric lightness she felt.

After a while he rolled to one side, still with one arm behind her head, fingers wrapped in her hair. She tumbled back from paradise, thoughts awhirl. *Was he satisfied with me? And did he understand my freezing up? Does he still even like me?* Summoning all her strength, she turned toward him. "So was I . . . you know, alright? I mean, did I do it right?"

"Darling, you were awesome. I have no words for it."

"Please don't ever let go of me," she whispered. "I want to stay in your arms forever, and ever, and ever. I'll follow you anywhere. I'll do anything for you. Just don't let go."

"I will never let go. And you don't have to do a thing but be yourself. You are the most beautiful, the most lovable, the most awesome girl—a woman now, excuse me—the world could imagine. And I'm the luckiest man in it."

She hugged him tightly. Then she sat up, shivering. The shell that held all the years of frustration with feeling different had just shattered inside her heart. She had to get it out. It might destroy everything. It might kill her. But she couldn't keep her secret from this man. "Erik, there's something I have to tell you."

She pulled the duvet up to her breasts and hunched her shoulders together. "I—I'm a transsexual."

Clasping sweaty fingers around her knees, she stared straight ahead. "It's why I was attacked. Some guy hit on me as a woman, before I had my operation. You can guess the rest. Oh, Erik, I'm so sorry. I should've told you long ago. It was selfish of me. But I loved you so much. I only wanted to be your woman. And to make you happy."

She finally turned toward him. He'd hardly moved. Now he sat up and slowly put his legs over the side of the bed, facing the window. With one elbow on his thigh, he moved his fingers over the stubble on his chin as he'd moved them over her back a few minutes ago. As she held her breath, he stood up and walked around the end of the bed.

She buried her head between her knees. *Oh my god, now I've done it. He hates me. I should've told him sooner. No, I shouldn't have told him now. Why did I have to? Aren't I a woman like any other? No, I'm not. Yes, I am. Anyway it's all over now. And so is my life.*

The light came on. "Hanna, who is this girl in the photo?"

She looked up to see him holding the photo of Elisabeth, which she'd placed in the center of her dresser.

"That's my sister. Mama and Papa's first child, you know—their biological child. Who died a little before they adopted me." Her fear held her in a vise grip. Now he would think of her as a usurper of this other girl's rightful place. The *real* girl.

He lingered with the photo, and she covered her face with her hands. Eventually she had to peek, to see when he walked out. Her head throbbed the way it had when she'd first heard of the Zwiebels' hatred.

Then he set the photo down with great care right where it had been, returned to his side of the bed, and crawled back under the duvet. His eyes were twinkling as they locked onto hers. "I'm sorry for your loss. She's very pretty. But you, my angel, are the prettiest woman in the world, by far. No competition from anyone."

She lost it then, her cheeks flooded with tears. But through them she could see a few on Erik's lashes also, glistening like pearls. *So he really understands me? It's going to be okay?* Her future reassembled, pieces flying back together like geese into a formation.

He sat up in front of her and took her hands in his. "Am I still the luckiest man in the world?"

They collapsed in a passionate, tangled embrace. But moments later Hanna froze again as Erik jumped up.

He looked very sheepish. "Sorry, I forgot to turn the light off."

They nuzzled and mumbled endearments for a few more minutes, entwined limbs exploring intimacy in the darkness. The next thing she was aware of was the singing of a lark. Ignoring a vague uneasiness, she put on a nightgown and carefully folded Erik's clothing. Then she began to prepare a batch of *Brötchen*.

After the coffee was gone and it was clear that he would eat no more, Erik cleared his throat. "Umm, Hanna, just tell me if any of this is out of bounds. It's hard not to be curious, and I know very little. I only read a newspaper article a few years ago about Georges Burou—the surgeon in Casablanca. Did you go to him?"

"No, I had it just after the assault—in Colorado."

"Your mother told me a little about Staunton's trial. But of course not the part about why he did it. It must've been very difficult for you when it was discussed publicly." He paused. "I'm sorry, that's probably far too painful."

She looked beyond him into a past that she still knew little of. "It's all right. Of course I couldn't read the news, and Mama protected me. Later, I asked her about it. She told me a few dribbles—kind of like titrating acid. People wrote letters to the paper saying they couldn't understand why the police thought it was a crime. One asked why Mama hadn't been arrested too, since *I* was the crime."

She tried to smile, but her lips only twisted under the tears. Erik rose and walked around the table. "It's totally understandable that you didn't want anyone here to know."

He put his hands on her shoulders. "I had many thoughts sitting on the edge of the bed. But it was simple in the end. She's as womanly as can be, she just made you deliriously happy, and you'd never have known if she hadn't told you. So, is there some reason why this little medical detail would matter?"

He tucked a strand of hair behind her ear. "That was an easy question to answer."

After he left, she sat on the balcony and tried to digest all that had happened. Only three months ago she'd felt that love was dangerous as well as unreachable. Now she had her own Prince Charming.

Yet, as she now remembered, she'd had a nightmare even after that blissful evening. The demons were far from giving up. Most of her memories were still sealed in mental mausoleums, harboring horrors whose very existence she wanted to deny. And her hope for a breakthrough after Staunton's arrest had only set her up for bitter disappointment.

She'd found a shield, but the battle would go on. What she needed to win it was not at all clear.

CHAPTER 20

SOON AFTER THE wedding in October Hanna and Erik moved into a house in Vaihingen, between the university and the train station from which Hanna commuted to the city. She made sure it had two child-sized bedrooms besides their own. After work she spent hours window shopping for cribs and baby clothes. But when she talked about children, Erik tended to change the subject to concerts, parks, and restaurants.

He'd assured her after their engagement that he didn't mind that she couldn't bear children. Just the two of them would be perfect. She told herself not to worry. He'd come around in time.

At the beginning of July, almost one year after their engagement, they took their places at the middle of a double-length table at the Gasthaus "Zum edlen Hirsch" to celebrate her graduation. Her dream of being a certified hairdresser, a *Friseurin*, was finally real. Another phase of her life had begun.

In addition to her relatives, all six girlfriends were there. Though they'd all gone their separate ways after secondary school, the bond remained. Doris had the seat next to Hanna. As desserts were disappearing she affected a perplexed expression. "Hanna, when the pastor joined you and Erik together, I don't think he meant physically. So how come we never see you apart?"

Hanna turned to her husband. "I think I'm getting a subtle hint here about this evening." Doris's dry wit was always just the right counterpoint to her own excessive earnestness.

Erik looked past her to Doris. "As long as she's home in time to find my slippers for me and turn down the bed, whatever you want to do is fine."

Hanna dug her elbow into his side. "Erik, Doris may not know you as well as I do . . ."

"I hope that's true," Erik interjected to general merriment. Hanna nearly melted into a puddle of cherry-red chocolate.

Doris, obviously struggling, managed a straight face. "Okay, Hanna, you're coming to meet my new girlfriend at the club tonight."

An hour later, Doris was dancing sensuously with her partner along with dozens of other women in a disco that pulsed with youthful energy. Hanna basked in the glow of the evening, sipping a beer. Her life felt whole. Her friend's apparent happiness mingled with the pride she felt in her achievement, and eager anticipation of the family she hoped to have soon.

It had been a long day. Erik was asleep when she got home, and she was ready to join him when the phone rang. Doris sounded seriously upset. "It looks like the truce with my mother just dissolved. She was spying on us at the club."

"Oh my god, that's awful. How did she even know you were there?"

"She knew I'd gone to your dinner and apparently followed us. She told me she'd been convinced ever since the Zwiebel fracas that you were a bad influence on me. Anyway, she's kicking me out of the house. I get to live in a *Jugendamt* dormitory until I'm eighteen."

Hanna recalled the cryptic comment she'd overheard at the train station. But that history was the last thing she wanted to intrude into her hard-won tranquility now. "I'm sorry, Doris. We should get together soon. I don't mean to be rude, but I haven't the energy to talk tonight. I'm really exhausted."

TWO WEEKS LATER Hanna rushed into a café near the Kernerplatz. Doris, whom she'd promised to meet twenty minutes ago, was sitting near the back with an empty coffee cup, her demeanor as dark as her black T-shirt.

It took Hanna a few moments to catch her breath. "I'm sorry, Doris. I'm getting ready to go to the Alps with Erik next week, and everything's such a rush. And things are a little tense between us. I've been pushing to adopt a baby, and he doesn't want to do it. I think he'd like to be a father, but he's doesn't like adoption."

"That's too bad. I hope you work it out."

Doris's curt rejoinder was jarring, but understandable. She'd surely have been annoyed if it were Doris who was twenty minutes late. "It's really odd, because we almost never fight. He won't talk about his feelings—he says, 'I'm not ready for that yet.' Once I asked 'Well, when *will* you be ready?' and he actually walked away. It worries me."

Hanna stirred milk into her coffee. "I love Erik madly. But I want a child, too. I want a whole family. I hope this isn't the beginning of some huge conflict in our marriage. God, that would be terrible. I don't know what to do."

"Family conflicts are the pits, aren't they?"

"I don't think this is going to be one. But I just said it might, didn't I? Oh, I don't know. I'm sure it will be all right. I want this so badly. I spend all my free time looking at baby clothes and planning the nursery. What color do you think is best?"

"I'm sure you and Erik will figure it out."

Hanna had never heard such bitterness from Doris, whose manner had evolved from chilly to stormy. A simple reconnection with a friend had turned into a major emotional engagement. "Doris, what's wrong? You aren't being your usual self."

"It's you who's not like you used to be. It seems like you're oblivious to everyone else."

Was a twenty-minute delay really being oblivious? "That's unfair—you didn't give me a chance. So, what's happening with you?"

"Construction school is good. I've always liked carpentry. My boss has even given me extra responsibilities as if I'd graduated already. But the dorm is a dump run by martinets."

"So that last fight with your mother was really final?"

"I told you that two weeks ago."

Hanna felt a brief pang of guilt. Probably she should be more concerned. But her worries about Erik and adoption occupied all her capacity for concern just then. "Well, I'm sorry. Seems to me you had fights before where she was threatening to throw you out, and it didn't happen. It must be awful. But you're probably much better off to be away from her."

Doris said nothing.

Hanna didn't understand why the woman she'd once considered a sister had become a stranger.

HANNA STOOD NEXT to Erik at the base of the thirty-foot cliff that she'd last seen nearly four years ago. A solid aluminum ladder glistened in the sun.

Erik put his arm around her. "Not even the cockiest of the students I used to climb with ever attempted anything that steep without a rope."

She rested her head against his shoulder. "Maybe I'm mistaken."

He pointed upward. "There's the scar in the cliff. You came through for your friends when they needed you, Hanna."

They continued in silence to the summit and sat to admire the view. The sky was cloudless, the rocks warm in the August sun. A light breeze barely ruffled their hair. The moment would have been perfect except for one little thing. One that scarcely ever left her thoughts.

"Are you imagining a child sitting between us?" Erik asked after a minute.

Of course I am. She gave him her most adoring gaze, filling it to overflowing with love that she hoped would overwhelm all his doubts. "She was pretty scared by the ladder. But on your back she felt safe. I noticed she was holding on to you for dear life."

His eyes met hers steadily. "Your motherly instincts have been apparent for some time."

He'd never encouraged her like that. "I know it's hard. But I'm ready for it." She held her breath.

"I'm ready, too."

"Oh, Erik." She flung her arms around him. "I'll make it work for us, I promise."

"I'd always assumed I'd be a father. But after you told me your background, I decided that might be more social expectation than real desire. Then I wondered if fatherhood would even be compatible with my work. And adoption is emotionally challenging—I wasn't sure I could handle it. I didn't immediately grasp how much motherhood means to you."

He looked toward the peaks, as if they might reassure him. "We should get started soon. It's a long process."

"Shall we go then?" Hanna said, feeling mischievous.

"Das Jagdhaus, or Restaurant Allgäu? We may not have so many chances in the future for a romantic dinner."

"Hmm, that's a hard choice. I guess the Jagdhaus will be the most memorable."

Hanna hummed a nursery song as she skipped down the trail, her toes barely brushing the stones. At the bottom of the ladder, Erik put his hands on her shoulders and held her gently for a moment. "If I didn't know better, Hanna, I'd say you look like you'd just told me you were pregnant."

She smiled through tears. "My heart says there's a baby somewhere that's ours."

As much as she loved romantic dinners with her husband, her thoughts kept darting toward what lay ahead. During the past year she'd learned every nuance of the adoption process. She knew what to say when the social worker came around to interview them and inspect the house. It was all ready. Petra Klinger had guaranteed her a one-year leave of absence from the salon. She was tingling with anticipation.

Near midnight she closed her eyes once more, hoping for sleep this time.

As the floor trembled, a young mother grabbed her sleeping baby from the crib and rushed outside. But it was not an earthquake. A giant man with cowboy boots, spurs, and a broad-brimmed hat towered over her.

The woman started to run. But a thick ring of red ants, too wide to jump over, surrounded the house. As she looked for a way across, the ring grew wider. She couldn't possibly get across it without being eaten. She turned back to the house, which crashed into a pile of rubble as the man struck it with a huge belt.

She woke up screaming, drenched in sweat. Erik turned and cradled her, still half asleep. "What's wrong, darling?"

She knew he knew very well about her nightmares. But he always asked in the same solicitous way. "I'm sorry, Erik," she said when she was able to talk. "Oh god, it was awful. I'm still such a hopeless wreck. And I'm waking you up again."

"Dearest, I'm your husband." Erik was fully awake now. "We look out for each other."

He turned toward her, supporting himself by one elbow. "Tell me about it. That's always the best place to start."

"It was different from usual. There was a giant, but not really a monster. Like a cowboy, but huge." She paused and shook her head.

"It was trying to get my baby, Erik." Her voice caught. "I couldn't protect her. I tried to run, but there were these huge ants blocking me. I don't know what that means. But then the giant knocked the house down. With the crib inside." The horror hadn't faded. "Oh god, it was too scary."

She rose and went to the little sitting room of their vacation apartment. Erik disappeared into the kitchenette. A few minutes later he brought two cups of tea.

She squeezed his hand. His quiet presence soothed her, but she still felt tense and closed in. "Erik, maybe I'm not ready after all. I can't be this way and have a baby."

"When it's time you'll be ready."

"I hope you're right." She twisted the ends of her hair in her fingers. "I know what to do. I've talked to Mama, I have books, I've thought about nothing else for the last year. Things will go wrong, but we'll know how to deal with it. Won't we?"

Erik pulled her closer. "Honey, your life hasn't exactly been a simple highway through paradise. Yet you've always dealt with it. I don't know what you know. But I'm here."

Finally, she let him kiss her, slowly at first, and then with passion that melted the constricting chains her unknown enemies had left around her heart.

He stood and held her hand. "Maybe we ought to get a couple more hours of sleep?"

When she shut her eyes again, she dreamed of shopping for a plush musical toy to play the perfect tune. She just didn't know what that was.

HANNA STUMBLED BLEARY-EYED toward the wailing across the hall. After six months she was supposed to be able to sleep through the night, but so far it hadn't happened.

Gently rocking Elisabeth in one cradling arm, she started water heating and removed the already-mixed formula bottle from the refrigerator. A few minutes later the crying abruptly switched to rhythmic sucking sounds as they sat in the darkened living room. These were her special moments.

Sometimes she fantasized that she was breastfeeding, holding the bottle as close to her nipple as possible and feeling the tiny head warm against her skin. Logic told her that Elisabeth didn't care, but she did. This was as close as she would get to experiencing the reward that most women got after the travails of childbirth.

It was one of many defects in her body that she was grudgingly learning to accept. Women came in different models, and not all of the differences were visible. Sisterhood was part physiology and part existential essence.

After a burp, she laid the sleeping baby in her crib and crawled back into bed. She smiled as she noted that Erik hadn't moved. Probably he could've slept through the cries if they'd been in the same room.

But he dutifully did the feeding each evening. The moment Elisabeth went from being a stack of bureaucratic papers to a real, crying, gurgling baby, his attitude had changed dramatically. Maybe men could feel the connection too.

Erik's reference to pregnancy had been remarkably accurate: the week-old infant arrived in their home a little under ten months after their Oberstdorf hike. He hadn't complained through all the adoption administrivia and the chaos that followed. But he didn't disguise his pleasure at the prospect of a quiet dinner that evening at the Hoffmanns.

Hanna wasn't so sure. Her parents had been living near the Südheimerplatz, less than fifteen minutes' drive from their house, ever since Hermann's company opened a branch in Stuttgart. Gisela eagerly embraced babysitting duties, allowing Hanna to spend a few hours each week at her salon. But a quiet dinner seemed improbable.

Gisela dismissed her qualms. "Hanna, darling, I've been a mother, remember? Don't worry about it."

She took obvious delight in getting a few spoonsful of applesauce into her granddaughter while Hermann watched, thoroughly bemused. By seven-thirty Elisabeth was fast asleep on their bed. Hanna went to check on her just before dinner and reappeared a moment later, motioning excitedly. "Erik, come!"

She pointed with her free hand as she led him into the bedroom. "You know you cross your legs the same way when you're sleeping?"

In the dim light from the doorway Erik's face was a luminescent gem. He stood quite still for a moment. "Do you think I could kiss her? I mean, I don't want to wake her."

"She'll have far sweeter dreams if you do."

He leaned over the bed, his lips brushing Elisabeth's cheek as lightly as a butterfly's wings. And Hanna's heart fluttered in harmony.

The *Schweinebraten* had scarcely been passed around before Erik spoke, his softly glowing mien still evident in the bright dining room. "Elisabeth is now in the sixteenth percentile for weight, and twentieth for height. But her sleep time appears to be right on the median."

Hanna rolled her eyes. "Just try to remember to actually put the bottle of formula into the hot water. Setting it on the counter like you did last week doesn't do much."

"Ah, the joys of a baby." Gisela kept a perfectly straight face. "Erik is adjusting quite well. I doubt that Papa ever knew Elisabeth's weight."

Afterward the men retired to the living room. Gisela poured more coffee for Hanna and herself. "This wasn't a scene I imagined when you came looking for a room."

Hanna savored a long, slow sip. "If only I could remember it. It's been such a long, strange trip from the hospital, when I was so frightened. But even the bad parts made me stronger. This is what I imagined for so long. I only wish I could've been pregnant."

"The joys of pregnancy are often exaggerated."

"But that longing will always be part of me—I want so much to be a normal mother."

"No one who knows you would ever think you weren't a normal mother, Hanna. As 'normal' as any of us."

"I guess I'll always be insecure about it. I wish I still had my old friends to talk to. They did so much for me during that first year here."

"Doris never called you back?"

"Not since summer before last. And Annika's gone silent too."

"Keep trying to get in touch. I know how much they meant to you. It may be awkward, but the sooner you talk the sooner you'll find a solution."

Hanna said little as they drove home with their sleeping baby. Though she didn't have a real girlhood to tell her daughter about, at least she'd been a teenager. But those thoughts always led back to Doris, and the enigma of a treasured friendship that had been tarnished and perhaps forever lost.

She awakened that night from her recurring nightmare about a giant attacking her house to find Erik sound asleep beside her. She slipped silently from the bed and padded over to Elisabeth's room. Her daughter was lying on her side, the furry foot of her toy kitten clutched in her tiny hand. The house was idyllically peaceful.

Hanna crumpled onto the carpeted floor, crying quietly. She didn't know if the tears came from joy or fear. Perhaps both.

THE FOLLOWING SUNDAY would be Elisabeth's first visit to a *Weihnachtsmarkt*. Hanna wanted to run the last few blocks to the strains of music drifting through the evening chill. But the little bundle cradled in front of her prescribed a more modest pace. Its occupant peeked out from under a pink wool blanket covering her cozy sling, snug as a joey in its pouch.

Soon they were ambling past the brightly lit stalls, where the seasonal tunes brought visceral harmony to the dissonant tones in Hanna's life. She carefully described the wax pine cones and tiny carved trees.

Erik regarded the bundle solemnly. "You realize she's remembering what you're saying for about a quarter of a second."

She looked down. "Elisabeth, did you hear that? Are you going to stand by and take it without complaining?"

A wide-eyed round face looked up and giggled.

Elisabeth contentedly sucked on a bottle while Hanna held their *Glühwein* and Erik fed her bites of *Bratwurst*. Closing her eyes, she imagined she was twelve, enthralled by the beguiling pull of mysterious memories dwelling in the very air she breathed.

The sound of a voice behind her made her jump a little. "Hallo, Frau Hoffmann." The face she saw on turning around was familiar, but she couldn't place it.

"Werner Jendrossek, and this is my wife Sophie." He smiled. "You probably don't remember me from the airport. You were a little nervous when I gave you that plaque."

"*You?* Oh my god, you remember me—I can't believe it—how nice of you. But wait—Jendrossek is the name of the chief of police in Waldenheim, too. You wouldn't be related?"

"One and the same. I joined the department just a few months after you came. But I left last year. Now I'm a private detective here in Stuttgart."

After Hanna controlled her astonishment and the spouses were introduced, she grew serious.

"Herr Jendrossek, do you mind if I ask you something? I've always wondered— after all, my friends *did* attack that man Zwiebel and his gang. But you ignored it."

"They got what they deserved. Indeed a law-abiding society can't tolerate vigilantism. But it also needs justice. You would've been hurt if they hadn't been stopped."

She looked at Elisabeth, now fast asleep. "I felt as if you were looking out for me."

"There's some truth to that. As a diver in the German Navy, I was a team commander in a lot of NATO exercises. Your cousin Richard Shelby had a similar position on the American side. Just before you came here, he told me about what happened to you, and asked if there was anything I could do."

She was grateful that Erik immediately asked him something about diving. She was following a fragile tether through the lonely depths of space to someone who had lent her silent support when she needed it the most. Her mother had only told her that she had a cousin who'd been nice to her. Yet another labyrinthine chamber in her opaque and perilous past.

"Hanna, here's my business card. You never know when you might need a good detective."

She tumbled back to earth. After that she had to ask another question. "So, when you said the embassy had contacted you, and the agents together made up that plaque—it was really just you?"

"It was really just your cousin. All I did was get it made, in a language you could understand. And become a border control agent for a day."

The enormity of his last sentence was too great for her to respond with anything more than a gaping mouth. He smiled slightly. "At some point I decided diving was too dangerous and went into the military police. The Immigration Office was quite accommodating to my request."

They said goodbye and sauntered on, holding hands tightly, Elisabeth dreaming, perhaps, of soft white Christmas lights and a kitten in her lap.

The next morning Hanna had to take her daughter to a checkup. Erik needed the car, but she didn't mind. She was actually looking forward to the walk to the train station in pleasant weather. Along the way they passed a construction site with a pair of sawhorses in front of the house. She shielded her eyes as a wave of anxiety hit her, and put all her thoughts on her child.

The sawhorses were still there when she returned. Her pelvis began to throb. At bedtime, every time she closed her eyes she saw the sawhorse being pushed under her. After some fitful sleep she awoke in pain so strong that she nearly cried out.

In the morning she knocked on the door. Doris answered, a carpenter's belt sagging around her waist. A flash of shock was replaced by a blank stare.

"Can I help you?"

A thousand thoughts and images raced through Hanna's mind, jumbled and incoherent, but her tongue—and her emotions—were frozen as if she'd glimpsed Medusa. The visage confronting her denied their entire friendship and invited no questions.

She finally decided to answer as if Doris was a stranger—which she effectively was. "Could you possibly keep your sawhorses inside the house?"

"I'm sorry we've disturbed you. Let me talk to the boss."

A minute later she came back. "There's no place inside for them."

Hanna swallowed hard. "Can you cover them with a tarp?"

"We need to have them available. Delays cost money."

"Doris, you know how much those things affect me. I know I told you."

"Look, I'm not the boss. Thanks to some rumormonger who apparently doesn't like lesbians, I've been demoted from that track. And I don't see any reason to go out of my way for your convenience. Just look the other way."

Hanna stood motionless for several seconds. Then she shook with unrestrained fury. "You stupid cow! How could you do this to me? You're as bad as Staunton."

She grabbed the doorknob and slammed the door with all her might. The tightness of panic clutching her chest and throat was so strong she wondered if she was having a heart attack. But she dismissed that fancy quickly.

This was merely another demon.

One she had some responsibility for. And no idea what to do about.

HANNA PUT DOWN her empty coffee cup. The lazy Christmas morning mood matched the stillness outside. The tree cast a relaxing charm from the corner, with no sign left of the gifts. Elisabeth's present from Hanna's parents, a black panther half as big as she was, had been firmly clutched in her arms as she went to sleep in Gisela's lap.

Each day normally left the living room in a debacle of rockers, dangling colored cutouts and music boxes. But Hanna always restored the space to immaculate order before dinner. When Erik offered to help after last night's elaborate feast, she shook her head. "Your job is playing with Elisabeth whenever you're here. And when the next one comes this summer you'll be really busy." This timing was pure hope. She'd learned from experience how difficult the process was.

"Doesn't all the housework get a little overwhelming at times?"

She shrugged. "This is what I wanted, Erik. A nest with beautiful children, an adorable husband who understands me, and a job where I can be helpful. That was my dream. What more could I ask for?"

"What if they get the impression that women are better at changing diapers?"

"When they get older, you can teach them to do the dishes. And laundry. And definitely vacuuming."

She paused. "Maybe cooking too."

As Erik smiled faintly, she put her arms around his waist from behind, resting her chin on his shoulder. "And I wouldn't mind at all if you made me another cup of coffee. For just the two of us."

This morning, the warmth of her freshly baked *Kranzkuchen* contrasted with the chilly scene outside. Silent friendly ghosts in fresh white dresses had taken the places of the trees, guarding each tiny yard.

She wanted to be forever cocooned by the comforting solace of this domestic idyll. Six years ago, after being adopted into her real family, she'd come as an immigrant to her own land. She was finally where she belonged.

And yet she wasn't. Why couldn't she learn so much as a word of English? In the milieu of her husband's friends and relatives this was especially embarrassing. And didn't she have a right to it? Maybe it was the language of the people who'd rejected her, but it was her language, too. They shouldn't be able to take a part of her away.

With Dr. Meissner's help she'd come to realize that William Staunton wasn't the only trauma in her life. Then she'd turned to her husband and family, hoping their unconditional acceptance would erase those obstinate barriers. But even as the seed of love had grown from fearful phantom to a luxuriant tree, another family of anxieties and nightmares persisted under its roots.

She could continue to deny its existence. "Erik, Elisabeth will wake up soon. What if I bundle her up and we take a little walk in the snow? It looks so beautiful."

"Well, it certainly will be when you go out in it."

Hanna looked aside and hid her smile. She could never decide which Erik she prized more: the suave, sarcastic physics professor and musician, or the hopelessly sappy and playful husband and lover. There seemed to be no other tones.

What more could I ask for? An answer to a very simple question: What was back there that still wields such power over me today?

Intuition told her that unknown past held the answers to how to become whole. Something still had a hold on her—or was she holding onto it?—that kept her from that wholeness. The scars on her back weren't the only ones. But could she truly know her real self? What would happen if she did?

She wanted the answers. She didn't want to face what it might demand of her to get them.

PART 3:
THE REAL ME

With the shyness of a small child
and the wisdom of a sage
I tell you now
there is no reason to be afraid

Kate Wolf, "Brother Warrior"

CHAPTER 21

Friday, 12 April 1985, Vaihingen

THE DOUR, CLIPPED tone of her daughter's second-grade teacher on Hanna's answering machine yesterday had been like a layer of frost on the promising spring evening. She arrived ten minutes early for the meeting the next morning.

The woman's expression was somber. "Elisabeth has been sullen and uncooperative for several days. But yesterday she was involved in a fight. This is, of course, a very serious matter."

Hanna waited. She was all too aware of Elisabeth's recent behavior.

"Neither of them would talk about it. But her anti-social behavior has coincided with an assignment to discuss family origins in class."

Hanna promised to resolve the issue promptly. But Elisabeth steadfastly refused to say a word about it. In the middle of dinner, she ran from the table after loudly asserting that the food was disgusting.

Erik sighed. "It's painful to say, but this is exactly what I was worried about."

Hanna could almost feel a rise in her blood pressure. Hadn't this argument been settled nine years ago? "In other words, 'I told you so.'"

"You said that, not I. But yes, I did. Adoption is noble, but it's fraught with emotional landmines. It appears we've stumbled upon one."

"Just remember I wouldn't be here if it weren't for adoption."

Erik stood up. "Come on, that's not the same and you know it."

"Oh, it isn't? Because I wasn't a child then—officially anyway?"

"It won't help to talk about that. It's Elisabeth's reaction that we have to deal with now."

"That's right. So, it would be nice if you could be helpful."

Without answering, he turned away and disappeared into his study. She called her mother. "Mama, what is this about? He's been so good with the kids. And I thought he'd gotten over his dislike of adoption before we started. But tonight, he wouldn't even talk about it."

"Adoptees tend to focus on the mother when they grieve for their loss. Maybe Erik is simply feeling left out."

"Gee thanks, that makes things *lots* simpler. How am I going to change that?" She put down the phone, suddenly feeling a flood of grief of her own.

Elisabeth and her brother Richard, who'd come three years later, were raised knowing they were adopted. Hanna had read them stacks of reassuring books. But what about her?

Sometimes, especially at Christmas when the tree was all decorated, she wondered about the couple who'd brought her into the world. She always put the thought out as if it were a rat in the kitchen. Tonight was different.

She called her mother again. "Mama, tell me again what you know about my biological parents."

"You didn't tell us much. You read us a letter that said they couldn't accept you. It was clearly very painful for you. Dr. Feinstein said you spoke to him about a probable childhood trauma, but you couldn't remember it even then."

Clearly, she wasn't going to remember it now. But the thought of that rejection squeezed her mind like a vise.

She struggled through each day, pushing a grouchy daughter to do homework, trying to stay cheery for Richard. She lived in constant fear of making a mistake with a customer.

Erik was no help. He began to work late, sometimes coming home as dinner was nearly over. He'd never done that before. Their cheery house began to resemble a funeral home.

Maybe that other trauma that kept snuffling around the edge of her consciousness like a bear in a dark campground had been even worse than she'd imagined. There was so much she didn't know about herself. Could it have been her fault that they'd rejected her? She must have disappointed them badly.

Everything she lived for was threatening to collapse. Her daughter hated her, her husband resented her. Sleep had become a scarcity. She clung to her work: if she messed up there, her reputation would be gone and that would be the end. But what did work matter if she wasn't a good wife and mother? Then who was she?

And how could she help Elisabeth feel accepted if *she* wasn't?

On the last Friday of April she woke up after two hours, barely able to breathe. In her dream, a panel of female judges, led by Frauke Zwiebel, had sentenced her to death for being a traitorous spy. The symbolism was overwhelming. Her bedroom seemed like an oppressive prison. Anxiety often veiled her life, but this was like a shroud.

She lay awake till early morning. Then she threw a few things into an overnight bag, including her slip-on walking shoes, and prepared breakfast. Before leaving for work she placed a note on the kitchen table.

Don't worry about me. I'll be back soon, I promise. I'm not sure when.

At three in the afternoon she was on the train for Oberstdorf.

IT WAS COLD and rainy when she checked into the first hotel she encountered after leaving the station. Room wasn't a problem—this was hardly a season for tourists. She got her nightgown on and fell onto the bed, exhausted and emotionally numb.

At breakfast, guilt over her horrendously irresponsible action mixed with weary relief at distancing herself from her troubles. Afterward, she pulled the shoes on and started up the broad trail that paralleled the cable car. She had to be careful. There was now a little fresh snow on top of the old icy patches. But she needed answers. Maybe the mountain had one.

Of course, she wished that the horror hadn't happened. She wished her body weren't so scarred. Or her mind. But was her life before it any better? She was scarred regardless of Staunton, assaulted by an entire society. She still couldn't speak English, or remember even a single scene before the hotel bedroom. And if her ordeal at the trial hadn't changed that, his arrest wasn't likely to, either.

She wanted to belong. But where?

A big part of the reason Elisabeth was miserable was because adoption made her stand out from her friends. She didn't want to be different. She wanted to fit in and be normal, like the other girls.

Just like her mother.

To the left, the crashing of snowmelt and rainwater down the boulder-strewn creek competed with the voice in her head, and she turned off on a small trail toward it. She picked her way carefully along the slippery rocky track next to the stream, occasionally showered by icy spray. Her shoes were sodden.

After a long scramble she came to a bridge. The chaotic cataract thundered over a small cliff above, vanished underneath, and crashed into billowing clouds on the rocks below. Hanna was mesmerized. For a while she was aware of nothing but the implacable power of nature.

When it began snowing, she realized she couldn't feel her feet anymore. A silent whisper, a ripple spreading on the motionless pool above her buried memories, told her this had happened before. Yet here she was, alive, with two good feet. Someone must have saved her.

Or maybe she'd saved herself.

She had parents who loved her, who'd stood by her through everything, no matter how weak and foolish she was.

A mother who'd never stopped believing in her recovery from the brink of death, who knew how to sing in the face of the devil.

A sister whose love had always bridged the faintly fractured wrinkle of time between them.

And a family. One she needed at that moment even more than they needed her.

She'd also had friends who'd accepted her as one of their own when she first came, alone and vulnerable, to this unfamiliar country. But she'd offended and lost them.

She started back. She could save herself again.

She wouldn't know her place in the world, where *she* belonged, until she confronted those unknown demons, and she would continue to be tormented until she did. How to do it was still a mystery. But she now knew how to get started. The insight was so simple—how could she possibly not have thought of it before? She turned and nearly ran back down the slippery trail, falling almost immediately, skinning her shins, oblivious to the pain.

It was Elisabeth Hoffmann who had made Hanna's new life possible. Now she could repay that debt. The rest of the world would always see her daughter as different. But through *Tante* Elisabeth that difference could become a special pride.

She wasn't dressed for the snow that was blowing thickly around her. Her wooden feet barely supported her, and she was shivering vigorously. She almost missed the fork in the trail. But even back on the road, each step was a struggle with the ice under the snow. Speed was essential as the wind picked up, but a fall could be her last. She hadn't seen another soul since leaving the town.

She wanted desperately to lie down and rest for a few minutes. The shivering intensified. That was a sign of hypothermia, and hypothermia clouded judgment.

Is there any sense in going on? Yes, I said to myself, summoning all my strength, you must keep going. Here you'll die. Juliane Koepcke's resolution murmured in the wind, a reassuring rhythm under its increasingly frenetic melody. She held onto its steadying strength.

Perhaps the widening of the narrow canyon was only an hallucination. No, there was the cable car base tower, vanishing a moment later into a solid white void. The path scarcely disturbed the featureless expanse of drifting snow. There was the switchback—or was it? If she was wrong she would never make it back alive.

You have a few more steps to go. Just a few more to the end. Don't give up now. Snatches of villainy from the courtroom mixed with Erik's witty endearments and her children's laughter. She could always take one more step.

Finally, her frozen feet felt the solid thud of pavement. Houses with people were only a few hundred meters further. After that came deserted intersections where she had to trust pure instinct. Then she was peeling away her soggy clothing, slowly sinking into the steaming bathtub, embracing the needles in her feet, grateful to the universe for giving back her life.

Making up with her family would be mortifying, but manageable. She had all the love it would need. Confidence was flowing into her veins along with the warmth of the water. She called home and got the answering machine. Probably they were out frantically looking for her. She left a message saying she would be back before bedtime.

She returned to what seemed to be an empty house. But on the table in the living room was an exquisite arrangement of Rohschinken, Emmentaler, Gravlax, capers, pickles, Schwarzbrot, and two glasses of Riesling.

Hanna stared open-mouthed at the tableau. A moment later Erik entered the room. Without speaking he guided her to the sofa and hugged her as if she'd been gone a year.

"I'm sorry, honey," he said.

She buried her face on his shoulder and wept with relief and gratitude.

Finally, she sat up. "You may forgive me. But Elisabeth won't be so easy."

"I think you'll find she understands more than you imagine. Last night I went into her bedroom to say goodnight and try to comfort her. Most of her stuffed animals were in the corner, as usual. But the little dolphin that I got her on my last trip was in her hand."

He laughed softly. "She still crosses her legs as I do, you know." Then he turned to face her directly. "She thanked me for it, which she hadn't before. And at that moment I understood that I was a real father."

With great effort Hanna suppressed more tears and smiled.

She learned that the children were with their grandparents. After relaxing with the hors d'oeuvres, she kissed Erik and went to her small room on the top floor. From her desk drawer she selected a greeting card with a lilac background. For a brief moment she wondered if her daughter would understand her plan. *She will if she sees your love.*

> *Dear Elisabeth,*
>
> *Your mom tells me you are enjoying second grade and doing great work. I'm so pleased for you!*
>
> *I want you to know how happy I am that you're with my sister and her husband. They're going to give you so much love forever and ever. I'm so proud they gave you my name!*
>
> *I know you're much too old for children's nighttime songs, but I asked your mom to make this tape for you. That song is special because it's the one your grandma sang when your mom was hurt. It helped her live.*
>
> *And you can always wear the pendant, and think of the three families that have been joined together to make one gem.*
>
> *With tons of love,*
> *Tante Elisabeth*

She'd found the perfect pendant in the jewelry shop near the train station. All she had to do now was to make the recording. She hung the photo of Elisabeth in the Nutcracker costume, the one she'd taken from Gisela, above her daughter's bed. She placed the envelope with the card on the pillow, and the tape on the bedside stand. She held onto the little box with its tiny bow.

The children were absolutely quiet when she and Erik picked them up. Nothing was said about Hanna's escapade. But when she came to say goodnight to Elisabeth, her daughter had already opened the envelope and was putting the tape into her cassette player.

Der Mond ist aufgegangen	*The evening moon has risen,*
Die goldnen Sternlein prangen	*the golden stars are shining*
Am Himmel hell und klar;	*in the heavens bright and clear*
Der Wald steht schwarz und schweiget,	*the forest stands black and silent*
Und aus den Wiesen steiget	*and from the meadow rises*
Der weisse Nebel wunderbar.	*a wonderful white mist.*

"You never told me that *Oma* sang that song to you in the hospital."

"It's hard for me to talk about that time. I learned that I'd lost something, but I didn't know what."

"That's right, you were adopted, too, weren't you? Do you miss your mother who gave birth to you?"

Hanna had prepared for this. "Because of my injury I don't know anything about her, honey. But I'm sure she loves me, just like yours loves you."

Hanna handed her the package. Elisabeth unwrapped it eagerly. She put the tiny heart-shaped pendant, with its triangle of amethyst, garnet and iridescent pearl, against her neck.

She smiled as she hadn't done in weeks. "Thank you, Mama."

"Goodnight, honey. Sweet dreams."

"Goodnight, Mama. I love you."

When Hanna came home from work a few days later, Gisela had brought the children to her house already. Elisabeth wasn't containing her excitement. She spread some papers on the floor.

"Mama, look, I made some pictures. And I wrote a story to go with them. Here's one of me and my other mommy. And this is Oma and you—when you were my age, see? And now in this one we're all together—Papa and Opa too. That's what the story is about."

Hanna knelt down to read the story.

Once there was a little girl who was all alone. She cried a lot. But a good fairy found her and took her to a mommy and daddy whose child had died. The girl grew up and they were very happy.

The child who had died came back to earth, because she was sad and she wanted to be with her parents. But she was accidentally put into the wrong tummy. Her mommy who gave birth to her realized this and gave her to the little girl who wasn't little anymore.

Now she had both a mommy and daddy again, and they all lived happily ever after.

The End.

"Mama, you're crying again! It's supposed to be a happy story."

"It is, darling, grown-ups are just strange, aren't they? I've never been so happy in my life." She hugged Elisabeth, who ran to her bedroom with characteristic eight-year-old energy.

Hanna made coffee and found some left-over cake in the refrigerator. She and her mother hadn't talked privately since her improvident venture. It was awkward, but plunging in directly was probably the best option. "I could've acted more maturely, I'm sure. Motherhood doesn't come with an instruction manual, unfortunately."

"Indeed, we learn on the job."

"Yes, but that whole thing brought up so many issues for me, that I've obviously not dealt with." She sighed deeply. "This is the first time I can think of that it hurt someone else."

"When you first came here, you depended on Doris Giesselmann and her friends a lot. I know you had a problem with Doris. But have you thought of reaching out again?"

Have I thought of it? Only at every child-raising crisis, when she longed to talk to them, let her guard down, drink a beer, cry with them. They'd been like sisters—who could've been with her, if she hadn't been so thoughtless with Doris.

"It's something I should've done long ago."

It would also give her courage to face all the other demons she'd ignored.

She filled the two cups again. "Werner Jendrossek, the old police chief in Waldenheim, is a detective now. Maybe he could help."

Gisela stirred milk into her coffee before speaking. "Hanna, as you well know, I kept many things back because of what happened in the hospital. Even after the trial, Doctor Beattie and I agreed that memories from before the assault were potentially dangerous. Then you got married and seemed so content, I felt maybe it was better to simply not disturb you."

She took a slow sip. "So, I hope you'll forgive me for not telling you sooner that Werner and your cousin were responsible for your coming to our house in Boulder."

She put a hand up, as if that could halt Hanna's heart-stopping astonishment, and told the story. "I have his letters at home, of course. But I can tell you what the last one says. *Your mother relayed the sad news to me. I don't know when you will either read or hear these words. But when you do, I want you to realize that courage to overcome adversity grows from hard experience. You've passed that test once. As more come, you'll know how to meet them.*"

Werner's cryptic comments seven years ago had just taken on a whole new dimension. Hanna was staring at the window, seeing far beyond it, searching for words that weren't there. "I should write to him. But I don't think I'm ready. Or worthy."

The next demon in line was clear. She called Werner. "You said a long time ago I might need a good detective someday. Well, you were right." She described her final interaction with Doris. "Without doubt I was a selfish clod. But I don't know what to do now. The 'demotion' thing needs your expertise."

His voice embodied quintessential professionalism. "Certainly. Give me two weeks."

The journey of a thousand miles no longer seemed quite so impossible.

TWO WEEKS LATER, she left work at two-thirty, though the meeting she'd arranged at the detective's suggestion wasn't till three. Maybe a little walk would quell the nausea that threatened to overwhelm her.

It had seemed so simple in his office. Doris's cryptic comment had come soon after she'd received a formal reprimand at work—on a project owned by Volker Zwiebel. A complaint had been lodged that she'd made offensive advances toward another woman. Two people had reportedly witnessed it.

Jendrossek hadn't been surprised to find that the complaints were entirely fabricated.

He'd discovered this using what he called "unorthodox methods." He didn't elaborate. He'd said only that his involvement couldn't be disclosed. But he had a plan through which she could exonerate her friend. A plan that involved her telling a complete stranger a story about those letters that was also entirely fabricated.

Now, as she stood on the corner watching the traffic light cycle through its colors, it no longer seemed simple. In fact, it seemed frightening beyond comprehension, almost like another attack.

The mere mention of Zwiebel's name had elicited a surge of loathing. She wasn't afraid of him as much as she despised him. Though he'd become a political bigshot now—chairman of the state section of the neo-Nazi NPD—she considered him a coward. But Karl Künstler, his lawyer friend who'd submitted the complaints, was a former Gestapo agent.

What would she say if he challenged her? Which he surely would.

Ten minutes to three. She was almost late. Her subconscious was obviously desperate to avoid meeting him.

The man she found at a table near the back of the café was probably in his sixties, tall with a prominent belly and a completely bald pate. Superficially he looked affable, but the gray eyes behind his wire-rimmed spectacles were as hard as diamonds.

"Herr Künstler?"

She didn't wait for an answer. The way he looked at her, as if she were a piece of dreck, was introduction enough. "My name is Hanna Hoffmann-Schoenberg. I'm a hairstylist. A customer at my salon recently started work in the *Arbeitsamt*, where Doris Giesselmann's personnel data are filed. As I'm sure you'll recall, you brought some complaint letters to that office several years ago, which led to a reprimand. It severely hurt her career."

She took a deep breath. "My customer, who is a friend of Doris's from school, has discovered that the letters are fakes, and she wants to erase this injustice. She asked me for help because she remembered the report of my being harassed by Volker Zwiebel in Waldenheim. I suspect you're also aware of that."

Hanna felt as if rivulets of sweat were running off her hands. But she planted them in her lap. She wouldn't be seen fidgeting in front of this living ice sculpture.

"She'd prefer a quiet settlement—she doesn't want to make waves in her new job. All you have to do is send a statement to them, saying that you've just discovered that the complaints were erroneous, and should be withdrawn. You needn't admit knowledge of fraud."

Künstler's dismissive sneer hadn't changed. "This is a fascinating story. Is there any reason that I should believe a word of it?"

"I think trouble could arise for you eventually if you don't."

He leaned back and smiled without a trace of humor. "Frau Hoffman-Schoenberg, you're quite tall. Close to two meters?"

She flinched, realizing without thinking about it what was probably coming. "Excuse me, what does my height have to do with what I just said?"

"The probability of a woman being that tall is extremely small. And with a voice that is not, if I may say so, a model of femininity. You mentioned the word 'fraud' a moment ago. I wonder who is the purveyor of fraud here."

She had no doubt that some people entertained such thoughts about her, unvoiced. She typically tried to compensate with a meek, hyper-feminine presentation. But in that moment her gut took over. She sprang to her feet, leaned across the table, and slapped him soundly.

"Herr Künstler, if the *Arbeitsamt* doesn't receive the retraction within the next two weeks, copies of those letters will be sent to the director along with the analysis that I described. And he will know who prepared them."

Künstler actually looked rattled. He didn't even straighten the glasses that she'd knocked askew.

She strode to the door, then stopped and turned. "My customer and I only want justice for Frau Giesselmann."

HANNA LEFT THE café with a slight tremble in her hands, her thoughts stilled by the rush of adrenaline. Not until she approached the *U-Bahn* platform did the enormity of what she'd just done percolate into her consciousness. She'd finally stood up to one of the bullies with no help from anyone—and it had worked. Well, she hoped it had. Anyway she'd survived, and was none the worse for it besides a little extra perspiration on her blouse. That would have to go straight into the laundry.

By the time she left the station in Vaihingen, a few doubts were creeping back. She wondered if she'd actually put herself in danger. *Could that black BMW parked by itself be a threat? Nonsense, that's silly.*

When the door opened in front of her, and a man jumped out and pushed her in, she told herself not to panic. But then a large hand closed around her left wrist, pulling it behind her back as her head crashed into the driver's headrest.

He might as well have placed a red-hot manacle on her wrist. Every nerve burned as it had from the shoelaces. And she knew that if he got her other hand, she would never escape.

She stomped blindly down on the floor as if stamping out a fire. She felt a toe, and he grunted and lost his grip on her wrist. She twisted and jammed the fingers of both hands toward his eyes. The attacker yelled. She'd hit home. He was holding his face with both hands.

She punched him in the groin. But he would surely recover—soon. For what seemed like ages, though it could only have been milliseconds, she considered her options. She'd heard the heavy click of the door lock, and finding the latch would take time.

Already she felt the car accelerating.

With every gram of force she could muster, she slammed her right hand into the middle of the window. She wondered why glass didn't cut her belly as she scrambled through the hole.

She remembered to tuck her head toward her chest as she hit the pavement, skidding forward, shredding clothing and skin. She felt the sticky blood in her hand and on her back. But she was out of the car, which she could vaguely hear roaring away far down the street.

Someone was standing over her. "Are you alive? My husband called the police. Oh god, are you all right?"

"I'm fine. Thank you."

The woman tore a piece of her dress and wrapped it around her hand. "You're going to be okay, I'm sure. You were brave. They'll be here soon. Don't worry."

Hanna wasn't really worrying. Probably she should be. But she was just happy to be free.

Listening to the inflectionless patter of the ambulance technicians, she passed out.

CHAPTER 22

SCENES FROM HER previous hospital stay filtered through groggy eyes as Hanna tried to make sense of the high steel-framed bed, vital signs monitor, and nurse hovering in the background. But why were her children there?

Richard jumped up and down, his face radiant. "Mama, you're so strong. You're like Superwoman!"

Then she remembered her frantic jump from the car. "Honey, I'm afraid I don't feel much like Superwoman right now. But thank you."

Elisabeth carefully held her bandaged hand. "Mama, you scared us. Promise me you won't leave us, please?"

The last vestiges of her disorientation faded. "Elisabeth, whatever I do, I won't leave you, ever."

Then she saw Doris at the foot of the bed, grinning from ear to ear. Annika and Clara were behind her. "Silly goose, don't you know enough not to jump out of a moving car?"

"I'm sorry, Doris." She'd never imagined that Doris's voice could be so musical. Nor that her attempted reunion would happen in a hospital.

"Your courage is the best apology ever. Who could've known what a hornet's nest we'd stir up with that man?"

"That man . . . ? Oh, Zwiebel, of course. But I couldn't figure out—how did he find out about you being a lesbian?"

"I'd love to know that. But he didn't win in the end. This incident is all over the news tonight. It'll be traced back to Künstler, whose fake complaints will be uncovered, and Zwiebel won't be able to hide his connection."

Hanna lifted her uninjured hand. "I'm sorry I can't hug you."

But it was Erik who took her hand. "I do wish you'd let me know before you go on another top-secret spy mission, honey. Maybe I could at least stock up on some extra bandages."

Her previous hospital room was a mixed memory—she'd gotten out okay, but not without a lot of pain. This felt like a haven of healing. "I'm so happy to have all of you. I only wish my parents were here."

Then she felt a pair of hands on her shoulders. Hands she knew instantly from the strength of their delicate touch. "I didn't want to get in the way of these strong youngsters, dear."

"Oh god, Mama. You're the worst comedian. You'll always be the strongest of us."

"I can attest to the truth of both of those statements," Hermann's deep voice sounded behind her.

"Hanna, do you know what a 'mitzvah' is?"

Clara was wearing the same necklace she'd worn when they met fourteen years before. The Star of David, inside a circle of tiny birds.

"I do, but why are you asking me?"

"I want you to come talk at my schul. Show the children an example of what courage really is. How you've overcome unimaginable trauma despite the odds. Really, you should be a teacher, Hanna."

"That makes me feel ignorant. I didn't realize there was even a schul here."

"It's not large, but we make up for it with feeling."

"It would be very humbling to do that, Clara."

As sleep crept in on the lullaby of soothing voices, the Marienhospital Stuttgart faded into Denver General. Dr. Beattie and Dr. Lamola mingled with her family and German friends. Her sister was there, excitedly describing student teaching at Stanford University. But outside an angry crowd in cowboy hats was yelling her name, and when she jerked awake, she thought she was in the hotel in Oberstdorf, still half-frozen.

Good or bad, her dreams would not stay buried. She could only follow them until she found their source.

A MONTH LATER she gave the talk to a group of eager children. Their questions spawned a greater number of her own. A nebulous portent was nagging at her psyche, pecking like a baby chick eager to be born. The melting spring snows of Oberstdorf had exposed yet another fleeting glimpse of that opaque past, dark as the night, shining out of reach.

The next day she removed the bandages, remembering finally being rid of the pressure garments thirteen years ago. She looked at her back in the bathroom mirror. Nothing much had changed. The assault had given her a sort of superimmunity, like Mithridates. Maybe Richard was onto something with his superhero comment. She let her hair drift across her face and tossed it back sassily with a sharp laugh.

Tomorrow was the first Monday after the summer solstice. She'd planned a walk and picnic in the woods with her family as a celebration of her complete recovery. But shortly after dinner, Erik informed her that he couldn't go. "A new laser system has come in, and the students won't rest till it's working."

On Sunday evening he's just learned this? But she suppressed her anger. It wasn't the first time he'd been absent-minded.

Then she had an idea. She knew the science teacher at Elisabeth's school wished the parents paid more attention to their children's education. He would probably love to have her take some of the pupils to visit a real laboratory after classes. And Erik wouldn't dare say no to her now.

And maybe she might learn more about what Clara had seen in her.

After school Hanna shepherded her charge of six second-grade pupils into her husband's laboratory. They donned protective laser glasses on their intensely earnest faces while she sternly warned them about the danger of not following instructions. Inside the windowless laser room, a student stood behind the optical table with its myriad of mirrors and lenses. His explanations left the seven-year-olds silent and awestruck.

She pointed to a rack of gray metal boxes. Some sported red LED displays, but others had large black knobs and white dials with red needles.

"What do these do?"

"Ah, those are the electronics. That's where we get the actual data. I mean, they measure the results of what the lasers do."

"The laser beams are pretty. But can you tell us the point, in just a few words?"

The student pointed to a fingernail-sized bluish chip. "This is a type of silicon, the stuff that computers use. When free electrons are excited by light—"

"That's enough for our level, thanks. This is awesome. But, Erik, you know there is one thing missing."

He waited for her to continue.

"There are no women in your group."

"Nor in the entire department. And I wish it weren't so. But I'm a university professor, not a school teacher. It's hard for me to affect that."

"Well, you should come visit elementary schools and show the girls what they could do." Even as she said it, she realized the incongruity. He was a man. They needed to see a woman in his position.

As she drove the children back, she was inundated with questions. With an academic education that ended with a vocational school for hairstyling, she wasn't well prepared to explain lasers to children.

But she wanted to.

She couldn't put these thoughts out of her mind as she went through the routine domestic chores that she always saved for her day off. She'd been to her husband's lab before. Why hadn't those instruments grabbed her attention then?

Maybe it wasn't the instruments so much as it was the children.

Or maybe it was the two together.

She was so distracted that she nearly burnt the *Schnitzel*. Before starting Richard's bedtime routine, she put a cherry *Streuselkuchen* in the oven and left strict instructions with Erik to remove it in twenty minutes if she wasn't back. He wouldn't forget that—it was one of his favorites.

Finally, she joined him on the balcony, where he'd set out the coffeepot and two cups alongside the dessert plates. The warmth of the day lingered after dark, and she turned the fan on.

"Hanna, I'm trying to imagine one other woman in this country who would think of bringing half a dozen seven-year-olds to visit a university physics lab. And then keep them from destroying anything. So far I'm coming up blank."

"Well, you get the medal for letting me. But honestly, Erik, didn't you see the light in their eyes? It was brighter than any of your laser beams."

"The next thing I hear, you're going to want some of those instruments for them. I'm not sure about the safety procedures for light sabers in elementary schools, though."

"I'll settle for the flashing blue light above the door outside your lab. That was cool."

She looked over the familiar tableau of housetops and trees. She didn't have everything. And tonight, she knew clearly what was missing.

Something that came straight from the other Elisabeth—and before her.

"Erik, do you think I could pass the *Abitur*?" Instantly she wanted to take it back.

"Of course. The *Volkshochschule* has preparatory courses just like you took before. You could finish in a year easily. But why do you want it?"

"I want to be a chemistry teacher."

Even in the dim light Hanna could see Erik's posture had tensed up. Now it slowly relaxed as she continued. "Second graders like you saw today are so full of enthusiasm. But then the girls lose it when they reach adolescence. It would be so fantastic to bring *them* into your lab. It's totally crazy, I know. I love what I do, and I'm good at it. Why would I leave it? And with two children to care for? The whole idea is insane."

She shook her head, as if to answer her questions. "But something is pulling me. Maybe someone like me could inspire them to follow their dreams. What do you think?"

"What I think is that you're the girl who is following your dream. I don't know what you saw in my lab instruments. But I saw what was in your eyes: You put children, gadgets, and curiosity together, and something was awakened. And it's not going back to sleep."

"You'll regret this—I'll be coming to you for help with the math all the time."

"Hanna, your tenacity was a part of what kept me there when you tried to break things off, almost exactly ten years ago. I knew you had a lot of demons to fight. And I felt it would be a privilege to be there with you."

He finished the last sip of his coffee.

"I know you're not done with the demons. And college chemistry will be hard. But not as hard as what you've already done."

"So, you really think it's okay for me to give my notice tomorrow? My god, what am I doing? It feels I'm like jumping into a hurricane."

"Well, maybe just a cyclone."

"Oh, yes, much better."

THREE MONTHS LATER, she said her final tearful goodbyes to Petra Klinger and her colleagues in the salon where she'd worked through all her adult life—engagement and marriage, the birth of two children, her life as a mother.

She'd left a home. She had to believe she would find another that meant as much.

Doris, Annika, and Clara met her at a nearby café. Over coffee and cake they chattered about the past, soaking in the pool of friendships forged through the odyssey that their leader had set out on long ago. The future was fraught with uncertainty. Doris had just become managing director of her firm. Clara had won her first political race and was on the city council. Only Annika seemed content—she was determined to work for Clara, no matter what the job.

Doris, who still had to return to Augsburg that evening, accompanied her to the subway. "Hanna, we've been through a lot together."

"I can't imagine my life without you. And I was such a bitch to you."

"Stop apologizing. Let's look to the future. It's thanks to you that no one at work can say a thing about who I sleep with now. And you'll have such a great time in college. You're absolutely meant for it."

"It's going to be so hard. I don't know if I'm ready for this, Doris."

"Of course you are. Listen—remember what I said when I first got to know you? Fourteen years ago."

Fourteen years? No way—has to be more than that. I guess we have been through a lot, haven't we? Hanna swallowed hard through a constricted throat. "You said I was going to change the world."

"Exactly. And look at you now. You're just getting started. By the way, Marlene and I have decided to have a baby."

Hanna stopped and came as close to shrieking as her larynx allowed. "Oh my god, that's fabulous! Congratulations to the happy couple. When?"

"Well, it isn't simple. It looks like Marlene will have to go to America to get a sperm donation. And of course, only she will be a legal parent."

"The law is horrible. But you know I think of you as married." She resumed walking. The complications of their lives united them. But those secrets had once torn them apart.

"Doris, did you ever tell Annika that it was her grandfather who killed yours?"

"How did you know that??" Doris clearly wasn't expecting that question.

"I was snooping in your room once when we were all working on the children's theater project, and you were called to the phone. I'm sorry."

"I should've told you myself, actually. Her father told her, after my reprimand. There's a whole other drama there—which also involves Künstler. That story will have to wait for another time. But it's made us all a lot stronger. And you'll appreciate Clara's response. *As the rabbis say, you are not obligated to finish the task, but neither are you allowed to desist from it."*

The girl whose precocious strength had been so vital to Hanna wasn't slowing down. "Do you realize we're walking in sync?"

Doris linked her arm with Hanna's. "Finally."

They arrived at Hanna's platform. "You never told me about your latest climbing adventures," Hanna said. "The next thing I hear you'll be on an expedition to the Himalayas."

"The Alps are enough. It's fun. And it challenges me."

"That's just what you need—more challenges." Hanna laughed, but then she furrowed her brow and lowered her voice. "Doris, be safe, okay? Selfish me wants to see you again. And again and again."

"Don't worry. I have to stay alive at least long enough to see how you change the world. Now get on the train, silly goose, or you'll miss it. *Auf Wiedersehen,* Hanna."

Looking at Doris through the window, Hanna found it quite easy to imagine arrows coming from those fingertips. It was her duty to emulate her warrior mentor. Without Doris, she wouldn't be where she was.

But she didn't like hearing Doris talk so nonchalantly about challenges. That woman never shrunk from one, no matter how hard—or dangerous.

She found the routine of her domestic duties unusually calming that evening. After the children were asleep and Erik yawned for the third time, he excused himself and left her alone on the balcony. The September air was slightly chilly but not inhospitable.

The Stuttgart *Volkshochschule* would be familiar terrain. She would even be a normal student now. English proficiency would be an issue, but not a roadblock. Dr. Meissner's formal psychiatric evaluation was acceptable to the *Pädagogische Hochschule* in Ludwigsburg, where she would go for her degree.

The thought of learning chemistry was feverishly exciting. The products she'd used as a hairstylist had always intrigued her. But there was something else. The multicolored laser beams in Erik's lab had reminded her of gems. Like her beloved amethyst—why was it purple? She longed to understand that. And she was convinced she could.

Only the college culture frightened her. Twelve years ago, when she'd first picked up a pair of scissors and begun to cut the hair of a mannequin, it was all she could do to keep her hands steady. But the students had encouraged and helped each other, trading tips and offering advice. It really was like a family. Like a family they sometimes bickered and played petty games, but then made up. They paid attention to each other's feelings.

College would be nothing like that. Her years of professional experience and motherhood would count for nothing. At thirty-six she would stand out from the much younger students, who would ridicule her ignorance. She closed her eyes, and a cloud of stern-faced professors loomed over her, lobbing questions that she couldn't answer.

She went to the living room and put on one of the tapes from Dr. Meissner's farewell present, turning the volume low. It was the Grateful Dead—that amazing group she'd first heard about in the middle of being tormented by Zwiebel. The first song was called "Ripple."

She closed her eyes and let the melodic folk chords seep into her tense muscles. Meissner had given her a translation which she'd memorized long ago. A mysterious road winding through life, laid out just for her. A pilgrim alone on this road. No one to lead and no one to follow. And yet—was there really no one? Could she even know? Did anyone know?

She'd started down a road toward some part of her self that she didn't yet know, that was a part of her yet still apart from her. Danger might lie around each bend. Yet there *were* people with her who cared about her.

"Hanna, dear—sorry, but it's morning." Erik was gently shaking her shoulder. "Honey, you really have to relax. It's going to be okay."

"Erik, I have confidence. I do. But it doesn't make the fear go away."

"It never will. But you can master it."

Perhaps she could. But not all of her fears were paranoid. Scars notwithstanding, she was still alive and healthy. But she'd also been lucky. The Zwiebels and Künstlers of the world clearly had no compunction about using their influence against her.

CHAPTER 23

Four years later: 2 July 1990

AFTER OPENING THE eighth thin envelope with its rejection of her application for a student teaching position, Hanna called the only person she knew who might be able to help her: Lothar Braunschweig, now director of all the *Volkshochschulen* in Baden-Württemberg.

College had been as hard as she'd expected, even with her now-retired mother helping with the children. Often she was up past midnight studying. Male chauvinism had been an ever-present companion. Sometimes she would think of days in the salon, when she felt confident of her skills and customers complimented her and walked out with a proud bearing and carefree smile. And she'd hide her tears with a book.

She never told Erik about these moments. She wanted to be strong for her husband and children. And now she'd reached her goal. She'd actually stayed for one semester beyond the required seven to take additional courses. Her exam results were excellent. Her recommendations were glowing. The hard work was about to pay off. She was going to be a teacher.

She'd arranged science demonstrations for several classes. There were so many possibilities. She could combine non-toxic colorless chemicals into a mixture that turned from red to blue and back again repeatedly. Or with a thermos bottle of liquid nitrogen and a petri dish, she could make a magnet hover over a little black puck in the dish in what seemed like pure, eerie magic.

It didn't matter that she couldn't explain nonlinear chemistry and superconductivity to sixth-grade pupils. They got excited about science. The teachers were grateful. But her interviews had gone nowhere.

Braunschweig gave her an appointment for 13 July. It was her graduation day.

She described her discouragement dispassionately. "I know there was an oversupply of teachers for a few years, and the ones laid off get preference. But it seems like there should still be enough openings. Is there something I should be doing differently?"

"Frau Hoffman-Schoenberg, first, congratulations once again on your impressive achievements. You've come very far since we first met. Now to answer your question, I did make some quiet inquiries with the help of a colleague."

He made a slight grimace. "Of course, the hiring process favors men as physical science teachers. But if a woman is hired, conventional standards of feminine attractiveness come into play. And height is not one of them."

Hanna felt a chill creep toward her heart. Hadn't Staunton and the Zwiebels done enough to her? Would she always have to watch out for the next reprobate who needed to thrust their misery onto someone else?

"Karl Künstler was never charged with a crime, but he was disbarred, and his accusations against you appeared in local news outlets. The principal at one of the schools you applied to, who is very conservative, attended some of the hearings. After getting your application, he spoke to his counterparts at other schools in the area, even though this is not permitted."

"Is there nothing I can do?"

"The *Transsexuellengesetz* gives you explicit legal rights as a woman. But a complaint is expensive and time-consuming—and perhaps emotionally damaging for you. I'm afraid your best option is to keep trying. You have a strong academic record."

It shouldn't be this way. How could physiology matter that didn't affect anyone? It couldn't even be known without some bureaucratic papers that almost no one had legal access to. Her chromosomes didn't define her as a teacher any more than they did as a mother.

More despondent than she'd been for ages, she went home to prepare dinner. She'd planned a festive celebration of her graduation—the first evening gathering with both her parents and in-laws for a long time. She didn't relish the thought of the false conviviality it would require.

They lingered over appetizers, talking about children and the stagnation in the German economy. Hanna's employment troubles didn't come up until the middle of dinner. She said nothing about her talk with Braunschweig.

"*Ach*, what blockheads. What are they thinking?" Gisela's tone left no doubt of what *she* thought.

Dagmar shook her head. "Unfortunately they don't have to give their reasons. Prejudice is rarely spoken outright."

"Well, then, maybe I'll just stay in school." The thought sprung out of nowhere. Hanna was shocked at herself. But why shouldn't she? Men did it.

Erik raised his eyebrows. "You mean to get a doctorate?"

"Why not? I'd do student teaching of undergraduates, right? Then I'd have more experience then the others as well as more knowledge. I could do it. Couldn't I?"

"If you want an objective answer you should ask an objective observer."

Hanna was now regretting her audacity. "But some professor has to be willing to take me on. My degree is from a teacher's college. And if being a ridiculously tall woman stops me from getting a job, how am I going to get that professor?"

Dagmar erased the smile that was playing on her lips. "Erik, would you pass the *Rostbraten*, please? Hermann, more of that superb Medoc wine? Isn't Professor Hoffman-Schoenberg's dinner simply delicious?"

"Hey, you're making fun of me now." But Dagmar's mischievous compliment struck an eerie resonance deep inside her. "So I just have to find him. Him—it won't be her, that's for sure."

She attacked the meat on her plate as if it had raised a vigorous objection. "*Some* man has to recognize the value of women in science."

Hermann raised his newly filled glass. "To my daughter, who's not once given up."

She acknowledged his gesture gracefully. If she did this, her parents would be the bastion she could hold onto. But that night as she turned restlessly in bed, it didn't seem so simple.

With little sleep behind her she went to the university and assembled every scrap of information she could find on the chemistry faculty. There was no point in looking beyond Vaihingen—she could never get to Karlsruhe or Tübingen every day and take care of her family.

Three of her five applications were declined within a week. But a few days later a woman called from the office of Jürgen Schubert and asked her to come in.

Schubert was a stocky middle-aged man with thick black hair and a severe demeanor. She sat stiffly in one of the well-padded visitor's chairs.

"I've got a couple of projects with open positions. But I think the one on impurities in three-five semiconductors would be the best fit for you, given your interest in crystals. Also solar cells are a currently popular topic."

She looked at him open-mouthed. "I—I don't need to take any tests?"

"My tests are the only ones that count in my group, Frau Hoffman-Schoenberg. And you pass."

He smiled slightly—a lot like her husband's smile. "I learned what I needed from your professors in Ludwigsburg. Proposing a forty-seven-step total synthesis of aconitine when a molecule needing ten steps would have sufficed was only one example. When do you want to start?"

"Umm, I guess I'm ready anytime . . ."

"Come back September third—after vacation. Here's some background reading. You should be ready to get right to work the first day."

As she left his office she alternated between ecstatic excitement and heart-stopping fear about twice per second. Graduate work would need self-confidence that she didn't trust herself to have. And her children and husband were still the center of her life. But through the laboratory windows that she passed in the hallways she saw a future that was calling her.

Difficult though it would be, she was ready to write to her cousin.

ON THE FIRST morning after Christmas break, Hanna savored a sip of her second cup of coffee before opening a journal from the stack on her small home desk. Her undergraduate experience hadn't prepared her for the sheer delight of freely exploring this all-absorbing intellectual garden.

She answered the jangling phone curtly. "Hallo, Schoenberg residence."

"Hanna, it's Papa." He paused briefly. "I'm at the hospital with Mama. She had an accident at the ski area yesterday."

Hanna sucked in her breath in a gasp that was more like a screech. "Oh, no. No! What . . . what happened? Will she be okay?"

"She's in critical condition. It's best you come over if you can. Marienhospital, same place you were."

"I'm on my way."

She arrived in twenty minutes. Though she'd grimly held herself together in the car, she lost it when she saw her father's tear-streaked face. She embraced him fiercely, wondering how often she must've taken his quiet steady strength for granted.

"Thank you for being here, Hanna." He mopped his eyes and blew his nose a few times before he could speak. "It was a freak accident—near the end of the day. She hit a patch of ice just under the snow, close to the edge of the track, and collided with a tree. At the local clinic they started to treat her broken leg. But they found her creatine level was over nine, which means total kidney failure. So she was brought here late last night. They operated already this morning, and may again tonight. She's sedated now."

Hanna stood with one hand gently resting on her mother's shoulder, trying to ignore the tangle of wires and tubes, imagining the closed eyes and rhythmic breathing as evidence of peaceful comfort. Her mind had little of either.

Barely three months ago Gisela had celebrated her sixty-third birthday, surrounded by a loving family. Two weeks later the families of East and West Germany had reunited, allowing relatives to visit whom she hadn't even met. This was the time for reaping the rewards of caring and patience.

Hanna tearfully promised to bring her family in the evening. Now she had to be alone.

She drove to the hikers' parking lot southwest of Echterdingen, drawn once again to the locus of the memory that had moved her so much, for reasons of which she understood so little. As now, the day had begun with the sun and ended in a storm, as the first news of the Zwiebels' hatred reached her.

Back in her silent house, she lingered in front of photographs of babies in their grandmother's lap. Her sister's teddy bear still sat on her dresser with her other stuffed animals clustered around like cubs.

She approached the desk she'd left so hastily, the coffee long since cold. On one corner lay the letter from Richard Shelby's wife. *I'm so sorry to have to tell you that Richard has advanced Alzheimer's disease. But his eyes lit up when I told him what you'd written. I think he understood.*

She'd come so far in the mission he'd helped launch her on. She wouldn't waver. But as she picked up the journal the text melted together. Finally she put her head down and bawled.

Erik agreed to come home immediately. But the children arrived from school first. Thirteen-year-old Elisabeth greeted her with obvious consternation. "Mama, you look like a ghost. What's wrong?"

There wasn't a kind or gentle way to tell her. "Oma was in an accident. She may be dying."

After hearing the details, Elisabeth went directly to the kitchen. "So, what would you like for lunch?"

Normally, Hanna fixed lunch for them. Now her daughter was going to show her who was grown up.

A few minutes later Erik arrived. He held her silently for a long time as she cried softly on his shoulder. Finally he steered her gently to the sofa. "I'll never forget how she trusted me when we first met."

"That was her character. She always looked beneath the surface of people. *Ach*, Erik, how can I go on? Oh, how selfish of me. But what am I saying? Of course she'll make it."

"Undoubtedly. When are the next visiting hours?"

"Starting at two. We should go soon. Let's make a little packet of treats for Papa. I can't imagine how it is for him."

In the kitchen she found Elisabeth already putting cheese and salami slices onto a roll. Her throat tightened again and she had to fight back another flood of tears. "You're a tribute to your namesake, Elisabeth."

"You helped each other when you met. Now we'll do it together."

GISELA WAS STILL unconscious that night. The next afternoon she was able to greet them weakly, but without much conversation. They spent the time quietly holding hands.

As visiting hours neared the end, a physician came by and took them aside. "I know this is hard to hear, ladies and gentlemen. But my job requires me to be honest. Her prognosis is getting worse. The kidney failure is combined with sepsis, and unless she gains strength we can't consider dialysis."

Hanna bit her lip. "Will she make it through the night?"

"Very likely. But it's hard to see beyond that."

When she got home she located the tapes that her mother had made for the earliest part of her recovery in Denver. Erik gave Richard extra attention while Elisabeth remained at Hanna's side. "Do you think she'd be able to enjoy any photographs?"

"I don't know, but we can try."

"I was thinking of how much that one of my aunt meant to you. It meant a lot to me, too."

Hanna nearly choked. The box of photos Gisela had shown her was where it had really started. She'd wanted so badly to be the girl in that dancer's tutu. And in a way, she had.

She had to leave her mother with the same gift of love and family.

When the family came the next afternoon, they found Hermann next to the hospital bed. Gisela's breathing was only faintly perceptible. Hanna held one feeble hand, emotions tangled by all she knew and didn't know, by what had happened and what might happen. "Mama, can I tell you a story?"

"I'd love that. What'll it be about?"

"It's about a woman who came to a strange country with her husband and young daughter. She barely knew the language. But she was gentle and strong. Gentle enough to pet a kitten, and strong enough to lift a horse . . ." Then she turned the tape player on to *Pipi Longstocking.*

After a little delay Gisela asked for silence. "Hanna, I don't need a doctor to tell me my time is short. Perhaps I should've told you this before. But it was too full of emotions for me."

Her eyes closed briefly. "We gave Elisabeth a Bild Lilli doll when she was seven—it was all the rage in Germany. Somehow it got lost in the chaos of moving, and of course she was devastated."

She gazed toward the ceiling. "I asked a friend in Germany to get a replacement, but she couldn't find the same doll. The Barbie company was about to take over. So she finally sent another one, called Miss Marlene."

Finally she turned toward Hanna. "That's the one you have."

She smiled at Hanna's gasp. "What I gave you from Elisabeth after the ski trip matched your age. Of course I have childhood mementos also; you'll find them soon. But when that birthday came, I felt you should have the doll. You'd told me what happened to yours."

"Mama, I don't know—" But her mother's eyes had closed. The room seemed a little darker, and Hanna's throat tightened. "Thank you." She turned the tape back on.

The end of visiting hours passed unnoticed. Soon after the tape finished, Hanna heard a distinct change in Gisela's breathing, and started singing the words she'd heard when she first came out of the darkness. And just like her mother, she didn't stop.

Wie ist die Welt so stille,	*How is the world so quiet,*
Und in der Dämmrung Hülle	*and in the twilight's blanket,*
So traulich und so hold!	*so cozy and so fair!*
Als eine stille Kammer,	*So like a quiet chamber,*
Wo ihr des Tages Jammer	*where you the day's deep sorrows*
Verschlafen und vergessen sollt.	*should put to sleep and all forget.*

She hoped her mother could hear her voice as she journeyed down that long tunnel of light.

She sat for some time in the dim light listening to the hum of the machines, oblivious to the departure of the spirit they were supposed to have preserved. She was about to press the call button when a nurse came in to check on an alarm. Only as she turned did she realize that Hermann was still right beside her. She fell into his arms and sobbed.

There were a hundred details to attend to in the morning. During the next few days she spent more time than ever before talking to him about their early times together. But she spoke at the service with a bittersweet feeling. She wanted so much to remember for herself.

HANNA CLOSED THE door to her lab at midnight, thankful that she'd asked one of the men in her group, a theorist who normally worked late, if he would give her a ride home.

Her research progress had come to a virtual standstill. She made simple mistakes repeatedly. In the middle of tuning the laser she would hear her mother's voice, and salty tears soon covered a mirror. After she cleaned up it might happen all over again.

And Schubert made it clear in one of their weekly meetings that he was not happy. "Frau Hoffmann-Schoenberg, it's entirely understandable that you would take some time to get back up to speed. But you've had more than two months. This is not the competent, hard-working student I brought on last fall."

He pushed her lab notebook back toward her. "If you need professional help, you should get it. I'm sure there are resources you can turn to. When we have this meeting next month, I expect to see the kind of progress you've shown in the past. Otherwise we'll have to have a serious talk about your future."

That was not the fitting memorial to her mother that she'd tearfully promised during the service.

She slipped into her house as quietly as possible and succeeded in waking no one. She looked to see if there was any bread for breakfast, though she already knew the answer. Then she set her vibrating alarm for five and put it under her pillow.

By seven the *Broïchen* were nearly baked and she'd just come back to the kitchen from finishing her morning routine in the bathroom. She put four eggs into the boiling water. Erik emerged from the bedroom.

"Erik, I was in the lab all day yesterday and didn't have time to shop at all. And this afternoon Richard is showing his drawings at an exhibition in the city. Can you get a few things for dinner on your way home?"

"I can't. I've got meetings till six. I changed my schedule already for you twice this week."

"Well, I'm *sooo* sorry. As if I don't do it all the time for the whole family." She opened the refrigerator and peered inside, trying to make a list in her mind, wondering when she would have the time for shopping. She would have to skip the departmental seminar.

She went part way up the stairs and yelled, "Richard, Elisabeth, where are you? Get downstairs—you're late already."

"Hanna, you need to manage your time better. You shouldn't be in the lab so late anyway."

She returned to the kitchen, eyes shooting daggers. "If you know the secret to my time management I wish you'd share it with me. But maybe not just when I'm trying to get breakfast ready for a family."

Shaking, she opened the oven door and removed a pan of overcooked *Brötchen*. Then she remembered the eggs, which were certainly hard by now. She flung the rolls into the sink.

Erik's hand gently touched her shoulder as she gripped the rim of the sink with both hands and sobbed.

"I'm sorry, honey. We'll be fine without breakfast this morning, I promise."

She turned and held him fiercely. "Erik, I'm not sure I can do it. Absolutely nothing went right yesterday . . ."

She straightened up and put her hands on his shoulders. "Look at you, now you'll have to change shirts. I'll get something from the refrigerator that the kids can eat on their way."

A few minutes later she drove to the store where she bought what she needed for dinner. It was a big block of her research time, but she'd realized that if she didn't relax a little she would break down completely. Not every problem could be solved by working harder.

Little steps, one at a time. This morning, that meant heating water and making a cup of coffee. Then drinking it slowly, savoring its warmth and strength and idly perusing a journal. No thoughts beyond the present.

Finally she was ready to turn the laser on. She went systematically through the procedure, writing out all the options she could think of. But nothing had changed from the night before.

Somehow she had to avoid getting frustrated this time. She stopped and left the building, walking aimlessly around the campus. She let her mind wander as randomly as her steps, shuffling erratically through the lab and her old salon with her mother's spirit at her side.

Clouds had gathered, and rain looked possible. She turned back. And almost ran to the library. And then to her lab.

A few hours later, lab notebook clutched under her arm, she was in her advisor's office. She took a deep breath. "Professor Schubert, I think I've found something."

His casual glance at her writeup turned quickly into serious study. Finally he looked up. "Frau Hoffmann-Schoenberg, this is quite remarkable. What gave you this idea? It isn't obvious."

Her explanation was going to seem naïve, but all she could do was tell him. "I went outside for a walk because I was frustrated. It was threatening rain, and that made me think of how dust nucleates raindrops. Which is a phase transition, of course, and then I wondered if maybe there could have been an impurity-catalyzed phase transition in my crystal. The spectrum matches the one from the literature quite closely."

His expression was intense and focused, as if her presence suddenly mattered a great deal to him. "Hanna, that's exactly how a good scientist thinks. Now, for a little while, you need to become a mechanic. That phase will be sensitive to pressure, of course. To study it properly you need an anvil, and I don't have a budget for it. But I think you can build one."

Filing toward the seminar room along with the other students at four, she wondered if she'd be able to pay the slightest attention. She'd regained her footing. Her professor had even called her by her first name.

But talk about pressure—Schubert would now expect her to follow through on the promise of a prominent discovery. And she was barely holding her life together.

CHAPTER 24

12 September 1993, Vaihingen

THREE YEARS AFTER she'd begun her doctoral research, Hanna was ready to begin writing. Though the experiments weren't finished, she knew the outline, background, and many of the references.

Following her near-breakdown, Schubert had asked her to prepare the introduction for a grant proposal that would help fund her research. A few months later, she'd written nearly the entire application, with only guidance and encouragement from her mentor. It had been exhausting, but she'd learned that she knew how to do this work. And she'd begun to believe in herself.

After that, her lab work became more and more the adventure she'd hoped for. She knew how to handle her own lab system, but she could help new students as well. Visiting lecturers at the department seminar would say "Now, that's an excellent question" before betraying perplexed disbelief when they looked at her closely. Schubert always smiled.

She traipsed back and forth between her office and the library the way she'd done for the research proposal. Stacks of papers sprouted on her desk like mushrooms. She scribbled outlines, threw them away, and started over.

The telephone interrupted her mid-September Sunday afternoon reading on the balcony, where she was trying to take advantage of the remaining balmy days of fall to relax her mind.

"Hanna, it's Marlene. Doris is dead. There was an accident where she was climbing."

This wasn't possible.

Der Tag ist schön! O sei nicht bang,   *The day is fine, don't be worried,*
Sie machen nur einen weiten Gang.   *They have only gone for a long walk.*

Friedrich Rückert had voiced her thoughts, one hundred fifty years ago, as if he were by her side now.

"Marlene, I—tell me what happened."

"She and Ruth Bowman—the sister of the woman you climbed with in Colorado—were doing the American 'direttissima' on the West Face of the Dru. It's one of the hardest in the Alps—only done free twice. They were close to the top, trying for the fastest ascent. There was a rockfall. Ruth is okay. There'll be a service there Tuesday—Paul said she'd told him that's where she'd want to stay if this ever happened."

A part of her had died with her mother, whose unflinching love sheltered her as she blossomed from her barren childhood. Now another part was gone. Doris had stood steadfastly with her through all those early battles as she attempted to reconcile her past and present.

Marlene was telling her more, something about television coverage and tributes from famous alpinists. In her distraction she heard only snatches. But twelve-year-old Doris's words echoed in her mind as though they were a soliloquy in Elfriede Jelinek's *Clara S.*:

"There've been strong women who changed the world in spite of all the bad things that men did to them. You're going to be one of them, Hanna."

You were the strong one, dammit.

Doris had started climbing after their adventure on the *via ferrata*. Didn't that make Hanna responsible for this tragedy?

"Marlene, we're coming to Augsburg. At least Annika and Clara and I. I'll call you back as soon as I can. I love you."

Her Sunday afternoon relaxation was obviously over. She called the other women and scheduled the visit for the coming Friday. But hardly had she hung up with Marlene when her phone rang. It was Heidi. Emma Giesselmann wanted to talk to her.

"I couldn't tell what her motives are. You don't have to do it if you don't want to."

Hanna didn't hesitate. "I want to honor Doris. She'd have listened, if her mother had ever called. She was that strong."

She knew from her aunt that Emma and her husband had quarreled bitterly and divorced in the winter following the fateful night club spying. Emma had then moved to Ulm. So she arranged her visit to Marlene to include a stopover in Ulm.

HER HOSTESS HAD changed a great deal. A face that had once been warm and gracious was drawn and brittle. Her thinning gray hair was unkempt, and she was still wearing a bathrobe in the middle of the day.

"Please come in." She motioned toward the sofa, where a cup of coffee was waiting, and sat down in the armchair at one end. Hanna mumbled something about it being a nice apartment.

"Thank you. It serves my present needs. You may recognize some of the furniture."

Hanna remained silent. Emma finally handed Hanna a thick envelope. "These are letters Doris received from Kirstie Wolf. Some of them were in an envelope that had fallen behind a dresser drawer. There were also a few that came after she left."

Hanna stopped herself from answering. If she wanted to learn anything, recriminations wouldn't help. She hadn't realized how close the two women were. They'd met at her wedding, of course, but then she'd been so busy with Erik. Not long before she'd given Doris a cold shoulder.

She couldn't turn the clock back seventeen years. But she could ask some questions.

"Frau Giesselmann, you were an outspoken advocate for women's rights. Your daughter was a woman."

"That's not fair. Lesbians and gays will want to get married if they're normalized in society. And that's the death of marriage."

"You never came to terms with your feelings about your father, did you?"

Emma's lined face grew more tired. "Of course, she would have told you about that."

"You were six years old. I'm sure you felt deserted, though it wasn't his fault. I understand your resentment. But it doesn't help to hate. Not Doris, and not me."

Seeing no response, Hanna continued. "I heard what you said at the train station, on the way to Oberstdorf."

Emma's shoulders twitched. "I was only trying to protect Doris."

Hanna watched her intently. And then it came to her in a flash. "And were you also trying to protect her when you called Volker Zwiebel and told him Doris led the dart attack on him?"

Emma jerked upright as if shocked. "How did you know that?"

"I didn't. Nor do I know how you knew—she said no one knew but us."

"It's true. I found out by reading those letters—you'll see that she told Kirstie a lot of things."

"And so you also told Zwiebel that Doris was a lesbian."

Emma slumped on the sofa. "Please believe me—I had no inkling he would do what he did. I only wanted someone to bring her to her senses."

They sat for a while in silence.

"Hanna, I've been so ignorant. And now it's too late."

Hanna stood up. "I'll give these to Marlene. Your home and hospitality meant so much to me in that first year. I won't forget that."

In the hallway she turned. "You can't change the past, Frau Giesselmann. Only the future."

She extended her hand. She had no right to speak for Doris. But for herself she couldn't leave any grudge if she could help it. She knew what that could do to a family.

Emma took her hand. "*Auf Wiedersehen,* Hanna."

"*Auf Wiedersehen.*"

Autumn leaves fluttered softly to the ground as she walked to the bus stop. Emma Giesselmann had played no role in her life for twenty years. Yet there was clearly a sense of something old making way for something new.

Although only nine months had passed between her wedding and Doris's eviction by her mother, there were more than a dozen letters. Once seated on the bus, she leafed through a few of them. A paragraph with her name grabbed her attention.

> *For me, having never known one, a mother is a mystical fantasy, a fairy who could right every wrong. That yours would take her own hurt out on you and Hanna is just heartbreaking. And I so much admire your bravery in standing up for Hanna in that toxic atmosphere.*

So much might've been different if she'd not been so insensitive to Doris.

Soon she was embracing Marlene while awkwardly holding a bag of groceries. Clara put them with the ones she and Annika had brought.

Hanna took the space the others had made for her on the sofa. "I'm so sorry. What can I say, Marlene?"

"We could argue about who's sadder." Marlene tried to laugh.

"Don't be silly. You're the one who was married to her."

"All of you knew her so much longer. And thanks, Hanna. I love the way you've always said that, even though the government won't."

"I try to be real."

"She had so much 'I don't care' in her. But she could be silly along with serious."

"Yes, what wouldn't I give to hear her calling me 'silly goose' now? Oh god, Marlene, this is too hard."

"She talked about the *Schildmaiden* a lot. She was so proud of you—member of the Bundestag, legislative assistant, graduate student in chemistry. We haven't seen Lena and Frieda and Amelie as much as the years went by, but she never forgot any of you."

"She was a leader we all looked up to—from childhood." Annika's red eyes betrayed emotions she normally suppressed.

Clara nodded. "I wouldn't be a politician without her. She pushed us all to do more than we thought we could."

They sat in silence for a while again.

"Hanna, what am I going to do? How will I raise Max on my own? I never learned how to meet new girls, you know. Doris was my life."

The question was another jab to her guilty conscience. And just as her intuition had guessed Emma Giesselmann's secret, it told her what to say now. *Crisis is always an opportunity—also for myself.*

"How about moving to Colorado?"

"Are you crazy? What would I do there?"

"Kirstie's a lawyer, and you're a paralegal. And the thing is—Boulder today has a strong lesbian and gay community. Not that there aren't homophobes. But I think it's one of the best places you could find to live."

"But I'm a German. I know nothing of U.S. law."

"Your English is excellent—Doris told me so. And Kirstie does environmental law, with many international aspects. You'd pick up what you don't know very quickly. I know you're fantastic at what you do. There's a spiritual connection here, Marlene."

"Wow. I've been so depressed, it just felt like there was no reason to get up except Max. To move somewhere totally different and start over—it seems insane. You really think Kirstie'd have a job for a German paralegal?"

"It's morning there. Let's call her. I'm paying."

Kirstie cancelled a meeting and listened without interruption to Hanna's impassioned proposal. Then she talked to Marlene while the three visitors cooked dinner and entertained Max.

"Hanna, this is crazy." Marlene looked almost shell-shocked as she sat down to the *Sauerbraten*, fried potatoes, and cabbage. "So sudden. But Kirstie says I'd be perfect to help expand her practice in a way she was thinking about, but hadn't figured out how to do."

She got up again. "It can't be real. What if she were doing this just as a favor? I'd feel terrible."

"Kirstie wouldn't do it if it didn't make business sense."

"Well, she's going to send me a bunch of papers. I have to see them, but it sounds like a dream come true. I won't forget this, Hanna. I'll pay you back somehow, I promise."

"Don't worry. Doris has taken care of it."

She returned Marlene's confused look with a faint smile. "Eight years ago Clara said I should be a teacher. Then I took some girls to my husband's lab and thought: They should see a woman in his place, as a professor. Yet I never considered myself in that place—until tonight."

She put down her knife and fork. "If Doris could risk her life to climb the most formidable pinnacle in the Alps, the least I can do is take a career risk."

THE THIRTY-FIVE-KILOMETER drive from Vaihingen to Tübingen led right through her old home town of Waldenheim. In occasional roller-coaster ups and downs it twisted through woods whose late autumn colors on her arrival in Germany had presaged the approach of winter. Today the tree skeletons stood starkly outlined against the early March sky, but daffodils already dotted bare patches on south-facing slopes. Spring was not far away.

Schubert had been skeptical. "There's no doubt you have the qualifications. Your work on that grant application was better than any other student I've had. Unfortunately, you'll soon run into a virtual brick wall of male chauvinism. You're also at least ten years older than a typical applicant for an *Assistent* position. But of course I'll support you."

Elisabeth, approaching seventeen, was more and more self-directed and responsible. Richard would still happily play all night with the Game Boy his grandmother had given him for Christmas just before her death. But between them she was beginning to feel some freedom, and a long commute was no longer out of the question. Albert Gleis, chairman of the chemistry department in Tübingen, had responded quickly to her application with a request for a research proposal. Then, with equal promptness, he asked her to come in three weeks after she'd submitted it.

"Welcome, Frau Hoffmann-Schoenberg. Let me introduce my colleagues, whom I've asked to assist me in assessing your qualifications. Professor Andreas Heubl joined five years ago, while Professor Stefan Hartz has been with us for over two decades. His research put the department on the world map."

He shuffled a couple of papers on his desk. "Professor Schubert's recommendation was very strong. Now we want to hear your response to a few questions."

Hanna seriously wondered if her vocal chords would accept the assignment. She hadn't expected an exam.

Yet she stood for two hours at the blackboard and fielded questions about her research proposal, and somehow the answers came. Many times she'd start with, "I'm not sure, but I think . . ." and as she began to say what she thought, the topic clarified.

"All right, we've put you through enough," Gleis finally said. "You definitely get a high grade on endurance. We'll talk among ourselves and I'll get back to you in a few days."

As she made her way home, Hanna couldn't keep a single rational thought in her head. Her mind had simply gone blank.

For the next week she tried not to think about the interview. Of course she couldn't think of anything else. This was the culmination of everything. The plans her parents had told her she'd made before the assault to be a professor of German literature. Her sister's plans, so cruelly cut short. Her mother's hopes.

The mountain she was climbing ended with a professorship. She owed this to everyone who had helped her along the way. This was her heritage and her obligation. She must not fail.

There was nothing she could do now but wait.

She made no progress on her thesis. She altered clothing and found new recipes. She sorted photographs and hung prints on the walls. She rearranged furniture in the living room, and then put it back the way it was. And she slept very little.

Gleis's call came just as she was beginning to prepare dinner.

"There's one issue I need to clarify. English proficiency is a necessity for a professor. You have a psychiatric diagnosis that you're incapable of learning it. Can you explain that for me?"

She felt lightheaded, on the verge of fainting, as she briefly related her medical history. The line was silent for a long time.

"I'm very sorry, because you're an exceptional candidate. But I can't change this requirement."

She closed the door to her bedroom and curled up on the bed. She couldn't go forward and she couldn't go back. Her grand vision was irretrievably shattered.

The attendant for the Physics Department stockroom went into a back room to get her order of nuts and bolts, which she needed for her laser system. As Hanna waited, she noticed a sign behind the counter:

"The impossible we do immediately. Miracles take a little longer."

Then the man returned and told her that the entire order was out of stock.

A gentle hand touched her shoulder. "Mama, what's wrong?"

She focused through bleary eyes on the bedside clock. She'd only been asleep for ten minutes, though she felt groggy and exhausted.

Her daughter was a teenager. She needed a mature voice to assuage adolescent stresses. Which her mother was not providing.

Hanna went to the bathroom and washed her face, after which she managed a short explanation.

Elisabeth seemed unfazed. "Mama, I know how much this means to you. But you know what you always tell us. Nothing wagered, nothing gained, remember? When you fall you just get up and go on."

She sighed. "You see? You should listen to your mother."

She didn't need more nuts and bolts for her experiments. And the stockroom had never had such a sign, nor did she recall seeing one elsewhere. Maybe her dream-eyes had been broken by stress. Maybe all her dreams were just lies.

She should've known the English requirement would eventually catch her. To quit now was unimaginable, yet finishing was equally so. She didn't know how to do miracles. She did know how to drop out.

The smell of burnt food reminded her that she'd been cooking. In the kitchen she found a pan that would need a lot of work before it could be used again.

CHAPTER 25

FIVE MONTHS LATER, Hanna opened the trunk of their rental car at a trailhead in Estes Park. As she grabbed her backpack, Erik opened his duffel bag and pulled out a climbing gear sling.

This was not part of the plan. "*What?* If this is a joke it's a pretty bad one."

They'd just come from the Aspen Center for Physics in Colorado, where Erik often spent a few weeks mingling with the best physicists in the world, enjoying intense conversations while walking in the shadow of the Rocky Mountains. After her hopes for a university position had been dashed, she'd insisted on joining him for half of it this summer, even though every day would rub the raw wounds of her disappointment in a new way.

She still didn't know if she could finish her thesis. Her progress was half-hearted, as she invented extra obstacles that then took ages to surmount. She needed a break—maybe the mountain air would do something for her. Hermann graciously agreed to look after her children.

Erik had been enthusiastic. "How about spending a week in Boulder afterward? We could visit Kirstie, and then go to Estes Park."

"Sure, as long as we take it easy. Neither my muscles nor my head are prepared for more. Maybe lying in the sun on a rock, like a lizard—that'd be nice."

So what was this gear doing here in the trunk of their car?

He put his arm gently around her waist. "Can we talk for just a minute?"

They found a log nearby to sit on. "It's true, I planned this outing in spite of what you said, and I owe you an apology. But please hear me out. I know the pressure you feel in the lab. I've been there. But those demons you've lived with so long—that part I can only guess at."

He pulled her hair gently back, and her tension ebbed. His sensitive touch always won her over. "I've been trying to listen to that quiet voice of intuition that you've tried to teach me about. And it says this will be a good experience for you. Can you trust me?"

Erik had learned to climb on student outings, and Hanna had followed him a few times during alpine vacations. She loved doing anything outdoors with him. She'd asked Doris to trust her like that on the *via ferrata*, hadn't she? She swallowed hard. "I can, and I do."

After a few short climbs she felt relaxed and ashamed of making a scene. Then they came to the base of a cliff that resembled a partially open book. Erik handed her the end of the rope from the top of the pile of loose coils at her feet. "This one looks perfect for your first lead."

"*First lead?*" Her pique returned.

"It's a classic crack, easy to protect."

She grimaced. Her mood didn't match what she knew was required of a leader.

The second in a climbing pair was completely protected. If she fell on a hard move, she could just try again. Nothing risked but pride. But the leader's decisions carried risk for both. And they had to be made without knowing all the facts, like: *What dangers are ahead, out of sight? Will I have the strength to keep going?*

It was a lot like the new life she'd taken on as a scientist. The new life she wasn't sure she could succeed in.

Adding more stress by leading a rock climb was *definitely* not appealing. But Erik was handing her the gear sling. "You might even remember it once you get going."

She looked at him curiously.

"It's the one you did when you came here three weeks after you became a Hoffmann and two weeks before you were assaulted."

"How do you know that?"

"Hermann told me where to find it. He has an excellent visual memory. It's just as he described it."

She stared up at the cliff. It did look vaguely familiar. And that made it doubly frightening. "Erik, you know how much I hate these memories I don't really have. I know it's irrational, but I'm still afraid of them."

"Honey, please give it a try. Humor me. I'll make it up to you somehow."

She resolutely ignored her pounding heart while she placed three chocks in the first ten feet. About twenty feet above the ground the face steepened and the crack widened to twice the width of her fist. Putting either hand or foot into it was useless.

She tried holding onto the tiny flakes on the sides of the book. She remembered Diana telling her about off-width cracks: wedge your arm or even whole body into it and wriggle up like a snake. Neither idea got her so much as an inch higher.

She was stuck, and near panic. Pain flared in her back. The chocks seemed far below.

She wanted nothing more than to be back on the ground. But climbing down looked harder than climbing up. And she couldn't bear the thought of defeat.

She couldn't stay where she was. Her legs were twitching up and down like a sewing machine needle. If only they were just hiking, as she'd wanted. No slipping there.

And there was the answer—simple physics.

She grasped one side of the crack and brought her legs up level with her hands, then walked her feet up the other side, pulling hard to prevent them from slipping. A few seconds later the difficult stretch was below her. She wedged her toe into the now much-smaller crack and stood comfortably, casually leaning out and surveying the landscape.

"Darling, didn't you say there was supposed to be a hard spot in here? I feel cheated."

"Well, you could redo it with your eyes closed."

The rest of the climb flew past effortlessly. She felt an urge to go ever-longer distances before placing another piece. As she topped out, she saw the last chock about twenty feet below. *You're crazy—you could have been seriously hurt if you fell.* But she merely tossed her bangs to one side and set up the belay.

When Erik arrived, he had the smile of a happy child. "Congratulations, Hanna, that was awesome."

He put his arms around her and held her close. As they separated, several wet streaks ran down his cheeks.

Minutes later they stretched out on a sloping rock at the base and nibbled on trail mix. A few fleecy July clouds cast random shadows over the meadow. She laid her head on his shoulder and pushed her hair away from her eyes.

Life really does go in circles, but they don't close in the same plane. They're more like spirals.

"When am I going to learn to trust my own abilities, Erik?"

"You're already doing it. All I did was give you a nudge. You just need to admit it to yourself."

He put his arm around her shoulders. "Jürgen's told me about your work. Don't be embarrassed, Hanna. Being self-confident isn't being cocky."

She turned and let herself fall into the depths of his eyes. There she found the forget-me-not, placed so delicately into her ponytail fifteen years before. And all the longing, vulnerability, hope, and trust that she'd felt in the Neckar River valley seemed to rise from the lupine, paintbrush, and blanket flowers in front of her like a magical white mist.

"Herr Schoenberg, I knew there was some logical reason why I married you. That, and of course your vast fortune, and the way you make coffee."

"It's been a pleasure, Hanna. And an honor."

As they wrapped themselves in each other's arms, Hanna felt their kiss was as passionate and tender as their first. There was life in the Colorado mountains after all.

She didn't know whether there was life after her graduation. But she was ready to find out.

AS FALL MOVED toward winter the cold gray days mirrored Hanna's mood. Erik was extra solicitous, and they ate out often. They were just putting their coats on to go to dinner on the Monday evening before All Saints Day when the phone rang.

"Hanna, it's Kirstie Wolf. Don't say anything—I have to read you this story from the *Denver Post* first. It's from this morning's edition—I only saw it seconds ago."

Distracted by their dinner plans, Hanna was only half paying attention. Then she jerked to attention as if she'd been on a puppet string. William Staunton had been arrested in Mexico, along with the rogue policeman who'd helped him escape. They'd been working as security guards for a drug cartel and organized crime syndicate in Zamora.

And they'd been found with the help of Werner Jendrossek, collaborating with a professor of criminology at the *Tecnológico de Monterrey*. He'd been there for the last three months.

Werner Jendrossek again.

She knew he spoke Spanish fluently, but how did he even know about her case, let alone learn all the secret details that he would've needed to solve it?

Kirstie was waiting for her to say something. The obvious something.

"So he'll be tried again?"

"There's no way he'll risk a trial. He'll accept a plea bargain, you can bet on it. He's going to jail, Hanna. And you'll have to be here. You have to make a statement."

Hanna mumbled something polite after Kirstie told her that the district attorney would be in touch with her, and hung up. She didn't welcome this news. She wanted nothing to do with that part of her life again. It wasn't going to help her now.

CHAPTER 26

EXACTLY SIX WEEKS later, Hanna found herself in the Denver District Court, jet-lagged and full of foreboding. Only the nebulous thought that this sentencing might bring her English back had induced her to come at all. Even so, without Kirstie holding her hand she'd probably have bolted out the back door.

Erik was supposed to be there. A symposium honoring him at the University of Colorado had been scheduled for the day after the sentencing, and he'd arranged other university visits ahead of it. When the court date was moved up three days, his new connection was apparently too close.

Archibald Grainger, presiding judge, peered over his reading glasses and turned toward the defense attorney. "Mr. Edwards, are you aware of any negative information concerning the defendant's competence that I should be aware of?"

"No, Your Honor."

"The defendant has satisfied the Court that he is thinking clearly, is not under the influence of intoxicants, has not been coerced, has had access to qualified counsel, and is competent to proceed to sentencing."

He turned to the prosecutor. "Mr. Kelly, does the victim wish to make a statement to the court?"

"Yes, Your Honor. She is in the courtroom. As you know, she is now a citizen of Germany. Ms. Kirsten Wolf will interpret for her."

Hanna approached the bench as if wading through water, more slowly with every step closer to Staunton. Behind him, she stopped.

"Kirstie, I—I can't do this." The sight of just the back of his head brought back a hint of the horror of the trial. How could she possibly face him?

Kirstie held her arm. "Hanna, I know how hard it was. I watched you. You faced him. And you can do it again."

Hanna looked at the judge. From his dispassionate expression he might have been moderating a panel on macroeconomics. "That was—I was . . ." She turned back, the taste of bile in her throat. Kirstie couldn't know how painful that had been. "Kirstie, where is my mother? I need my mother."

Hanna strode toward the rear of the nearly empty courtroom where her desk had been, gasping for breath as though she'd run a race. She turned toward the exit.

Kirstie blocked her way. "Hanna, please."

Hanna searched with jerky motions for an escape route. But Kirstie stood firm. "I'm sorry. Dear God, I'm sorry. But you can't stop, Hanna. Not now. You have to finish it. It's just one more step to the end. Don't give up now."

Hanna stood rigid for a moment, and then probed in her purse until she found the stuffed kitten. Clutching the little toy tightly, she set the purse on the prosecutor's desk and walked resolutely forward. It wasn't only for herself she was doing this. *You are not obligated to complete the work, but neither are you free to desist from it.*

"Good afternoon, Ms. Hoffmann-Schoenberg." Grainger's voice was businesslike. "Please try to relax. I know you cannot ignore the presence of the defendant, but you are here to talk to me. The court would simply like to hear your thoughts about the penalty that may be prescribed for the crime, which Mr. Staunton has already admitted."

Hanna looked down, caressing the kitten, composing a shield of family pictures around her—or was it a weapon? Finally, she raised her head. The words came slowly but her voice was clear and steady.

"Your Honor, twenty years ago I sat in this same room as the memory of what Mr. Staunton had done to me returned. The pain of that memory seemed almost as much as the pain of his attack. Nevertheless, I described it to the court, so that justice could be done.

"But it was not done. Despite all the efforts of the lawyers, and the detectives, especially the woman standing next to me, still translating into the language he took away. The jury tore my wounds open, and Mr. Staunton walked away.

"Then he attacked me again, by escaping from prison and denying me justice a second time. Forever, I thought.

"I'd fallen deeply in love with a man who was the antithesis of Mr. Staunton. A man who instead of torment, offered me tenderness. Who instead of tearing me apart, sought to make me whole. Who instead of trying to take my life, gave from his own. Mr. Staunton's second attack almost took me from that love, and from my life with love.

"But that man—now my husband—refused to give up. Because of him, the work that my mother, the doctors and nurses at the hospital, and so many others, had done was not in vain. Mr. Staunton failed, because he succeeded."

Hanna looked directly at Staunton, her gaze unwavering.

"I don't know, and I don't care why you did it. What I know is that you should never be able to do it again. I don't care what else happens to you. I don't care about vengeance. But you should never, ever, be able to cause another innocent person harm."

She turned back to the bench. "I thank the court for this opportunity."

Grainger was as nonchalant as before. "You owe us no thanks. You may sit down now next to the state's attorney."

When they were seated he continued. "Mr. Staunton, I accept your plea bargain request for a security rating consistent with the Cañon City prison rather than the harsher maximum-security facility in Florence. I note that the charge of first degree kidnaping with its minimum life sentence has been dismissed.

"The minimum and maximum terms set by statute are five and fifty years for first degree sexual assault, and four to forty years for first degree assault. For the former offense I impose a sentence of thirty to fifty years, and for the latter twenty to forty years. You must serve at least the minimum term before any possibility of parole.

"I reject your request for these to be considered a single criminal act, with concurrent sentences. They were separate acts, and your sentences shall run consecutively."

He banged his gavel. "Court is dismissed."

For Judge Grainger the sound of that gavel was routine. But for Hanna it marked a boundary. No new languages had appeared. She was the same woman as a few minutes ago. Yet she wasn't. Never before had she spoken so forcefully in public. A burgeoning power was pushing impatiently against a barely intact shell, muttering opaque promises of something to come.

Whatever it was, she was no longer afraid to find out.

The bailiff opened the door. Karen Dickenson, John Alda, and Manuel Barrios were waiting with Marlene. Hanna rushed to throw her arms around them—the district attorney and detectives who'd done their best for her when everything seemed hopeless. Then she grabbed Barrios, who was in uniform, by the shoulders.

"Manuel, *Cómo sabías*—how did you meet Werner?"

"Your friend Marlene introduced us. She said she owed you one."

She quickly covered her gaping mouth. So, karma was real after all. Also, guardian angels. She wondered if anyone had done such a thing for her cousin during his wartime trials.

From her to Richard to Werner to Doris to Marlene and back home through Werner again, another spiral had closed.

"You must tell me all about it. We go to dinner now, yes?"

They had just gotten drinks in the Brown Palace Hotel restaurant when a harried-looking Erik arrived and slid quickly into the vacant chair. "I'm sorry. Airlines could give a little more attention to preventive maintenance. But I guess better late than never."

Dickenson poured some wine in Erik's glass and raised hers. "A toast to the survivor. May you prosper even more, Hanna."

"Thank you very much. I'm grateful. I do feel more optimistic somehow."

Erik turned toward her. "Maybe more than optimism. There's really a change in your face, Hanna. A light that I haven't seen for a long time."

If there was a light in her face, it came from the fire that had begun to burn after she gave that speech. A resolve, kindled from the crucible of pain that she'd stared into without flinching, to claim her life—all of it. From the beginning.

Irrational though it was, she'd subconsciously expected that lost language to break through like the sun after a storm. There wouldn't be another chance. It was as if Staunton got in one last triumphant lick even in defeat. It hurt. And it made her angry.

The conviviality of the group was a helpful distraction. But this thing was gnawing at her like a rat. She couldn't let him win. And she didn't know how to stop him.

BY TEN THE next morning they had dropped from the treeless slopes of the Continental Divide into the frigid windswept farmland near Fraser. Three days in Steamboat Springs, one of Colorado's best ski resorts, awaited them before Erik's symposium.

Hanna knew that, seen up close, an entire rainbow of colors would sparkle in each tiny facet of the perfectly white snow. Yet she couldn't look. "I know it's beautiful. But I'm terrified. I suppose it's from the past again."

He squeezed her leg. "Hang on. I know the resort is a good memory. Your mother told us about it herself."

"Can't we go faster?"

He gave her his trademark faint smile. "We're already five miles an hour over the limit. I don't want to push my luck."

Her spirits indeed lifted as soon as they approached the town. Already while renting equipment she felt her tension ebb. After dinner they strolled around and she imagined the Alps. The courtroom and William Staunton seemed far away.

Clouds moved in the next day, and it snowed heavily overnight. When the upper lifts opened in the afternoon, they were near the front of the line. After carving perfect parallel curves in lazy swoops through the pristine powder, they stopped to savor the silence. The dark evergreen forest stood in black contrast to its white drapery.

As if cued by a conductor, a sharp crack abruptly transformed the tranquil scene. A billowing cloud of snow outside the resort boundaries thundered down the steep slope. Hanna pointed. "Erik, look, isn't that awesome?" Then she nearly choked. Below the cloud, the avalanche had almost engulfed two tiny figures.

Erik almost pushed her. "Go, Hanna, you're far faster than I am."

For a split second she questioned if they were still above the intermediate lift station. Maybe the ski patrol already knew. But she couldn't take the chance.

She shut out all thoughts, focusing only on the snow in front of her. She imagined herself in a giant slalom race. Her body felt supple and graceful. The trees flashed by in a vague blur.

It's still not enough. But I'm already afraid of falling. Her throat was dry as desert sand.

Gradually she became aware of a voice guiding her. She dared not look, but she was absolutely certain that right next to her was another woman, short brown curls flying in the wind. Confidence flowed into her muscles as if from a drug injection. Her anxiety disappeared.

She skidded to a halt at the lift station and yelled "*Hilfe*" before collapsing, lungs on fire and legs turned to jelly. A moment later she frantically pantomimed an avalanche for the head of the ski patrol, shouting "*Schnee—Unfall—Tief!*" He pulled out a resort map, and she pointed to the location. He nodded and jumped onto the rescue toboggan as it roared toward the hill.

When they returned after forty-five minutes, her husband was with them. "Both men were buried, but the dogs went right to the spot. You probably saved two lives. The patrol couldn't believe your speed."

Hanna hesitated, but only a moment. "Erik, promise me you'll never tell anyone I said this. But I swear my sister was with me. Right beside me."

He hugged her. "Your sister is always with you, Hanna. As is your mother."

The sense of the unfamiliar power that had appeared in the courtroom returned. Maybe it had never left. Perhaps that's what had carried her safely down the slope. Her family—parents, sister, husband—was like a towline connecting her to the past. A past that seemed determined to be in the present.

They had just finished dinner that evening when a wiry man with a ski patrol badge on his shirt approached their table. "Please excuse my interruption, but I believe you're the woman who reported the avalanche victims?"

Erik translated and Hanna stared blankly for a moment. "You're the chief? I'm sorry I didn't recognize you."

"No problem. I guess I'm mistaken about you, too. You look exactly like a girl I gave a week of lessons to some twenty-odd years ago. Really awesome student— placed third in a race afterward. But she was an American."

Her chest tightened against a pounding heart. "*Ach,* you remember *me*?"

"Wow, this is getting into Twilight Zone territory. You're Hanna Hoffmann, but now you only speak German?"

His astonishment was amusing but also unsettling. What *could* she say about the life of trauma and transformation behind that innocent observation? She didn't really understand it herself. She certainly didn't know how to discuss it with a stranger.

She invited the man to sit down. "It's a long story. I was born in Colorado, but was adopted by a German couple. There was an . . . accident, that affected my language. I moved to Germany, and met my husband. "

To her great relief he didn't probe for details. After a few minutes he got to his feet. "Hanna, I hope you don't mind my saying this. I'm just a ski bum. But back then, I thought there was some sort of struggle going on. You were so intense, so—focused. Like you were trying to prove yourself against some unkind critics."

He leaned forward, resting his hands on the chair back. "But there's no room for self-doubt when you're skiing at thirty miles an hour. Whatever you've been doing in Germany, I think maybe no more proving. Anyway, good luck to you."

After he left, Hanna looked squarely at her husband. The man was right. She didn't need to prove anything to anyone anymore.

"You were right, Erik. My speech changed something in me. I have so many feelings. And I have a plan. I'm going to write another speech—which you will give."

The maelstrom of hot and cold emotions stirred up by Staunton's sentencing were a geothermal spring in a glacier-fed mountain stream. Currents of icy determination mixed slowly with bubbling passion, carrying occasional bursts of some repressed fiery force deep underneath. Staunton could take her dream job from her, but he could not take her self-respect.

"I want to tell my story, in my words. On my terms. Without fear. The symposium is your day, but you could give an introduction about me. Tell them that more than half of us are assaulted during our lifetimes. That fourteen were murdered in the U.S. last year. And here I am—not giving up. I want the story of the violence that was done to me to be a triumph. And I want to support other transsexual women. I want to say we don't have to be ashamed. And do it in the place where it all began."

"Your courage never ceases to amaze me. I'd be happy to—I'll do it at the end. There may be some people who won't understand, of course."

"To hell with them. This is about who I am. About my pride. Damn the consequences."

AS ERIK SPOKE of the depths of her trauma, Hanna watched the furtive glances toward her with detached bemusement. She'd seen them earlier at the reception. An off-the-shoulder dress nearly always got that reaction.

A part of her still dreamed of smooth, unblemished skin and a fashion-model figure. But years of professional acceptance, fond compliments from her husband, and children who cared far more about the freshness of the bread their mother baked than how she looked, had quieted that voice to a background whisper.

Twenty-three years ago, standing in front of a hospital mirror, she'd begun an argument. *This isn't the real me,* she'd said, looking at her scars and ungainly figure. *But this is the real me. A woman with a beauty of her own, and nothing to be ashamed of. And the world should know that.*

"Then over the years, her academic inclinations, buried by the trauma she endured, reasserted themselves. Next month this former hairstylist will defend her PhD thesis on phase transitions in semiconductor crystals."

The applause was nice, but it was only a background rhythm to the frenetic melody playing in her mind. The transition that had unlocked success for her thesis involved mere atoms. Now, pieces of her psyche itself were fluctuating wildly, seeking new connections, convinced of an equilibrium structure they hadn't yet found.

The Real Me was still emerging.

After the applause quieted and people lined up at the podium, a cluster formed around her table. Professor Carl Hänsch, organizer of the symposium and close friend of Erik's, came over and offered to translate. A woman who'd attended the Aspen Institute was in front, wide-eyed and open-mouthed. "Hanna, how amazing. I never imagined when I met you that you weren't a woman."

The burst of anger was gone as quickly as it came. There was so much ignorance. People needed time to really understand. She smiled brightly. "Linda, I *am* a woman. And I always have been."

Linda blushed. "Oh, I'm so sorry. I didn't mean it that way."

"Es macht nichts. Für me *ist* today a—" She gasped and covered her mouth briefly. "A very nice day."

Hänsch raised his eyebrows and smiled slightly. The others appeared as shocked as she felt. She finally unrooted herself and ran over to Erik as fast as her kitten heels allowed. "Erik, what think you? How sound I? Tell me, tell me!"

A broader grin than she'd ever seen on his face slowly followed the short flash of surprise. "You sound like a German learning English, Hanna. You're not ready to be a spy yet."

She held his hands and whispered, still in English, "We can now together lead, Herr Schoenberg."

In response he slipped one hand under her hair and briefly brushed her cheek with a feather-light kiss. "Side by side."

Feeling a glow that threatened to burst into a flame, she returned to her social duties. Half an hour later the crowd finally thinned out and left only Carl, who'd seemed completely unfazed by her transformation as he discreetly helped her find words she stumbled over. "Hanna, what are your plans after your thesis is done?"

At first she hesitated. But this was someone who'd been a guest in her living room, playing with her children while she fixed dinner. She had to trust him. So she told him of her previous application to Albert Gleis, and the aftermath. "Now I don't think there are any more open *Assistent* positions within commuting reach."

"Keep looking, Hanna. Your tenacity in this journey tells me you'll succeed."

She repeated his words frequently to herself on the flight home. She wanted so badly for them to be true. But the prospects seemed nonexistent. She would find an industrial job—secondary school teaching would always remind her of her failed quest.

On Monday she went dutifully into the lab to begin translating her thesis. It was a struggle. Sometimes the words were there, but she was constantly thumbing furiously through the dictionary.

At home, tired and despondent, she was ready for bed early when the phone rang. It was Albert Gleis. "Frau Hoffman-Schoenberg, good evening. I apologize for the late call. We only took the final vote two hours ago. It's my pleasure to offer you a position as an ordinary professor of chemistry, with a time-limited appointment. After six years, if your achievements are sufficient, you'll be given a normal, tenured, professorship."

Her vocal chords simply would not respond to command.

Gleis finally broke the silence. "We had some very intense meetings over the weekend, after Professor Hänsch called me with the news that you were now speaking English fluently. We were close to extending an offer for our one opening, and we don't anticipate another for a few years. The timing couldn't have been better."

"But . . . isn't the *Habilitationsschrift* still a requirement?"

"That's the traditional process. But there's been a lot of discussion recently about the concept of an *Assistenzprofessur* or *Juniorprofessur*, which Germany actually had in the early 1970s and dropped. I'm betting it will come back within a few years, but academia moves slowly. In the meantime, no law prevents us from doing it on our own if we so choose."

With her still-heavy accent she asked, "Would you like to hear me say something in English?" It was all she could think of.

She'd never heard any professor laugh the way he did then. "What a pleasure to hear that. Your appointment won't begin formally till the start of summer semester in April. In the meantime, you have to defend your thesis, and after that we can pay you as a research associate."

She hung up slowly and deliberately, afraid she might frighten the news away. Then she leapt down the stairs three at a time to where Erik was reading and flung herself into his arms. "I got it," was all she could say before choking up.

He held her the way he always did at the tenderest moments.

After her thesis defense she went to dinner with her extended family at the same restaurant where she'd become engaged. Nine people, ten settings. Hanna felt the fulfillment of the moment like ripples on the shore of a mountain lake, traveling from the past to boost her gently into the future.

From graduate students in Gleis's lab, she learned that the story Erik had related was now well known. She had to remind herself of what she'd told him. *I want the story of the violence that was done to me to be a triumph. I want to say we don't have to be ashamed.*

CHAPTER 27

Four years later: Friday, 9 April 1999, Tübingen

HANNA FOLLOWED HER two graduate students out of the light-tight laser room and closed the door behind her. "Do the two of you want to join me for a beer? This has been a hard week. And I can actually relax for a couple of minutes. Erik is out of town, and Richard has gone skiing with friends for the weekend."

Once seated in a Gasthaus on the edge of the university campus, she took a notebook from her purse. "Look, there has to be a solution. The laser is stable. We prepare the materials the same way. Yet the data are scattered all over the map. Let's list the steps, one by one, and try to find the weak link."

She glanced up in time to catch Jutta's and Rainer's stares. "You didn't think you were going to get a *free* beer, did you?"

An hour later she closed the notebook. "Okay, that's enough. We'll figure it out. Maybe Eva's data on the new system will help."

After having dinner with a friend, Hanna was greeted at home by two clearly annoyed cats. She fed them and found her place in the novel that she'd started months ago. Usually she got through a few pages before falling asleep. Tonight she couldn't focus at all. Thoughts of work intruded insistently.

It had been two weeks since Albert Gleis had told her of the faculty complaints.

She was sure the instigator was Stefan Hartz. He'd made no secret of his opinion that her publications were insufficient. It didn't seem to matter that the first one appeared in the highly selective *Physical Review Letters*, and the second in the *Proceedings of the National Academy of Sciences*, where papers had to be communicated by members. Hers had come through Nobelist Manfred Eigen.

It was true that she'd gotten a slow start. Jutta Kornfeldt, the first woman student the department had ever had, came in the summer. With one post-doc and a few undergraduates, they worked together for a year before Eva Hollenhorst signed on, giving her the label of "the women's lab" until Rainer Hausmann joined the year after.

Now, four years after she started, she had eight students and post-docs, and several projects. But the pervasive male chauvinism aside, Hartz had been especially cool. And she knew why. Her close faculty collaborator Andreas Heubl had told her about his comment. "This delusion about being a woman is a mental illness. I don't think he can become a solid scientist unless that changes."

Her rash decision to come out to the world through Erik's speech had gotten her this job. But it might also take it away.

She'd never even considered confronting Hartz, afraid of making things worse. Instead she'd doggedly worked even harder, hoping that would be enough. But Gleis had given her an ultimatum: five papers, published or accepted for publication in top-tier journals, by the first of October, a year and a half earlier than the original decision date.

Jutta's work could easily yield four papers, but so far it was a confused mess. Only Rainer Hausmann's forthcoming paper could be counted on to meet that deadline.

She loved being a mentor. And the pupils at the schools she visited were as excited as she'd ever hoped for. But that didn't get her any more publications.

She was being unreasonable. She'd accomplished a huge amount of her dream. What did a professorship matter? She could still inspire young pupils with an industrial research job.

But it did matter, and nothing she might tell herself was going to change that. She gave up on the novel and went to bed, tossing restlessly.

A little girl crawled out of the rubble of a collapsed house and started walking with her cats toward a mountain. Some men on horses shot at the cats, but they had disappeared. One man trained his rifle on the girl. "Thought that was a clever disguise, huh," he said. "Now we're gonna expose you. Too bad you won't survive." He cocked his gun.

The girl put her hands on her hips. "I dare you to try. You're cowards." She threw a rock toward the men. The horses started bucking and the men dropped their rifles.

Hanna woke up, groggy. Her entire body hurt. At first she thought little of it—nightmares were part of her life. But then she realized with a shock that this one was different. The girl had challenged the men and won—at least temporarily.

Of course it was completely irrational to think that a dream foretold the future. But it made her feel better. She needed every smidgeon of confidence she could get.

The bedside clock read 1:10. She lay down again and tried to concentrate on the novel.

She wished her mother were there.

THE DIFFIDENT KNOCK on Hanna's office door might easily have gone unnoticed, but she was expecting it.

"Come in, Jutta. You're one minute early, but I'll forgive you." Hanna grinned at the young woman who came in carrying a large laboratory notebook. "Did the free beer last week stimulate some new results?"

"I think so—maybe." Jutta gingerly handed her the notebook. "Every point is right on that line now, over four orders of magnitude."

Hanna looked intently at the graph for nearly a minute before looking up. Her facetious reference to free beer may not have been so far off from reality. "Jutta, this is fantastic. Absolutely fantastic. How did you do it?"

"Well, we've talked about temperature control several times. I remembered how I'd take layers of clothing off while skiing, and thought maybe multiple layers of different insulation systems might help. It did: I was finally able to control temperature to better than a thousandth of a degree. And after that I got this data."

"Jutta, you know quite well this is what we've been looking for, and you've got it—there's no 'thinking' about it. This makes everything fall into place. You could be ready to defend your thesis in a few weeks."

She took her glasses off. This was just cause for an exuberant celebration, but her student looked positively funereal. "You should be jumping up and down. What's wrong?"

Jutta looked up at length from her lap and stopped folding and unfolding her fingers. "I—I've been depressed, it's true. I guess I felt I wasn't doing as well as I should."

"You don't need to apologize for the time you took. Problems in science aren't solved on a schedule."

Hanna put her glasses back on and made a mental note to get used to them. "I'll bet my next grant your depression has a cause outside of work, and you don't want to tell anyone. But I want you to tell me."

She leaned across her desk. "Right now, think of me not as your professor but as your friend, and specifically an older woman friend."

The quietly passing seconds told of the turmoil Jutta was struggling to contain. Finally she raised her head and pushed her hair away from her face. "It's true there's something . . . A few months ago I was raped," she whispered.

Hanna swallowed hard. The memory threatened her like a tsunami, a deadly calm before an inexorable spasm of pain. Her invitation to cross the boundary of formality between professor and student may have been ill-advised.

But she couldn't go back. She took the glasses off again. "I understand. I've been there."

Jutta looked astonished. "You have? Really? I mean, I'm sorry, I didn't mean I doubted you. I just thought . . ."

"You thought you were the only one. And realizing that you're not is the first step. There are reasons why women remain silent about it. Neither society nor the legal system are friendly. But that silence is itself an attack on the spirit. So, let's start with you telling me about it."

She left to tell her assistant not to allow any visitors, and came back with two cups of coffee. Half an hour later she gently guided a red-eyed Jutta to the hallway.

"Remember my cousin's words: *You have to decide which path to take: the one that is right for you, or the one that they say is right for you. It is, in the end, your decision alone. You will never regret making the right one.*"

"Thank you, Professor. I believe I'm ready to speak up. I'm sorry about the mess this makes for you."

"That's my concern. I'm ready also."

She returned to her office and shut the door carefully. Many decisions, not just one, had brought her to this desk. Battling her trepidation daily, she'd pushed ever upward, led by the girl who was looking for her home. At the hair salon and with her family it seemed like she'd found it.

But the girl said something was missing. *I remember a radio, and some purple crystals.* So she kept going, attaining the same skill with a soldering iron as she had with a curling iron. Rising from the pile of trash where she'd been tossed by a transsexual-hating misogynist, she'd become a professor and role model for girls and women.

So why wasn't she home yet?

As she'd done every workday for three months, she glanced at the envelope with its return address in shaky handwriting: "Mr. & Mrs. Charles Shelby, P.O. Box 1282, Ft. Lauderdale, Florida." And as she'd done every day, she turned away and tried to forget it.

Why her birthparents wanted to contact her now, after twenty-eight years, she couldn't imagine, nor was she sure she wanted to know. Especially not today, with her previously merely uncertain career prospects completely extinguished.

Jutta's breakthrough had unlocked those four papers. Added to Rainer's, that would be enough. But there was one problem: Rainer couldn't write the paper if he wasn't part of her group.

She'd hadn't hesitated. This was her duty, and not only to Jutta: to every woman who had ever been devalued and denigrated for being who she was. They were all in this together.

She'd have to provide proof. She believed Jutta without hesitation, but some of the men wouldn't. After talking with Eva Hollenhorst, the only other person Jutta had told, she mapped out a plan.

At three in the afternoon she was in the office of her department chair. "Albert, I'll come straight to the point. I've learned that Jutta Kornfeldt was raped in January, at a private event after the department's New Year's Eve party. She was inebriated and unconscious when it happened. There were no witnesses, but the perpetrator told two other men what he'd done. He also gave her spiked drinks."

She drew a deep breath. "He is one of my students—Rainer Hausmann. I'm discharging him from my research group as of today."

Gleis was quiet for a long time. Finally, he said, "Hanna, you have a reputation in the realm of science for demanding impeccable proof. I would expect the same of you in law."

She watched him closely as she told him the results of her investigation. If she got his support, she wouldn't worry about the others.

His expression was tired but resolute. "You've done your part. I'll take the proceedings from here."

Hanna stood up, still tense but relieved. "Thank you, Albert."

On the wall of his front office was a poster of a snow-covered mountain. It had appeared there several months ago, but it had made no special impression on her before.

She pointed to it as she passed his secretary's desk. "Is that Ragged Peak?"

"Yes, how did you know?" The woman looked astonished. "He took the photo at a conference in Aspen last summer. He was sure no one from Germany had ever been there before."

"He might be wrong." She was from Germany. And surreal as it was, she would swear that she'd not only been there, she'd been inside that mountain. Now she felt like she'd climbed it, and was about to stand on its summit.

Back in her office she stood for a long time in front of the photo that she'd taken long ago in her husband's lab, of those electronic instruments with their old-fashioned black knobs and white dials. She'd never understood her fascination with them, and she didn't now, but she was certain they were connected to Ragged Peak.

GLEIS PRESIDED OVER a department faculty meeting three weeks later.

"The content of the investigation is contained in full in the report which you have, so I won't go over it now. The question is simply the decision to be taken. The department has an official policy of encouraging more women to participate in science. We cannot tolerate this behavior. The chair's recommendation is that Herr Hausmann be expelled."

"Albert, I don't agree." Heads turned toward Stefan Hartz and his imperious voice. "It was a party with copious consumption of alcohol, and the alleged victim was inebriated. That was her responsibility. Nothing in this report shows that she refused to have sexual intercourse. I don't wish this man's reputation besmirched with an unwarranted charge. What he did was not unnatural."

For a moment Hanna's vision blurred. She heard a car door slam, and an old motor stutter to life. Then Earl Williams, his stern voice as clear and strong through the intervening forty-three years as Hartz's.

"Johnny, yer dad told me what he found'ja doin'. Now you lissen to me. Yer old enough to know what's what. A boy actin' like a girl ain't nothin' to play about. That's bein' a pervert—no better'n the garbage. Jis plain sick and foul.

"Yer dad was kind jis givin' you a thrashin'. The men in town, 'specially the young guys, ain't gonna be so kind. They'll bash yer head in if they catch you doin' that. So if you wanna stay alive, don't you ever even think that way again, you hear?"

Holding his terror like a rattlesnake, Johnny stood up in the depths of Hanna's soul. Maybe his father *had* been kind. But Johnny didn't know that. He'd thought he was about to be killed. And then this man had told him that people everywhere would do that if they found out about her.

It couldn't be an accident that Stefan Hartz had used the word "unnatural." And if his objection wasn't meant as an indirect attack on her, why hadn't he raised it in private? This meeting was supposed to be a formality.

It was merely one more in the lifelong litany of denials of her human dignity that had begun with the one she'd just remembered. But this one was about to get a different response.

She stood and walked with purposeful poise to the front of the room. Next to Gleis she stood absolutely straight, completely unashamed of her height for the first time she could remember. Her curled-under bob and sand-beige sheath dress were the epitome of feminine professional fashion. But her face might have been sculpted from stone.

She made eye contact with each of the men, one by one. Only then did she speak.

"Professor Hartz, I will not share a workplace with someone who believes that a woman can be responsible for her own rape. If she has not consented, then she has not consented."

She looked directly at him. "If you retract your statement and apologize for making it, I will forget that it was ever made. Otherwise, I will publicly ask for your resignation."

A minute went by. The silence that reigned in the room went from oppressive to painful. Men shifted uncomfortably in their seats, but no one spoke. And Hanna's gaze did not waver.

Hartz stood up. "Chairman Gleis, I wish to retract my statement and apologize for the insult. I second the chair's recommendation regarding Herr Hausmann."

"My word is my word," Hanna said and returned to her seat. Her heart rate took a little longer to return to normal.

The next five months would probably be unpleasantly tense, but she'd made the decision that was right for her. And Hartz might even have done her a favor. Maybe there would be more cracks in her memory vault.

CHAPTER 28

HANNA CHATTED AMIABLY with Andreas Heubl as the auditorium filled up. Most of the faculty were there. Jutta's oral examination promised to be a fitting conclusion to Hanna's academic career.

During the last two months Jutta had finished the four papers. That wouldn't save Hanna's job. But she could still send her student off with the highest acclamation. And she'd keep Gleis's respect if she remained professional to the end.

She was surprised at the discussion. Some of it suggested knowledge of Jutta's work that wasn't in her presentation, although only Heubl and Gleis had copies of the papers.

Finally the public audience filed out. The discussion between Hanna, Andreas, and a third professor lasted only seconds. Jutta was invited back, and fidgeted while the men signed her thesis.

Hanna was last. "Congratulations, Dr. Kornfeldt. I'll come by your party in a few minutes. Enjoy the weekend, and on Monday we can make the final revisions before sending your papers off."

She returned to her office. She couldn't ignore that envelope forever. Her birthparents were part of her family, good or evil.

She sat down and rested her chin on her hands. In her mind, her childhood had been in that cozy, languid German village, where she played and attended kindergarten, knowing nothing of scars, nightmares, and a misfit body. She knew it wasn't real, and yet it was.

Life before the assault was like an archeological dig, a city lost in history. Over the years, weaknesses in the wall of amnesia had allowed fragments to emerge, shard by splintered shard. Now the wall began to fissure like a frozen mountain lake in the morning light, revealing traces of childhood memories woven with imagination.

She saw a small boy sitting beside a placid tree-lined creek below a sandstone cliff, making flower chains from dandelions and putting them in his hair. A doll, wrapped in purple velour and propped against a log, looked on.

Then the creek became a dry ravine through a maze of twisted, toppled trees and thistles. The boy ran frantically away from a rusty hay baler through a field of red ant hills.

His parents sent him to bed for being disobedient. During the night he snuck out to an amateur radio set and asked someone in another country if boys could be girls there.

As the sun rose, he strode away toward a distant peak, followed by two cats. Beyond forested foothills a rainbow hung over a rugged massif, marking a magical realm inside which he would be a real girl. But the mountain, like the rainbow, receded as he walked. After a time, a single bluebird detached itself from a flock and disappeared over the rainbow, leaving him standing by the ravine in torn, greasy pants.

As Hanna watched, she felt once again the agony of her torture. Behind the erupting memories were deadly sharp, jagged barbs that tore at her soul, as menacingly as her attacker's belt and shoelaces had torn her flesh.

Then she heard the voices of her husband and children through the fog of pain, reminding her that she had a family who loved her, students who looked up to her, and colleagues who respected her. The rainbow broke into a cloud of brilliant sparks of light that gathered into amethyst stones in a necklace on the doll her parents had given her.

In front of the case holding the doll were the pen and letter opener that her son had made many years ago for her birthday.

As she ran her fingers lightly over the delicately carved wood handle of the letter opener, tracing the inscription which read, *Für Mama, in Liebe, von Richard,* the wall evaporated like a cold night's mist in the midday sun.

She remembered the taunts, the insults, the fear of being discovered. The quashing of her soul's yearning over and over again, the denial of her self day after day. The menace that lurked behind friendly facades, forbidding her from ever going where she felt she belonged.

And through it all: the silent, secret nurturing of a seed of something better.

Then she finally understood: Staunton's brutal attack simply condensed into a few hours what a hostile society can do during a lifetime of dehumanizing denigration.

Ellen Beattie's diagnosis had been right. Those memories had ruled her entire life from their fear-sealed vaults, haunting her days as much as her dreams. The assault was only an episode.

But now their sting was gone, their power vanquished. They were a part of her but apart from her. The voice of Pam Preston reverberated from the corridors of the university in Boulder to those in Tübingen.

"You are who you are, and you're okay. That's the starting point."

And the end point.

Hanna slit the envelope open and removed the letter.

Dear Hanna,

I hope this letter reaches you. We sent it to your university office since we have no other address.

At a gathering of ex-Coloradoans we met a former physics professor from the University of Colorado. We got together for dinner, and he told us of this amazing woman he'd heard about in a lecture by her husband. Though he didn't remember your name, we knew it could only be you. He helped us locate you.

Hanna, we have agonized times beyond counting over what happened. If we had gone up to you at Dorothy's reception and said something polite—maybe that we didn't like the way her grandmother was talking and that you didn't deserve that, no matter how much we disagreed—would things have turned out differently? We will never know. We wish we did.

We couldn't change our fundamental beliefs, but we could have just said, "We love you all the same, even if we don't understand what you're doing." So simple. But by the time we realized that it was too late.

As I'm sure you know, we were influenced by Daniel's views, which remain rigidly rejecting even now. It was because of him that we didn't even reach out when you were in the hospital—something I've never stopped regretting almost every day since. We retired to Florida to live with him and Phyllis and our grandchildren. But our disagreement has been a thorn in our relationship, so much that we finally had to move to our own apartment.

Hanna, we'd like to say we're sorry. It won't make up for the past, but it is what we can do.

Sincerely and with the love that we always had for you,
Mom and Dad

Hanna saw herself laying a broken doll tenderly into a little grave, longing for a pretty dress, singing through tears what her mother had taught her in German.

Schlaf, Kindlein, schlaf,	*Sleep, baby, sleep*
der Vater hüt't die Schaf,	*the father guards the sheep*
die Mutter schüttelt's Bäumelein,	*the mother shakes a little tree*
da fällt herab ein Träumelein.	*and down falls a little dream.*

She was ready to say farewell to that little girl and hello to Professor Hoffman-Schoenberg.

The letter was obviously written by her mother, but she saw her father's face in the page. She looked him straight in the eye. *I know now you didn't mean it,*

Daddy. You had your own fears and hurt, didn't you? It was the world you lived in. You couldn't help that. I hope you're okay. I am.

She returned the letter carefully to the envelope and tucked it into her purse.

Doris's mother had said to her, "I've been so ignorant. And now it's too late." But for her and her birthparents it was not too late.

Hanna dabbed at her eyes with a handkerchief and briefly fussed with powder and blush before leaving and locking her office. She quickly located Jutta's party in an area outside the building where students often gathered for lunch when the weather permitted, and accepted a plastic cup of champagne from Jutta.

"Prost," she said as she raised the cup, "and congratulations. You were a star, by the way. The men were competing to praise your performance. Not that that was a surprise to me."

Jutta's face turned serious. "Professor Hoffmann-Schoenberg, just a few months ago I would've found something self-deprecating to say. But now I know I don't have to do that. I did earn it. I really think I did."

"You certainly did, Jutta." Gleis's voice came from directly behind Hanna, who jumped in surprise. She turned and made to reply, but he was quicker.

"Besides congratulating your student, I came to ask if you're willing to accept the leadership of the search committee for a new opening we've authorized. Stefan Hartz nominated you for that job. He did hint that he'd enjoy working with you if you were inclined to invite him."

Hanna took a sip of champagne, buying time to digest the meaning of this bombshell. But her mind was still completely blank when he handed her an unsealed envelope.

> *Dear Frau Dr. Hoffmann-Schoenberg,*
>   *It is my pleasure to inform you that the faculty has approved your permanent appointment as a professor in the Department of Chemistry.*
>   *Sincerely,*
>   *Albert Gleis*
>   *Chairman*

She looked up slowly. She'd never seen Gleis smile so broadly.

"Immediately after that faculty meeting about Rainer, Stefan came to me and asked to see the drafts of Jutta's papers. He kept up on all her progress, and recommended that we offer you tenure. But we were only able to take the final vote this morning after everyone else read the latest drafts."

"I guess Papa's going to have to keep making his own breakfast after all."

"Elisabeth! Aren't you supposed to be in class still?"

"Yes. But as you can see—I'm not."

Richard stepped out from around the corner. "She came home to make breakfast for me. And to remind you that I have a graduation party tomorrow—at your house, by the way."

She stared at the two of them as if they were ghosts. "How did you know all this would happen today?"

Gleis answered before they could respond, still grinning. "Perhaps it bordered on hubris. But I had little doubt that the faculty would follow my recommendation. So I invited them."

Hanna sighed. "I guess I'm the only person in the university who didn't know about all this already?"

Richard was almost as tall as Hanna, and had to stoop a little to get his arm around his sister's waist. "Not true. At least one physics professor doesn't know. He's at home fixing dinner for you, in hopes of cheering you up. Opa's there too, but hopefully not in the kitchen. We haven't checked the smoke alarms recently."

In spite of her best efforts a tear escaped. Everyone who had brought her through that reverie of pain—family, students, colleagues—was right here in real life. Finally, a dream that she didn't need to bury.

She'd been so close with Erik's speech. *This is the real me: a woman with a beauty of her own, and nothing to be ashamed of.* But the world could only understand that when she stood up and fought for it—fearless, fierce, and whole.

The final step to the summit.

ACKNOWLEDGEMENTS AND NOTES

"It was the best of times, it was the worst of times."

Charles Dickens must have had a crystal ball. Transgender women and men have attained prominent positions in nearly every profession, yet still do not have even basic protection against employment discrimination in many states. Transgender children increasingly have parental support, yet are seeing a veritable assault from some state governments. Denigration, bullying, and rejection remain commonplace, and extreme violence is never far in the background.

This experience is not unique, and indeed transphobes often promote racial and other types of bigotry. There is nevertheless reason for hope: Young people are increasingly respectful of human dignity regardless of physical characteristics of any kind. I am optimistic that the physical and psychological trauma depicted here will soon fade into the mists of humanity's difficult history. The loving support of families is vital in this quest, and I am grateful for having so much of that. My children are my delight as much as can be imagined.

Six years elapsed from the first conception of this book until its publication. In the journey of a thousand miles, the first step is often to ask for help. Without five extraordinary writing coaches I could not have arrived.

Margot Silk Forrest, primarily a non-fiction expert, bravely took on this scientist whose prose resembled eighteenth-century German philosophy. It is with the most profound gratitude and respect that I consider her my elementary school teacher in writing. After that came Amy Sue Nathan, Sheila Athens, and Elizabeth Sumner Wafler, all of whom kept saying "Dig deeper into Hanna's emotions;" I hope I got the message. Bettina Eschenhagen gave both literary critiques and vital inputs involving German law and the educational system. When John Reid (at Blackwater Press, through their Manuscript Assessment Service) informed me that I'd reached a "publishable" stage, I felt I'd finally entered the promised land.

My heartfelt thanks to beta readers Barbara Waugh, Cynthia Valdez, Cindy Brine, Dottie Unwin, Rabbi Charles Familant, Christopher and Kirsten Shockey, Shannon Ellis, Jane Hickman, and Sho Tsuji. Many others encouraged me along the way: Jennifer Finney Boylan, Dr. Lynn Conway, Dave Margoshes, and Dr. Pamela Gaynor (formerly Pearson) deserve special mention. I apologize to all those I've not named given space limits; I had the benefit of a very big village.

Some notes about terminology: I have used the word "transsexual" rather than "transgender" in order to be true to actual usage in the time frame of the story. The latter is standard now, but it was almost unknown in 1970, and saw little use until at least the 1990s. Our knowledge has evolved significantly; for example, the non-binary identity was not appreciated until recently. I highly recommend the website of Dr. Lynn Conway (professor emerita at the University of Michigan, and a trans woman with an extraordinary and inspiring life story); it is still today the gold standard for accuracy, clarity and depth on gender identity issues.

The book also uses the term "sex reassignment surgery." This too, was standard at the time, though it is now more clearly understood that "transition" represents an affirmation of gender and not a reassignment (that happens only in the eyes of the law). There is no evidence that anyone's gender identity changes after birth, although our awareness and/or acceptance of it certainly does. Some surgeons, particularly in Thailand, still use the terms SRS or GRS.

VIOLENCE AGAINST TRANSSEXUALS

Some readers may be unaware of just how serious this violence still is. https://en.wikipedia.org/wiki/List_of_people_killed_for_being_transgender gives a very abbreviated list of the several tens of women murdered each year (the Wikipedia page for "Transgender Day of Remembrance" provides more information). The following two cases exemplify some of the elements of the story.

On May 27, 2003, during oral sex, [Jatin] Patel became aware of scarring on [Shelby Tracy] Tom's body that he recognized to be from gender confirmation surgery and became enraged, strangling Tom to death… Patel's defense argued that Patel's encounter with Tom caused him to feel rage, betrayal and personal violation, …[he] was sentenced to a total of 9 years in prison. Wikipedia, https://en.wikipedia.org/wiki/Murder_of_Shelby_Tracy_Tom

Islan Nettles was beaten to death in Harlem just after midnight on August 17, 2013. The killer, James Dixon, was not indicted until March 2015, . . . confessing that he had flown into "a blind fury" when he realized [after flirting with her] that Nettles was a transgender woman. . . . [He] received a sentence of 12 years' imprisonment. Wikipedia,https://en.wikipedia.org/wiki/Islan_Nettles

Jayna Sheats grew up on a Colorado ranch without electricity, neighbors, or schools, but obtained a ham radio license when she was seven. After language and psychology studies in Colorado and Germany and a PhD in chemistry from Stanford University, she became a researcher and entrepreneur, publishing 60 scientific articles and book chapters, and started three companies. As creator of Hewlett-Packard's e-Inclusion program she worked with Dr. Muhammad Yunus in Bangladesh on telecenters for the poor. Today she lives with her children in northern California, hikes frequently in the redwoods, and writes novels involving social justice and triumph over trauma.

Visit Jayna's website at https://jaynasheats.com.

9 781960 373076